Praise for the works of
TOM DEITZ

"Few writers match personal crisis
with epic conflict as effectively."
Dragon

"His characters live and breathe and pass easily between the realms of reality and fantasy."
Lynn Abbey, author of *Unicorn & Dragon*

WINDMASTER'S BANE
"ENCHANTING . . .
Holds the reader spellbound!"
Fantasy Review

FIRESHAPER'S DOOM
"Full of fun, wonder and m_____e"
Roger Zelazny

THE

"A S_____K . . .
You won't want to ___ ___ding for a minute!"
Sa__ News

Other Avon Books by
Tom Deitz

WINDMASTER'S BANE
FIRESHAPER'S DOOM
DARKTHUNDER'S WAY
SUNSHAKER'S WAR
STONESKIN'S REVENGE
THE GRYPHON KING

Coming Soon
in the **SOULSMITH** *Trilogy*

DREAMBUILDER
WORDWRIGHT

SOULSMITH

TOM DEITZ

AVON BOOKS • NEW YORK

SOULSMITH is an original publication of Avon Books. This work has never before appeared in book form. This work is a novel. Any similarity to actual persons or events is purely coincidental.

AVON BOOKS
A division of
The Hearst Corporation
1350 Avenue of the Americas
New York, New York 10019

Copyright © 1991 by Thomas F. Deitz
Cover art by Tim White
Published by arrangement with the author
Library of Congress Catalog Card Number: 91-92060
ISBN: 0-380-76289-7

First AvoNova Printing: November 1991

AVONOVA TRADEMARK REG. U.S. PAT. OFF. AND IN OTHER COUNTRIES, MARCA REGISTRADA, HECHO EN U.S.A.

Printed in the U.S.A.

RA 10 9 8 7 6 5 4 3 2 1

For "The Group"—who kept me sane one summer:

Jennifer Campbell and Shawn Carter
Eric Clanton and Chuck Gillespie
Ron Helm and Reid Locklin
Heather Pritchett and Linda Smit
Matt Smith (who made me retype Chapter 18)
and, in absentia,
Buck Marchinton and Paul Matthews
(that's two times, guys)

Wish you coulda been there, Jamie

Acknowledgments

Beulah N. Deitz
Gilbert Head
Adele Leone
Buck Marchinton
Paul Matthews
Chris Miller
Brad Strickland
Sharon Webb
Charles Wiley

SOULSMITH

Prologue: Wheel of Fortune

Federal Prison, Homestead Air Force Base,
Homestead, Florida
Monday, February 19—9:30 A.M.

Dion Welch read auguries in rock-and-roll like some people read Tarot cards, and in very much the same manner. It was a far bigger "deck," of course, and of necessity expanding all the time; but during the twenty years since he had finished law school, he had taken to affixing specific meanings to particular songs in certain contexts—and had discovered that the first song he heard on a given day almost always set the tone for the subsequent twenty-four hours. All he had to do then was note the next ten tunes as they came up, consider them in relation to the classic Celtic cross spread of the Tarot, and *voilà*: a pretty good notion of how the day was going to progress.

The day he'd been convicted, for instance, the first song he'd heard was Elvis's "Jailhouse Rock," followed immediately by Sam Cooke's "Chain Gang" and Hendrix's rendition of "All Along the Watchtower." Those three, especially in that conjunction, had been more than sufficient to give him a pretty fair idea of his impending fate—which reality had subsequently borne out.

For Dion Welch, LL.D. (University of Florida, class of 1970), Ph.D. (ditto, 1971) was also a convicted embezzler and (some said) thief. That the crime which had engendered the financial investigations that had wrought his downfall— spiriting a certain Jacksonville millionaire's favorite genetically engineered sow to Dion's Fernandina estate for a six- month vacation, during which interlude Dion had coinci- dentally caused a remarkable litter to be sired on her by his own prizewinning boar, before returning her (womb and pedigree intact, if not inviolate)—was essentially victimless, had not seemed to matter to a probably purchased jury. (The Lord of the Pigs had inconveniently been the brother-in-law of a well-known state senator, whose interest in the affair Dion had, unhappily, seriously miscalculated.) There were limits, it seemed, to even Welch-clan money, power, and influence.

That, Dion had discovered most bitterly.

Still, things could have been worse. He was in a very upscale federal prison, for one thing, meaning he had decent quarters, acceptable meals, adequate facilities, and a rea- sonable amount of freedom he had manipulated into a num- ber of exclusive perks. And for the last several weeks, he'd even had no roommate—which, if his good fortune held (and it probably would, since he had considerable influence in such matters), might possibly be a long-term situation. Especially as he was in all regards a model prisoner and was bucking hard for a speedy parole.

For the moment, though, he had other concerns.

He had known when his eyes popped open just past mid- night, with some distant sleeper's anguished, nightmare cries still echoing faintly in his ears, that unless he missed his guess a major revelation was almost certainly going to find its way to him come morning. He could not say *how* he knew, for it did not pay to be too analytical about such things; but Dion had learned enough in his forty-four years to place implicit trust in certain sorts of hunches. It was a skill he had—or an art; one of several possible manifestations of what the senior members of his family had always simply called ''luck.''

In any event, he'd checked his watch, confirmed it was past midnight, and flicked on the radio. The hourly weather report was just ending on WYFX Miami, which meant he'd be able to catch the next song in its entirety—an important consideration. He'd waited expectantly through two minutes of commercials, then caught the first dark chords of that day's Significator: the Animals' ''We Gotta Get Outta This Place.''

He'd stopped listening after that, too absorbed in pondering the tune's implications—for the first song determined the subject of the rest of the reading. Thus, he had known immediately that whatever was lighting up the psychic circuit boards did not refer to him. *That* song, with its theme of adolescent dissatisfaction, implied the yearnings of a *young* man—which, in spite of his looks, Dion no longer was. Other tunes had reinforced that notion: the Chambers Brothers' ''Time Has Come Today'' covering whoever the reading was about, and David Bowie's ''Changes'' in the slot for What Lies Ahead. The Doors's ''The End'' in position ten, signifying What Will Be in the Celtic cross, had been the clincher. For that shamanistic anthem signaled in no uncertain terms the passing of one phase of a young man's life and the beginning of a very different other. Never mind that it was also rife with sexual innuendo of the most incestuous kind—which was also something Dion knew a bit about.

The upshot of it all was that he had become so intrigued by the accumulating weirdness that he'd violated his own long-standing prohibition and started collecting a second series of tunes as soon as an appropriate Significator to represent himself (Dion's ''Where or When,'' as it transpired—which could have hardly been more obvious, which in turn meant this was gonna be a biggie) cycled around the next morning.

That sequence had been full of threats, cautions, and foreboding—and was still unfolding when events began to overtake expectation.

The song for What Lies Ahead—Cher's "Dark Lady"— had just begun when Dion heard footsteps approaching from the corridor outside.

Even without the musical premonition Dion would have known one set belonged to a woman simply from analyzing her tread. The pace was rapid but controlled, indicating a style of hurry atypical of masculine ambulation; and the material comprising the soles made a sharper slap than any man's shoe leather would have produced—never mind that it was accented with a click of heel and that the force that drove those smack-clicks was insufficient for most men's weight.

There was a man with her, of course: Warden Wheeler, if he'd caught the rhythm right. (And the latest cut, Cream's "Crossroads," was very coincidentally off an album called *Wheels of Fire*—which in turn reinforced the omens predicting change.)

The footsteps slowed a short way off to the left, and Dion dialed the radio down to the merest whisper and relocated himself from his chair to his bunk, pausing only to add a black T-shirt and a pair of socks to the ragged jeans he was already wearing. A glance in the mirror on the white enameled wall showed him passably presentable, if perhaps more artfully unkempt than was the norm for middle-aged inmates. Still, the effect would probably put him in good stead with a female visitor: his hair black and thick and spiky (though shorter, of necessity, than he would have preferred); his features angular and slightly dissolute, perfectly matching his elegantly lean body. And his eyes, which were the key to any woman's heart—*they* were dark blue and held a feral sparkle that hinted at too many drugs, too much expensive alcohol. Too much sex.

Except that he had never indulged either of the first two vices, and the latter only when convenient, preferring the giddy madness of his own brilliant mind at play. And he was certain it was going to get a major league workout real soon.

By looking *through* the bars instead of *at* them, Dion saw the warden—sure enough, it was Wheeler—and the woman before they saw him.

Wheeler mumbled something, the woman nodded; keys rattled in the lock, and Dion found himself sharing his cell with a remarkably attractive dark-haired woman in her mid-thirties, dressed in a severe business suit that did not complement the soft curves of her face.

"I'm Alice Bartlett," she announced primly, meeting his eyes with a challenging glare that suggested she had dealt with criminals far less innocuous than his own country-club variety. "I'm with Roberts, Owens, Michaels, and Stevens—"

"—Attorneys at Law," Dion finished. "Juries found for my clients over yours seventy-eight percent of the time." He indicated his still-warm chair. "I'm afraid the accommodations aren't what you're accustomed to," he added, sparing a wink for the warden looming outside, "but do sit down."

Ms. Bartlett grimaced, but accepted Dion's offer and sat staring at him narrowly, as if deciding whether to speak to him or bite him.

"Dion Welch at your service." Dion grinned. "I suppose you knew that."

"Yes."

"I don't attack women either, at least not when I'm guarded."

"I didn't think you did."

"Pigs are more my thing, actually."

Ms. Bartlett's glare intensified. "So I'm informed."

"Ah, so you've seen my record?"

"Yes—what's left of it. There seem to have been . . . deletions."

"Power failures in the midst of transcriptions, so I've heard. And a number of suspicious fires—affecting far more records than mine, I might add."

"Still very convenient, *I'd* say."

"So would I."

The woman uncrossed, then recrossed her legs. "I'll get right to the point, Mr. Welch: I believe you once arranged for the adoption of a certain young man—he would have been an infant when it happened."

"Several, actually," Dion replied neutrally. "It's an occupational hazard—you know how it is."

"This one's named Ronny: Ronny Dillon. He lives in Tampa—or did until recently."

A shiver shook Dion at that, though reason told him that the omens should have sent off bells and whistles if anything bad was afoot with Ronny—unless he'd misread them. "The End" *could* mean Death, after all—even War, when juxtaposed with martial songs like "Eve of Destruction" or "Sky Pilot." And the Significator *had* indicated a *young* man, which, at seventeen, Ronny Dillon certainly was. Dion tried to picture him as he had last seen him at a regional swim meet two years ago: a slim, handsome lad of average height but with the strong chest and shoulders, good muscle definition, and dark tan that marked lifelong aficionados of water sports. He also had blue eyes, dark hair cut very short to ensure less drag in the water, and had shaved his legs even when there had not been, at the time, much need to.

"Mr. Welch?"

"*Did?*" Dion whispered aloud, not bothering to suppress the ensuing chill.

"Still does, I suppose," Ms. Bartlett corrected stiffly. "If he can be said to live *anywhere* just now."

"Which means?"

"He's had an accident, Mr. Welch. Two, actually, though one didn't physically involve him. The first was two days ago—he was on his school's swimming and diving team, and— But I suppose you knew that, since my informants indicate that you've kept pretty close tabs on him— ever since you arranged for his adoption. Not counting the *last* year, of course," she appended a tad too pointedly.

"The accident?" Dion prompted, while the radio quietly whispered "In the Midnight Hour," specifically the line in which the amorous narrator's love comes "tumblin' down."

"No, let me guess," Dion continued. "He had a fall."

Ms. Bartlett looked startled. "How'd you know?"

Another grin. "I have a way of guessing, I suppose you could say. Besides," he added, "it only makes sense. Both swimming and diving are potentially risky activities, and since I know Ronny doesn't drink, do drugs, or drive like a maniac, it only stands to reason that the sort of accident most likely to claim him would involve one of those sports. Since you've indicated that he's *not* dead, and since it's difficult to actually injure yourself swimming per se, that only leaves diving; ergo he fell."

"Touché," Ms. Bartlett replied, smiling in spite of herself at Dion's practiced wit. "Except that I didn't *say* 'injury,' I *only* said 'accident.' ''

"Touché in turn!"

Ms. Bartlett took a deep breath and pondered a small notebook that had found its way into her hand. "We need to get serious, Mr. Welch. Like I said, Ronny had an accident. You were correct, too; he *did* fall while diving. According to his best friend he'd been having a lot of trouble sleeping lately, apparently due to some kind of recurring nightmares. This kid says that right before the fall he found Ronny sitting with his head against his locker sound asleep. He was stark naked—still had his suit in his hands, apparently. And when this friend asked Ronny what was up, he said something about having just had *another* nightmare."

"What *kind* of nightmares?" Dion asked carefully, feeling a vast uneasiness slipping up on him.

"Of dying, apparently. Or, to quote his friend quoting

him: 'It was like what dying—what *being* dead—must
really be like.' There was some mention of Ronny hearing
voices, too.''

"What *sort* of voices?''

Bartlett looked at him askance. "A voice telling him life
was futile, that since everything ends sooner or later anyway, he should spare himself the pain of living and go ahead
and die.''

Dion bit his lip and nodded, but did not press the point,
though he had a good idea what was up—and why the omens
might not have warned him. "And the fall?'' he ventured
at last, careful not to let his growing apprehension show.

"Well, according to his friend, Ronny snapped out of
whatever was bothering him and went ahead and climbed
to the ten-meter platform. Once there, things looked fine—
until all of a sudden he began to waver, like he was dizzy
or something. He started to climb back down—and apparently simply lost his balance and toppled off. He
glanced off the railing of a lower platform—got a mild
concussion from it, too. But what's much worse is that
that impact knocked him so far back that he grazed the
side of the pool with sufficient force to essentially rip off
his right kneecap, while shattering it and most of the bones
around it, which—''

"Which effectively puts an end to his Olympic aspira-
tions, never mind local competition.''

"Exactly.''

"And his parents got killed on their way to the hospital.''

"You saw the paper, did you?''

"Nope, never touch the things, and I only listen to *music*
on the radio.''

Ms. Bartlett stiffened, looked a bit unnerved, but managed to mask her discomfort with a frown. "Well, you're
right again,'' she managed. "And I have to *ask* again: how
did you know?''

Dion only smiled cryptically. The pieces were coming
together almost more quickly than he could sort them now:

song sequences from several days past that he still recalled, all bearing implications so cryptic that he'd simply abandoned hope of figuring them out—until now.

Like Herb Alpert's "The Lonely Bull," which had turned up in the This Lies Ahead position the day before yesterday—the day of the accident. *That* hadn't made any sense at all—except that now he considered it, a bull often signified a car, and *could* mean something as specific as a Lamborghini (which used a bull on its badge), an AMC Matador (possibly, though that was a stretch), or a Ford Taurus. And Ronny's folks had a Taurus; Dion had helped arrange the "lucky" lottery win that had paid for it. And since the second accident had not directly involved Ronny, it stood to reason it had to have involved those closest to him—and the likeliest way the bull could have tied in was through the Taurus.

Of course, there was no way he could explain any of this to the woman. So he simply went on smiling and eventually mumbled a rather noncommittal, "Just makes sense."

"How so?" Ms. Bartlett countered instantly.

Dion shrugged. "Well, if his folks were alive, you wouldn't have come to me. It's as simple as that." Which effectively passed the buck back to Ms. Bartlett.

"Uh, yeah, I guess it does," she acknowledged, looking flustered and confused—which amused Dion immensely. "They were on their way to the hospital," she went on a moment later. "They ran a stoplight and hit a much bigger car."

"Air bag didn't help?"

"There was a secondary impact from the side. It was . . . messy."

Dion nodded sadly. He'd known the Dillons for more than seventeen years; had even dated Harriet Dillon briefly—when she was still Harriet Moreland. She'd been his sister's roommate in college.

"So . . . ?"

"Figure it out, Mr. Welch. You seem to be good at that."

"Very well," Dion replied, flopping back on his bunk and steepling his fingers on his chest. "Ronny's hurt and his adoptive parents are dead and the Dillons were the last of their line. They have no siblings, cousins, in-laws, or living parents. As the person who arranged Ronny's adoption and subsequently kept an eye on him at the bequest of his biological mother, I am therefore the closest thing the boy has to next of kin. Therefore, you either want money for medical bills—which I doubt, since I know for a fact that he's well provided for and insured out the wazoo—or else you want me to put you in touch with his mother, which I absolutely will not do."

"Not necessarily his *mother* . . ."

"Well, *I* obviously won't do as a guardian, and my brother Gil—who also used to check up on him from time to time—is right out, 'cause he's even deeper in the clink than I am—you *did* know about him, didn't you? And why he's out of the running as well?"

"Rape, wasn't it? A sorority girl at that college he used to teach at?"

"Right. My last trial, too—and one of my very few failures."

"Which brings us back to a guardian for Ronny Dillon."

"And?"

"Very well. Since you insist on having it spelled out for you, the boy's godmother is someone named Erin Welch—your sister, isn't she? And also Harriet Dillon's roommate at the University of Florida, unless their records have *also* been tampered with. She visits Ronny from time to time—or so the neighbors tell me. We've even found *pictures* of the two of them, though none were very recent. I believe he usually calls her Aunt Erin."

"Correct."

"Well, the Dillons' will leaves custody of Ronny to her."

"Not the will *I* did for them!" Dion flared. "It specifies quite clearly that a consortium of family friends is to make any custody decisions—with Ronny's consent, now that he's nearly of legal age.''

"Ah, but *I* did a new one for them last year!" Ms. Bartlett countered triumphantly. "I took over as their lawyer when you became . . . unavailable. We decided that custody by committee was simply too cumbersome in the event of an emergency. I convinced the Dillons to name Ronny's god-mother, since that's what they're for anyway.''

It was Dion's turn to stiffen. *This* he hadn't foreseen at all, not even a hint—though, he supposed, the optimum time for such things to have shown up in the omens had passed long ago. Still, he should have known something was up—unless, as he sometimes did, he'd misinterpreted the signs. Or unless there was another influence at work— a possibility he did not want to consider because it implied that Ronny had attracted the attention of someone he should not have. Which meant that a *really* messy situation could be evolving—one that Dion had hoped to forestall.

"And . . . ?" Dion managed finally.

"Unfortunately, we can't seem to locate an *address* for this Erin Welch—*nobody* can, apparently. In fact, there seem to be *no* records of her whereabouts after college, at least not that anyone I know can access. And the home address she listed *then* was only an Atlanta post office box, which has long since been reassigned. There's not even a number in the Dillons' phone book. That's why I'm asking you: I need an address for her, something to go on.''

"No," Dion stated flatly.

"But *why*? It's what the Dillons wanted. Don't you trust your own kin?''

"Not to raise children, I don't!''

"But she's got a son herself! Nice kid, too—according to the neighbors who met him when they used to come down and visit.''

"Neighbors can lie." That was to throw her off the track. Dion had known the boy—his name was Lewis—since the day he was born, and liked him just dandy. He should have kept an eye on those neighbors, though; evidently they'd seen more than he'd given them credit for.

"*Another* reason then?"

"Okay," Dion said bluntly. "I'll lay it on the line: If Ronny goes to live with my sister, there's a very good chance he'll end up dead. Barring that, he's almost bound to wind up crazy as a peckerwood."

"Get real, Mr. Welch!"

"I *am* real! I'm as real as anybody you'll ever meet, and a hell of a lot more alive!"

Ms. Bartlett stood abruptly and fixed him with an icy stare. "There's more to life than being alive."

"No," Dion snapped, "there isn't!"

"And you *really* refuse to tell me? I can subpoena records if I have to—or get court orders. She has to have an address listed *some*place."

"Oh no she doesn't." Dion grinned triumphantly. "You won't find a thing on her—or me—or my brother Gil—and especially not now that I know you're looking! You're *extremely* lucky you located *me*—and a year from now you wouldn't even have been able to do that!"

"And *how*, pray tell, do you expect to accomplish such *wholesale* annihilation?"

Dion's reply was a cryptic smile.

"I still have one *other* option," Ms. Bartlett said at last, with a challenging twinkle in her eye Dion did not like. "This brother Gil you keep referring to. I hear he *likes* to talk to ladies."

"He likes to do *lots* of things to ladies—as I'm sure you've *also* heard."

"That's fine," Ms. Bartlett said even more icily. "My uncle's a warden up where he's staying—and *he* likes to do things to men."

"It's only pain and humiliation. Nothing he can do'll touch the real Gil."

"Ah, but your brother's also inordinately fond of you, isn't he, Mr. Welch? And I *also* have a warden friend *here*—

a fact I'm sure your brother would find very interesting. How *else* do you suppose I arranged this private an audience?''

Dion rolled his eyes and stood, extending his hand chivalrously. "I don't think we have anything else to say to each other." He smiled. "Ms. Bartlett, it's been a pleasure.''

Bartlett's reciprocal handshake was the shortest on record. "I'll be in touch, Mr. Welch. Sleep well.''

And with that Warden Wheeler unlocked the door.

She *would* be in touch, too, Dion knew—one way or another—for the next song was "See You in September.''

He also knew his brother would tell Ms. Alice Bartlett everything she wanted to know. The omens confirmed it, when he recast his future that evening: "I Heard It Through the Grapevine" in the slot for Influences Coming into Being and "Do You Want to Know a Secret?" in the space for What Will Be. And the clincher, the omen for Hopes and Fears: The Zombies' "Tell Her No," but interrupted halfway through by the DJ, thereby reversing the meaning.

"Tell her *yes*," Dion muttered to himself, as he conjured up the mental game of chess he'd been playing with himself for two days now. Then: "No, please God, let Gilbert tell her *no*!''

PART I

CRUCIBLE

Chapter 1

Peer Pressure

Welch County High School,
Cordova, Georgia
Friday, April 6—2:30 P.M.

"Hold it . . . hold it . . . wait . . . okay, it's ready! Any time now!"

But Ronny Dillon already had the tongs in an asbestos-gloved hand and was easing the crucible of molten silver away from the nearly invisible flame of the blowtorch clamped in a specially designed vise beside the worktable. As his instructor's final directions subsided into the dull mumble of youthful voices that pervaded Welch County High's barnlike industrial arts annex, he smoothly swung the ceramic vessel around ninety degrees, then carefully tipped the pouring spout above the foot-high plaster-filled steel cylinder that rested atop an asbestos-covered counter beside him. Liquid metal flowed in a red-white stream, gurgling and fizzing as it invaded the cavities that had housed a purple wax master form until he'd cooked it away in the kiln the day before. A thin, sweet, acrid odor filled the air.

Ronny held his breath for the ten or so seconds the pouring lasted, releasing it only when the mold was full. A shallow dome of glowing metal like a superheated bubble lingered for an instant, centering the smoke-stained plaster, then slowly began to darken. There was practically no overflow. He checked the crucible before setting it down beside the mold and nodded in satisfaction. Good: he'd figured the amount exactly right. Not a trace of what had once been four of Aunt Erin's mismatched antebellum spoons remained unused.

Behind him, his teacher, Mr. Wiley, shut off the torch with an audible *whufft*, then joined Ronny at his work station. "I don't know why I even bother coaching you." Wiley sighed, lifting a blond eyebrow in resigned bemusement. "I should know better by now—but I still don't see how you do it."

"Do what?" Ronny was genuinely curious. As best he could tell he'd done nothing particularly remarkable. All lost-wax casting amounted to, after all, was following a relatively straightforward set of procedures.

"All of it!" Wiley snorted, full of good-natured exasperation. "Getting your molds right the first time, knowing exactly where to put the sprue and how big and long to make it; figuring out precisely the correct amount of metal to melt straight off by eye and *never* having any left over; temperatures; time over the torch—the whole nine yards!"

Ronny's reply was a disinterested shucking of his gloves. "Dunno," he grunted, which was as much response as he generally granted anyone since his accident had forced him to move in with his godmother and her son, here in the wilds of north Georgia. "Just feels right, I guess."

"And you're *sure* you've never done any metalwork before?"

"I told you when I signed up," Ronny replied shortly, scowling as he waited for the button of metal atop the plaster to turn black. "Took a semester of jewelry-making back in Florida," he added irritably, when Wiley showed no sign of leaving. "Never got further than cutting circles, etching, and twisting wires, *okay*?" His gaze never left the steel cylinder.

"Any sculpture?" Wiley persisted. "Your wax master models are as good as any I've seen *anywhere*, never mind high school."

Ronny grimaced sourly. All he needed now was to let himself get distracted and screw up.

"I'd appreciate an answer, Mr. Dillon."

Ronny shot Wiley as much glare as he dared. "I've always liked fiddling around with models, I reckon. I guess I'm used to dealing with small, intricate stuff." He wiped his hands on his holey jeans, as if in dismissal.

"Well, whatever it is, you've sure as heck got a knack for it."

Ronny's reply was to seize the mold with a fresh pair of tongs, swing it another ninety degrees, and dunk it unceremoniously into a galvanized steel basin full of water. A veil of steam immediately engulfed his arm to the elbow, coupled with the frying, sizzling hiss that meant heat and cold had joined battle for control of a defenseless chunk of plaster. Ronny kept it submerged a full minute, then retrieved the spoils from what was now a vat of very murky liquid—and breathed a sigh of relief. Good, he'd done that right too: the sudden cooling had shattered all but a few stubborn fragments away from his new creation.

Several of his classmates had gathered around to watch by now, each holding his breath in anticipation. Wiley was too: as much a kid as the rest of them—which, given he was only in his mid-twenties, didn't require much of a stretch. A chorus of appreciative gasps hissed around him as Ronny gave the prickly object a few quick swipes with a small paintbrush, followed by a careful pair of prods with a sculpting stylus. And then, quite suddenly, his latest masterpiece stood revealed. He examined it critically for perhaps a minute, then passed the object to his teacher.

"Jesus," Wiley murmured, studying the hand-sized figure that glittered before him like an enormous tropical mantis snagged by some biologist's tweezers. "There aren't even any bubbles to speak of!"

"They're just small, that's all," Ronny countered quickly, so enthralled by his own success he forgot to be sullen. "See, there's one in the hair, and one along the edge of the shield . . ."

Wiley screwed up his eyes about as far as anyone could and still look human. "If you *say* so," was all he could manage. He returned the silver figure to Ronny.

"What's that supposed to be?" Rory Smith wondered from the other side of the counter. "Some kinda *Conan*?"

Ronny ignored his classmate's obvious ignorance and eyed the fruit of the last three days' labors with aloof detachment. Not Conan, no; but he really couldn't blame Rory for not knowing the difference, since he was fairly certain the guy's exposure to matters fantastical was exclusively through rented videotapes. And especially since the figure Ronny had so artfully crafted actually *was* a barbarian warrior of sorts.

Maybe six inches high, it depicted a slender, long-haired, angle-faced man clad in intricate breastplate, helmet, vambraces, and greaves, but bare-armed and -legged, and flourishing a huge (i.e.: three-inch) broadsword one-handed above him, while a shield trailed behind in the other. What *looked* like a six-inch-long ribbon of grass terminating at the figure's feet was actually the sprue—the channel down which the molten metal flowed to reach the mold itself— and disguising it that way was another of Ronny's clever touches. In fact, about the only thing that *didn't* betray original thinking was the pose itself; he had lifted it shamelessly from a paperback book cover. But the actual execution from sketch through wax model to finished product was all his own.

Without further delay, Ronny turned and limp-hopped the few steps back to his worktable. His crutch was leaning against one side, and he snagged it as he sat down. A few deft twists of the sprue, which had been designed and positioned as an attachment agent, and he had secured the figure just below the frontmost of the padded horns atop his crutch.

Wiley raised his other eyebrow, muttered a final "Reckon there's nothing *I* can teach you," and stalked off to see how his less accomplished students were doing on *their* casting projects.

Not well, Ronny conceded sadly, as he disengaged the figure from the crutch and rummaged in the drawer under the tabletop until he found a fine-toothed file the size of a toothpick, a soft cloth, and a smidgeon of jeweler's rouge, with which he set to refining his new creation. Most of his eleventh-grade classmates were hard-pressed to comprehend the basic soldering or braising they'd been attempting when Ronny had joined the class two weeks before. *Those* he'd mastered in roughly a day apiece, surprising no one as much as himself. There was no way he could explain his facility, either; working with metal had simply *felt* right. More than once Ronny had found himself wondering why he'd never noticed such an obvious knack before. He supposed it was because he'd had more ego-gratifying priorities—like swimming, like diving, like all the shattered dreams of his former life.

Wiley had been impressed from the start, of course, and had made any number of slightly inane comments about good hand-to-eye coordination being a survival skill and therefore probably hereditary—and had been keeping a more than casual eye on his progress ever since.

Ronny wasn't wild about the attention. Since he was a city boy new to a rural school, and newly handicapped besides, his intention had been to maintain as low a profile as possible until the end of the school year, whereupon he intended to spend a nice lazy summer getting his head back in order. Which meant, in the meantime, keeping talk to a minimum; making good, but not outstanding grades; answering in class only when specifically called on; and not asking questions himself, even in those rare subjects (like trigonometry) when he found himself utterly confounded.

Trouble was, he couldn't *help* showing off when it came to working with metal; the only alternative was to consciously hold himself back, and that violated every principle he'd ever been taught. "Determine a goal and go for it," his father—his *late* father—had said. "If you have a gift, you have an absolute obligation to God, yourself, and your fellow man to use it to the fullest with the last atom of your being."

And to think that a month ago he had not even suspected he could do it! Shoot, two weeks ago they'd practically had to force him to sign up for shop because there were no other classes open for such a late transfer as he. And even at that, had his godbrother Lewis (what *else* could you call the natural son of the godmother/guardian with whom you were living?) not insisted the teacher was a good guy and made Aunt Erin practically fill out the schedule card for him (both thinking—rightly, as it turned out—that activities that kept his hands busy would serve him better than those that merely occupied his rather self-absorbed head), he would have wound up learning accounting or something equally stultifying.

In *that*, at least, he had been fortunate.

Another *whufft* and a blast of heat from behind meant that someone else was taking a turn at the torch: rendering down their own conglomeration of scrap metals. He tried not to look that way; tried to ignore his classmates, to key only to the task at hand. Tried most earnestly *not* to meet scores of adolescent eyes that at once regarded him with begrudging admiration (some of them would get As too, but on that scale, Ronny was due two or three at once), and yet were obviously (and not unreasonably) consumed with jealousy Ronny made little effort to alleviate. None of them truly liked him, he knew, though most were civil—probably out of consideration for Lewis, whom many of them seemed to regard with an almost superstitious awe that Ronny hadn't figured out yet. But he didn't much care anyway, because he really wasn't in the market for friends right now. Not when any one of them could fall and get killed just like that; not when the roads were full of cars, any one of which could snuff someone's candle without the slightest warning.

And of course there were the kids who actually deigned to feel *sorry* for him! Those were the ones that got to him most: the ones who could walk and move freely and pity him, when not *one* of them had a clue how much Ronny was missing.

Like his entire future: there one day, all bright and shining as this silver; and then gone the next, dashed to pieces on the edge of a Florida pool. That he now owned a two-story Tudor in Tampa and had his name on a good-sized bank account, courtesy of inheritance, was little consolation. There were legal administrators for them, and he couldn't touch them until he was twenty-one in any event. What he couldn't touch *ever again*, however, was the dream he'd held dear for as long as he could remember: himself on the ten-meter platform at the Olympics. That it might well have been the *Atlanta* Olympics—practically in his backyard, which would have ensured that people he knew and cared about (*had* known and *had* cared about, rather) would get to watch—merely made the loss of the dream that much more bitter. Now he'd probably get to hobble in on his crutch and watch Aaron Loomis (if his former best friend was extremely fortunate) go for the gold in his stead.

Unbidden, tears welled up in Ronny's eyes, as they still did far too frequently. He wiped them on his polishing rag and hoped no one noticed, then scowled at his crutch once more.

His crutch! He regarded it with a mixture of resentment and appreciation. Resentment that he had no choice but to use it (a shattered—indeed, largely absent—kneecap that, coupled with a broken tibia and major ligament damage, limited leg flexion to the few degrees necessary to drive a car made that a certainty). But appreciation too, since his hostility toward its antiseptic utilitarianism had been the genesis of the current wave of creativity. He had to stump around with a crutch, huh? Had to have people stare at him and feel sorry for him? Well, so much for that! He'd *use* a crutch, then—but it would be the best, the flashiest, the most bizarre crutch in the world, and *he* would make the whole damned thing! He had worked out the basic design already, and was well along on the wax master form (all this at home during his copious free time). It would be simple of line yet baroque in detail. And he would form the main section of it from one piece of aluminum like those complex alloy castings the Italians were always using in their Ferraris and Lamborghinis. Why, just yesterday Wiley had surveyed his drawings and said he thought his design would work in theory, adding that—and these were his exact words—"It looks less like an appliance than a piece of abstract sculpture, combining the functional elegance and organic form of bone, with the mechanical precision of engineering."

And it would be completely overrun by as large a phalanx of miniature warriors as class time and availability of silver spoons allowed. The one in his hand would merely be their captain.

It would take a long time, too, he knew. But that did not concern him, because with diving gone, there was a vast echoing emptiness in his soul that he doubted would ever be filled.

Still, a month ago, flat on his back in a hospital with what was left of his knee screwed full of surgical steel and cased in plaster, there had been nothing in the world he cared about.

Today there was *one* thing.

But when the ringing of the bell signaled the end of class, he knew that was not enough. Sighing, he quickly stashed his warrior in his backpack, then secured his supplies in his locker, slipped a faded blue denim jacket over his black

Indigo Girls T-shirt, and ventured out into the end-of-day chaos of Welch County High.

It was a long way from the industrial arts shop to homeroom: a *bloody* long way. Or at least it was when you had to navigate every slope and staircase with a crutch under one arm and an overladen backpack encumbering the other. Never mind doors that were designed with *two*-handed people in mind, or the inevitable adolescent sadists who tried to trip him, not because he was crippled, but because he was the new kid and—Ronny was ashamed to admit—more than occasionally a sullen, uncommunicative asshole.

The worst part was the eyes: eyes following him down the corridors, lingering over his every halting step but never meeting his own blue gaze—though the fact that he tended to stare fixedly at the ground certainly didn't help. Still, he caught an occasional encouraging comment—mostly from girls. "Looks like Kevin Bacon" was his favorite—if only the follow-up hadn't been "Yeah, but *he* can't dance." Or the ego-shattering double-edged sword of "He's a real fox—or would be if he hadn't got his hind paw hung in a trap!"

As if good looks made a turd's worth of difference anymore. Oh, he lifted weights and worked out on Lewis's rowing machine when he could, so that he'd burned off most of the flab a month in the hospital had given him, leaving him lean and hard and with a good part of his tan intact. And his hair was finally growing out, there being no reason to keep it short now that he wasn't swimming—resulting in a high-tech, burr-headed effect that Aunt Erin said was quite flattering. But would any of it do him any good? Would anyone ever go out with him again, now that he had such an obvious limitation?

He was still pondering that when the last of the stragglers swept by him, leaving him alone on the breezeway that connected the upper and lower buildings. And the lower door—the heavy, glass-and-steel, two-handed door—was already closing ahead of him. He stumbled forward to catch it before it latched, on the theory that if he could reach it before it secured itself, he could just squeeze inside without making a production out of it. Unfortunately, that was not to be. The door shut, the hardware clicked, and he had to fumble with both pack and crutch (securing the latter under his chin) in order to manipulate the recalcitrant mechanism. Of all the doors in school he hated this one most, for it was awkward and heavy and sluggish all at once. He had just gotten the latch to cooperate and was bracing to give it a good yank, when he found himself thrust backward and the pull bar wrenched from his grip. He stumbled, and certainly would have fallen had not a hand closed around his upper arm to steady him.

"Sorry," a female voice gasped—Southern-slow, but without the twang that made too many of his classmates sound like refugees from "The Dukes of Hazzard." Full of sincerity too, though he had no idea how he knew that.

He glanced up reluctantly and found himself gazing into the frank brown eyes of a remarkably pretty girl: slim and dark-haired, and wearing an Indigo Girls T-shirt identical to his above new jeans. Her brow was knitted with concern, but as their exchange of gazes lingered, her expression smoothed and—wonder of wonders—she smiled at him. He could almost literally feel its warmth.

"You are okay, aren't you?" the girl went on breathlessly. "Jeeze, but I hate it when teachers keep on after the bell, don't you?"

"No problem," Ronny mumbled, ignoring the girl's second query while he rearranged his load and edged toward the door she was still partly blocking.

The girl stepped aside to let him pass, but lingered a moment longer.

"You're *sure*?"

"Yeah," he replied, "thanks."

"You're staying with Lewis Welch, aren't you?"

How had she known that? he wondered. It implied that she'd noticed him before, whereas he'd never seen this girl in his life. He'd *certainly* have remembered.

"Uh, yeah, sorta," he told her. "His mom's my . . . uh, my godmother. My folks . . . uh . . ." He swallowed, looked down. "Uh . . . they kinda died. I had to move up here."

"Where from?"

"Tampa."

"That must've been neat. I—" The girl broke off in mid-sentence, blushing furiously. "Oh, I'm sorry! I meant living in *Florida* must've been neat."

Ronny shrugged and managed a smile, hoping to ease the girl's obvious discomfort without betraying too much of his own in the process. "It was."

"Lew's a good guy. I really like him."

"So do I." Which was true. Lewis was in fact the only true friend Ronny had in Welch County.

"Must be real strange—growing up by yourself, and then having to become part of another family, and all."

"How'd you know I grew up by myself?"

The girl smiled cryptically. "I'd have heard if there were any others. News travels fast when it's about the Welches."

Ronny blinked stupidly, wondering whether that was meant as a compliment or an insult. The Welches commanded a huge amount of clout locally, that was a fact (the county had, after all, been named for some multiply-great uncle of Lew's who had founded it). And if he hadn't learned anything else during the two weeks he'd been around, he *had* discovered that being a Welch—or on the good side of one—mattered a *lot* in certain circles. It was hard to get used to, though: being an adjunct to a prestigious local clan—especially when the sept he was connected with was by all accounts the black-sheep branch. And it was doubly confounding when somebody mentioned it and he had no idea how he was supposed to respond.

The girl saved him the risk of a reply—by the simple expedient of checking her watch. "Oh, crap," she wailed in alarm. "I am *so* late."

Ronny smiled wistfully. "Don't let *me* hold you up."

The girl blushed again and glanced down, which brought her gaze in line with his chest. "Like your shirt!" She chuckled. Once more she flashed him that dazzling smile.

"Huh?" Ronny stammered. Then, "Oh . . . right."

"You like the Indigo Girls?"

"Some of their stuff."

"So do I."

A bell chimed. Ronny glanced up apprehensively. "Catch you later?"

"I hope so."

And then, somehow, they were both continuing on their way.

Once inside, Ronny turned and thumped along backwards, gazing through the door's thick glazing to trace the mysterious girl's progress up the breezeway. She moved nicely, but without the self-conscious pretentiousness a lot of pretty girls affected. And he wondered why he suddenly had the oddest feeling that she was thinking about him as well. Why, he could almost imagine the thoughts running through her head: *Nice guy—I wonder if he's taken. Maybe I ought to ask Marilyn.*

Ronny halted dead in his tracks.

Who the hell was Marilyn?

Marilyn *Bridges*, perhaps? She was the only person of that name *he* knew, in which case that was a good sign, because he'd been pretty impressed with *that* Marilyn. Marilyn Bridges had actually gone out of the way to say "Hi" to him on his first day in this new school—as best he could tell, even before word got out that he was associated with the obviously popular Lewis. So if this girl was *that* Marilyn's friend, it augured well for her.

But how the hell had he known?

Maybe he'd been mistaken, and the girl had merely been talking to herself as she sashayed away—though she'd have to have been speaking pretty loudly for him to have heard her through plate glass and steel. He shook his head. Probably he'd been daydreaming again: making up conversations he wanted to hear. He did that a lot, especially in situations where he didn't know many people and was shy about breaking the ice.

But then a cold, sick dread assailed him from out of nowhere, making his stomach flip-flop and chills race over his body. *Maybe he was going insane!* He hadn't had the nightmares lately—not since his accident. But could it be that—

"*Mr. Dillon*," a voice thundered so close behind him he nearly lost his balance again, "don't you have somewhere you need to be?"

Ronny whirled around on his good leg and nearly fell for the second time in as many minutes. "Sorry," he mumbled to the assistant principal he found himself facing. "I got delayed."

"You *must* have! I mean I realize you have a, uh, *problem*, Mr. Dillon, but that doesn't mean you can take advantage of . . ."

Ronny tuned out the rest and stumped away. Only then did it occur to him that he didn't even know the girl's name.

Or did he? Why did he have the strangest suspicion it was *Winnie Cowan*?

Lewis Welch was alternately checking his watch, peering expectantly at the door, and talking ninety miles an hour to everyone in earshot when Ronny finally made it to Miss Maybelle Shepherd's homeroom—bare seconds before the final tardy bell chimed. The *next* bell, due in approximately five minutes, would signal the loading of the first of two series of buses, and the one after that would dismiss commuters: those who drove their own cars, as he and Lewis took turns doing—it had been Lew's turn today. Walkers would go last, which didn't make a lot of sense to Ronny, though he supposed it had something to do with making it less likely they'd be mowed down by the zooming Trans Ams and low-flying Mustang GTs that seemed to be standard fare among the more affluent juniors and seniors.

Lewis's grin and inquisitively lifted left eyebrow easily countered Miss Shepherd's pursed lips and ominous scowl as Ronny thumped over to his front-row seat and flopped down in it—last of her delinquent sheep to return to the fold. The room was abuzz with conversation, even more so than usual, and Ronny could pick up odd snatches—phrases like "*Where'd* you say?" and "Meet you there" and "Wonder if my folks'll let me go," all of which made not an iota of sense, except as they implied that something more interesting than usual was evidently up. He'd *never* seen that much excitement up here. And Lewis, naturally, would be certain to know all about it.

In defiance of Shepherd's strict edicts, Ronny immediately twisted around in place, curiosity about what was happening vying for attention with his already-pending questions about the mysterious dark-haired girl, whom Lew was also sure to have the scoop on.

Lewis, who could be devilishly quick at times, preempted him, however. "'Bout *time* you got in," he chided, thwacking Ronny gently on the nose with the Bic pen he'd been using to doodle on his notebook. "I was afraid I was gonna have to leave you."

"Leave me?" Ronny asked stupidly. "How come?"

"'Cause we've gotta boogie, man! Gotta go over the river and through the woods; gotta—"

"Boogie?" Ronny interrupted. "Where? Lew—what the hell's going *on*?"

Lewis's blue eyes rounded in mock astonishment, preposterously guileless and young in what was already a remarkably youthful face. With his curly blond hair and oversized white shirt he looked amazingly like a Renaissance angel. "You mean you really don't *know*?"

"If I knew, I wouldn't have asked, would I? By the way, do *you* know—" Ronny checked himself, abruptly aware of easily a dozen sets of eyes and ears all intent on his conversation with Lewis.

"Do I know what?" Lewis wondered innocently.

"Never mind." Ronny snorted in disgust. "I'll ask you later."

"I bet he ain't never *heard* of 'im," Jay Garrett opined loudly from one row over and two seats back. He squinted at Ronny speculatively, a-drip with that redneck arrogance Ronny so thoroughly detested. "*Have* you, Dillon?"

"Heard of *who*?" Ronny asked, before he could stop himself. The smart response would have been to ignore Jay and whatever secret had got him and most of the rest of the class riled up—it couldn't be *that* big a deal, after all. But now he'd slipped and set himself up for what would doubtlessly be yet another round of teasing.

Jay leered across Lewis. "He *don't* know, does he?"

Fortunately Lewis interceded and spared Ronny further perplexity. "The Road Man," he whispered conspiratorially, eyes a-twinkle with secret knowledge. "I'll give you the scoop in the parking lot."

At which point a bell obligingly rang, taking the last of the bus riders with it. Miss Shepherd went with them, it being her turn to oversee that stage of the loading—whereupon the rest of the class immediately abandoned their seats and scrunched closer in to Ronny and Lewis.

"And you *really* ain't never heard of the *Road Man*?" Mandy Stevens gasped from Ronny's right, fidgeting with the keys to her classic '66 GTO. "Boy, you *must've* had a mighty queer raisin' if you ain't never heard about *him*!"

Lewis fixed the girl with a good-natured glare which effectively silenced her. She stuck out her tongue, but then grinned broadly—and sincerely, Ronny thought. On the other hand, Lew *was* a Welch, whatever that implied. Ronny wondered if he'd just witnessed some type of subtle one-upmanship.

Lewis winked at him.

"Who's the Road Man?" Ronny repeated, trying to ignore the smirking Mandy.

"I'll *tell* you in the car!"

"*Lewis!*"

"It'd be bad luck to say more right now, okay?"

The ensuing silence told Ronny he would get no more out of Lew until he was good and ready. He would have turned around and stared stonily at the floor had a contemptuous guffaw not drawn his gaze over Lewis's shoulder, to see Chuck Matthews leering at them across the basketball that was his eternal fashion accessory, never mind that the season had long since passed.

"Since when does a Welch needed to worry 'bout *bad* luck?" Chuck wondered loudly, staring straight at Lew.

Lewis did not reply, but Ronny saw him bite back a retort. That was the downside of being a Welch: people liked you— or went through the motions of liking you; they kind of *had* to, though Ronny hadn't exactly found out why, except that it was considered propitious to have a Welch in attendance at any given function, and that no major rite of passage was ever enacted without one. But that same nebulous notoriety also ensured a certain amount of resentment and distancing that for some reason reminded Ronny of what must have existed between serfs and peasants in the Middle Ages. And occasionally, apparently, that resentment boiled over, most often in a small faction that lived in the extreme northern part of the county, as Chuck and Jay both did.

"We don't have luck," Lewis finally growled, unable to restrain himself. "We make do with what comes to us, same as everybody."

"Seems like an awful lot of comin', then," Chuck shot back sourly, and Ronny suspected he was witnessing a resurgence of some long-standing feud only thinly buried. "Seein' as how your mom don't do nothin' all day 'cept stay home and paint, and still drives a Continental, and all."

"Luck don't work *too* well," Junior Warren chimed in, having shifted a seat or so closer in support of his basketball buddy.

"Why not?" Chuck asked in a tone of mock innocence, and Ronny saw him exchange mirthful, knowing glances with Jay. He wished Ms. Shepherd would return, but she was probably still standing guard beside the loading zone.

" 'Cause money and houses and cars or not," Jay went on gleefully, when Lewis showed no signs of answering, "the boy *still* ain't got no daddy—*do* you, Mr. Lewis Welch?"

Lew simply glared at them, and Ronny had to fight the urge to thwack the crap out of them with his crutch, but refrained—out of consideration for his friend.

Ronny didn't understand it all. *He* deserved most of what he got because he brought it on himself by acting aloof and weird. But Lewis . . . Bastard or not, why would *anybody* have it in for Lew? He was bright but not show-offish about it; he was talented (could play a mean twelve-string, sing on key, and draw rather well); he had good, if somewhat trendy taste in clothes; and he was nice-looking, if a bit small for his age, but well-built for all that, with the hard, clean muscles that had helped him to a regional wrestling championship the year before. He also had a sunny disposition that not even vicious teasing could cloud for very long, a disposition exactly mirrored by the curly blond hair and light blue eyes that—Ronny had heard more than once—must have come from his unknown daddy, 'cause surely no Welch ever looked like that.

As to what Welches *did* look like—Ronny had no idea. The only one he'd actually met besides Lewis was Aunt Erin, who was tall, slim, and redheaded.

Lewis had not responded to Jay's last remark, but Ronny could see hurt in his eyes. Fortunately another bell sounded, signaling the departure of the drivers, which put an end to further discussion.

Once in the hall, Lewis automatically ducked ahead of Ronny to run interference, as the roughly ten percent of the student body who drove stampeded for their mounts. Ronny tried to make the best progress he could, hating to slow his friend—until he noticed that Lewis was also hanging back. Roughly thirty seconds later, they were outside and heading toward Lewis's new red Ford Probe halfway down the parking lot on the juniors' side. The lot was almost empty already, but Lewis neither spoke nor increased his pace until they reached the car.

Ronny waited expectantly by the passenger door, but Lewis did not unlock it. Rather he was glancing around as furtively as Ronny had ever seen him.

"Quick—this way!" Lewis hissed, apparently satisfied that some coast or other was clear. Not waiting for Ronny's reply, he darted across the nearer horn of the school's U-shaped driveway and entered the dark pine forest which surrounded Welch County High on three sides. A froth of bluish-white pine needles closed behind him, hiding him completely.

Ronny, finding himself alone, had no recourse but to follow. Sparing a distrustful glance toward the school building, he limped as fast as he could across the road and into the welcoming cover.

"Lewis, what in the *hell* are you doing?" he called, seeing no sign of his friend.

"You haven't figured it out yet?" Lewis chuckled, appearing so suddenly by Ronny's side that he jumped. "We're walking home today!"

"*Walking!*" Ronny cried. "Lewis, I don't *feel* like walking!"

"No, you *feel* like being sorry for yourself—like you always do. But there's a *reason* for it today."

"You gonna tell me?"

"If you're good."

"I'll stick my crutch up your butt if you *don't*!"

"Now or later?" And with that Lewis broke into a grin that quite disarmed Ronny.

"Dammit, Lew, level with me, okay?"

"Okay, okay!" Lewis sighed, bending closer. "We're gonna take the overland way home—and zip by and see the *Road Man*!"

Ronny stiffened. "Will you *cut* this secretive crap?" he

gritted. "Who the *hell* is the friggin' Road Man? And why was it bad luck to tell me back at school?"

"I'm not gonna tell you if you don't come with me."

"I don't like this, Lew," Ronny grumbled. "Besides, there's something I need to ask you."

"I thought you wanted to hear about the Road Man."

"At this point I just want to hear *anything* straightforward and coherent."

Lewis halted and waited for Ronny to catch up, then matched his steps one-for-one. They were still only ten or so yards from the highway, but already the branches had thinned out some, though the ground continued to be carpeted with pine needles. Fortunately, thus enclosed, they were largely immune to the occasional sharp bite of April wind.

"Talk," Ronny said flatly. "Or I turn around and leave."

"Okay, then," Lew began. "As to why I said it was bad luck to tell you at school, that was just so you'd shut up and stop asking questions that were only gonna make trouble for you—I was heading off bad luck for you, so to speak." He paused then, looked thoughtful. "As to who the Road Man is . . . well, it's hard to say."

"*Lewis!*" Ronny warned, deftly thwacking him on the butt with his crutch without losing stride—which surprised both of them.

"Well, I *can't* say, not really," Lewis protested. "I . . . guess the safest way to put it is that he's a kind of tinker or something. Comes through here 'bout every nine years, or so—I barely remember the last time."

"*And . . . ?*"

Lewis cleared his throat. "Well, see, what he does is he just travels around the South with this Gypsy-kinda wagon, only it's pulled by goats; and he sets up shop in a vacant lot or a meadow or some such, and makes things and fixes things. Folks come from all over to see him, and he preaches a little and makes a little money from selling his picture, which is supposed to cure what ails you."

He paused then, bent close. "Some folks say, too," Lewis confided, "that he's a witch—or a conjure man. Say he witches off warts and makes love potions, and aphrod-itiacs—"

"*Aphrodisiacs!*"

"Whatever that stuff is."

"Yeah."

"Right . . . Well, anyway, he's supposed to be in town, supposed to be over at Swanson's Meadow. And—"

"Where'd you hear this?"

"Eddie Lunsford came back from lunch and told it. Said he saw 'im."

"So what're we doing roaming around in the woods, then?"

"Why, it's *obvious*, man! This is a *shortcut*!"

"But why do we need a shortcut?"

"To beat the folks in cars, silly! This way *we'll* get there first!"

"But why—?"

"Because it's supposed to be lucky to be first to have your picture made with the Road Man, stooge!"

"I thought you didn't *need* luck."

"Want a better answer?"

"If you've *got* one!"

"Because I bet Jimmy Powell twenty bucks I'd be the first."

"And let me guess: you—"

"Right. I don't dare put that much pressure on poor old Lady Luck."

Ronny stopped and stared at Lewis, who spun around to face him. "How did you know that's what I was going to say?"

"You mean you *didn't* say it?" Lewis's face was serious.

"You interrupted me."

Lewis turned once more, resuming his progress. "Maybe I read your mind."

"Bullshit."

"Wasn't there something you wanted to ask me?"

"As a matter of fact, yes."

"Well, this would be an awful good time to ask it."

And *that*, Ronny thought as he began to frame his questions, had sounded less like an invitation than an evasion.

Chapter 2

The Machineries of Joy

West of Cordova, Georgia
3:30 P.M.

Ten minutes into their journey through the woods, Ronny had become so frustrated by the rapid pace Lewis had established that he scarcely cared that he still hadn't worked up sufficient nerve to pose the one question that was foremost on his mind regarding the promising Winnie Cowan: namely whether or not she was attached, and if so, to whom.

That *was* her name, however; this Lewis had assured him upon hearing Ronny's surprisingly detailed description, much less curious about how Ronny had come into its possession than Ronny himself was. Her folks had moved up from Atlanta roughly ten years earlier, when her dad had lost his job at the Doraville General Motors plant. They now ran a convenience store on the western edge of Cordova, at which Winnie had been obliged to spend nearly all of her free time until her younger brother, Kelly, had been deemed old enough to take over a full shift a few months before. She was very quiet and made excellent grades, but had been almost invisible until the last year or so when she'd begun to blossom. Since then she'd been making a good name for herself for her consideration, unpretentiousness, and even temper.

All of which was pretty encouraging. But Ronny had to be careful how he phrased any inquiries about possible romantic entanglements, because he had always been very secretive about that aspect of his own personality and didn't want to appear too "interested" lest Lewis catch on and tease him. He liked Lew a lot, but he valued his privacy more.

Still, he wouldn't learn anything by being cautious, and with that resolve firmly in mind, had actually opened his mouth to ask if Winnie were dating anyone, when Lewis glanced at his watch, announced that they weren't making adequate progress, and picked up the tempo to a near-jog that took all of Ronny's concentration and most of his energy to maintain, what with the encroaching twigs and branches and the uneven forest floor. That he could nearly match Lewis stride for stride, even with his various impediments, was a source of considerable pride, because it proved that he hadn't lost *all* his physical prowess. But the altitude— or so he chose to believe—left him desperately short of wind.

"Just one more little hollow and we're there," Lewis panted, easing ahead of Ronny to push through a screen of white-pine branches.

"*Already?*" Ronny wheezed back, more out of breath than he liked from navigating the steep forest track they'd just descended. Having grown up in the flatlands, he wasn't used to mountains yet, and had forgotten that it sometimes took as much effort to go downhill as up, because you had to constantly restrain your momentum. "I thought Swanson's Meadow was a long way from school."

"As the road bends," Lewis replied, holding the branches aside for Ronny to maneuver past. "Not as the crow flies! That's why I wanted to come this way. We ought to have an easy fifteen-minute lead on the other guys, since they'll have to come through town—either that or take logging roads, and they can't drive fast on them. There really are advantages to checking out maps."

Ronny consulted his watch. "Yeah, but it only took, like, *ten* minutes."

Lewis shrugged. "Well, we made good time—but then I always seem to make good time in the woods."

Ronny shot him a dubious glance, but kept his silence. "You coming or not?"

"Soon as I get my dratted crutch untangled." The open V where the fork met at the rubber tip had gotten fouled by a low-lying briar, forcing Ronny to sit down awkwardly (he could not kneel) to extract it.

Lewis gave him an arm up, but that was their last delay. They had reached the bottom of a shallow hollow that sported a yard-wide trickle of stream so pocked with low, flat stones that even Ronny had no trouble crossing it with dry feet. The woods opened out ahead, gradually giving way to knee-high grass along a gentler slope, at the top of which blue sky glimmered between the trunks.

"There's one more thing I need to ask you . . ." Ronny gasped, as he toiled up the rise behind his friend.

"Just a sec," Lewis called, obviously intent on something more esoteric than Ronny's desire for gossip.

The last few yards were the steepest, so that the boys did not actually see the meadow until they were practically in it.

"Made it," Lewis crowed. "And right on time."

Ronny limped up beside him, grimacing as a sharp twinge of pain shot through his injured knee. He rubbed it absently, feeling the bulge of brace and Ace bandage through his jeans, and decided to postpone his final question.

Roughly thrice as long as it was wide, Swanson's Meadow occupied approximately five acres. It was screened by forest on three sides, while the fourth—one of the long axes—fronted the main highway through town, which lay two miles away to the east. More pasture faced it across the road, accented by the mouldering gray shell of a derelict farmhouse, its roof collapsed into its upper story.

"That's the old Swanson homestead," Lewis volunteered, inclining his head that way. "Deserted now, but that's what gave this place its name. We own it," he added. "Or Uncle Matt does."

"Does he own *everything*?"

Lewis nodded disinterestedly. "Just about. He does favors for folks, and they do favors for him, and he likes to collect favors in land. Somebody dies intestate, he usually makes their heirs an offer."

"And let me guess: it's bad luck to refuse."

"Something to that effect."

"So where's this so-called Road Man?"

"Good question." Lewis shaded his eyes to survey the area. It looked empty: a greenish-yellow splash of tall grass broken here and there by scraggly hollies.

Ronny directed his gaze further to the right, squinted, then pointed with his crutch while he wobbled on one foot. "Over there, I think: right past where that finger of trees kinda pokes into the field. Isn't that some kind of wagon?"

Lewis followed his line of sight. "Shoot—you're right. I thought that was an old shed behind a bunch of bushes."

Before he realized it, Ronny was in the lead. He skirted along the north edge of the meadow, keeping the slope to their right, and noted that the treetops were level with them, which would serve to obscure their approach—especially since they were both in jeans and dark jackets. *Why* Ronny thought stealth was important, he didn't know. Maybe it was the sense of adventure it imparted. Or perhaps, he forced himself to admit, he was a little apprehensive.

But if that was the case, Lewis was too. In fact, his godbrother was clearly hanging back. Not overtly, but certainly not maintaining the brisk pace he had set through the woods.

And there was no earthly reason for such trepidation. It

wasn't like the Road Man was unused to visitors, after all. Indeed, from what Lew had told him in the forest, he couldn't get along without them. And Lew himself admitted to having seen the Road Man on the tinker's last foray through—though Lew had only been eight years old at the time, and didn't remember a lot about it.

Except the smell, which he had described vividly.

The same smell Ronny was catching strong whiffs of now.

It was the sickly musk of goats, mixed with the odor of smoke, and as they drew closer to the line of trees that screened the camp, Ronny could hear occasional bleats and the distinct *tink-tink-tink* of metal on metal. It was still hard to see, however, which perplexed him. But then again, what they had taken to be the camp *was* on the fringes of the forest and much the same color, and the sky had, of a sudden, grown cloudy, so that the entire landscape had faded to a kind of colorless, murky haze. And their route had been such that the trees were now directly between them and what they'd assumed to be the camp.

Ronny did not realize he had reached the first machine until he was almost on it. What he had taken for a man-sized bush from as close as ten feet, proved to be an elaborate fan-shaped structure of bamboo and pine twigs laced together with lengths of twine in two colors and string in three. Various bits of metal gleamed dully here and there, and the wind brought the gentle whirr-click of mechanical movement. Closer examination showed that the active components were largely pulleys and gears connected by drive belts of either leather or braided yarn. It was not clear what drove the apparatus, but a trio of grimy plastic pinwheels projecting from the top were spinning slowly.

"Jeeze!" Lewis whispered. "What's this supposed to be?"

"Search me," Ronny replied, scrutinizing the spindly contrivance more thoroughly. "Oh, I see . . . Look!"

He pointed to where, at a yard's remove from the closest

pinwheel, a shaft was rapidly spinning. Affixed to the shaft was what was undoubtedly a bottle brush, and stuck onto a similar shaft next to it was a brass candlestick of the sort often found in import shops. As the shafts rotated, the two brushed against each other, with the result that the candlestick was being gently but thoroughly polished.

"Neat." Ronny chuckled.

"Yeah," Lewis replied dubiously.

"But strange."

"How so?"

"Because I think more energy's going out than coming in."

Lewis studied the machine a moment longer, then nodded. "You're right!"

They lifted inquisitive eyebrows at one another, exchanged shrugs, and trudged on.

The next machine stood precisely at the end of the finger of woods and was constructed in much the same manner as the previous contraption, except that it included a tad more metal and had a framework of rusty iron rebar joined together without obvious welds. It too seemed to be pinwheel-powered, but this time there were five—made of roofing tin—and the spinning brush had metal bristles that were gradually scraping the hair from what was obviously a goatskin.

Ronny did not pause to examine it, for by now they were on the fringe of the Road Man's camp.

A smaller adjunct to the actual meadow, it too was screened by trees on three sides. The grass was much shorter, though, and patches of mud showed through here and there. To the right was a frail-looking stockade lashed together out of more bamboo and rebar, behind which Ronny could see the horns, heads, and widespread ears of an indeterminate number of black-and-white goats.

And straight ahead, maybe twenty feet away, was the rear of what they had first taken to be a shed and now saw was a small enclosed wagon, rather like he'd seen Gypsies

use in movies. The side they were facing contained a narrow
window—he thought. It was hard to tell for certain, because
the entire surface was so thoroughly encrusted with artifacts
of every description it was impossible to ascertain clearly
where augmentations began and underlying structure ended.
A great deal of the clutter consisted of small bits of metal,
either naturally finished, rusted to a uniform red-brown, or
painted; among which Ronny recognized several small appliances, including a rather new blender. But there was also
a stereo turntable set on its side and a multitude of pulleys
and gears, from rusty relics that had to have come off Twen-
ties-vintage farm machines to shiny new ones that could
have driven the engine accessories of any number of late-
model Toyotas. In addition, there were bundles of rebar,
there was aluminum tubing, brass tubing, and PVC tubing
in both black and white. There were phonograph records,
Coke bottles, beer bottles, beer *cans*, blue glass insulators,
five sizes of pistons in stair-step increments, a woman's
dress shoe, two children's sneakers, four squirrel skins, a
stuffed raccoon, and a mirror five feet long and four inches
wide. And that didn't even count the small stuff, like buttons, beads, bottle caps, brushes, screws, nuts, bolts, and
rivets. Finally, there were lengths of wood, scraps of
leather—and bones. *Lots* of bones: vertebrae by the score,
long bones, short bones. Three skulls: one of which was
definitely a goat; one probably a dolphin; and one, sporting
three-inch fangs, either lion or bear. There was also a large
bleached turtle shell, and the pelvis of a cow centering what
Ronny hoped was the window. Discs of blue stained glass
spanned the circular openings, giving it the appearance of
an outrageous mask. Only one wheel was clearly visible
from their angle, but Ronny thought it was made of one
complex metal casting—rather like an Italian sports car's
alloy road wheel on steroids. And there were pinwheels
everywhere, in all sizes, colors, and materials, so that the
entire rear of the wagon seemed kinetically alive.

There were more machines, too: mostly spindly contraptions ranged in a circle around the wagon and made of every conceivable substance, though bamboo and rebar predominated. Ronny and Lewis did not even bother to examine them as they crept closer. None of Lew's cronies had shown up yet, which Lewis whispered was odd.

And then the *tink-tink-tink* that had been so pervasively steady that Ronny had tuned it out ceased abruptly, and they saw the Road Man himself.

He appeared suddenly, rounding the corner from where he'd been occupied up front. He was facing them but not looking their way—which gave the boys a chance to give him a thorough appraisal unobserved.

He was tall, easily six foot three or four, and very muscular—obviously so, since he was wearing nothing but patched and faded jeans and cheap sneakers. His pecs, biceps, and shoulders were particularly impressive, as was his very thick neck. Both Lewis, who wrestled, and Ronny, who had been a swimmer, knew enough about bodybuilding to be more than casually impressed, for this was the body of a man who clearly valued strength and knew how to apply it. It was impossible to tell his age, but his skin looked smooth—what they could see of it; for in addition to the curly red hair that matted his chest, belly, and arms, he also sported a number of tattoos. Ronny couldn't quite make them out, but they seemed to be monochromatic and fairly linear.

The hair on the man's head was likewise curly, wiry, and very red, and would have fallen past his shoulders had a scrap of velvet ribbon not secured it into a greasy-looking ponytail. And as for his face—it too was ageless; he could have been anywhere between twenty-five and fifty. It was a square face, and angular—very masculine, but rendered less threatening by the short, turned-up nose that from some angles made him look almost like a child. He was staring intently at the ground, so Ronny couldn't see his eyes, but something told him they'd be blue. He also wore a plain gold ring on his right pinkie; and at least two baubles depended from his left earlobe.

"Jeeze!" Ronny whispered. "Is that him?"

"You got it!"

It was then that the reason for the Road Man's approach became apparent, for even as the boys watched, he unzipped his fly and proceeded to urinate copiously on the ground. By unspoken agreement, they held their breaths, fearing that any sound or movement would attract the mysterious man's attention when they least desired it.

Fortune was with them, however, and a good half-minute later the Road Man shook himself dry, turned, and sauntered back out of sight.

Ronny vented a sigh of relief, which Lewis echoed.

"Still want your picture made?" Ronny teased in a whisper. "Boy, you could have got a real good 'un there!"

" 'The Road Man Walks His Weenie.' " Lewis chuckled softly.

"More like salami, I'd say . . ."

"Shhh. He'll hear you."

"So? We came to see him, didn't we? He's *got* to hear us sometime."

"But *now*? He'll know what we saw if we show up now."

"So? He's a man; so are we. Men take leaks. All three of us know that."

"I don't know . . ."

"You're just scared."

Lewis frowned thoughtfully, then nodded. "Yeah—maybe I am."

"No reason to be."

"How do *you* know?"

"I just do."

"Ron . . . I know this was my idea, but . . . well, maybe I'm not so sure now . . ."

But Ronny wasn't listening. Ignoring Lewis, he skirted right, beyond the circle of machines, then angled in again from the direction opposite that which the Road Man had so recently anointed.

As he rounded the corner of the wagon, he finally got a view of the forge: a complex but portable affair involving a foot-operated bellows virtually lost within an intricate stand which supported a large iron barrel sliced in half horizontally, then hinged and placed on its side. Even from several yards away Ronny could feel the heat and smell the thick black smoke that billowed from a makeshift chimney on one side. A tree stump a yard beyond supported a good-sized anvil, and as Ronny watched, the Road Man grasped a sooty handle on the edge of the cylinder with his bare hand, dragged a thin, foot-wide wedge of some glowing material from inside with a pair of sooty tongs, transferred the object to his anvil, and commenced to pounding on it with what looked a great deal like a sledgehammer's head lashed to a cow's thigh bone.

For easily a minute Ronny watched spellbound, fruitlessly trying to figure out what the man was making. Lewis, who had only then joined him, was edging away already, but Ronny thumped him on the leg with his crutch and beckoned him back. Not bothering to see if his friend complied, he set his jaw and limped forward until he was scarcely two yards from the anvil.

"Afternoon," he ventured, then succumbed to a fit of coughing brought on by a sudden shift of wind which steered the smoke his way.

"Afternoon," the Road Man replied, his voice unexpectedly light and gentle.

"Afternoon," Ronny repeated, inanely. "I'm Ronny Dillon. I . . . that is, my friend and I heard you were here."

"You're the first," the man observed, still not looking up. "Want a picture?"

"Sure."

"Got a camera?"

Ronny and Lewis exchanged embarrassed grimaces.

"N-no," Lewis stammered. "We . . . uh . . . we didn't

know you were gonna be here until it was too late. We came straight from school. I didn't think to go get one— figured you'd have one, or . . ." He lapsed into an inarticulate mumbling.

"Somebody else'll get the luck then."

Lewis shrugged nonchalantly, but Ronny could tell he was pissed at being toyed with.

"We . . . we thought you might *have* some," Lewis continued awkwardly. "You know, like maybe some we could buy, or—"

"Folks usually bring their *own* cameras."

"We . . . didn't think."

"You'd of been here a minute ago, you could of got a shot of me takin' a piss. *That'd* be one to show your mamas!"

Ronny stifled a giggle. "Yeah . . . I guess it would."

The Road Man did not reply. Intent on his work, he still had not acknowledged their presence with eye contact. And this close, Ronny could see that what he had taken for tattoos were exactly that—except that instead of hearts and wings and the names of women, they looked like intricate engineering drawings interspersed with smaller, even more complex designs that strongly resembled printed circuits. The exception was the circular medallion on his shoulder which faithfully and exquisitely depicted Da Vinci's *The Measure of Man*. Ronny had been correct about the earrings too; except that there were three—one a plain gold stud, one some sort of purple crystal wrapped in wire and secured with a safety pin through the lobe, and a larger one made up of tiny gears that circled endlessly, powered by another of the ubiquitous pinwheels, this one no more than a half inch across.

Finally, what he'd taken for simple patches on the Road Man's pants proved to be more bits of metal; sewn, riveted, or otherwise fastened wherever the fabric had worn thin. And there were a few kinetic assemblages as well: watch-sized gears meshing along his thighs, rubber-band–powered pulleys sliding slowly across his hips. And there were what were undoubtedly scribbles and sketches in dark ink.

Ronny studied the Road Man's technique intently, aware only of the movement of the man's hands, as deft thwacks with the osseous hammer first dished the wedge of dully glowing metal, then chased it with barbarically flamboyant leaves and flowers.

"Northwest eighth of a cauldron," the Road Man muttered without solicitation, whereupon he gave the work three more whacks and dunked it unceremoniously into a nearby vat of water—which also happened to be the air cleaner from a '58 Ford. When the resulting steam had subsided, he wiped his hands on his thighs and—finally—met their eyes. As Ronny had expected, his were blue. What he had *not* expected was that they would be so piercing. Indeed, he felt as if the Road Man were gazing right through his skin and into his soul. He shuddered suddenly, fearful of what this peculiar stranger might find there.

The Road Man lifted a ruddy eyebrow almost sadly. "No pictures?"

"Sorry."

"Your loss more'n mine."

"We . . . we just wanted to drop by and see what was up," Lewis stammered.

"That's what folks usually do, all right. Or what they usually do first. Sooner or later they all come by—'specially the women." He winked at the boys and clutched his crotch. "Sho' do like them women. *Cleave* to 'em, I do—just like the Bible says—cleave to 'em right in the cleft!" He thumped a suspiciously square bulge in his hip pocket emphatically.

Ronny was at a loss. The Road Man obviously knew a vast amount about metalwork, to judge by the ease with which he had pounded out that piece of metal—and Ronny was certain he could learn a great deal from him if the guy'd let him stick around. But he was also physically intimidating, utterly tactless, and appallingly vulgar, which made

Ronny more than a little dubious about the whole affair.

"You a cripple, boy?"

Ronny jumped, not realizing he'd been staring at the Road Man's tattoos. He scowled and nearly spat out an especially virulent comment about how the answer to that ought to be pretty obvious. "You could say that," he managed.

"*Huh?*"

"I said, 'You could say that'!"

"If it ain't worth shoutin' from the mountaintops, don't say it a-tall—that's what I say!"

Ronny's scowl deepened and he eased a step backward. "Thanks for the advice. I reckon we'd better be going."

"What's your hurry? Stay a while. Shit, stay for supper. I might even let you watch me take another leak."

"No thanks."

The Road Man roared with laughter.

Ronny glared at him a moment, then spun around and did his best to stalk away. Lewis followed quickly.

"Ain't got no sense of humor, have you?" the Road Man yelled at their backs.

Ronny ignored him.

"To thine own self be true!"

And still Ronny paid him no mind.

"*That's a nice piece of lost wax casting you've got there . . .*"

Ronny froze in mid-step, wondering what this obviously crazy man was talking about. Unaware he was doing it, he risked a glance over his shoulder—his *right* shoulder, his *crutch* shoulder, and then he understood.

The Road Man had been referring to his miniature warrior: the one that was fixed to the rear horn of his crutch. He frowned. Had that been there all along? He was certain he had removed it at the end of shop class and stashed it inside his backpack. Or had he only *intended* to do that? He'd been awfully preoccupied lately; had undergone a lot of reversals, lots of stress, lots of surprises. Perhaps he was wrong; maybe he only thought he had stashed the figure.

"Ronny, come *on*!" That was from Lewis, tugging at Ronny's other shoulder. Out of the corner of his eye, Ronny could see the Road Man, arms folded on his chest, leering at him.

"No," Ronny replied softly. "Hang on a sec."

"*Ronny!*"

But Ronny did not listen. Squaring his shoulders, he strode back toward the Road Man's camp until he was once more facing the stranger.

"Nice work," the tinker said very simply. "I thought somebody ought to tell you that."

"Thanks."

"*Crude*, but nice."

A scowl smothered Ronny's smile a-borning. "I suppose *you* could do better?"

"Faster'n a goat can fart."

"Prove it!"

The Road Man's eyes widened, but not in anger, and not as much as Lewis's did in horror or Ronny's own did, in amazement at what he'd so stupidly blurted out.

The Road Man chuckled softly. "I don't have to prove *anything* to *you*."

Ronny locked gazes with him, giving him challenge for challenge.

"Can you make a machine that skins chickens?" the Road Man hissed from between brilliant white teeth. "Can you contrive an engine that'll bring the rain? One that can have orgasms? One that can carve hieroglyphics? One that can sing Etruscan? One that can translate Linear B?"

Ronny hesitated. "Nobody can make things like that."

"*I* can."

"Prove it, then. Put your money where your mouth is— come on, where are they?"

"If I could make stuff like that would I keep 'em here? Folks pay money for things like that, and money's the name of the game."

"And you don't have even one?"

"Maybe one."

"So show me!"

The Road Man merely laughed again. "Come back tonight and see."

"Why tonight?" Ronny challenged. "Why not *right now*?"

"Because I'm about to have a lot of company."

Ronny glanced around. The highway thirty yards behind him was empty for a good quarter mile on either side. He raised an eyebrow in mute accusation.

"The first one will be a Pontiac."

"Jesus!" Lewis gasped beside him, tugging once more on Ronny's sleeve. "Look!"

And sure enough, at that exact moment a pale gold blur burst into view at the end of the long straight to their left. Ronny held his breath until he could see the car more clearly. It was Mandy Stevens's classic '66 GTO.

"Better run on," the Road Man yelled behind them. "I might say something would embarrass you otherwise."

The boys needed no further urging.

"See you tonight?" the Road Man roared again, by which time they had covered easily half the distance to the highway.

Before they had reached the road, the pavement was practically choked with cars, most of which pulled over to one or the other sides to emit a veritable battalion of teenagers. Jimmy Powell was in the forefront, most tenured of Lewis's host of buddies, and almost Ronny's friend as well. Jimmy shook a lock of dark hair out of his face and fished for his wallet. Lewis merely grinned and stuck out his hand.

"You win." Jimmy sighed. "Soon as I see the picture."

Lewis's face fell. "Uh . . . I didn't get one. I thought he had 'em to sell and all."

It was Jimmy's turn to hold out his hand. "Then you owe *me* twenty bucks."

Lewis reached for his right hip pocket—and froze, an expression of utter confusion distorting his face.

"Lew? What's wrong?"

"Nothing," he whispered shakily. He withdrew his hand, and stared at what he held.

Ronny craned his neck to see as well, and felt a chill strong as an electric shock. For Lewis was clutching a still-developing Polaroid photograph of himself standing across from the Road Man. Ronny was there too, but mostly cropped out of the frame.

"Jesus!" Ronny whispered.

"Yeah!" Lewis replied. "Wonder how I got that?"

Ronny shrugged. "Doesn't surprise me. Guy as clever as he is probably had a camera hidden somewhere, a little maneuver, a bit of sleight of hand, and *voilà*—instant photo."

"If you say so." Lewis did not sound convinced.

"Or maybe he read your mind," Ronny teased.

"Here's your money," Jimmy grumbled, slapping a twenty atop the photo.

"What took you so long, anyway?" Lewis asked him. Ronny noted that most of the other visitors had already passed them by and were making their way through the grass of the meadow, lifting their legs high, as if they were wading.

"What *took* so long," Jimmy countered, "was that we got friggin' *lost*!"

"Lost! How could you get lost? You've been riding these roads for seventeen years!"

"*I* got lost," Mandy inserted. "The rest of 'em was followin' me. I *knew* you'd try to head off overland, so I took me a little shortcut of my own down some loggin' roads my daddy showed me one time. Only 'bout a mile or so, max, and I'd only been through there two weeks ago when me and Raymond was out . . . never mind. But anyway, I just got lost. Somebody'd done some work in there or something, and I kept runnin' into turns I didn't remember, and I like to never have got out."

"Tough luck!"

"A fat lot *you* know about it!" Mandy snorted and stalked away.

"You boys leavin'?" Jimmy wondered when she had gone.

"Reckon so," Lewis replied.

"Like a ride back to school to pick up your car?"

Lewis checked his watch and glanced at Ronny. "Nah. We're closer to home here than to school anyway, so I reckon it'd be just as easy to walk and collect the car tonight."

Ronny shot his friend a scathing glare. "*Lewis!*"

"*What?*"

Ronny started. This was the first time Lewis had ever raised his voice to him. Probably the guy was wired, he thought. *Something* had sure as hell unnerved him. "Never mind," Ronny said sullenly. "I could use the exercise."

Lewis was all smiles again. "Good job, man!"

Ronny surveyed the surrounding landscape. It was a part he had only passed through once or twice, and then by car. He hadn't really been paying attention. "So which way's home?"

"That way," Lewis said, pointing across the road and past the derelict Swanson house toward another dark line of trees that lay beyond a field. "We'll swing through the edge of Uncle Matt's place, pick up the river path on the other side, and a half mile up that ought to do 'er."

Ronny regarded his crippled leg dubiously. "I dunno, Lew, that's an awful lot of walking. The doctor said—"

"And *I* say it'd do you a world of good," Lewis finished. "—Or don't you trust your luck?"

"I'm not sure *what* I trust anymore," Ronny muttered, and fell silent.

Chapter 3

A Route Obscure and Lonely

East of Cordova, Georgia
3:50 P.M.

"Boy, *he* was a strange old bird!" Lewis chuckled glee-fully as he and Ronny skirted the pair of lightning-blasted walnut trees that had once marked the extreme northwestern corner of what had once been the Swansons' expansive yard. Ronny merely grunted in reply. He had hoped they might swing further left to investigate the house (a rambling two-story with kitchen elling off the rear, in the style that was called Plantation Plain), but that would have required a considerable detour, which Lewis was apparently not in-clined to make.

"We'll check *that* out another time," Lewis added off-handedly, inclining his head in the general direction of the ruin. "There's not really much to it, now that you can't get upstairs."

Ronny blinked in surprise. Once again Lew had preempted a statement he was on the ragged edge of voicing—though he supposed that given the proximity of the building it was not an unlikely observation. "What was so great about the upstairs?" he asked, to cover.

"Well, it was a good place to make out, for one thing," Lewis replied. "Uncle Matt owns the place, so there wasn't any worry about trespassing, plus you could see a fair way off, and the stairs were creaky, so nobody could sneak up on you."

"But couldn't folks see your car?"

"Not if you walked—which I usually did. Or parked around back, where the bushes would hide you. We'll have to spend the night there sometime."

Ronny rolled his eyes dubiously and followed his friend, angling through a field of broomsedge toward a line of forest perhaps an eighth of a mile away. "It's . . . it's not haunted, is it?"

Lewis nodded vigorously and grinned. "Of course it is!"

Ronny was almost taken in for half a second, then returned the grin. "You let folks *think* it is anyway, right?"

"More or less. But speaking of thinking: What did *you* think about the Road Man?"

Ronny shrugged—a gesture made difficult by crutch and backpack. "I dunno. He was . . . weird, I guess. Real off-putting—grouchy and all—yet I couldn't help but kinda be impressed by him. Like, all those machines that ran on wind power were really sharp, and I would swear—I would *swear*, Lewis—that every one of 'em put out more power than it took in, which is supposed to be impossible. I definitely want to look at 'em again, maybe talk to him about 'em too. And that stuff he was working on when we got there! Shoot! He dished out that piece of cauldron in about fifteen seconds, and that would have taken me at least half an hour, never mind the decorations!"

"And how do *you* know so much all of a sudden?" Lewis leapt over a shallow stream, which put Ronny behind once more.

Ronny used his crutch to pole-vault over, then hopped the few steps it took to catch up. "I . . . just *know*, I guess.

I mean I *have* had a jewelry course—took one back in Florida. And once you've mastered a technique, I guess it just gets easy to assess other people's skill. I mean, you're that way with guitar and all.''

"You've certainly embraced that with open arms—metal-work, I mean.''

A heat of anger flushed Ronny's face. "I have to embrace something, don't I? I certainly can't embrace what I used to—or *who* I used to either, since I'm up here and she's down there. And nobody up *here's* bloody likely to want to embrace me!''

"That'll change.''

"Bullshit!''

"It will, trust me.''

Ronny was on the verge of bringing up the question of Winnie Cowan's availability again, but decided the juxta-position of that to their previous discussion would be a little too obvious. Instead, he lapsed into a sullen silence, broken only by the swish of grass against their legs and Lewis's rambling assessment of their encounter with the Road Man, which was basically that he wasn't at all like Lewis had remembered, that he'd been badly put off by the man's demeanor (Lewis was on the fastidious side when it came to language and matters scatological), that he felt really stupid for assuming that the Road Man would have a camera—and that he *loathed* being made to feel stupid.

For his part, Ronny merely soldiered along, tuning out most of Lewis's chatter as he pondered a number of things, not the least of which was the Road Man's comment about his miniature warrior.

"Nice work,'' the Road Man had said.

Damned right it was!

"Lew?'' Ronny asked abruptly, breaking in on Lewis's ongoing monologue.

"Yeah?''

"Did I have that little figure on my crutch when I was in homeroom?''

Lewis glanced over his shoulder in the general direction of the crutch. "Heck if I know. I didn't *notice* it, but that doesn't mean anything. I wanta check it out when we get home, by the way. If it impressed the Road Man, maybe it'll impress me. Mom'd probably like it too—her being an artist, and all."

"I'm serious, Lew."

"So am I. But truly I didn't notice it. Then again, I wasn't *looking* for it. It's nearly the same color as the crutch, anyway."

"It is not! It's silver, the crutch is steel!"

"Looks like steel to me!"

Ronny stopped to examine the tiny figure. It was no longer atop the crutch, but seemed to have slipped down the rear leg almost to his waist—evidently he hadn't fixed it securely enough. "Crap!" he grunted in disgust.

Lewis halted, then jogged the few yards back to rejoin him. "What's the matter?"

"It's . . . it's tarnished all to hell," Ronny groaned. "Some kinda stuff must have got on it at the camp, 'cause it's got this yucky gray crust all over it." He dragged a red bandanna out of his pocket and proceeded to rub the silver warrior's head vigorously. A glance at it and a squinting inspection of the bit of cloth, and Ronny breathed a sigh of relief. Whatever it was wiped off easily. He sniffed the rag and got simultaneous impressions of pollen and smoke.

Lewis raised an eyebrow. "Well?"

"Search me," Ronny muttered, and resumed his trek.

The clouds had grown heavier by the time the boys reached the rampart of scrubby oaks that marked the southern boundary of the former Swanson property. A line of welded wire fencing blocked their progress there, but Lewis dealt with it by the simple expedient of leaning on one of the decaying locust posts that supported the rusty spans until the rotten wood broke. A long section of fence obligingly sagged toward them, and Lewis stamped the center section flat enough for Ronny to make his way across, which he did easily.

What they entered then was not truly forest, though they had to fight their way through a fine tangle of flowering blackberry briars to discover that. Rather it was a grove of widely spaced oaks of a species that was much more common farther south. The branches sprawled for a considerable distance horizontally, and a good many swept close to the ground. Ronny half-expected to see the long wispy beards of Spanish moss that surely would have adorned them in his native Florida, but here in the mountains, he had to make do with mistletoe instead. The leaves were just starting to come in, and it was easy to spot the darker green clumps among the frothy branches.

Lewis led them east along the southern edge of the grove for several hundred yards, then turned right into an open, and rather hilly, field. It had been recently plowed and the long brown furrows stretched nearly to the horizon to both left and right. Ronny was on the verge of asking what sort of crop grew thusly when Lewis preempted him again.

"Corn," he explained. "Uncle Matt uses it for grocery money."

"We're on his land, then? I've only seen it in passing, and not from this side."

Lewis nodded, gestured to his right. "Cardalba Hall's over there."

Ronny squinted into the westering and increasingly murky light, and could just make out roughly half a mile away a clump of dark evergreens crowning a low knoll surrounded by an even mix of forest and riverbottoms. The dull gray roofs of an imposing mansion were barely visible through the lacy branches: three matching gables above a sloping, two-story porch roof, with a second, longer gable at ninety degrees atop them, producing what was in effect a four-story house. Faintly visible beyond was a glimmer of paler green that marked the growth along the Talooga River.

"In this part of the county you're *usually* on Uncle Matt's

property. As you noted, he's rather fond of land.'' Lewis
was walking more slowly now, for which Ronny was mightily grateful.

''And what he doesn't own, Aunt Erin does?''

''Not really. We've got plenty—enough to regulate the
kind of neighbors we have—but Mom's not really into land,
not the way Uncle Matt is. It's practically an obsession with
him.''

''Just enough to make her comfortable?''

''Something like that.''

''And it takes a *hundred* acres to do that?''

''Hundred and twenty point six,'' Lewis supplied. ''I
hope you're not complaining.''

''Not a bit,'' Ronny countered. ''I like my solitude just
fine. It's just a little weird there being so much of it and
all. And Aunt Erin having that nice house and the nice car
and not ever working for it.''

''She works for it, believe me—or did.''

''It's not inherited?''

Lewis shook his head. ''Not much of it. She got a bit
from her mom's estate when she died, but the rest was just
clever investments.''

''Enough to *retire* at thirty?''

''She bought computer stocks when they were cheap—
while she was still in college. And she's always seemed to
have a knack for knowing when to sell 'em right before
they were gonna crash. It's kind of a hobby of hers—playing
the market, I mean. She's also made killings on Chrysler
and Ford.''

''And the art? I mean I know she sells paintings.''

Lewis gestured at the field around him. ''They're to her
like this is to Uncle Matt: spending money.''

''At ten K a pop?''

''Does it bother you?''

''No, it's just that . . .''

''What?''

Ronny halted and glared at Lewis, forcing his friend to

turn and retrace his last half dozen steps. Lewis's face was guileless, confused. "What?" he repeated.

"Oh . . . everything, Lew!" Ronny cried in frustration. "It just gets to me, I guess. I mean, there I am happy as a clam in my own little world, and then bang-thud-swoosh, here I am up to my nose in rednecks—not you, but you know what I mean. So I go in all set to be picked on, 'cause that's what rednecks do to city boys like me, and they *do* pick on me some, but mostly they just treat me like I'm some kinda . . . some kinda *god* or something! And all because I'm stayin' with you guys—all because I'm some kind of honorary Welch—when I don't have an ounce of Welch blood in me. I mean just 'cause Mom was Aunt Erin's roommate in college doesn't mean that—"

"Would you rather they picked on you straight?" Lewis inserted smoothly. He stamped out a small circle in the soft earth and folded himself down into it. A pat of his hand next to him invited Ronny to join him.

"I dunno . . . *No*, of course not!" Ronny stammered, following Lewis's example, grateful for the break. "But at least I'd know how to handle that, for chrissakes. I *can* fight if I have to, but I'm not used to being worshipped. I want folks to like me—*or* hate me, if it comes to that— because of what *I* am, not 'cause of who puts meals on my table."

Lewis regarded him for a long moment. "You may not believe this," he whispered finally, "but I understand—I really do."

He smiled then, and Ronny could not maintain his anger—especially when it had not been directed at Lew in the first place. Ronny flopped his free left arm on his friend's shoulders. "Sorry, man."

Lewis patted the hand. "No problem."

"Something still puzzles me, though," Ronny ventured cautiously, as his eyes once more drifted toward the distant mansion. "Well, several things, actually."

"So shoot."

"Well, first of all, what's the deal with the Welches—
your Welches—and this being Welch County and all—beyond the obvious, I mean. Aunt Erin always tries to sidestep
that when I ask her. You guys got some kinda secret, or
something?"

"No secret," Lewis replied, "not that I know about. But
our folks have been here since at least the late seventeen
hundreds, so they say. Seems one of the ancestors struck
some kinda deal with the Cherokees long before they were
rounded up and sent off, so that when the first settlers came
along they found this nice little tobacco plantation already
thriving."

"Not cotton? I thought all plantations raised was cotton."

"Not up here, the climate's wrong for it. But anyway,
when there got to be enough settlers to name the county, it
only made sense to name it after the guy who more or less
founded it, so it became Welch County—well, actually, it
was officially part of Union County for a long time, though
the folks over here never claimed it, since they were here
first—but when the war came along, it broke off for good."

"Which war?"

"War Between the States, stooge! The War of the Rebellion—the War of Northern Aggression."

"You sound like a Rebel, boy!" Ronny teased, cuffing
Lewis's arm.

"Well, I'm not—really. But I don't like other people
telling me what I can or cannot do with my property."

"Even when that property's a man?"

"They didn't think of them as men then."

Ronny regarded Lewis incredulously. "I hope you don't
mean that."

Lew grinned again. "I don't. I'm merely repeating Uncle
Matt's party line."

"He's a bigot, then?"

"Not in the usual sense. But the family—I guess it
would've been his three-times-great-uncle, but I'm not exactly into genealogy—did lose an awful lot of slaves.

'Course they lost a lot of *everything*, including most of their
land, which they had to sell for taxes—and *not* just on the
plantation, they paid the taxes for everybody in the frigging
county! For three years running! *That's* what ate up most
of the plantation, and it's why Uncle Matt's so land-hungry
now—it's kinda an obsession of his, I guess. 'Course the
family never made a big deal about it, and most folks don't
know that now, but it pisses me when they talk about us
being so lucky that nobody seems to remember that.''

''So what did they do after that?''

''Well, basically, they had to switch professions. It's all
real estate now—and building, and insurance, and bank-
ing.''

''They own all those businesses in town?''

''Most of 'em. Don't *run* 'em; just take a cut of the profits
and keep everybody happy. There's not really a *they*,
though; there's just Uncle Matt—the Master of Cardalba
they call him sometimes. Apparently there's one every gen-
eration. If he's got any brothers, they take their hunks of
their mom's inheritances and split.''

''Their *mom's* inheritances?''

Lewis grimaced uncomfortably. ''I don't know a lot about
it, since my Mom won't talk about it much. But as best I
can tell there's some kind of weird fixation the family's got
about inheritance. See, the Master of Cardalba usually gets
the estate and most of the money, but it's traditional that
as soon as he moves in he makes a will and leaves the
money to his *sister's* kids.''

''His *sister's*? Why?''

''Just tradition, I reckon. Something to do with being
able to prove your sister's kids carry your blood, but *not*
being able to prove your own do.''

''So . . . what *does* your Uncle Matt do?''

Lewis rolled his eyes expressively. ''I honestly don't
know, except that he does it at home. We . . . we don't get
along real well anymore.''

''What happened?''

A shrug. "Well, to be perfectly honest, I don't know the answer to that either. All *I* know is that as long as I've been around, Mom and him have been on the outs, so that anything else I've sort of had to pick up on the sly. All I've been able to find out is that he tried to control her life, and she wouldn't let him; and he tried to get *her* mom—his sister—to intercede, only he couldn't 'cause *his* mom wouldn't let him."

"His mom? Who's that?"

"Aunt Martha."

"Never heard of her."

"Most people haven't. She doesn't get out much, except to travel, by which I mean overseas for months at a time."

"Sounds neat! I'd like to meet her."

"No you wouldn't."

"Why not?"

" 'Cause she's a bitch. She picks on Uncle Matt—and that's saying something."

Ronny looked puzzled. "And Aunt Erin's Matt's . . . sister? No, wait, you said . . ."

"*Niece*," Lewis corrected. "Mom's mom's name was Donna. I guess I should really call him Great-uncle Matt." He paused then, and rose gracefully to his feet, dusting a film of earth off his butt with a swipe of his hand. "Look, Ronny, I truly don't want to talk about this now. It's really complicated and all. I promise I'll lay the whole thing out for you later."

"Tonight?"

"Maybe."

"Okay . . . but can I ask one more question?"

Lewis sighed expressively. "Sure."

"Why is the plantation called Cardalba? What does it mean?"

"I have *no* idea," Lewis replied instantly. "And that's the truth."

"Any relation between it and Cordova?"

"You said only one question."

"Right—but *is* there?"

"Cordova's a corruption of Cardalba."

"Which means what? What language is it?"

"I have *no* idea! Now, look, Ronny, can we just drop it?"

"Long as we pick it up again, fine," Ronny replied. And by that time they were moving on.

As it turned out Lewis was finally persuaded to offer enough additional explanation for Ronny to figure out that when they'd exited the oak grove and headed southeast across the corn field, they were cutting across one corner of the original Cardalba Plantation. The eastern boundary was marked by a loom of pine forest so dark it gave Ronny the willies, especially now as it had begun to sprinkle, which cast the entire landscape in a pall of gloom. Lewis was giving it a wide berth, too; but Ronny was finally getting sufficient feel for the territory, most of which he'd seen from afar from the road across the river, to have a strong suspicion that the straightest way home led through those ominous trunks, not around them.

He said nothing, however, nor was he surprised when a short while later they topped a gentle rise and found themselves facing a chest-high stone wall of the sort Ronny had often seen in episodes of *All Creatures Great and Small*—except that this one wasn't in Yorkshire.

"Bloody hell!" he muttered, as Lewis headed toward it. "We're not going over *that*, are we?"

"I'll give you a hand."

"Can't we just go around?" Ronny sighed.

"You mean go through the woods?"

"Isn't that the straightest way?"

"Yeah, but . . ."

"But what?"

"But . . . well, let's just say I'd really like to avoid the woods."

"I'll *bet* you would!" came a low male voice from the other side of the wall.

Ronny nearly jumped out of his skin, and Lewis too looked more than a little surprised. But then Lewis's face clouded and he marched up to peer over the top row of stones, leaving Ronny to stand blinking bewilderedly among the dirt clods.

"Okay, Anson," Lewis gritted, "I don't need any grief from you."

Anson? Ronny wondered. *Anson who?* But then someone poked his head above the wall and he knew whom Lewis was addressing.

It was Anson Bowman; Ronny would have recognized those piercing blue eyes, that crisp-angled chin and mane of wild black hair anywhere. It was a cruel face for one so young, or would have been had Anson not also possessed an upturned nose that was almost perky, and a thin black mustache so silky and spare it undermined any pretensions to machismo it—or the black leather jacket he always affected—might otherwise have evoked.

Though Anson was officially a senior at Welch County High, Ronny had it on good authority that he only showed up when he felt like it. Why Anson hadn't either dropped out or been expelled, he could not imagine. It certainly sounded like a good idea to him, since Anson was one of the small group of rowdies-cum-bullies (that also included Chuck, Jay, and Junior) who haunted the breezeway between classes: smoking, laughing, and hurling insults and obscenities at anyone unfortunate enough to fall under their baleful scrutiny. Ronny had been their prey more than once—not to the point of blows yet, but he suspected that day was not far off.

But what on earth was Anson doing *here*? And more to the point, what were he and Lew going to do about it? Though Anson hadn't responded to Lew's implicit challenge yet, the already heavy air was suddenly rank with latent confrontation.

Ronny held his breath and waited.

"I'm where I'm *supposed* to be," Anson drawled easily,

flopping his hands on the topmost tier of stones, oblivious to the heavy drops that were now splattering across the chunks of red-brown quartzite. "What's your excuse?"

"You're supposed to be *here*?" Lewis replied, his voice a-drip with sarcasm.

Anson's brows lowered dangerously. "I'm Mr. Welch's yardman. This is Mr. Welch's yard."

Lewis's gaze drifted casually to the right—straight toward the knoll that supported Cardalba Hall. The nearest of the trees that bounded its proper precincts was still over a quarter mile distant. "A pretty *big* yard, I'd say."

"It's still the yard," Lewis countered. "Leastwise it still gets mowed—and I'm still in it. You wanta do something about it?"

Lewis did not honor Anson's taunt with a verbal reply. Instead, he vaulted atop the wall in one fluid motion, then leapt to the ground on the other side. Ronny was at a loss as to how to follow, at least with any grace, then decided that grace or no, there was a good chance Lewis might soon be in need of him. With that in mind, he secured the silver warrior in his backpack, gritted his teeth, and flung his crutch across the wall. It required a bit of a struggle to join it, since the wall was chest-high and he could not bend his right leg more than the few degrees necessary to operate a car, but eventually he was able to scramble over. An instant later he thumped down beside Lewis. He landed badly and felt an excruciating stab of pain as something grated in his damaged knee. He stifled a cry completely, allowing himself only the smallest of grimaces.

Lewis handed him the crutch he'd retrieved for him, but never left off staring at Anson.

For his part, Anson clenched his fists and slowly backed away. Not in cowardice, Ronny saw in an instant, but to give himself room in case anything happened. "*You're* trespassin'," he snarled.

Lewis regarded him coolly and advanced. "I'm a Welch, this is Welch property; what's *your* excuse?"

"You're the bastard son of a disowned Welch daughter," Anson shot back, standing his ground. They were now maybe a dozen yards inside the wall.

"At least I wasn't sleeping on the job."

"Sleepin'?" Anson screeched. "By God, *I* ain't been sleepin'!"

"Then what were you doing lying on the ground?" Lewis asked, wagging his thumb toward an obviously body-shaped impression in the close-mown grass near where Ronny had touched down. It was green as summer, Ronny noted, which struck him as odd. On the other hand, Mr. Matthew Welch was obviously pretty well fixed, and could doubtlessly afford whatever he wanted in the way of fertilizers.

Anson did not immediately answer, and Lewis seized the moment, grinning wickedly. "Only thing *I* know you lie down for besides sleeping is playing with yourself!"

"You don't know much then." Anson snorted.

Lewis's face contorted with mock contrition. "Oh, you're right!" he replied apologetically. "I should have said only thing you lie down *by yourself* for besides sleeping's playing—"

"Look out, Lew!" Ronny's yell drowned out the last of his friend's sentence.

"Don't need to," Lewis replied casually, having neatly sidestepped the overhand jab Anson had launched at him. The failure to connect threw Anson off balance, and he staggered past his intended victim. Lewis tripped him as he went by, then gave him a sideways shove with his forearm for good measure. His eyes were grim, though, and Ronny knew he had doubts about his ability to win what looked very much like an inevitable confrontation. Lewis wrestled competitively, true, but Anson was taller and rangier and had reach. If he relied on his fists and could stay on his feet, there was a good chance he might emerge the victor— which Ronny could not allow. Gritting his teeth against the pain dancing through the remains of his knee, Ronny stumped up to stand shoulder-to-shoulder with his buddy.

Anson was still picking himself up—Lewis was being excruciatingly chivalrous about the whole affair, which Ronny thought preposterously foolish—when Ronny caught sight of a dozen white-furred blurs streaking their way across the expanse of lawn from the direction of the half-hidden mansion. He nudged Lewis gently with his elbow, but a nod from his friend indicated that he too had seen what approached.

By the time the first deep-throated bays reached them, the streaking shapes had resolved into long, thin-bodied hounds, rather like the borzoi his unwillingly abandoned sweetie Anita had liked to show—except that these weren't quite as tall (though perhaps they were females or pups). And except for the fact that every single one of them was pure white with blood-red ears. Ronny barely had time to wonder what Anita would say about such an odd color combination, when Lewis poked him hard in the side.

"Easy," he murmured. "They only *look* dangerous. I've got a different kind of son of a bitch to take care of," he added calmly, glaring at the once-more-upright Anson so furiously that Ronny half-expected one or the other of them to burst into flame and burn to ashes.

But Anson wasn't listening. Even as he dusted himself off, he glanced over his shoulder—and let out a low curse. He immediately headed toward the nearest bit of wall, but the pack (which was *remarkably* fast, Ronny thought) had split into two sections by then, one of which forged ahead to cut him off before he was halfway there. He whirled around and changed direction as best he could—which set him on a collision course with Ronny and Lewis.

Ronny was on the ragged edge of following Anson's example and bolting, but Lewis restrained him with a cautioning touch on his elbow. "Cool it," he whispered. "Those are Uncle Matt's guard dogs. I don't know what they're doing out, but they shouldn't give us any trouble— not while you're with me."

"What about *me*?" Anson gasped, shakily joining them

as the rest of the pack circled in. Ronny simply tried not
to appear frightened, in spite of a nearly overwhelming
desire to turn tail and run. Maybe it was the dogs' uncanny
coloring—for truly he had never seen ears that red. Or
perhaps it was the way their black lips curled back from
their teeth in evil-looking grins. But then he knew why these
dogs had unaccountably terrified him. It was their eyes.
They were blue—as blue as his own. And he had never in
his life seen eyes so intelligent—canny as wolves, and a
thousand times more subtly cruel.

Lewis continued to stand his ground. "They know me,"
he whispered where only Ronny could hear. He knelt on
one knee then, and extended a hand tentatively toward the
nearest hound. "Here . . . Cadwallader, aren't you? Come
to your old buddy Lewis. Yeah, that's a good boy."

Ronny almost couldn't believe it. The wildness in the
lead dog's eyes quickly faded. It took a tentative step toward
Lewis, then another. He could hear Anson's sharp intake
of breath behind him as it paced closer, then realized he
was barely breathing himself.

Another pace, and another, and Lewis's hand never wav-
ered.

And then—abruptly—the dog lunged.

Lewis jumped back in alarm and would have fallen had
Ronny not somehow managed to steady him. A quick check
showed the traitor Cadwallader staying where he was, but
the rest of the pack was advancing behind their leader, and
fanning out on either side.

"Shit!" Anson gasped.

"Yeah," Ronny replied dubiously. "You said it."

"I don't get it!" Lewis whispered, as they continued to
ease away. "They usually like me. They've *never* acted
like this before."

"Maybe they've finally figured out what a conceited asshole you are," Anson sneered.

"Give it a rest," Lewis shot back. "We've got a mutual
problem right now."

Anson did not reply, and Ronny was just as glad, for the dogs were still approaching, still forcing them to retreat across the long empty acres of the "yard."

"Last time I listen to you, when you say you wanta walk home," Ronny growled in Lewis's ear.

"Not now," Lewis gritted. "Absolutely not now." Then, "Oh, Jesus! Look!"

Ronny wondered what he was talking about, until a gasp from Anson drew his attention to the right. He turned that way—and saw that the semicircle of dogs that paced them on that side was slowly and inexorably drawing closer. And then, so quickly Ronny had not even time to cry out, the endmost hound bounded forward—straight between Lewis and Anson. The ones behind it followed immediately, and before Ronny knew what had happened, Anson had been neatly cut off from him and Lewis.

He expected them to attack Anson then—but they completely ignored him, and picked up their pace in Ronny and Lewis's direction. Faster and faster they came, with their strange blue eyes ablaze, and their long white teeth gleaming brightly.

Closer and closer, and then Lewis shouted, "Run!"

In spite of the logic that told him it was the stupidest thing he could do, Ronny did his level best to obey his friend's order. He couldn't run, for his leg was too stiff—and now too painful—for that. But he could half hop, half pole-vault, half hobble, and by the combination of all three make considerable speed.

He was aware of Lewis jogging along beside him, his face more full of disbelief than fear; of Anson falling away behind; of Anson's abrupt shout of laughter, born no doubt of the discovery that he was being ignored, that the cocky Mr. Lewis Welch was being pursued by his own uncle's dogs on that very same uncle's land.

That was peculiar too, Ronny thought. But no more so than the fact that the dogs had not yet attacked. They could easily outrun either him or Lewis, yet they had not. Instead, they seemed content merely to lope along behind them. The dogs were herding them, he realized. Herding them toward the wall on the river side of the yard.

He had just started to inform Lewis of this, when Lewis turned to him and nodded. "Yeah, I know. I saw it too."

"Any idea why?"

" 'Cause they don't want us in here, I suppose. Something must be up with 'em though; 'cause usually they like me."

They were nearly to the wall by then, and a backward glance showed Ronny that the lead hound was picking up the pace a tad. Lewis tapped him on the wrist. "You run on ahead if you can, and get over the wall. I'll try to hold 'em off if I have to."

"But Lew . . ."

"Just *go!*"

Lewis gave Ronny a slap on the butt, and Ronny had little choice but to hobble the last few yards and fling first his crutch and then himself over the wall.

He landed at the top of a bank of thick grass above a narrow, dusty path that ran beside a wide, deep river lavishly overhung with willows: the Talooga, without a doubt. A glance at the sky showed it absolutely thunderous, though the rain was still falling only in random patters—which was all Ronny needed.

"Lew?" he called, glancing back up the bank. "Are you okay?"

No answer.

"*Lew?*"

"Watch out!" And with that Lewis vaulted one-handed over the wall.

Neither boy needed coaching to get as far down the path as they could, but they had not gone far at all before Lew slowed and turned around. Ronny did too, wondering what Lew was about when there was no reason at all dogs that size couldn't easily leap a wall as low as the one they'd just crossed.

But pursuit had evidently ended, and by straining his ears, Ronny could barely make out the swish of grass against multiple pairs of long legs, and then, a short while later, a single, much more distant bark.

He shivered, and resumed his awkward way up the path. Lewis joined him.

"*That* was odd," Lewis panted, and Ronny noticed he was shaking.

"Yeah, tell me about it."

"I just don't understand; those dogs used to *like* me."

"I don't know," Ronny replied. "Maybe they smelled goats on you or something; you know, from our little visit with the Road Man."

"Give me a break." Lewis snorted. "No way I could have picked up that much odor in the little while we were there. I didn't even *touch* anything, for God's sake."

"You got any *other* suggestions?"

Lewis shook his head as they trudged on down the lane. The rain continued to hold off, but a silence had fallen upon them.

"That Anson really is an asshole," Ronny ventured at last.

"Yep."

"Any particular reason? Bad family life, or—"

"Born that way, I guess. We used to be friends, but that was a long time ago."

"What happened?"

"I don't want to talk about it."

"Where's he live, anyway?"

Lewis pointed eastward down the riverside path. "That way, 'bout two miles, across the river."

"I'll give it a wide berth."

"Smart man."

Silence.

Silence—and a much sharper prickle of rain.

"There's one other thing you ought to know about Anson Bowman," Lewis announced abruptly, when ten minutes' travel had brought them in sight of the narrow stone bridge that opened onto the stony path which another quarter mile and a scrap of woods further on emptied into Aunt Erin's backyard.

Ronny glanced sideways at him. "What?"

"Well, you know that Winnie Cowan you were asking me about a while ago?"

Ronny perked up immediately, though he was careful not to show it. "What about her?"

"She's Anson Bowman's girlfriend."

And then the sky exploded with thunder.

Chapter 4

Lucky Finds

Cardalba Hall
7:30 P.M.

"Just initial all three pages and sign the last one," Matthew Welch murmured, trying very hard to mask the anticipation in his voice with the soft scrape of documents shuffling. "Full name, please, and both copies, and then I'll countersign, and we'll be all fixed."

He leaned back in the red leather recliner that dominated Cardalba Hall's oak-paneled library and peered across his silver-framed glasses as Gerald Burns gave the top sheaf of papers one final scan before affixing his signature above the appropriate line at the bottom of the third page. The pen he used was of gold fitted with a white ostrich plume, and the ink was the finest India squid. The small table the sheafs of pure rag paper rested on was of carved and gilded rosewood and had once belonged to the last tsarina. Now all three—pen, ink, and table alike—were the property of Matthew Welch: his to use, to withhold, or to share as caprice inspired him. Just now, he was inclined to be expansive.

Nothing was too good for his clients—especially when what they were signing over to him was land.

"You vetted these past your lawyer, didn't you?" Matthew asked casually, as Burns turned his attention to the duplicate set. "We don't want any problems."

Burns applied his final signature with a flourish, then slid the papers around for Matthew to countersign. "Sure did."

Matthew shook the pen to clear the point, careless of the thick Oriental rug that covered the polished oak floor, or the lanky, red-eared hound resting its head on its paws atop it. "And he's clear about the agreement?"

"Clear as glass," Burns replied, smiling as he ran a knobby hand through hair white as Matt's, though he was younger. It was an honest smile too, free of guile or distrust or apprehension. "I take these deeds and have my lawyer stash them in his safe-deposit box. If, when the time comes, I'm satisfied with the results of your . . . efforts, he pulls them, files them at the courthouse, and the land's yours. And . . ." He paused, almost shyly, ". . . if I'm *not* satisfied, I notify him, he pulls them in *your* presence and shreds them."

"Correct on all counts," Matthew affirmed, matching Gerald's smile with a more wolfish one of his own. He blew on the final signature to dry the ink, then folded both sets of documents, trussed them with black satin ribbon, and slipped them across the table to his visitor. "That's a fine piece of property," he continued. "I want you to know that I really appreciate what you're doing."

"Land's land, and I've got plenty," Burns replied with a nonchalant shrug, retrieving the packets and settling back into the twin to Matthew's chair. "I'll never miss that little corner of riverbottom. But I've only got one boy, and I want him to do as well as he can. An acre's a small price to pay for luck."

"And you understand why we had to set up our deal this way?" Matthew rose with a grace that belied his sixty-two years and crossed to a sideboard to retrieve a Waterford sherry decanter and two matching glasses. Tiny spectrums sparked and slid across the room as the light caught the hand-cut crystal.

Burns stood to accept the drink Matthew poured for him. "Sure I understand. If you provide your service first, and execute it acceptably, and I then renege on our deal, you have no way of reclaiming your investment, so this is a way of assuring I won't simply abscond with the goods, as it were. If, on the other hand, I'm unsatisfied, I need assurances that you won't—ah—take advantage of *me* by claiming you fulfilled your part of the bargain when you didn't."

Matthew grinned broadly and clicked his glass against Burns's, then swished the wine around the sides and swallowed slowly, letting the flavor sift through his entire mouth. "You should have been a lawyer yourself."

Another self-effacing shrug. "I thought about it—never had the money, I guess."

"You should have come to Uncle Ben then—or to me, even. We could have pulled some strings."

Burns suddenly would not meet Matthew's eyes. "Dad never did things that way. He always said a man made his own luck."

It was Matthew's turn to shrug. "Ah well, it doesn't really matter now, does it? But my Uncle Ben, who was like a daddy to me, always said that if a man's got something his neighbor needs, he ought to share it—so that's what I do. And if folks feel like they need to recompense me a little with what *they've* got more than enough of, why, that only seems fair." He paused for a second sip of sherry, which he savored as expressively as the first. "That's the whole trouble with the world today anyway. There's more'n enough stuff to go around, but somehow it doesn't always work that way. Not a supply problem as much as one of distribution. I just try to help out a little."

"And I appreciate it."

"Like I told you, it's a pleasure. I appreciate your confidence."

Burns took a sip in turn, and Matthew saw him steal a glance at his watch.

"Time to pick up the wife?"

The faintest flicker of surprise ghosted across Burns's weathered features. "Uh, yeah, actually. Her day to get her hair fixed, y'know?"

"I know," Matthew acknowledged sympathetically, though he had never been married himself. "Over at Jessie Westcox's, isn't it? Isn't that who she switched to?"

Burns polished off his sherry and set the glass down on an intricately enameled trivet. His surprise had shifted toward alarm. "Y-yeah, last week, as a matter of fact. Her and Mable had a fallin' out over some kinda foolishness. I reckon news gets around."

"I reckon it does," Matthew acknowledged offhandedly, noting how his casual tone was already soothing Burns' unease. "I'm always picking up some little tidbit or other like that. Don't even know where I heard." He grinned again—a little too toothily for sincerity—then inclined his head toward the decanter. "Want another?"

Burns shook his head. "I've *got* to be goin'."

"Stay with us!" Matthew insisted, intoning the age-old formula of Southern hospitality that no one ever actually accepted.

"Sorry, but I really can't. Like I said, I gotta be travelin'—might even ride by and take a gander at the Road Man on my way. I hear he's back in town."

Matthew froze. His face darkened perceptibly. "Now that I *hadn't* heard. Where's he set up? You know? It better not be on any of *my* property!"

"I don't blame you for that!" Burns assured him. "But no, I think he's set up over at Swanson's Meadow—the part you *don't* own."

Matthew tried to appear unconcerned, though Burns's news bothered him more than he liked to admit. Still, there was no sense in letting it show. He had an image to protect, after all. There was no point in letting the rank and file know that the Master of Cardalba was anything less than perfect, and *certainly* not that anything as insignificant as a rumor could upset him.

"Well, if you won't stay, at least let me show you out." Matthew sighed, following his guest toward the massive oak door that let into the upper hall. The last light of day filtered in through the stained glass fanlight above the front door, further inflaming the already brilliant colors of the red-and-blue Persian carpet there.

Matthew slipped ahead of Burns to unlock the front door. In spite of its weight, it moved smoothly on well-oiled hinges, requiring only a finger's touch to manipulate. He eased aside for Burns to pass through, and extended a hand.

Burns took it with a nervousness that had not been present earlier. "Thanks," he said. "It's been a pleasure doin' business with you."

"The pleasure's mine," Matthew replied as Burns stepped onto the porch.

Matthew remained where he was, silhouetted in the doorway until Burns had traversed the four front steps and the avenue of cubical boxwoods that lined the walk. One of the hounds came out to sniff his retreating guest, forcing the man to execute a startled hop that made Matthew chuckle. Only when he saw the brake lights of the dark blue Cutlass blink on at the end of the turnaround did he close the door.

Well, *that* was done, he thought, smiling gleefully at the ease with which Burns had been persuaded to meet his price. Most Masters would have done something like that for far, far less—his late Uncle Ben probably for free. But he saw no point in such altruism—not until Cardalba Plantation had regained every bit of its former glory.

A movement to his right drew his gaze that way, to glimpse his own reflection gazing back at him from the gilt-framed mirror by the door. It revealed a tall, slim man clad in a dark blue business suit worn without a tie. A bit florid of complexion, perhaps, but clear-skinned and bright-eyed nonetheless. And even as he studied his alter self, a stray beam of sunlight pierced the pervasive clouds and crowned his pure white hair with a halo-like glory that reminded him of Saint Thomas in the painting in his bedroom.

He smiled. Such glory was not out of place.

Still, he was troubled about the reappearance of the Road Man, if for no other reason than that he represented an element of chaos in what was otherwise a largely ordered world—which order Matthew by and large controlled. And Matthew did not like rogue elements. For the moment, though, he had a much more imminent problem in the form of the bargain he had so lately sworn to fulfill.

Exactly two minutes later, Matthew was back in his library, but three elements had changed from his most recent tenure there. One was that all three doors were now locked—he had turned the brass keys himself. Another was that both shades and drapes had been pulled across the single tall, many-paned window that looked onto the front porch.

And the final alteration was the person occupying the red leather chair so lately vacated by Gerald Burns it was probably still warm.

She called herself Lenore, and Matthew was content to leave it at that, though he knew both her true first name and her last. She was between fifteen and sixteen, and there were pictures in a number of California post offices listing her as missing, presumably a runaway, and giving a description that was two years out of date. *That* child had dark, haunted eyes, hollow cheeks, and the fearful, wasted expression which collectively screamed "abused." But now, under Matthew's tutelage, she was blossoming into quite a beauty. Her hair had grown out and was trimmed in feathery layers that were far different from the severe, boyish style she'd affected when Matthew had happened upon her on one of his infrequent gambling jaunts to Lake Tahoe. And her face and figure were filling out nicely and she looked absolutely smashing in the new designer jeans and burgundy silk blouse she was presently wearing. She *appeared* happy, contented, and healthy—as much so as a steady diet of good food and all the electronic recreation money could buy and technology could stuff into a two-room suite could provide.

Whether that was *sufficient* was debatable; for she was also, for all practical purposes, a prisoner in Cardalba Hall: forbidden to pass beyond the yard the red-eared dogs patrolled, but otherwise free to roam the sixteen-odd rooms of Matthew's house—excepting the library, his suite, and his mother's.

She was not, however, as most folks would also have assumed, either Matthew Welch's housekeeper (though she did cook a lot because she liked to) or his mistress.

In fact, the latter was an impossibility, for Matthew needed her exactly as she was: completely (and remarkably, given her background) inviolate sexually.

She was, in short, a virgin.

She was also Matthew Welch's footholder—which function she had just been summoned to fulfill.

Matthew helped himself to his second sherry in half an hour and offered another to the girl. She accepted it dully, with a barely audible "Thanks."

"I'm *sorry* to interrupt your movie," Matthew apologized with a touch of sarcasm, referring to the brand-new videotape of *Edward Scissorhands* Lenore had been engrossed in when he had retrieved her, rather unwillingly, from her room. "But the sooner I get started with this, the sooner it'll be over and we can both return to our own lives."

"No problem," Lenore replied softly, her blue eyes never leaving him as Matthew settled into his chair. But there was a hint of resentment there, Matthew noted. It wouldn't be long, he imagined, before she would take flight as well. They all did, after a while; old men and women were scarcely fit company for teenage girls, at least not once they got used to having everything they wanted *except* friends their own age. He knew: *he* could have used a friend or two when he'd been Lenore's age.

If only the Wind would show him the girl's hidden Voice—that way he'd know what to expect and when. But it would not; that was one of the limitations of the Luck: most folks kept their Strength and gave their Voices; but footholders kept their Voices and gave up their Strength.

Sighing, Lenore rose gracefully from her chair and folded herself down on the thick carpet before Matthew's recliner, displacing the hound that had parked there. Matthew, meanwhile, had removed his expensive Italian slippers and was working on his socks. Lenore shifted to accommodate him as he eased his feet into her lap. They looked oddly vulnerable: pale and old—far older than his face, which could have been anywhere between forty-five and seventy.

"This shouldn't take long," Matthew whispered, as he shifted in turn to a more comfortable posture.

"No problem," Lenore repeated.

But Matthew was already electing not to hear. A final sip of sherry and he began.

Placing both hands on the arms of the recliner, he leaned back, inhaling deeply as he let his lids drift closed. The dim light helped there, the warmth of the room outside matching that the sherry lit within. He breathed twice more, inhaling slowly through his nose and exhaling even more gradually through his mouth. The air smelled of dust and old books, of sherry and the herbal shampoo Lenore used on her hair. Twice more he repeated the ritual, willing himself to relax, aware only of the weight of his own body— and of Lenore, who in some subtle way he could not begin to understand, fed him Strength.

His breaths were growing shallow now, his eyes rolling back into his head of their own accord as he entered the trance his Uncle Ben had long ago taught him not to resist— in spite of the fact that in the initial levels, it was very much *like* dying. He knew: Sharing Ben's death had been the last step in the ritual that had made him Master.

But he was already past that phase, and alone in the dark.

Except that it was *not* dark now, for his memories were awake, both those he had himself acquired, and those others the Wind had brought to him and which he had made his own. Those had color and shape and texture, and he sorted them, but did not find what he wanted. Further then, still to no avail, so that he finally had to do a thing he intensely disliked. Steeling himself, he slipped a month or so into the future, then searched out the Winds that blew from a particular schoolroom. A number of students sat there, waiting apprehensively at alternating desks, as they were handed pencils, sheets of paper covered with slots to be blacked in, and thicker booklets which they were sternly ordered not to open until the presiding officer (it was Quintin Carter, Matthew noted, last year's Welch County High Star Teacher) told them to. The words *Scholastic Aptitude Test* were printed across the covers. Matthew shifted his gaze then, examining the tense adolescent faces that filled the room, until he found the one he wanted. It might have been Gerald Burns himself, as he had been when younger, for this boy had much his father's features, though smoothed by youth and framed by hair that was thick and riotously curly. The boy wore a red-and-white athletic jacket, on which was affixed additionally the letter A.

Matthew watched as the boy waited, could sense his unease, and along with it a blending of confidence and doubt. A moment longer he held back, until he was certain that the booklet the boy had been passed would not be exchanged for another. Then by a means even Matthew did not understand, he inserted his consciousness inside the examination book and read it. It took only seconds, for Matthew did not bother to comprehend what passed before his mental eyes. It was enough that every page and question and problem was locked away in his memory.

An instant later, and a second tensing of will, and he had returned to his own time, his brain now laden with knowledge he could not himself recall.

But he was not the one who needed it. Matthew shifted slightly, drew more Strength from the patient Lenore, and sent his mind on the one final journey. It took less than a minute for him to find Burns's boy. He was cramming for his S.A.T.s between glasses of milk at the kitchen table, his thoughts full of algebraic functions and geometric relationships—and of his impending date with his girlfriend.

It was not the optimum time, Matthew knew, but he was both confident and impatient—eager to fulfill his bargain and so gain another parcel of land, which would give him strength of another kind: the security that came from knowing he had regained a small bit more of what had been lost. Still, he was much practiced, and so it was with no particular difficulty that he insinuated his consciousness among the boy's memories—and there planted every word he had read in the examination book.

The boy resisted for an instant, but his parents and two sisters were otherwise occupied with one of the evening Atlanta newscasts, and so did not see his eyes go briefly blank or hear his sharp, startled gasp.

And by then it was over.

Matthew drew away, confident now that as he crammed for his exam, the boy would recognize anything in the booklet Matthew had foreseen, and give those items more attention. He could not *make* him succeed, of course, because the Luck didn't work that way. But what he *could* do was to make the boy aware of the information to key into, and in an already first-rate scholar, that would be sufficient. Ronny Burns would ace his S.A.T., and Matthew would be richer by an acre.

And if the boy chose to ignore his father's wishes and *not* study, why, that would be his problem—*his* bad luck for going against a Welch's advice.

And speaking of wishes, maybe it was time to see how the rest of the county was faring. The Wind brought him *many* Voices, after all, but those that came strongest were wishes—and hatreds and fears.

He drifted then, let his mind settle into his body and simply Listened. Alvin Lawston over at the Exxon station was wishing it would get to be nine o'clock, so he could close up and go home. Sarah Bostwick sitting in her red LeBaron beside the pump was in turn wishing Lawston would get the lead out of *his* feet and pump *her* unleaded faster instead of staring off into space. Austine Hartwell was wishing she hadn't said what she had to her former best friend, Samantha Jones; and Samantha Jones was wishing she had Austine Hartwell on *her* end of the phone line so she could pass on a little piece of her mind. Jeffrey Ash was wishing his date would finish putting on her makeup so they could get on to the single surviving drive-in in town, at which time he would make his most determined assault yet on her virtue; and that same date, Andrea Stancil, was alternately wishing she'd never agreed to go out with Jeffrey at all, and hoping desperately he wouldn't take no for an answer quite so easily. There were others, too: a couple of thousand in fact, but the messages were all essentially the same.

It was business as usual in Welch County.

Except—there were two more Voices he wanted particularly to investigate.

With that in mind, Matthew Listened first in the direction of Swanson's Meadow. There were a *lot* of Voices there—which he expected if what Burns had told him was true about the Road Man making his once-every-nine-years appearance. And most of those Voices were saying about what he expected: a combination of nervous humor, anticipated ridicule, and uneasy distrust.

But the Voice that *should* have been there, that because of its very alienness should have trumpeted like brass through the Winds, was completely silent.

And *that*, Matthew thought, was exceedingly odd. Of course, he had never actually Listened for the Road Man before; the last time the mysterious tinker had passed through the county he had not been *the* Mr. Welch, not been *the* Master of Candalba. And, truth to tell, he'd had other concerns on his mind then, not the least being his confirmation into the Mastership from his dying Uncle Ben. As for the Road Man's *earlier* visits—well, he'd somehow managed to be out of the county during most of them. All he'd actually witnessed was the post-partem chaos—and that family crises always tended to coincide with the tinker's forays through. He hoped this one did not portend the same.

Still, with very few exceptions, the nearest being Lenore, but otherwise confined almost exclusively to the more paranoid members of his family, he could *usually* count on getting at least an Echo from anyone he Listened for locally. And he was not. The Winds were empty, silent, full of nothing out of the ordinary. As if the Road Man were not there at all.

Yet the Road Man *had* to be present, because Gerald Burns had said he was, and because an even score minds of all ages were thinking about him right then—were *looking* at the very source of that confounding Silence, even *talking* to him, for God's sake.

But why hadn't he heard that before? Surely someone in the Clan would have noticed it before. Unless they did *not* know—or unless the Road Man hadn't *been* Silencing those other times. *Or* unless they hadn't *wanted* him to know— except *that* made him sound paranoid, which was one thing he definitely was not.

It was a matter worthy of investigation, that was for certain, but not now. He had Listened to the future, and Looked there as well, and both were preposterously tiring— especially as he was not as strong now as he once had been. He would check one final Wind, then retire.

A final deep breath, and he Listened to a place much closer to hand—across the Talooga and less than a mile upstream. It was his niece's estate: Erin Welch's house. But he did not seek out his sister's daughter, because he knew her Voice would be hidden from him behind the shield of Silence she always maintained around herself and her bastard son—though how she had learned that art to such perfection, when she had supposedly disavowed all traffic with the Luck and its trappings, he had no idea. It was one of the few frustrations—and few failures—in his long and productive life. And even the Master of Cardalba was entitled to a *few* failures.

Especially when there'd been successes as well, and not that long ago: Erin Welch had been ill for two weeks back in February, and during that time she'd let her Silence slip enough for him to slip a few Words past her—only a few, and only occasionally, but enough (he hoped) that the cumulative terror of their immediacy would drive Lewis Welch insane. Not that he had anything *personal* against the boy, of course; only that he represented a threat to another plan of Matthew's, which was just about to come to fruition. And since actually *killing* the lad was out of the question for a number of likely *and* unlikely reasons, he had chosen the next most viable option. Unfortunately, he hadn't had quite enough time for his nighttime Whisperings to take full effect, and even his successes had had a peculiar feel to them, as though his Voice was shouting across a great distance.

And *something* odd had been going on over there lately, as well. Erin's Silence had become *particularly* strong since her recovery, as if she were extending that shielding beyond its usual limits. He'd meant to investigate further, but had to be careful about how he used his Voice, lest his mother catch him at it. Still, now might be a good time for exactly that.

Erin's Silence was back in place, of course; but Matthew had Listened around it enough recently to discover a few thin places—perhaps a function of that same curious expansion he'd detected lately. It was at one of these he paused, and caught, for the first time in over a month, faint but clear the Voice of Lewis—his grandnephew, and the boy he had sworn to drive mad. The lad was playing a video game and recalling a recent adventure he'd had with someone named Ronny. It involved the Road Man, Matthew realized, which excited him. But with that excitation, he lost his subtlety, and Erin became aware of him and thrust her Silence out at him, forcing him to withdraw. He Heard anger, the same sort of threat Erin had directed at him before.

And as soon as he blinked himself back into the library, he heard the sharp-edged voice of his mother snapping, "Scoot, child. I need to have a word or two with my boy."

Lenore was already withdrawing, peering fearfully over her shoulder at the tall, thin, gray-haired woman who stood directly behind her, glaring at Matthew from behind steel-rimmed glasses the same color as both her eyes and the fine velvet suit she was wearing. Matthew could sense the Strength drawing away, returning to the much lower pulse that always filled him when he did not have Lenore to augment and recharge him.

Miss Martha Welch was not pleased.

"Scoot!"

Lenore, who had been edging toward the hall door, finished that journey in two long strides and a hop. The door had not yet slammed behind her when Martha started in on him.

"You've been at it again, haven't you?" she shrilled in a voice that sounded far older than her face would indicate— she was in fact eighty-two. "Making *deals*," she continued, before Matthew could insert a single word. He hated it when she did this, not the railing alone, but catching him Between, when his thoughts were muddled. "Making deals and swindling honest folks out of their property! Why—"

"It's a service for a service," Matthew countered sharply, a raw, bitter edge to his voice. "We've been over this about once a week since I took over the Mastership."

"Yes, and Brother Ben'd be spinning in his grave if he knew what you were up to! A Welch, a goddamned *Welch* taking that much property for that little Luck! Why, I never heard of such a thing!"

"Well, what *else* am I supposed to do? Give it away for free?"

"Your uncle did, and his uncle before him. Every Master of Cardalba there ever was did—except you."

Matthew shrugged arrogantly, gestured expansively around the room. "And how do you explain all this? Are you saying this represents *nothing* but two hundred years of goodwill?"

"Absolutely," Martha snapped. "And Luck like it's supposed to be, too: what goes around comes around, and all that. You do a good thing *of your own free will* and if folks appreciate it, they do something for you in turn—but you don't ask them to. Sometimes they leave you property in their wills, but only if *they* want to, not if you coerce them into it, like you did to that poor man just now—and don't think I don't know every word that went on down here behind closed doors! And if they *don't* appreciate it, then you write it down in the debit colum and forget it—chalk it up to laying down—"

" 'Treasures in Heaven,' " Matthew finished for her. "I know, Mother. Except that I don't believe in Heaven."

Martha helped herself to Lenore's former chair and continued to glare at her son. "Well, you're blatantly abusing a God-given talent, and no good'll come of it, that's for damned sure!"

"I don't believe in God either."

"I know. What's important is whether or not he believes in you."

"You've been reading too many cheap magazines."

Martha snorted. "Don't dodge the issue. I know more about these things than you do, and you're doing wrong, boy. I know absolutely, positively that you're doing wrong."

"Have you Listened to the future, then?"

"You know I can't do that." She rose abruptly, stalked over to retrieve the sherry decanter, and took a healthy swig straight from the heavy crystal. "And speaking of things people *won't* do,'' she continued, ''I think it's past damned time you Activated your heir.''

Matthew rolled his eyes. They were back to that, huh? He wondered what had gotten into the old bitch that she'd chosen today of all days to dig up both their ancient bones of contention.

''Do we have to go into that now? I have a headache.''

''I shouldn't wonder! Prowling 'round in people's heads.''

''I was *only* Listening—and not even you can object to that—it's part of the job! Besides, what I did for that boy's going to help him.''

Martha grimaced sourly and took another hit from the decanter. ''I'll concede that, though there are much more subtle ways the same results could have been achieved— but don't sidestep the issue.''

''What issue?''

''The heir! When are you going to start laying the ground-work for Lewis's initiation? He'll be eighteen in less than a year. His Luck's probably already manifesting.''

Matthew twisted uncomfortably—an odd gesture in one of his mature years and normally patrician demeanor. He was on the spot now, and he knew he dared not lie. ''It's not going to be Lewis,'' he stated flatly. ''I've finally decided that. Erin obviously doesn't want him to be the one, and—''

Martha's eyes nearly popped out of her head—which Matthew would have welcomed. ''Who, then?'' she interrupted. ''Poor Donna's children: your *proper* heirs? Dion's got two years to go on his sentence, even if he gets paroled, never mind that he doesn't want anything to do with you; and poor Gilbert's so far in the jail he's *under* it, and he doesn't want the Mastership either, even if it would accept either of them now, which it probably won't, given that they've both undergone the rejection ritual. Erin's not a virgin, so *she's* out, which leaves *her* son: the only other one with true Welch blood—at least that we have access to.''

Matthew shook his head. ''There's also Anson.''

''*Anson!* You mean to tell me you'd actually consider your bastard's bastard a proper heir? Besides, you *know* what he is.''

''He's my blood through and through is what he is. I know, I had all the tests run, right down to the DNA. I don't think that the other really matters, long as we're careful.''

Martha was gaping incredulously, as if the revelations Matthew was making had never occurred to her. ''But the succession always goes through the female line—through the Master's sister's sons, or *her* daughter's sons. It's the only way we can be *absolutely* sure of the bloodlines.''

Matthew smiled cryptically. ''Ah, but is that *law*, or *tradition*? What about now that we can *prove* descent genetically?''

''That's the way it's always *been* done.''

''And our ancestors used to take heads, pickle them in cedar oil, and parade them around on holidays, but we don't do *that* anymore.''

''That's a matter of legality, not . . . karma, or whatever we're calling it now.''

''See, even you're confused.'' Matthew chuckled grimly. ''Besides, Erin's kept the boy wrapped in Silence for every day of his seventeen years—though how she's managed to accomplish *that*, I haven't a clue. She doesn't *want* him to be heir. Shoot, if she had her way, she wouldn't even want him to be a Welch. He's not predisposed, even if he has been Fixed.''

''So much the *better* if he doesn't know what he is. If he doesn't know he's heir to the Luck, he's less likely to covet it, and if he's already well-adjusted and happy, he's more likely to use the Mastership wisely.''

''All of which can also be said of Anson Bowman.''

''Bullshit. The boy's a bully and an arrogant asshole.''

"As you would be too if somebody called you a bastard every day of your life."

Martha smiled sweetly. "Hasn't hurt Lewis."

"That you know of!"

"I won't have it!" Martha retorted. "It will be Lewis, or it will be nobody. If the tradition can't be upheld, the tradition dies. Folks'll just have to get by on their own Luck—most folks do anyway."

"That's 'cause most folks who have it to spare don't get paid to use it."

Martha fell silent, while Matthew gazed at her triumphantly. Her eyes were narrowed, though, and her brow wrinkled with thought—though even then it was not as wrinkled as eighty-odd years should have made it. Finally she looked at him slyly.

"There's one *other* possibility."

Matthew leaned forward with an air of feigned interest. "And who, pray tell, might that be?"

"You know as well as I do."

"You mean the other heir? The apocryphal Unknown Heir? That's *bullshit*! Just because Uncle Ben one time *thought* he Heard a Welch Speaking from afar."

"*And* because Erin very conveniently contrived to go into labor in Florida when none of the family were around except Dion, who always keeps his Silence up, and who would not take an oath, even though he was present at the delivery— officially, at least, to set the boy's triggers, since Erin was in no shape to do it."

Matthew sighed. "Okay," he said slowly. "If it will make you happy—if it will make you go away and leave me alone with my headache—I will check again. I doubt it will work, mind you, but I will make the attempt." He glanced at his Rolex, which informed him it was fast approaching nine-thirty. "But I have *got* to rest some before I can do that. Passing around the Luck takes it out of a body."

"I'm sure," Martha growled sarcastically.

"Be glad you're female."

To Matthew's surprise Martha was giggling. "What's so funny?" he asked.

"I can't help it, but—well, just think how much *more* complicated the whole mess would be if men *also* lost their chance at wielding Luck when they lost their virginity. Then we'd have everybody jockeying for position right and left."

"Or holding out." Matt laughed in spite of himself. "But if that were the case there'd be no Listeners in short order, because no one would be willing to make the sacrifice."

"Celibacy for power?" Martha snorted. "I'd have chosen that in a second, had I been given the choice."

"Which you weren't, by the dubious virtue of a convenient bribe to a local lad, so I hear. Now scat. I've got some resting to do—and then some heavy-duty Listening."

But Matthew Welch did not wait to carry out his mother's will. As soon as her footsteps were echoing up the stairs toward her second-floor suite, he pressed a button she did not know of that was conveniently concealed beneath his chair. A bell obligingly rang in Lenore's sitting room (which was as far from his mother's lair as he could manage), and a short while later, his footholder returned. She looked grumpy and out of sorts—tired from the ordeal he had lately put her through—and from having her evening's entertainment interrupted twice in an hour. Nevertheless, she obligingly resumed her place at his feet, and it was then a simple matter to slip into trance once more.

This time, however, Matthew quickly tuned out the local Voices, letting them fall away one by one until only the soft whisper of the Wind remained, undisturbed save by the occasional Silences, the strongest of which rose around the ever-vigilant Erin. At first he simply drifted for a while, Listening further and further out, catching other Listeners—or those with Luck of other kinds. But none bore the tell-tale signature of Welchness. He strained his Strength then, Listened even further afield, distantly aware of Lenore's gasp as his efforts taxed her far beyond what she was accustomed to. Eventually he brushed the Silence that was a sleeping Dion, felt it stir in alarm and harden as if by reflex; then Heard the naked Voice of Gilbert awake and so alert and spiteful Matthew fled from it lest it know him and trap him there.

He'd been right, then; there was nothing. The Winds were empty, brought him no lost Welch Voices crying out their loneliness.

None at all.

Except . . .

His return brought him near Erin's house once more—and this time he found, for the second time that evening, a weakening in the Silence she had raised around herself and her son. No, he was wrong: it was less a weakening than an actual rupture, and Lewis's Voice was leaking through again. He had put his video game aside and was now engrossed in a horror film of some kind. But there was something odd about his Voice Matthew had not noticed before, as if it had a sort of echo, like a second Voice harmonizing with it.

A second Voice!

The force of that realization was equivalent to shouting in his own Voice. Which meant that anyone in ten miles who could Listen very likely Heard.

Someone did—presumably Erin—and flowed into the Silence and sealed it until it once again resembled a dome of opaque glass rising firm above the Winds.

Matthew's eyes popped open.

''So there *is* another heir!'' he whispered to a near-unconscious Lenore, as he snatched the half-empty decanter and impulsively drained it. ''And his name is Ronny Dillon!''

And Anson Bowman, who was born of the seed of Matthew Welch, and who had been standing on the porch outside the library window ever since he had first heard voices and paused there while on his way to the front door where he had planned to ask for an advance on next week's already remarkable yardman salary, had heard almost every word both Matthew and Martha had spoken. *And*, since the window shade had not been inspected for bug nibbles lately, had also seen a fair bit as well. Suddenly, he felt very, *very* lucky indeed.

Chapter 5

Food for Thought

Erin Welch's house
Saturday, April 7—2:05 A.M.

(. . . darkness—and a distant, insidious murmur . . .
a man's voice, a soft drawl, that gently lulls awareness to
rest . . .)

" . . . *You* will *die—sooner or later; sooner or later you*
will *die . . . You will be* nothing! *You will have* no *senses,*
no *memory,* no *dreams,* no *ambitions,* no *desires . . .*

" . . . *You* will *die . . . Sooner or* later *you will . . .*

" . . . *A hundred years hence, all who ever knew you will
have vanished . . . The files that tally your deeds will all
have been deleted . . . Your very* bones *will have drifted
down to dust . . ."*

" . . . *Why not negate it now . . . ? Why endure the battle
when all effort comes at last to nothing . . . ? Why hope for
joy when it is fleeting . . . ? Why flee from pain that need
not be endured . . . ?"*

A heartbeat skips: a spark of panicked pain gone so quick
it does not register. Ronny forgets to breathe—which wakes

a familiar tightness in his lungs that becomes the one lone
stimulus some vigilant neuron can fix on . . .

   "*Die!*"

Ronny sat bolt upright in the darkness, uncertain if the
dreadfully familiar word still ringing in his ears was the last
gasp of his fading nightmare or his own barely audible
responsive cry. Probably the former, he concluded, since
whatever it was had not disturbed Lew, who snored on
undisturbed in his twin bed across the mazelike clutter of
the spacious bedroom they—at Aunt Erin's insistence—
shared. Ronny blinked into the moonlit gloom, could just
make out his foster brother sprawled across the covers on
his stomach, bare to the waist and clad in red sweatpants,
right arm draped so far off the side of the bed his knuckles
brushed the floor.

Ronny shuddered and pulled the single quilt up around
his own naked shoulders. It couldn't be happening again,
couldn't! The nightmares had already cursed him once, had
shattered his world and then left him—so he thought; as if
they had completed whatever vicious mission had been
theirs. But now, just when he was finally becoming able to
sleep without fear again, they had returned.

Or had they? What he had awakened from hadn't quite
felt like one of his earlier nightmares. *They* had been *too*
immediate, *too* real; this had seemed more like an ordinary
dream about an extraordinary unpleasantness, perhaps one
born of his own fear rather than the nebulous external influences he'd half-suspected had been at work before.

Except that it hadn't quite felt that way either, for there
had been the merest trace of some alien element, as if—
there was no other way to put it—something had *sensed* his
dream and begun poking at its edges from outside.

One thing was for sure: he was too wired to get back to
sleep anytime soon. He poked the tiny button that illumi-
nated his watch and saw to his dismay that it was only a
little after 2:00 A.M., which meant he'd only been asleep
maybe an hour—he and Lew had stayed home that night to

catch an obscure horror movie on an even obscurer network
in preference to being social. Not that he was very social
anyway, beyond the occasional party Lewis dragged him
to.

So the dream had come to him in the first stages of sleep,
in good old R.E.M. He wondered if that was important and
shook his head, too befuddled to resort to higher reasoning.

Which still left him in a quandary regarding what to do.
He considered making a snack, but the noise that would
necessitate could easily rouse Aunt Erin, whose bedroom
was next to the kitchen and who was, he had discovered
early on, a very light sleeper. All he needed now was *her*
asking him those pointed, disturbing questions about what
was bothering him, the same sort she'd plied him with about
a million of on the long drive up from Tampa. He'd told
her about the nightmares then, though he hadn't really
wanted to. But he certainly didn't want to talk about them
again now.

TV was out for much the same reason—either the big
Sony in the den, which would once again disturb Aunt Erin,
or its smaller cousin in this room, which would undoubtedly
awaken Lew. And reading was a no-no as well.

Still, he certainly couldn't lie there and fidget all night.

A walk, then? Yeah, maybe that was it. The moon was
just past half full and waxing, and its light was filtering in
through a fair number of windows throughout the house, so
that if he walked barefoot and carefully, he could probably
make it outside without awakening anyone, even with the
damnably cumbersome crutch.

Without further ado, he slid noiselessly from bed and
reached for his clothes, then thought better of it. Lew might
hear and intercept him. But the clothes he had worn earlier
that day, which had gotten soaked by the rain that had
terminated his and Lew's ramble through the fields, were
still in the dryer in the utility room, and his soggy Reeboks
were there as well. True, that room also adjoined the
kitchen, though on the other side; but in deference to the

noisy appliances it contained it had been given an extra layer of sound insulation, so that if he could once make it there undetected, he could almost certainly change inside without risk of being overheard. Besides, it had its own outside door.

One thing he *would* need, however, was his security card. Aunt Erin was an attractive woman living virtually alone in a semi-remote area in a large house full of valuable antiques and more valuable paintings. She was reasonably well off and heavily into computer stocks; thus, she had the place pretty well armored with electronic safeguards.

Sighing softly, Ronny reached for his wallet, snagged his crutch, then made his way across the thick carpet toward the door. It opened soundlessly—fortunately it had not quite latched when Lew had closed it—and, clad only in his blue bikini briefs, he entered the hall. A few soft, halting steps, and he had reached the kitchen. He turned right there—left would take him to Aunt Erin's sanctum—and made his way to the utility room. That door was the hardest—it, and muffling the crutch's thump—but he'd always prided himself on moving smoothly and silently and, even disabled, was still fairly adept at stealth.

So it was that barely more than a minute later he was fully dressed in the distressed jeans, denim jacket, white Reeboks, and Indigo Girls T-shirt he had previously shed there. A pause for his crutch (with its silver augmentation now thoroughly cleaned and reaffixed), a swipe of his security card through the slot by the door, and he was outside.

Night rushed up to greet him, silent and starlit, if still slightly damp after the afternoon's brief downpour. The overall effect, however, was of springtime freshness: delicately chilly, but awash with the scents of newborn foliage. Without consciously thinking about it, Ronny found himself following the concrete walk that flanked the driveway, noting absently how neat the few remaining raindrops looked as they glimmered and quivered atop the sensual, newly

waxed curves and planes of Lew's Ford Probe, which the
two of them had retrieved after supper.

The walk petered out a short way further on, however,
to merge with the trail he and Lew had taken from Matthew's
place. It also ran by the river, and Ronny had the sudden
notion that perhaps a walk beside running water would relax
him. It was a fair hike, especially for someone whose knee
had not entirely recovered from the workout he had already
given it that day, but that did not concern him. He was wide
awake, after all; there was no school tomorrow, and the
scrap of woods that lay between Aunt Erin's house and the
river looked both mysterious and inviting. Shrugging for no
particular reason except to confirm his decision, he marched
into the forest.

It did not take nearly as long as he expected to traverse
the parklike stands of oak and walnut, so that before he
knew it, he had crossed the arched stone bridge and was
once more following the path beside the Talooga, with the
looming willows on his left and an overgrown field beyond
a fringe of pine trees to his right. He'd guessed correctly,
too: the combination of moonlight and the lulling burble of
the river was relaxing—so much so that before he knew it,
he had come much closer to Cardalba than he'd intended.
The wall-crowned slope that marked the formal boundary
of Matthew Welch's inner environs loomed to his right,
butting right up against a finger of the forest Lew had wanted
to avoid earlier.

Ronny paused there a moment, torn with indecision, alert
for hint of the proximity of Matthew Welch's guard dogs;
then squared his shoulders and strode (as best he could,
given the footing) straight beneath the dark needles. By
keeping the wall barely in sight to his left, he was able to
make his way with surprising haste without getting lost—
quickly becoming aware of the field becoming ever more
distant to his right. He'd been wrong about the woods,
though: they were not threatening at all. Indeed, they seemed
to exude an air of calm that was, if anything, even more

soothing than that he had felt on the path beside the river. He wondered about that too: about why Lew had wanted to avoid them and wouldn't explain why.

Once again, it did not take him as long as he'd predicted to navigate that bit of forest (perhaps assisted by the surprisingly sparse ground cover and the relatively flat terrain). The result was that less than ten minutes after he had entered, Ronny found himself standing at the edge of the overgrown broomsedge field behind the old Swanson place.

And up ahead, ringing softly through the night, came the faint but clear sound of metal tapping on metal.

Ronny could not resist. It was a long way back home, he realized suddenly, but the Road Man's camp was not much further on, and since he was nearly there anyway, he saw no reason not to extend his ramble a little more.

Five minutes later he had crossed the Swansons' field and stood on the edge of the highway. Two minutes after that, he was approaching the Road Man's camp.

The smithing sounds were definitely louder too, and clearly coming from the forge side of the wagon, which meant that whatever was causing them was obscured by that fantastically decorated bulk. But Ronny could see flames flickering between the wheel spokes, and as he drew closer, make out a puff-and-grunt that accompanied the rhythmic pounding.

He had just reached the circle of "machines" that fringed the encampment proper when something caught his attention. He froze where he stood and rubbed his eyes, thinking at first that what had given him pause was merely a function of the uncertain light. But he was wrong.

These were not the same machines he had seen earlier; none of them were. The fabrications he'd encountered that afternoon had looked flimsy in the extreme: jury-rigged contrivances of wood and scrap metal and odd bits of rusted or corroded junk. But *these* man-high constructs gleamed and glittered in the moonlight, their lines taut, their structures gossamer weavings of shining chrome and polished copper and shimmering aluminum. Every juncture (it was hard to tell if there were actual welds) was completely seamless, and the gears and sprockets within moved almost soundlessly, in contrast to the noisy clank-and-clatter Ronny had previously observed. As for motive power—well, Ronny wasn't sure, but there were none of the ubiquitous pinwheels. What *was* present, though, was a delicate, flowerlike array of silvery metal dishes, all joined to miniature electric motors and pointed toward the waxing moon. Ronny stared at the nearest machine in mute amazement, completely unable to divine its function, except that there appeared to be something alive prisoned in the lace-metal sphere that spanned the space between the machine's tripod legs. It was fascinating—but staring at toys, however well-wrought, was not what he had come for.

But why *had* he come? Well, the Road Man had said to return that evening, but he'd been unable to. Lewis had made some vague mention of their earlier visit over dinner, whereupon Aunt Erin had first bristled, then clammed right up and forbidden them to return to the strange tinker's camp, and "*certainly* not at night." The mysteriously appearing photo had merely been the icing on the cake.

Maybe he should leave, then; maybe he should turn tail and run. But what if the Road Man caught sight of him? What if he left a trail? It would be all too obviously his in the soft earth of the meadow, what with the crutch's telltale third footprint. Then he'd *never* be able to face coming back.

Sighing, Ronny eased between the nearest two machines.

Which was fortunate, because the Road Man chose that moment to stop working and amble around the corner of the wagon. For the second time in about a minute, Ronny halted dead in his tracks, but this time it was because the Road Man had seen him and was limping toward him.

Ronny regained sufficient control of himself to respond in kind and began hitching forward as well, but he had not gone two steps before another mental alarm brought him up short once more.

Was this the Road Man? Though much the same size as the person he had met earlier, *that* man had been tall, rugged, and muscular—and so sweaty and dirty and besmirched and besooted he'd looked like an utter tramp. He'd also smelled. *This* man, though, was so clean he practically shone in the moonlight, and the red hair that had been so wild before had been washed and combed to a fine, smooth gloss.

But most disconcerting was the man's apparel. When Ronny had last seen him, the Road Man had been wearing jeans and scuzzy sneakers, but had been shirtless—a reasonable enough condition for one doing hard work by a forge in Georgia spring heat. This man, however, went barelegged and barefoot—and in fact, seemed to be clad only in a long-tailed, long-sleeved, pure white shirt of old-fashioned cut. Whether or not he wore anything *under* the shirt, Ronny couldn't tell, nor did he have particular desire to know. He was also limping, and Ronny was trying hard to remember if the person he'd met that afternoon had been. He shook his head. He didn't think so.

The man was no more than four yards away by now, and neither of them had spoken. Indeed, the Road Man—if it *was* him, and Ronny was somehow beginning to doubt that it was; either that, or he'd been remarkably unobservant that afternoon—was staring at him with some perplexity, as if he'd never seen Ronny before in his life. Ronny cleared his throat uncomfortably, aware that he too was gaping like an idiot.

''Who are you?''

Ronny started. The voice, too, was wrong, though he couldn't tell exactly how. Perhaps it had a finer, clearer edge to it, like a brass bell as opposed to one of bronze.

The man took a step closer. ''Who are you, I say?''

Ronny took a deep breath and advanced in turn. That near he could make out the man's features clearly enough to have little doubt it was the man he had visited before, though somehow transformed into a sleeker, glossier version of himself. "I . . . I'm Ronny Dillon," he stammered. "I . . . was here this afternoon. The guy with the little cast warrior you liked, don't you remember?"

The man's perplexed scowl shifted into an outright frown. "I've never seen you before in my life."

Ronny was still balancing between the urge to snap off a tart reply and the desire to simply turn and leave, when he noticed the man gazing toward the small cast warrior. He followed the line of sight, and saw the tiny barbarian agleam in the moonlight, sword shining sharp as any razor, mail and armor so aglitter with highlights they looked like diamonds overrun with spilled water.

"That's good work," the man observed flatly, not looking at Ronny. Without asking permission, he crossed the intervening distance and reached out to touch the casting. Ronny held his breath, but the man offered no threat. This close his skin gleamed like new ivory, the tattoos were like the most delicately incised scrimshaw amid the now nearly invisible red hairs, and he smelled not of goats and smoke, but of incense and cinnamon.

"Glad you like it," Ronny managed, shifting his weight awkwardly, as even the gentle pressure of the man's touch on the figure threatened to overbalance him. "But, uh . . . are you *sure* you don't remember me? I was here and . . . and you saw the little warrior, and you said to come back tonight."

The man turned his gaze curiously toward Ronny. "That was the Day Man; I'm the Man of the Night."

Ronny was on the ragged edge of asking what the difference was when he caught himself. The answer to *that* was obvious. By asking, he'd only show himself a fool. On the other hand, it was late, he was far from home talking to someone whom he was beginning to fear was not entirely in his right mind, and he had no inclination whatever to either match wits *or* be toyed with by anyone.

"This is old metal," the tinker stated abruptly. "I'd like to see it in the light." And without further comment, he turned and made his way toward the more brightly lit side of the wagon.

Ronny hesitated. Logic said to get the hell out of there. But his sense of wonder had been awakened now, and his newfound fascination with smithcraft. Without really intending to, he found himself following . . . whoever it was.

The area in front of the wagon *was* more brightly lit, and Ronny saw that the forge had been completely cleaned and scrubbed. There was no sign of the tree-stump-and-anvil, but in the place it had occupied stood a waist-high, foot-thick cylinder of what looked like solid glass, with, lying athwart it, a single feather as long as his arm and apparently made of pure gold. And much to his surprise, the only source of light was the flames of a small cooking fire a little farther on, above which depended from a spit a triumvirate of gold-colored pots, one of which was steaming.

The Road Man helped himself to a seat on the middle step of the three that bridged the gap between wagon door and ground and looked at Ronny. "I want to hold it," he said, almost plaintively.

Ronny hesitated at first, then grimaced and balanced on his good leg while he unslung the crutch and disentangled the warrior. Grasping it in his right palm, he crossed the intervening few paces and passed it to the Road Man.

The man snatched it roughly, and Ronny feared to see it crumpled into an unrecognizable prickly mess until the man's fingers parted again to show it intact, whereupon he proceeded to poke and prod it as if it were some tiny new machine he had just discovered. For his part, Ronny merely stood patiently by and tried not to appear apprehensive.

"You can eat if you want to."

Ronny nearly jumped out of his skin, then collected himself and glanced dubiously toward the fire. He started to say something like "No thanks, I'm not really hungry," when his stomach obligingly gave the lie to that by growling loudly.

"Better eat," the man urged again without looking up.

Ronny made his way to the cookfire and peered at it distrustfully, uncertain how to proceed. Both the tripods that supported the spit from which the pots depended and the spit itself were likely to be hot, never mind the pots themselves (and how was it they weren't blackened by the smoke, as every utensil he'd ever seen used for open-fire cooking had been?). Ronny attempted a squat by setting back on his haunches, his game leg stiff before him. A quick check of his pockets produced a red bandanna, which he folded twice, then used to lift the spit.

It was an awkward motion, though, and he lost his balance and toppled toward the flames. Before he damaged himself, however, a hand seized him roughly and yanked him in one smooth arc to his feet. Something hard smashed into his palm, and it took him a second to realize it was the miniature warrior.

"Here," the man snapped. "I can't believe someone as clumsy as you could make something as delicate as that."

Ronny gaped stupidly, staring first at the still-intact figure, then at the Road Man who was lifting the spit from the fire with his bare hands. The merest bit of steam emerged from his closed fingers, and Ronny thought he heard something sizzling and was *certain* he caught a whiff of cooking meat.

"It's all in the technique," the man noted offhandedly, limping past Ronny and resuming his place on the step, which was barely wide enough for him to deposit the cooking vessels beside him, whereupon the odor of meat became that of charring timber. "Everything in the world is a matter of technique," he continued, deftly removing the lids from the pots one by one. He speared the spit through the middle of a conveniently dangling cow vertebra and inserted two fingers into the nearest vessel. "I said you could eat."

"I'm . . . I'm not really hungry."

"You were a minute ago. Your stomach growled and you were only too glad to investigate my cooking."

"I . . . was just being polite."

"No, you're being polite *now*—polite and distrustful. Before you were being honest. I'll take an honest man over a polite man any day. And any man who trusts another's nothing but a fool."

Ronny was still hesitant.

Meanwhile, the Road Man was applying himself to his meal with a vengeance by the simple expedient of alternately scooping masses of food from each of the pots in turn with his fingers. It was appalling etiquette, but for some reason here in this odd camp, surrounded by the fragile machines, it too had a curious sort of primal elegance.

When the Road Man had sampled the contents of each pot for the second time, he sucked his fingers delicately. "I could show you a thing or two about technique."

"You *could*?"

"Doesn't mean I *would*."

Ronny's face fell.

"It involves a few tricks of the trade."

"I . . ."

"But if a man's gonna show his secrets, he's got to trust the man he shows them to, and that man's gotta trust him."

Ronny rolled his eyes and tried to grin resignedly. "But you just said that any man who trusts . . . oh, never mind, you win."

And with that, Ronny stepped forward and, seeing no other utensil, followed the Road Man's example and inserted two fingers into the nearest pot—and gasped immediately, for the dark paste inside was boiling hot. It was only by pure force of will that he managed to withdraw his hand without too extreme a grimace. The substance wasn't easily recognizable, either—some kind of pounded-up root, possibly. It had a strong, pungent odor, with—Ronny sniffed it once more and nearly choked—a definite underscent of skunk musk that made him gag as he got a third whiff. Still, his audience with the Road Man appeared to have become a trial of one-upmanships, and he'd never been one to back away from a dare. An instant later, he had sucked the stuff off his fingers and somehow got it down. It was awful, too, for the skunk aspect exploded inside his mouth, masking all others (and the *only* familiar taste he'd detected in the first place was something like horseradish). And the stuff was hot in the bargain, hot as the hottest jalapeños he'd ever tasted. He could feel himself breaking into a sweat.

The Road Man had obviously anticipated that reaction, and Ronny smelled rather than saw (for his eyes were scrunched closed with tears) a cup of some liquid thrust below his nose. He took it gratefully, too concerned with his tormented tonsils to worry about further abuse. Fortunately, the first sip cooled him, and the second—it tasted like mint-flavored wine—put his mouth once more at ease.

"Too hot for you?"

Ronny nodded ashamedly. "Sorry."

"Try the next one—it's cooler."

Ronny did—rather reluctantly, in spite of his desire to save face.

This course—globules of what might have been meat in a gelatinous sauce—was even worse than the previous mess had been, though less because of taste than texture. Indeed, the flavor was actually quite good, if rather tart and bitter. But the stuff stuck to the inside of his mouth and clogged his throat and seemed to take actual pleasure in globbing up on his tongue so that he came even closer to losing his gorge than before. It took all the control he had to get the stuff down, and even so, it took several attempts, as the substance was so intent on remaining cohesive he had to swallow the whole mass at once.

The last dish was the worst, because where the first two had been distressing because of flavor and consistency— but were otherwise unrecognizable—this one was disturbing because he *did* know what it was: stewed earthworms.

Ronny had been brought up in a well-off home by open-minded and widely traveled parents. He had eaten good bit of unusual cuisine in his time—everything from escargot and curried squid through birds' nest soup to Chinese ducks' feet. And he knew logically that far stranger things—including earthworms—were standard fare in odd corners of the world.

Which did nothing at all to alleviate the revulsion he now felt as he regarded the red-brown shapes on his fingers.

Still, it had become a matter of honor, so he steeled himself, closed his eyes, and chowed down. He did not chew, though, and fortunately did not have to. And even more fortunately, the stuff actually tasted quite good, so that it took only a few swallows to empty his mouth. A swig of the peculiar wine cleared his pallet.

"Want more?" the Road Man asked, grinning. "There's plenty."

"N . . . no thanks, I'm full." Ronny replied, and only then did he realize that he actually was.

"You're crippled," the Road Man stated flatly.

Ronny felt a flush of anger. Hadn't they already covered that point once that afternoon? He certainly didn't want to bring it up again now! On the other hand, he didn't dare offend the Road Man too much, lest he jeopardize any hope of instruction.

"How?" the Road Man continued, without waiting for him to reply.

Ronny would not meet his eyes. "I don't want to talk about it."

"*How?*"

"Look, I fell, all right? Now, do you *mind*? Can we talk about something else? I need to be going anyway."

"*Fell?* How *far*? Falling's no way to cripple a man."

"I *don't* want to talk about it, okay?"

"How far?" the Road Man repeated, as if he had not heard.

Ronny could not contain himself. "I fell off a goddamned ten-meter diving platform," he raged. "I got dizzy and I fell and completely destroyed my right knee. What's left is so full of pins and plates you could probably pick me up with a magnet.''

''And this happened . . . ?'' The man's voice was softer, Ronny noticed, but he was too irritated to care. This was not what he had come for, though what *had* brought him here was a mystery as well. Divining the secret of the photograph, perhaps?—though he was pretty certain that was merely a case of sleight-of-hand. No, more likely it was the hope of picking up a few hints on technique. Yeah, that was surely it, in which case he *had* what he came for— or a promise to that effect, in any event.

Ronny merely shook his head.

''Sounds like bad technique to me,'' the Road Man observed cryptically.

''What about *you*?'' Ronny shot back. ''How'd *you* get *your* limp?''

The Road Man gazed up at him guilelessly. ''What limp?''

Ronny blushed to his ears. The light had been bad. Perhaps he hadn't seen the Road Man limp at all, in which case he'd just made himself an utter fool. Before he knew it, he was staring at the man's legs. Bare in the moonlight from foot to hip (for the man *was* wearing only a shirt— Ronny had discovered that to his embarrassment when he'd sat down), the man's legs showed no sign of any wrongness. Muscular, but well-shaped; pale, and with the hair almost invisible in the moonlight, there was no indication of scars or disfigurement—unless, he realized, they were cleverly masked by the tracery of tattoos that swirled and twisted around them.

''*What* limp, boy?''

''Never mind.''

''I mind!''

''I thought I saw you limping earlier.''

''Limping doesn't mean a man's crippled.''

''I never *said* you were crippled!''

"Means the same."

"Never mind! Look, I'm sorry, okay?"

"Sorry's a mighty weak salve to smear on an insult!"

"I think I'd better just split."

"Suit yourself."

"I will."

And that last had been unnecessary, Ronny told himself as he began backing away. But something had just clicked in him. Maybe it was the man's continued obtuseness, his teasing. Perhaps it was the fact that he had sized up Ronny's flaws pretty accurately in about five minutes. But whatever it was, he suddenly had no desire whatever for the Road Man's further company.

"You're welcome to dinner." The Road Man chuckled as Ronny continued his retreat.

Ronny did not reply.

"You're *welcome!*"

Ronny had reached the circle of machines.

"I'll tell the Day Man you came by!"

"Don't bother."

"I'll tell him to teach you technique."

"Don't *bother!*"

"I'll tell him I've never seen anything like that little figure in thirty-six years on the road."

"You're not that old!"

"Then I'll also tell him you're a fool! But come back tomorrow anyway. He'll be waiting—and bring your own food next time!"

Ronny was beyond the machines then, past the flicker of the firelight. But only then did he turn his back on the wagon and softly whining machines. And only when he reached the highway did he realize his eyes were misting.

All right, Dillon, get your act together, he told himself, wiping his eyes on the bandanna he'd earlier stuffed in his pocket. *No sense crying over the first hard words some arrogant asshole son of a bitch of a tinker lays on you. Guy's probably crazy anyway!*

But Ronny did not believe that, and was already stealing glances back toward the Road Man's camp. The tink-tink-tink had resumed, and he could just see the man's silhouette against the fire. Almost he turned then; almost he returned— but something else told him no, that he'd spent enough time chasing foolish notions for one night.

But he felt oddly refreshed, strangely alive, full of peculiar energies on the verge of awakening. His senses tingled, seemed somehow more focused and acute. He could actually *feel* the spaces around him: the yellowish-silver of the moon in the heavy dome of sky; the long flat line of the highway at his feet, vanishing over rises to right and left; the flat crescent of the meadow behind him, with the forest rising dark behind; the less clearly defined fields across the road, with the scraggly trees and sharp-angled roofs of the Swanson house the only defined landmark.

That too was a mystery to be explored.

Tink-tink-tink came the Road Man's hammer behind him.

And thus Ronny was caught, suspended for a moment between two mysteries.

And then he decided.

Not bothering to check for traffic, he crossed the highway at a rapid hobble. But instead of continuing on into the fields around the derelict dwelling and retracing the route he had already traversed twice that day, he made his way along the shoulder of the road until he was nearly opposite the first of the line of ragged cedars that had once led up to the Swansons' doorway.

He was still trying to decide if he really wanted to continue down that enticingly sinister avenue when the clear silence of the night was broken by the roar of a distant automobile being driven hard and fast—and quickly approaching from behind. Ronny could not resist a backward glance, and did so—just in time to see a set of high-beams rake across the top of the rise at the end of the straight, then lance down the road beside him. He could not tell what sort of car it was in the increasing glare, but thought it was something fairly low and sporty.

He also felt very alone and vulnerable, out there in the middle of nowhere far past midnight, with no one around for half a mile save the unreliable Road Man. Best to try to ignore it, then; best to act like you knew what you were doing and keep on your way. The odds were in his favor, after all.

But Ronny lost the gamble, because instead of passing him by at a roar as he had hoped the car would do, he heard the motor begin to wind down and very soon became aware of his shadow stretching ever longer before him, followed close on by the crunch of tires on gravel to his rear. There was no sense in running, not with his ruined leg. He was caught, there was no way around it; he would have to face whatever was up.

The car proved to be a two-year-old Pontiac Trans Am, dark green or black, with heavily tinted windows and an aftermarket exhaust system Ronny imagined rendered most of its antismog hardware nonfunctional. He could not see the driver, not even when the car eased alongside him, then passed, and pulled over a few yards beyond. The driver killed the lights, shut off the low thunder of the healthy V–8.

Ronny considered bolting then, but by that time the door had opened and a figure had emerged.

It was Anson Bowman.

Seeing no other viable option, Ronny stood his ground, figuring that if something *did* happen, he'd be more likely to find aid (even from the Road Man, perhaps) here on the side of the road than farther afield.

For his part, Anson did not speak at all. He simply ambled along at an easy, self-conscious pace, pausing now and then to kick at some invisible impediment. He was better dressed than when Ronny had seen him earlier, and more neatly groomed. But that hateful leer was still in his eyes.

"Evenin', Dillon," Anson mumbled, when no more than three yards separated the two young men.

"Hello, Anson," Ronny replied carefully, keeping a close watch on both Anson's hands and eyes, grateful for the occasional forays into "bad" neighborhoods he'd had when he was younger.

Another yard covered, and Anson stopped and folded his arms. "You're out mighty late for a city boy."

"So are you."

Anson was standing with the moonlight streaming into his face, and Ronny saw his eyes narrow. There was also a new, but familiar, odor on the night breeze: the scent of alcohol. "Any particular *reason*?" he slurred.

"I couldn't sleep."

"Don't get smart, boy!"

"Don't boy *me*, Bowman!" Ronny flared. "I doubt you're a whole lot older than I am!"

"I'll talk to *you* any way I want to, you crippled little scumbag!"

Ronny bit back a scathing reply and tried a different tack. "Look, Bowman, you barely know me. You don't have any reason I can think of to dislike me, and I'd just as soon we kept out of each other's way, okay?"

"No."

Ronny was still formulating his next argument when Anson suddenly crossed the remaining few feet and straight-armed him flat to the ground. He stood over him, glaring down at him.

"You've been messin' with my woman," Anson snarled. "And nobody messes with Anson Bowman's women!"

Ronny's mouth popped open before he could stop it. What was Anson talking about? But then he knew.

"I've talked to her *one* time!" he shot back. "For about thirty seconds when we met in the breezeway . . . !"

"That's thirty seconds too many!"

Ronny was trying to get up, but just as he managed to return to a sitting position Anson flung himself atop him, pinning him to the ground with his weight, legs astride his stomach, arms forcing his shoulders down into the gravel. Having no other option, Ronny flailed upward with his crutch, but Anson blocked him easily and wrenched it from his grip to fling it away to Ronny's right.

For nearly a minute they strove there, arms braced between them, with Anson remaining on top but Ronny giving little ground.

"You're a strong little son of a bitch, I'll grant you that," Anson gasped, as Ronny used all the force at his command to rise, but to no avail. He couldn't use his leg for leverage, and Anson was taller than he and heavier.

"Yeah, you're a strong little asshole—but you ain't strong enough to steal my woman!"

"I don't *want* to steal your woman," Ronny gritted, though he realized as soon as he said it that it was a lie.

"Then why was you talkin' to her?"

" 'Cause she talked to me! Just 'cause you talk to somebody doesn't mean—"

"Shut the fuck *up*!" And with that Anson released his grip on Ronny's shoulder long enough to slam his right fist into Ronny's jaw. Pain flashed through Ronny's head, and with it came the thin, coppery taste of blood.

"Look, Anson, what in the hell's wrong with you?"

"*You* are, you asshole! Ain't no woman ever turned Anson Bowman down, and it's all your fault."

Ronny couldn't believe his ears. Lewis hadn't told him how long Anson and Winnie had been dating, only that they were. From that, and what he knew of Anson's personality, he'd assumed the worst. But now . . . maybe there was hope for him after all.

"Get *off* me, you asshole," he grunted, redoubling his force, and this time he succeeded in thrusting Anson away. "You're drunk, Anson; you're drunk and pissed off. But get the hell away from me or I swear I'll have the cops on you."

"You and who else?" Anson sneered, as he regained his feet.

And from somewhere the answer to end all answers came to him. "Me and the Welches, Anson; me and the god-damned Welches. And I don't think even you'd want to stand against *them*."

Anson's reply was masked by the whiz of another car accelerating onto the straight, and that was all Ronny needed to take evasive action. Anson was standing by then, but Ronny was still lying on in the roadside gravel; thus, it was a simple matter to roll the few feet into the shallow ditch to his right. That left Anson as the only obvious target for the rapidly approaching vehicle.

Ronny saw it pass and waited, hoping in vain it might be the local sheriff. It wasn't, but Anson had evidently either lost his nerve or his taste for violence and had returned to his Pontiac.

For at least five more minutes, Ronny lay bruised and breathless on the side of the road. He was *not* thinking about Anson Bowman, though; he was thinking with renewed optimism about Winnie Cowan.

Chapter 6

Lies on Toast

Cardalba Hall
Saturday, April 7—8:45 A.M.

Matthew Welch, who had been staring at the same blind white eye of poached egg for the last ten minutes without touching it, was beginning to think that Luck was less a blessing than a curse. Well—not the Luck, precisely, but the aftereffects of using it, as he had done in one form or another until somewhere around 6:00 that morning. It was not unlike a hangover in that it stole his appetite and made him feel queasy and bleary-eyed and muddleheaded—never mind the headache. Except that no hangover in Matthew's experience *ever* filled his head with the static of low-level Voices all babbling at once, because he'd been so tuned to them for so long he could not *stop* himself from Listening—and didn't dare draw further Strength from the long-since-depleted Lenore.

Still, it had been worth it.

By a deft prowling through unguarded memories scattered throughout the county he had ferreted out a great deal about

117

this Ronny Dillon. Like the fact that he had been living at Erin's house for several weeks without Matt even knowing. Like the fact that Erin had apparently tried to *further* conceal that knowledge from him by inserting sub-Silences cloned from her own into two-thirds of the memories in town: quite an accomplishment, actually, for one who was supposed to have no more than the standard, minimal Strength women survived their forced deflowering with; *and* who officially frowned on any use of the Luck in the bargain—never mind that it was also a remarkably subtle and clever deception. Like the fact that Matthew's mental assaults on Lewis had evidently somehow gone awry and targeted this Ronny person instead.

That was curious too, though Matthew supposed it had something to do with the literal interpretation the Luck sometimes affected. His *conscious* mind had been focused on Lewis; but the Luck lived mostly in the *sub*conscious, which meant that it occasionally responded to what he *actually* wanted, not what he *thought* he wanted. And evidently his subconscious had been wanting to madden the Heir more than it wanted to madden Lewis, who was, as best Matt could determine between the lines, Ronny Dillon's long-lost *younger* twin.

More reading between the lines had confirmed a number of additional suspicions, paramount of which was the one his mother had intimated the night before: namely that his dear niece Erin had been in some sort of collusion with his equally dear nephew, Dion. Unable to hide her pregnancy in a family full of Listeners, she had nevertheless managed to conceal the fact that she was carrying twins until she had time to spirit one away—presumably to be raised among infidels and remote from the (so *she* would have expressed it) corrupting influence of the Luck. That would be just like her too, with her talk of renouncing the Luck (that seemed a tiresomely recurring theme among all Donna's children), and her near-obsession that her (until lately) only son grow up normal—which Lewis had been doing very nicely without any intervention from Matthew at all. On the other hand, it would also be exactly the rebellious Erin's style to risk sacrificing one son to tradition (though she was obviously trying to circumvent even that) so that the other could grow up in blissful ignorance of his heritage (or—as Matthew was wont to consider it, given his headache—his curse).

There was one saving grace, however: while Matthew's efforts at driving Lewis mad had not succeeded, they *had*, quite inadvertently, found sufficient purchase in his unknown older twin to cause the boy to topple off a diving board and thoroughly lame himself. That, in turn, implied that the boy's Luck had not activated yet, which Matthew fervently hoped was true, since the Luck would never lodge in anyone who was less than physically perfect. Lewis *was* perfect, however; they'd all seen to that: Erin's son had every tooth, foreskin, and vestigial organ he'd been born with, and it was probably too late to bother trying to change that now. But Anson had them too; *he* had seen to that.

Which meant that Lewis *still* had to be disposed of (or at least be rendered unviable as a contender for the Mastership), and probably this Ronny Dillon as well, since, in spite of his optimism, Matthew wasn't *certain* how the Luck would respond to its prospective host being for all practical purposes *deliberately* mutilated. Besides, there was a tiny chance the Luck had *already* begun to take hold despite his injury, the boy being as old as he was— there was a gray area about such things. And while, as Martha had pointed out, neither lad was either preconditioned for the Mastership or greedy for it, he knew the time was not far off when the first stirrings of Luck might very well assert itself and *force* them to seek understanding of the changes at work in their minds, thereby blowing the whole kettle of fish sky-high.

Lewis *was* the rightful heir, after all, at least according to tradition. Certainly he had exactly as many Welch genes as Anson did. And he would definitely make an excellent Master if exposed to that notion carefully (as Erin, fortunately for Matthew, was *not* doing). Except that Anson was the fruit of *his* body—and that counted for a heck of a lot. Whether it was enough to justify destroying (even temporarily) the mind of a perfectly innocent boy (or two) in favor of another who was less obviously deserving, he did not want to contemplate. What was important now was that Matthew be able to do what *he* wanted to do, not what three thousand years of tradition said he *ought* to do. Besides, there was always a chance he could cure the boys of any Wind-borne madness *after* Anson had been confirmed. In the meantime, he had to do *something* now, and do it quick—before the Luck started manifesting in all three of them.

Matthew was still pondering this (for even he had *some* respect for the traditions), and still staring stupidly at his egg (which Lenore had now supplemented with toast, bacon, fresh-squeezed orange juice, and coffee), when his mother swept into the kitchen.

Martha Welch looked immaculate, as he did not, and he knew that she would instantly recognize the signs of an all-night Listening. Still, she'd practically demanded a less ambitious one—thus, since he *had* performed that one too, he would not officially have to lie.

Not about that, at any rate.

Martha fixed him with her morning steely glare, which was only slightly softer than the one she affected in the afternoon, and joined him at the round breakfast table in the gentle light of the east-facing kitchen. Matthew merely grunted an acknowledgment of her presence and turned his gaze elsewhere, as if he hoped to find shelter from his mother's scrutiny among the gleaming copper pots, stainless-steel pans, and iron skillets.

"Learn anything?" Martha's query was sharp, loveless— but then, it had been a long time since she had shown any love for him.

"Some."

The glare intensified. "I'm in no mood for obtuseness this morning, Matty."

"Neither am I. In fact, I'm in no mood for conversation of any kind."

"Hard night at the Listening post?"

"You try Listening to half the Voices and all the Silences on the Eastern Seaboard sometime."

"I wish I could. Unfortunately, I'm limited to family, and that only if they're not Silencing—as I'm sure you know."

Lenore brought Martha her traditional pecan waffle and bacon, and was filling the old woman's personal black stoneware coffee mug. She was also staring at Matthew curiously.

He knew why, too: most of the local Listening he'd done last night he'd done on his own, without her help since his earlier efforts had already worn her out. Not that she'd have been able to Hear any of the things he did, anyway; she was as Deaf as most normal people were. But he rarely worked alone, and usually only when he was up to something, and he knew that she knew that—which was one more reason to get rid of her fairly soon, if she didn't take flight herself.

Matthew forced himself to relax, then grinned wolfishly at his mother.

Martha merely scowled and doused her waffle with pure maple syrup, then proceeded to further subdivide the nearest quarter into a precise wedge. She ate with vigor, the light glinting off her silver fork in a way that made Matthew's head hurt even worse.

A sip of coffee, and then the words Matthew had been dreading.

"Okay then, did you find an *heir*?"

"You mean besides Lewis?"

"Of course!"

"No."

Matthew thought his mother's ensuing silence lasted too long to be entirely uncontrived. But when she spoke again her voice was lighter, as if she were no longer concerned with the matter at all. "Well, it's worth an attempt every once in a while," she muttered between sips of coffee.

And Matthew could breathe easier. It was not easy to lie to his mother. Fortunately he'd kept it to one word, and since he wasn't absolutely *certain* who Ronny was, that had made up the difference. Any more she'd have been able to sense in a trice.

"I'm leaving in an hour," Martha announced flatly.

Matthew perked up immediately, both his physical discomfort and his latest batch of duplicities forgotten. Gray eyebrows rose toward white hair. "Oh?"

Martha nodded. "I was certain you wouldn't care, so didn't think it worth my while to inform you until I had to."

Matthew couldn't suppress a relieved smile. "So what's the unfortunate destination this time?"

"Does that mean it's my turn to be obtuse?"

"If you like. Obviously it makes no difference to *me* where you go."

"I'm thinking of Cypress. But first I have to fly to London."

"I presume you've already called a cab?"

Martha checked her watch. "It should be here in fifteen minutes."

Almost by reflex Matthew closed his eyes, sifting the Winds.

"He'll be three minutes late because he didn't count on the train coming through; and he'll be grouchy because of that. And he's also scared of you, and that'll make him worse. So *don't* try to engage him in conversation."

"I never do."

And that, Matthew decided, as he finally worked up sufficient stomach to nibble a corner of his toast, was just as well. And while she was gone, he'd try to figure out what to do about Erin's sons.

Chapter 7

Forbidden Fruit

Erin Welch's house
9:30 A.M.

Ronny *normally* thought very highly of his godbrother. Lew was bright, handsome, clever, talented, charming, and generally pleasant to be around. Most of the time they got along famously, or at least as well as young males could when they'd both been heirs apparent to their respective domains and then suddenly found themselves forced to share living quarters—which Erin Welch had insisted they do for the first few months of Ronny's convalescence. Most guys, in fact, would have considered themselves fortunate to have a roommate like Lew.

Ronny considered himself fortunate too—except on Saturday mornings, when Lew absolutely could not resist playing Tigger. Nor was *this* morning any exception. It was therefore with more than a little irritation that an already bruised and beaten Ronny Dillon got his introduction to the weekend sunlight by being pounced upon and tickled unmercifully, when he could easily have used another two or three hours of shut-eye.

"Rise 'n' shine, Ronny m' boy," Lew cried gleefully, leaping onto Ronny's bed and straddling the small of his back while he expertly found the sensitive spots at the juncture of Ronny's ribs and armpit and began to dig in. "Rise and shine and meet the day. The sun's out, the sky's blue, coffee's in the pot, and it's the weekend—two whole days to have fun in, two whole days away from Welch County High!"

For his part Ronny, who seconds before had been sprawled dreamlessly across the top quilt, merely grunted and tried with little success to simultaneously drag his pillow across his throbbing head and clamp his arms sufficiently close against his ribs to trap Lew's far-too-accomplished fingers. Lew had the better angle of attack, however, and simply wrenched his hands free and shifted his assault to the sides of Ronny's even more susceptible tummy, where no amount of countermeasures could prevail.

"Jesus shit, Lew! Leave me alone!" Ronny finally managed to gasp between grunts and giggles, when Lewis relaxed his attack after perhaps ten seconds of outrageous writhings on Ronny's part. "Leave me alone—I mean it!"

"Do you?" Lew giggled in turn, resuming hostilities. "Ah, but Tiggers *never* leave anyone alone. They're *always* up and about. Only way to avoid having a Tigger attack you in the morning is to sleep in full plate armor—or get up before the Tigger!"

"Get *off* me," Ronny pleaded again, his voice muffled by the pillow over his head. "I feel like three-day-old crap this morning."

Lew gently lifted the pillow and peered down at him. "You really do?" he asked disappointedly.

Ronny slitted his right eye open. "I really do—sorry."

Lew commandeered the pillow and climbed off Ronny's back but continued to sit on the side of his bed. "Ah well."

He sighed with theatrical exaggeration, thumping the well-padded bundle. "There's always tomorrow."

"Gimme a break!" Ronny made a dive to reclaim his shield and in the process twisted onto his side, so that he was facing his godbrother. His knee twinged smartly, but he ignored it.

Lewis was on the ragged edge of reengaging battle when his cheery, teasing expression faded to one of alarm. "Oh, Christ, Ronny—what the hell's *happened* to you?"

Ronny blinked at him in perplexity. "What d'you mean?"

Lewis bit his lip, then nodded sagely. "Well, if I didn't *know* better, I'd *swear* that you had a black eye."

Ronny sat bolt upright and ran a hand tentatively across the left side of his face, which sure enough felt remarkably tender. An instant later he was out of bed and scrambling for the bathroom. Lewis followed close on his heels and was gazing curiously over Ronny's shoulder when he switched on the light and peered into the long slab of mirror.

"Oh, God," Ronny moaned. "Jesus, what am I gonna tell Aunt Erin?"

"Aunt Erin, hell!" Lewis whispered, easing Ronny around so he could inspect the damage firsthand. "What are you gonna tell *me*!"

Ronny shrugged free of Lewis's inquisitive fingers. "Never mind. Just don't ask."

"But I *have* to! And Mom's sure gonna ask. And you *know* you can't lie to her!"

"Can't I? I'll . . . I'll say I ran into the door in the night."

"Yeah, sure, and she'll see right through you. *Nobody* can lie to Mom. She's always been able to catch me at it, and you're no better a liar than I am."

"But I can't . . ."

Lewis reached past Ronny to turn on the taps of the nearest of the two oval sinks set in the long marble counter below the mirror. He tested the water experimentally while Ronny continued to stare stupidly at his reflection. It was a first-rate shiner, no doubt about it, and the range of colors it displayed was already quite extraordinary—the yellows and purples were especially striking. He touched it cautiously and winced, then felt down along the angle of his jaw and found more pain and a smaller bruise there. That brought his hands into his line of sight, and he realized then that the backs of both of them, plus his right elbow, bore numerous scrapes and abrasions—residue, no doubt, of last night's scuffle in the gravel.

Meanwhile, Lewis had disappeared into the bedroom. When he returned a moment later, he was holding the dirty jeans Ronny had unceremoniously dumped when he'd crept back into the room somewhere around four in the morning. Without a word, Lew closed the bathroom door, flipped the toilet lid down, and sat there, gazing accusingly up at Ronny. Ronny noticed for the first time that Lew's hair was damp, his bare, compact torso squeaky-clean above a different pair of sweats than he'd worn to bed the night before—legacy of a shower Ronny had obviously slept through. And one glimpse at Lewis's eyes, and he wished he could have slept through what was coming. "You got in a fight, didn't you? You went somewhere in the middle of the night and got into a fight."

Ronny nodded solemnly.

"Who was it?"

"Never mind."

"Who *was* it, Ron? Nobody beats up my friends without paying the price, and for sure nobody beats up my foster brother!"

Ronny was still probing his face. "I said I didn't want to talk about it, so just leave it, okay? What I've got to figure out is what to tell Aunt Erin."

"Well, you can't lie to her, I've already told you that."

"Not even if *you* say you heard me run into the door in the night?"

Lewis shook his head. "Sorry. Besides, there's the small matter of your clothes being in our room when they *should* be in the dryer, not to mention how they happened to get dirty again. No way we could sneak 'em out *this* late.''

''Oh, shit—I forgot about that!''

Lew grinned in satisfaction. ''See—you can't even lie to me.''

Silence, while Ronny rinsed his face in cold water. He was feeling better now, less muddleheaded.

But Lewis showed no signs of leaving. Finally Ronny turned toward him. ''Look, are you gonna sit there and watch me take a shower? I'm *not* gonna tell you, and that's that.''

''It was Anson, wasn't it? You went off somewhere and ran into Anson.''

Ronny was too shocked to mask his surprise. ''Yeah,'' he whispered. ''How'd you know?''

Lewis pointed toward the ridge of Ronny's cheekbone where, faint but clear, the unmistakable outline of the letter A was etched among the bruises. ''Because we ran into him yesterday and he had an attitude; because he doesn't like me and apparently therefore doesn't like you. And because I happen to know he wears a signet ring that looks like that.''

Ronny grimaced sourly. ''Christ!''

''I'll bet I know what sent him off, too,'' Lewis continued. ''I'll bet you dollars to donuts he somehow got wind of you and Winnie Cowan.''

''What *about* me and Winnie Cowan? I've barely talked to her, Lew!''

''Barely's enough in Welch County, bro. And barely's more than enough for Anson Bowman.''

''Evidently.''

''Now,'' Lewis said primly, ''why don't you tell me all about it?''

Ronny did, begrudgingly, leaving out nothing except what he had threatened Anson with there at the last, about invoking the luck of the Welches. Since he neither believed in it himself—nor understood it at all, for that matter—and since any mention of it obviously made Lewis uncomfortable, he saw no point in opening up yet another Pandora's Box. One per Saturday morning was plenty—and it wasn't even ten o'clock yet.

Lewis's response was to sit quietly—still on the toilet seat—and nod sympathetically. He remained there while Ronny went through the motions of shaving. "Well, I'll do what I can to soften Mom up," he said finally. "But no way you'll be able to avoid confrontation. Frankly, I think the direct approach would be best—throw yourself on the mercy of the court, as it were."

"Whatever," Ronny replied absently. "Now scat—I've gotta grab a shower."

Lewis puffed his cheeks and rose, then paused in the doorway for one last quip. "Too bad Mom's not as blind as Justice is supposed to be," he mused philosophically. "That'd take care of all your problems."

Ronny took a very long shower, but twenty minutes later he still had not contrived a foolproof defense.

For almost two minutes Ronny thought he might be able to escape breakfast with his secret intact. As he approached the kitchen, he could hear Lewis chattering gaily about some inconsequentiality or other, with background noise courtesy of the sizzle of something frying and the Black Crowes' newest turned low on Lewis's radio. As Ronny drew closer, he got a whiff of his two favorite odors in the whole wide world: sugar-cured bacon and fresh-brewed coffee. More to the point, though, for one of guilty conscience and troubled soul, was the fact that Aunt Erin had her back to him; and Lewis, who was already seated, had thoughtfully left the chair closest to the hall door vacant for him. Which meant that if Ronny sat just so, his injured side would face away from the watchful eyes of his guardian.

Lew looked up when Ronny entered, and Ronny squinted at the bright morning light, which was made even brighter by the clean white walls (where they weren't covered with

Erin's Day-Glo geometrical paintings), black-and-white tile flooring, and gleaming appliances, none of which bore a speck of stain or grime. The TV was on, tuned to the channel that scrolled yesterday's closing stock reports across the bottom of the screen. Ronny eased down in the chair and leaned his crutch against the door frame. He raised a quizzical eyebrow in his friend's direction, but was rewarded with an irresolute shrug.

Aunt Erin had heard him by that time (there was no sense trying to hide the sound of his approach, after all—that would *really* rouse her suspicions) and glanced around to flash him a quick, warm smile. Ronny managed to hide his war wounds with a feigned yawn and scratch of his head.

"And how are *you* this morning, Mr. Sleepyhead?" she asked lightly.

"Sleepy," Ronny grunted, snagging the coffeepot from the middle of the round breakfast table and pouring a healthy portion into a black china mug someone had already set out for him.

Erin turned around to resume her frying. "Bacon in a sec, guys. Want a waffle, Ron?"

"No thanks," Ronny replied as casually as he could. "I'm not real hungry this morning."

"Suit yourself," Erin tossed back.

Ronny vented a sigh of relief that he rapidly converted to a second bogus yawn.

"So what are you boys gonna do today? Looks like a mighty fine day to do *something*."

"Don't know," Lew replied quickly, rolling his eyes at Ronny as if to say, *Let me do the talking*. "Might go into town and see if any comics came in yesterday."

"Sounds good." And then, in the lower voice both boys had learned to dread: "Well, you'd better *not* let me hear about you hanging around with the Road Man!"

"Oh, give me a break!" Lew snorted. "What's *wrong* with dropping by again? All the kids in school were there yesterday. And from what I've heard he's basically harmless—I mean what *can* he do if there's other people around? And believe me," he added, aiming a warning glare at Ronny, "there's *no* way I'd go if there *wasn't* somebody else there. I'm curious, not stupid."

Aunt Erin turned around and stared fixedly at her son for maybe ten seconds without saying a word, and Ronny couldn't help thinking what an attractive woman his god-mother was: tall and slim, red-haired and green-eyed, with just enough angles among the soft curves of her face to give it an edge of authority. She was forty, but could easily pass for fifteen years younger. She also tended to dress like someone much younger—as she was doing now in a pair of distressed jeans Ronny suspected were some of Lew's old ones altered only by the oil-paint stains she had added, and a green R.E.M. T-shirt.

But there was no mistaking her anger when it got fired up, for youthful beauty or no, Miss Erin Welch was not a woman to be trifled with.

"You're *not* to go near him—either of you. Is that under-stood?" And Ronny was certain the temperature in the room immediately dropped at least five degrees.

"Is that *clear*?" she repeated.

Ronny nodded minimally and tried to keep his mark of shame out of her line of sight, and Lewis had just opened his mouth to reply when the phone rang—the two short and one long bursts that meant it was for him. Venting the smallest of sighs of relief, Lewis rose and sprinted for the adjoining living room, eschewing the nearer portable phone in the kitchen.

And Ronny found himself alone in the lion's den.

Fortunately, the bacon had diverted Erin's attention again, so that Ronny thought he might be off the hook, until Erin turned the stove off, flipped an even dozen slices onto a paper-toweled plate, and set the whole mess in the middle of the table—whereupon she helped herself to the seat at Ronny's left and stared straight at him.

"Where'd you go last night?"

Ronny merely snagged a pair of slices, took a sip of coffee, and evaded her eyes.

"I'm *talking* to you, Ronny. I'd like an answer." Her tone wasn't harsh or threatening, but somehow the words carried the force of flashing steel.

Ronny still did not reply.

"I can wait here till tomorrow morning if I have to," Erin continued calmly. "And I can ask you every five minutes between now and then. I can also lock every door and window in this house with two buttons on this little doodad," she added, patting what Ronny had taken for a calculator hanging from her belt. "*And* if you break out, I can chase you down in my car, which is faster than yours. If *that* fails, I can set the cops on you, and if they put you in jail, I'll continue asking you there. So you might as well save us both a bunch of trouble and level with me now."

"Jesus!" Ronny grumbled, stabbing listlessly at the nearer slice with his fork.

"An important Hebrew prophet with possible ethereal connections," Erin shot back promptly. "But I don't recall that we were discussing theology."

Still Ronny kept his silence.

"Very well," Erin replied after perhaps half a minute. "You went to see the Road Man. You went between two and four A.M., and you wore the clothes I washed yesterday afternoon. He fed you something god-awful because I can smell it on your breath, and he probably asked you to come back because that's what he does. Now, do *you* want to tell me about the shiner?"

Faced with such a fusillade of accusations, Ronny found himself with no choice but to recount the whole embarrassing incident, which he did. But to his surprise, Erin's only response was a surprisingly understated "That boy's gonna be a problem."

Somehow Ronny had managed to finish breakfast in spite of his grilling. "Can I go now?" he asked hopefully.

Erin shook her head. "No, Ronny, I'm sorry, but I need to ask you one more thing."

"Okay . . ." Ronny replied dubiously.

"Ronny, I . . . I have to know: Have you had any . . . *more* unusual dreams lately?"

Ronny wondered what had brought *that* on, and nearly told her "No," since last night's manifestation hadn't quite been like the others. But somehow, under the force of his guardian's steady gaze, he found himself saying "Yes"— and proceeded to blurt out a second tale of nocturnal deception, this one of how he'd awakened in the night with the residue of a nightmare haunting him, and how *that* had led him to wander abroad in the wee hours.

Throughout it all, Erin said nothing, though she occasionally bit her lip or nodded. When he had finished, she merely regarded him curiously for a moment longer, then said, very softly, "If you have any *more*, I'd like to know about them. And I'd appreciate it if you *didn't* tell Lewis; do you understand me?"

Ronny bit his lip. "Yeah, sure."

Erin's mood brightened immediately. "Now then," she announced briskly, rising from the table, "let's see what we can do about the damage." She crossed to an eighteenth-century Spanish cupboard and began rummaging through a drawer full of miscellaneous medical supplies.

Lewis chose that instant to return and immediately reclaimed his seat. He made eye contact with Ronny, then pointed toward his cheek and sketched a question mark in the air. Ronny nodded and shrugged, and that put an end to the matter.

"Who was on the phone?" Erin asked, as if nothing had transpired.

Ronny saw Lewis relax from relief. "Marilyn Bridges."

"And . . . ?"

"She wanted to know if me and Ronny wanted to go swimming up at her place. I told her we'd be there."

"*Swimming!*" Ronny choked, as a score of conflicting

emotions threatened to overwhelm him. "Dammit, Lew, what're you trying to *do* to me? You *know* I swore off that stuff! It hurts too much to even *think* about it anymore, much less be around it—and besides, it's too bloody cold anyway!"

"Well, we probably won't actually go swimming," Lewis conceded. "But there's a waterfall up past her folks' house, with a kind of hollowed-out streambed below that can be dammed off. Lots of rocks around to lie out on, which is probably what we'll really do—after we've helped rebuild the dam, of course."

"Of course."

"It's a kind of tradition, actually," Lewis continued. "First pretty weekend in April, Marilyn invites all her friends up to help rebuild the dam, and those who are brave take a fast dip, and the rest sit on the rocks and get sunburned and laugh about how stupid the others are."

"Sounds like fun," Erin observed in a tone that suggested she approved.

"So, Ronny m'boy, you wanta go?"

Ronny shot his friend a stony glare. "Do I really have to answer that?"

"Well, if you *don't* show, I'll have to tell Marilyn some kind of outrageous lie, which I'd undoubtedly get caught in. Besides, she specifically asked me to invite you."

"Well, you can tell her that I don't think it'd be a lot of fun to sit around and watch other people play in the water, when I can't!"

"But you *can* play in the water," Lewis protested. "You just can't swim—and I bet you could even do that if you tried."

"Yeah," Erin chimed in. "Besides, don't you think you're being a little childish about all that? Swimming's good exercise, for one thing, which would actually *help* your leg, as I'm sure you've been told. And the water'd partly support you, so it shouldn't hurt you much just to wade around in it."

"She's got a point," Lew acknowledged. " 'Course it's *your* life, so if you *want* to keep on feeling sorry for yourself, 'stead of trying to solve your problem, *I'm* not gonna try to stop you."

"No," Ronny stated flatly. And with that he rose awkwardly to his feet, groped for his crutch, and made for the den.

"I think Winnie Cowan's gonna be there," Lewis called behind him.

Ronny went. He did not want to, but Lewis had truly given him no choice. Besides, it was a fine day, and Lew was in such a preposterously good mood Ronny couldn't help but be infected by it. *And*, of course, there was the small matter of one Winnie Cowan, who, he had reason to think, might not be as firmly allied to the troublesome Anson as his godbrother had intimated.

But Winnie Cowan was *not* there when Lewis eased his Probe onto the grass behind the half dozen other cars that flanked the long steep driveway adjoining the Bridges' glass-and-timber mountainside showplace—for Ronald Bridges was second vice-president of the bank Matthew Welch owned, and liked to flaunt it.

Nor was she in evidence when Lewis led the way to the patio out back where the rest of the doughty dam-builders were being fortified with grilled hamburgers that Ronny barely tasted.

Nor when Marilyn finally suggested it might be time to change, whereupon everyone except Ronny trooped inside, leaving him alone with an increasingly sullen disposition and a spectacular view of half of Welch County and all of Cordova he was in no mood to appreciate.

Nor when the whole host of them trekked single-file up a narrow mountain trail that took all of Ronny's determination to navigate and resulted in him falling behind and arriving thirty seconds after everyone else *and* out of breath.

And she *still* had not appeared when the more venture-

some members of the crew (including Lewis, there were
ten of them, all juniors or seniors except for Amy Smith's
sophomore brother), braved the frigid, knee-deep water at
the base of the falls and commenced to excavating stones
that had tumbled from last year's dam, while the more
frostbite-shy scoured the neighboring banks and laurel thick-
ets for suitable new additions. For his part, Ronny eased
down on the largest of the gently sloping boulders that
overlooked the incipient pond and tried *not* to enjoy the
scenery.

Unfortunately, that proved difficult, and he was more than
a little impressed that a family could actually own such a
spectacular piece of landscape. They were already a very
steep quarter mile up Shackelford Ridge from the Bridges's
house, which itself was halfway up the mountain, but somewhere higher still the Talooga gushed from the earth and
commenced an eager, bubbly journey toward the valley
below. And right here it chose to tumble over a series of
boulders and into a V-shaped ravine that was flanked on
both sides with broad, yellowish boulders interspersed with
clumps of laurel and rhododendron. If nothing else, the
ambience was soothing—the influence of ionized oxygen
molecules, Ronny's rational half informed him. In spite of
himself, he found his eyes getting heavy. Since the only
other person who'd been anywhere near him had already
given up on engaging him in conversation in favor of the
giggling group below, he allowed himself a single conces-
sion to the occasion and stripped off the red Tattooed Dogs
T-shirt he'd picked up in Athens on the drive up from
Tampa, then rolled over onto Lewis's immense purple-and-
white beach towel to sun himself. A moment's consideration, and he removed his sneakers as well. But he did not
doff his jeans to reveal the gym shorts he'd worn underneath
at Lew's insistence. No sense flouting the ugly conglomeration of flesh-tone bandages and metal bracing that was
an eternal reminder of his infirmity.

And before he knew it, he was dozing.

A fair bit of time had evidently elapsed when he awoke once more, for the shadows creeping across the rocks had definitely lengthened. But there was no change in the excited voices below, and only the fact that he *thought* he could hear more determined splashing hinted at substantive progress at all. Someone was playing the new Neil Young, too, and the nasal vocals were an oddly incongruous element amid the softly buzzing calm.

He had scarcely closed his eyes again, when he felt a shadow fall across his face, just as a foot prodded him gently in his naked side.

"You're gonna burn if you don't put some lotion on."

He froze. Where had he heard that voice before? And then he knew. He opened his eyes, trying not to appear either surprised, expectant, startled, or—when he had confirmed who it was—happy. Which meant he gaped stupidly.

At Winnie Cowan.

She was standing directly between him and the sun, and as best he could tell she was wearing jeans, a sleeveless blue pullover, and sneakers. She was also smiling.

"I've got some sunscreen, if you want," she offered, holding out a bronze squeeze bottle that he could just barely see by shading his eyes against the glare.

He almost refused, choosing to lapse into his solitary dream in preference to expending the energy necessary to engage in the sort of delicately prying conversation he'd need to ascertain how affairs lay between her and Anson, and how he might fit into the situation.

But then Winnie turned her head enough for him to get a good look at her face—and he nearly cried out. For she too had been gifted with a black eye. And Ronny knew instantly who had caused it.

"We . . . appear to have something in common," he stammered, and immediately felt like a complete jerk. That was the *worst* thing he could have said, because it called attention to something he doubted Winnie wanted attention called to, and because it instantly brought the conversation around to serious matters.

In reply, Winnie flung down a yellow-and-green striped towel and sat down beside him.

"Let me try again," Ronny mumbled. "How 'bout it I start out by saying 'Hi.'"

"Hi." And there was definitely a flicker of appreciation along with it.

Ronny heaved himself up and rubbed his shoulders where, to his surprise, a bit of telltale warmth *was* evident. "Thanks for waking me." He yawned. "I thought I had some tan left over from Florida, but evidently it's not as much as I thought."

Winnie craned her head sideways and regarded his back critically, and Ronny was glad beyond reason that he'd been working out lately. No way he'd want to bare his bod to someone he was interested in when it might not measure up.

"You're okay, I think," she whispered. "But I really do believe I'd put something on my shoulders if I were you."

Ronny tried to twist his head around enough to check for himself but failed.

"Here—" And a soft hand brushed the crest of his right shoulder blade with the utmost delicacy. "And here," which brought a matching touch to the other. And then, almost unbelievably: "Want me to do it?"

"Yeah," Ronny replied, trying not to sound too eager. He dipped his head far forward and waited for the recurrence of Winnie's touch. When it came—gentle, but sure—he gasped at the pleasure. It had been months since a girl had touched him like that, and longer yet since one he cared about had. He was still a virgin, technically—mostly because Anita, who had been his most recent squeeze, had had definite, if rather high, limits. Now, though . . . well, he was suddenly grateful for the concealing power of ragged blue jeans.

Which surprised him, because it indicated he was a lot

more interested in Winnie than he had thought he was.

"I didn't know you were gonna be here," Winnie said, as she continued to smear the oil into his skin, and Ronny thought she sounded a little bit embarrassed. The odor of coconut eased into the air.

"I didn't know I was, either, until Lewis made me."

"This is a nice place, though; I really like it up here. I just wish I hadn't had to miss the cookout, but . . ."

"What?"

"I . . ."

The pause made Ronny glance behind him—to catch a shadowing of Winnie's expression, as if she had already said too much and was wondering whether it was wiser to soldier on or retreat. But then she set her mouth and continued, "Well, I don't suppose there's any point in making a secret out of it, is there? Since the evidence is out there for everyone to see and *somebody's* sure to be tactless enough to ask questions. But . . . well, I was kinda pretending to sleep late, so my folks would be gone when I got up."

"And I bet I know why."

The stroking of his back ended, and Winnie slid forward to sit beside him, legs drawn up, arms folded around the knees on which she rested her chin. As she continued to gaze out into space, Ronny realized that not only did she have a black eye, but that her upper arms were patterned with what could only be the bruises left by viciously clutching fingers.

She did not immediately respond to Ronny's comment, however, and he was certain he'd committed another faux pas until she finally sighed and spoke once more. "What was yours called?"

Ronny tried to grin offhandedly, as if it didn't matter. "Well, I was *gonna* say it was called the bathroom door, but . . . the fact is that it was . . . it was Anson Bowman."

"Mine too," Winnie admitted in a troubled voice. "But . . . what could Anson possibly have against you? You're

Lewis's guest, for heaven's sake and—well, let's just say I'm surprised that even *Anson*'d risk upsetting the Welches.''

"We're back to that, huh?" Ronny grumbled. "But yeah, I was out walking last night, and he kind of ran into me—with his fist.''

"Oh, Christ," Winnie moaned. "I'm sorry, Ronny—and I bet it's my fault, too, 'cause he and I had a really bad argument last night, and he accused me of flirting with you. But . . . but that was *late*. You couldn't have been walking out *that* late.''

"Wanta bet? You'd be surprised how late somebody'd be out when they can't sleep.''

"But where were you? You don't live anywhere near either me or Anson.''

"I went to see the Road Man.''

"Oh, gee, Ronny, he gives me the creeps.''

"Yeah, well, he kinda does that to me too—but I still think he's *real* interesting.''

"But what's he like? I mean, I've heard some stuff from the other kids, but they don't express themselves very well. Somehow I think you can.''

Ronny shrugged and tried not to blush. "Well, I can give it a try, I guess.''

And somehow Ronny spent the next several minutes relating a somewhat edited account of his two encounters with the mysterious tinker.

"And is that the little metal guy you were talking about?" Winnie asked when he had finished. She inclined her head toward the crutch Ronny had tried to make inconspicuous beneath a fold of towel.

"Yeah.''

"Can I see it?''

"Sure.''

A moment later the miniature barbarian glistened in the palm of Winnie's hand.

"And you really made this?" she breathed, her voice all

awe and admiration, but with none of the resentment that usually accompanied that reaction in shop class.

"Yep, every bit."

"You really, *really* did?"

"Absolutely."

"Well, Ronny Dillon," Winnie said with conviction, "I think that's really, really *neat!*"

"Thanks."

Silence then, as Ronny waited for a follow-up line that never came.

"Can I ask you something?" he murmured finally, when the silence became too awkward.

"Sure."

Ronny cleared his throat. "Well, uh . . . let's see. Maybe *you* can tell me since Lewis won't, but . . . well . . . what exactly is this deal about the Welches?"

"What do you mean?"

"Umm, like, why is it that everybody's so hung up about 'em? Why does everybody treat 'em like . . . like they're some kind of gods or something? What's all this about luck and all?"

"Hasn't Lewis told you?"

"Well, he promised to tell me a bunch last night and then didn't. Mostly he just makes jokes and says it's nothing. Shoot, I've never even met his uncle Matt, and he's supposed to be the number-one honcho around here."

"Yeah." Winnie sighed. "I guess he's fairly important."

"And? I mean, why? What makes him so special?"

"Well," Winnie replied with conviction, "according to most folks, he's *responsible* for the luck around here."

"The luck? What the—'scuse me—what the hell's the friggin' luck?"

Winnie's brow furrowed. "I . . . I'm not certain, actually. I didn't grow up here, so I didn't exactly learn this stuff from birth. But the best I can tell is that the Welches have been here since before there was even a county—had some kind of private treaty with a Cherokee chief, or something, before they were all removed. Apparently the first settlers who came in when they opened up the former Indian territory—I guess this would have been the early eighteen hundreds—found this plantation already thriving. It was called Cardalba, and eventually a little town grew up at the edge of it, which somehow got turned into Cordova 'cause that made *some* sense and Cardalba didn't make any.''

''But I've *heard* all that,'' Ronny persisted, trying not to get too frustrated. ''What about the *luck*?''

''Well,'' Winnie continued, ''it's hard to say *what* it really is, but as best I can figure, the Welches were always pretty powerful, since they controlled a lot of money and land—slaves too—so it just made sense for folks to want to get in their favor. Eventually word got out that if the Welches liked you, they'd do stuff for you in turn; you know, use connections and all—they had a lot of money and I guess knew a lot of important people. Something like that, anyway, 'cause things just seemed to work out better if you were friends of theirs—and maybe treated them a little bit special once in a while. And naturally it just made sense for those people who wanted to hedge their bets to invite the Welches to parties and christenings and stuff.''

''Naturally,'' Ronny muttered. ''But what about the *luck*?''

''I was *talking* about the luck. That's all I know. It just *is*—it's another way of saying connections, I guess. Just a polite way of saying that.''

''You think there's anything *more* to it? Stuff to do with land, maybe?''

Winnie frowned thoughtfully. ''I think the land thing's new. As best I can tell, Mr. Matt's the one who really got a bee in his bonnet about land and wants to rebuild the estate to its former limits and all that. See, they lost a lot during the War Between the States and it's taken them a long time to regain it 'cause not everybody thinks trading luck for land is fair.''

''But some do anyway, right?''

"Some folks are scared not to."

"Scared? Why?"

" 'Cause of those same connections, I guess. Maybe they're afraid old Matt'll sic the Mafia on 'em, or curse 'em, or something."

"And could he?"

"What?"

"Curse them."

"I don't believe in that kind of stuff, not really."

"That doesn't answer my question."

"Why do you ask?"

"Well . . . let's just say some pretty weird things have been happening lately."

"Like what?"

Ronny bit his lip thoughtfully and almost told Winnie everything. Why, even in the last twenty-four hours a lot of pretty weird things had transpired—like that business of knowing her name when he shouldn't have, like the ultra-quick trip through the woods. Like the peculiar behavior of Matthew Welch's guard dogs. Like his dream. Like the whole hazy business with luck. And that didn't even count the numerous perplexities that revolved around the Road Man.

And then he realized how preposterous the whole thing would sound. Shoot, it sounded pretty wild to him, and he'd *been* there. And there *was* such a thing as coincidence in the world, never mind the tricks memory could play, even after only a few hours—he was already beginning to wonder if events had occurred as he remembered they had. It was better, then, Ronny decided, to keep silent.

"I can't tell you," he sighed at last. "I'm sorry, but . . . well, I haven't quite got my head straight about all of it myself, and I guess I just don't know you quite well enough yet to hit you with really wild stuff. I suppose I'm afraid I'll sound stupid."

"I can understand that."

"But really, do you think there's anything to it? Beyond folks brown-nosing, I mean?"

A shrug. "I don't see how there could be."

"Then why do you treat me like I'm some kinda"—he started to say "freak" and caught himself barely in time—"some kind of *celebrity* or something, just 'cause I happen to live with the Welches?"

Another shrug. "Just habit, I guess. I guess I like to hedge my bets too."

"Just one more question: have you heard anything else odd about my—about *Lew's* family? I mean I'm not fishing for gossip or anything, but . . . well, you seem like a pretty straight shooter, so I was just wondering."

Winnie looked intensely uncomfortable. "Well, they say that the head of the family's always called either Mr. Welch or the Master of Cardalba—that's kind of odd."

"Okay . . . go on."

"Lew *truly* didn't tell you any of this."

"Some," Ronny admitted. "But I think he's been holdin' out on me. I'd like to hear it from somebody else, in case there's something he conveniently left out. Maybe you could just start with the family history, or something."

Winnie bit her lip, but continued, though she really did look scared. "Okay, then. Well, I think the way it works is that the Master of Cardalba before Matthew was his Uncle Ben Welch. Ben had a sister named Martha, who I think still lives over at Cardalba Hall with Matt, who's *her* son. And since Ben didn't have any kids anybody knew of, when he died he left most of the estate to Matt, who was his favorite nephew."

"Did Martha have any other children?"

"Maybe, but I don't think they live around here any-more."

"Then who's Donna? I think Lew mentioned somebody named Donna?"

"Oh yeah, you're right. Donna was Matt's sister, and she had—I think it was *three*—kids. One was named

Dion—he was a lawyer or something, until he got into some kind of trouble and landed in jail. And the other one was called—''

"Gilbert," Ronny supplied. "Dion was my folks'—my *old* folks'—lawyer until he got disbarred and stuck in the slammer. I met him a couple of times, actually. Not a bad guy—looks a lot younger than he is, and was a hell of a good musician. Only met Gil once. He was okay, but kinda creepy.''

"So I hear," Winnie said darkly.

"But how does Aunt Erin—Lew's mom—fit into all this?''

"Lew's mom was Donna's only daughter.''

"But where's Donna now?''

"You don't know?''

"Would I have asked?''

"She's dead. She killed herself two days after Lewis was born.''

"How do you know—about the two days, I mean?''

" 'Cause I've heard it since I moved up here: 'Poor Donna Welch: killed herself two days after her grandson was born.' ''

"One more question, and I promise I'll hush.''

"Ronny . . . I don't know if I *want* to talk about this anymore. It makes me feel kinda . . . funny. Like somebody was listening in or something.'' She rubbed her arms then, and Ronny was certain he saw goose bumps dimple the smooth flesh there.

"Oh well, never mind.''

"No, it's no big deal, I guess. I mean I'm acting pretty stupid.''

"You're sure?''

"Yeah, go ahead.''

"Okay, then . . . well, why is it that they're all Welches? I mean don't *any* of 'em ever get married? Or do the women just keep their maiden names, or what? Oh, and while we're at it . . . who *is* Lew's father?''

"*That's* a good question, the last one. I've heard not a word, either. All I know is that Lew's mom was supposed to have gotten pregnant while she was off at college, then showed up here with a baby. And *her* mom—Donna, remember?—died right after and left her some money. I think she invested it in stocks or something, and made a killing that way. She's never dated again, that I know of, or—" She stopped in mid-thought, looking puzzled. "You know, now I think of it, you're right: I don't believe I've *ever* heard of a Welch getting married. They have kids and all, but I've *never* heard of one having a husband or wife. I wonder why that is."

"So Lew's Uncle Matt isn't married either?"

"Not that I know of. But I *do* know he's always got some kind of mistress. Some kind of young girl hanging around."

"Does he have one now?"

"I don't know. I haven't ever actually been there. This is all stuff I've heard."

Ronny shook his head. "Jesus, but that's a bunch of stuff to puzzle through—and it looks like we'll have to finish up some other time. Looks like we're about to have company."

Winnie, who was considerably shorter than he, craned her neck enough to see that a line of well-drenched laborers had commenced trekking up from the now-completed dam. A few—a very few—had remained to swim a few symbolic laps. Lew was one of the latter, and even at this distance, Ronny was positive his friend's skin had a distinctly blue tinge.

"Will there *be* another time?" Winnie asked abruptly.

"Sure . . . if you want there to be." And then, without warning, Ronny blurted out, "But what about Anson?"

"Anson and I are finished," Winnie stated flatly. "I don't want any more to do with somebody who treats me like he does. I should have known better than to go out with him in the first place, but . . . well, he can be *really* charming when he wants to be. And he truly is good-looking, and he's kind of a big shot, though not the way Lewis is, and I guess I got tired of waiting for anyone else to ask me out, so when he did, I said yes.''

''But it's over?''

''Well, I've still got his ring . . .''

''You gonna keep it?''

''Not after last night.''

''Wanta—that is, would you like to get together again?''

''Yeah,'' Winnie said slowly, ''I would. But we're both gonna have to be careful.''

Ronny took her hand then, felt the electricity of her touch. But he also noticed she was crying.

Chapter 8

The Worm Turns

Cardalba Hall
1:45 P.M.

Anson had been staring doubtfully up at Cardalba Hall for nearly five minutes before he finally assembled sufficient courage to take a deep breath and stalk the fifty-odd yards from the lower turnaround, where he'd left the Trans Am so as not to attract undue attention before he'd got his act together, up the line of boxwoods, past three white hounds that chose to ignore him, to the mysterious portal of Matthew Welch's citadel.

And he felt really stupid about it too, because not a day gone by he'd had no compunction at all about parking outside the carport (Old Man Welch hardly ever drove his burgundy Lincoln Town Car anyway), stomping up the side steps, and sauntering loudly across the porch to inquire about yard-keeping instructions at the front door. Mr. Welch had always greeted him in person, too, and had always been more than cooperative, giving him small tasks, long deadlines, and an inordinate amount of pay in relation to the effort he expended. Shoot, it was only just now spring, and the previous yardman had already done a bang-up job clearing out the winter's detritus and tending to whatever bulbs needed planting early. All *he'd* had to do was scout the grounds with a weed-eater and chew up the odd ragweed or dandelion—and, once a week, walk the perimeter of the outer wall in search of stones that had come adrift.

Yeah, it was definitely a cushy job, and until the day before, Anson had always been puzzled by the ease with which he had snared it—merely a discreet help-wanted advertisement in the local newspaper his mother had called his attention to. There had been a phone number (which proved to be one of several unlisted lines Matthew Welch maintained in his sprawling mansion), and before he knew it, he had found himself talking to the mysterious Master of Cardalba for the first time in his life.

That had been a month ago, and he'd not thought much about it then: Mom was advertising editor of the Welch County *Witness*, and so was in a position to hear about available odd jobs before anyone else. And since Welch County had a healthy tax base anyway, there was always plenty of money to go around. Why, last summer's construction job (laying floor tiles in the high school's new art annex) had earned him enough by itself to pay for half the Trans. Of course his mom *had* called in a marker or two to get him the car at cost, just like her cousin at the insurance company had got him a discount there . . . and, well, he'd figured he pretty much had it made.

And now he knew why. It was *not* Mom's job or Mom's connections. It was Matthew Welch pulling strings behind the scenes for the bastard son of a bastard son he had never acknowledged. And frankly, Anson didn't know whether to appreciate the old asshole's wiliness—'cause he'd certainly had not the vaguest inkling that his never-seen, never-referred-to father was Matthew Welch's by-blow—or resent the fact that he had been robbed of the respect due one of his heritage by the small technicality that, blood kin or no, he did *not* have the magical name that so easily opened doors of opportunity.

Until yesterday, when heretofore unformed speculations had suddenly begun to come into focus. Until yesterday, when he'd finally begun to get a handle on the nature of the—he could say it now—family Luck.

He still wasn't *sure* exactly what that was, but from what he'd pieced together growing up, plus what he'd insinuated from between the lines after his eavesdropping session last night, he had a pretty good idea where the Welch clan's success came from.

Magic, some folks would have called it, or something *like* that. And a part of him wondered at his easy acceptance of such a preposterous notion. Except, he realized, he'd been conditioned to accept the unlikely from the Welches all his life. After all, personal paternity problems aside, things were just a little *too* good to be true in Welch County. Too many people were *too* prosperous; the high school teams were *too* successful; the crops *too* bountiful. Businesses never went under, and even the weather could usually be counted on to cooperate. He couldn't remember the last time an important local event had been rained out.

And *he* was part of it now. He was himself a *Welch*—certainly as much as Lewis was, who actually had the name.

Oh sure, he was also apparently a pawn in a subtle and obscure power game between Matthew and his mother—one he only vaguely understood. But *he* could play games too. And he was about to roll the first die.

He had reached the front steps by then: four granite slabs rising toward a break in the carved wooden railings of the two-story porch, with the projecting bay-windowed parlor off to the left. And before he had truly composed himself, he was ringing Matthew Welch's door chime.

He waited a full minute before punching the brass button again, for Cardalba Hall was nothing if not spacious, and Mr. Welch was getting on in his years and surely couldn't move as fast as a young buck like he was. A further half minute's wait ensued, at the end of which he heard the soft shuffle of footsteps approaching. And then the door opened to reveal Matthew himself.

"Why, Anson!" the old man exclaimed in what Anson suspected was genuine surprise—though from the little he'd picked up yesterday, he doubted it was possible to *really* get the drop on him once he was alert to something. "Come in, my boy, come in!"

Anson did, noting to his satisfaction something he had not noticed before, which was that he was a good three inches taller than Mr.—he stopped himself: best get used to altering his way of thinking—than his *grandfather* was. And with that in mind, he stood up straighter still, seeking thereby to press whatever small psychological advantages he could.

For he was not seeing Mr. Welch about work, he was seeing him on far more personal business.

"Thanks," Anson muttered absently, as Matthew ushered him first into the hall, then left into the front parlor, which was where he commonly received drop-in guests.

"Sit, make yourself at home."

Anson did, flopping languidly onto the overstuffed velvet of an antique sofa. Though he had gradually assumed a degree of familiarity with Matthew the last few weeks, he was still awed by him—and suddenly acutely aware of how incongruous he must look sprawling there in the jeans (though they were clean new ones without holes) and red T-shirt that had seemed perfectly acceptable at school. Even Mr. Welch's burgundy sweater and tan cords were more formal.

"Sherry?"

"Sure."

Matthew busied himself at a small table to the left of the door, then returned, handed Anson an obviously expensive cut-crystal glass, and claimed the wing chair opposite. He looked tired, Anson thought, as if he had not slept well the night before.

But if that were true, it was not reflected in the jaunty tone he assumed when he spoke—or else he was covering it well. "So, young Master Bowman, what can I do for you? Surely you haven't gone through your paycheck in one *day*! Even *I* can't spend *that* quickly."

"Uh, no sir, not really."

"You need more work, then? I'm sure I can find *something* for you to do if I prowl around a bit. The Lincoln could use a . . ."

"That's okay," Anson replied, trying not to appear nervous. He was used to having his own way, enforcing his own will on buddy or girlfriend or foe alike. He was· *not* fond of kissing ass, never mind the subtleties of beating around the bush.

"So what *do* you want, then?" Welch's tone had cooled noticeably between questions, and Anson wondered if the old geezer suspected he was up to something. Then again, maybe it was just the tiredness seeping through.

Anson cleared his throat and stared at his black-booted feet. "I . . . I guess I need a little help with my luck."

Matthew's eyes narrowed, suddenly all business. "And what makes you think *I* can help you?"

Anson tried to mask his apprehension with a sip of wine. "Well, I've heard you've got connections—*really* good connections."

Welch steepled his fingers before his nose and regarded Anson critically. "And what, pray tell, might you want . . . connected?"

Anson took another deep breath. This wasn't working at all. Matthew was growing cooler and more distant by the second, and Anson had the distinct sensation he was being played like a fish on a line. He also had the uncomfortable feeling that a gentle breeze was wafting across his memories, pausing now and then to eddy around this one or that.

He didn't like it either, and without really thinking about it, willed it to stop.

Matt's left eyebrow lifted at that—Anson caught the reaction, but had no idea what it meant.

"Silence is not a very informative answer," Matt noted
pointedly. He put an odd accent on *silence* too, which disturbed Anson even more. Maybe he should just abort this
interview now. He had heard enough to have some leverage,
he thought, but perhaps that was *only* enough to be dangerous—to himself.

Yet somehow he found himself speaking.

"I'm havin' some trouble with my girlfriend," he blurted
out. "We had a fight last night, and I'm really bummed out
about it, and I was just kinda curious about . . ."

"Yes, go on."

"Well . . . I guess you know I don't have a dad, and
you're the only older man I really trust much, so I was
hopin' you could maybe give me some advice."

"What sort of advice?"

"Some way to make her like me again. She . . . I think
she's startin' to get this thing for this other guy, and—"

"Does this girl have a name?"

"Of course."

"Would you like to tell me what it *is*?"

"Winnie Cowan."

Matthew puffed his cheeks thoughtfully. "And this other
fellow, this lad you think may be a rival?"

"His name's Ronny Dillon."

Matthew's mouth popped open with a start, and Anson
would have given a lot to know what the old man knew
about his erstwhile rival that had prompted *that* strong a
reaction.

"I know who the girl is, but I've never actually met her—
keeps to herself a lot, doesn't she?"

"Yeah."

Welch's eyes narrowed once more. "And the Dillon
boy?"

"He's new in town. Moved here from Florida 'bout a
month ago—but shoot, I'm tellin' you stuff you already

know, aren't I? Since he's livin' with your nephew and all.''

"*Grandnephew*; Lewis is my grandnephew. But actually, I haven't met this new boy yet. I don't get along well with Lewis's branch of the family; they're a touch too . . . ah, *willful* for my taste—though that's just between you and me.''

"Yeah, right," Anson grunted, doubtful if anything at all was being accomplished beyond a certain degree of verbal fencing. "But *is* there—"

"—Anything I can do?" Matthew shrugged. "I'll have to do some investigating first. In fact," he added, with a sly lowering of his eyebrows that Anson did not like, "I'd need to meet her. After all, I only have your word on this. You might not *be* the right man for her—there *is* a right and wrong about that sort of thing, you know. And I'd hate for *anyone* to be bound to someone they didn't like against their will—it would be bad luck for them, and I don't deal in that kind of thing. *Or*," he continued, "she might not be worthy of *you*—it takes mature judgment to determine those things sometimes.''

"Then you won't help me?"

"I didn't say that."

"So you'll . . ."

"I'll consider your request and contact you again. We can discuss payment later."

"Oh yeah, I kinda forgot about that. How much—"

"It will be in services."

Anson found that he had no reply.

"Is there any way you could bring her here?" Matt asked in a much lighter tone that implied the bargain had been concluded. "There are no activities in town anytime soon that require my presence—not until May, at any rate, which I imagine is longer than you want to wait."

Anson frowned. "I don't know. Like I said, we had a fight. She may not be willin' to go anywhere with me."

"You should apologize then. All women love that; it

gives them a feeling of control. Let her think she's doing you a favor in forgiving you, and then take over from there.''

"Well," Anson said finally. "I reckon I'll give it my best shot."

"Fine," Matt replied. "I believe we have a deal." (Though Anson wasn't sure exactly what he had committed himself to.) "And since I've got you here, I might as well outline a couple of projects for next—"

A telephone rang in another room.

"Sorry." Matthew sighed, rising. "I'll be right back."

Matthew was *not* right back, however, and Anson found himself slipping into a dreamy languor. It was the warmth of the room that did it, he decided, the dusty afternoon light sifting in through high windows onto antique furniture.

He had finished his sherry and was on the verge of resting his head on the sofa's arm, when Matthew stepped inside and informed him that this was an important overseas call and he was going to be tied up for at least thirty minutes; that Anson ought to stick around if he could; and that he was welcome to more sherry.

Anson obliged himself, and had barely resumed his seat when the hall door eased open once more. He jerked awake reflexively—and was both surprised and pleased to discover that the intruder was a girl. She was quite pretty, actually, in a punk-Gypsy way, though Anson tended to like his women with more meat on their bones. But what was she doing here? And then he recognized her: it was the girl who'd held Matthew's feet when he did . . . whatever it was he had to do to conjure the Luck.

"Oops, I didn't know anybody was in here," the girl murmured softly, not meeting his eye—which was fine; Anson liked 'em shy. It made the chase more challenging. He also got the distinct impression she was lying.

"What makes you think *I'm* anybody," Anson shot back smoothly, with his patented wicked grin. Flirting was a skill he had long ago mastered. It ingratiated you with a majority

of women, gave you a little mystery—and sometimes even
led to more . . . *interesting* diversions.

"Oh, I'm sure you're *somebody*," the girl teased back—
which mixture of innocence and guile piqued his curiosity
even more.

"Actually," Anson said, "my name's Anson."

"I *thought* that's who you were. I've seen you outside
some. You do yardwork for Mr. Welch."

Anson nodded solemnly. "Yep, that's me. —But you
know who I am now; what's your name?"

The girl leaned back against the door, and Anson heard
it click closed. A metallic snap meant that she'd locked it.
Anson was instantly on guard, though he tried very hard
not to let it show. "I didn't mean to startle you just now,"
she said in a drifty-lazy kind of voice, ignoring Anson's
question.

"Uh . . . well, I thought you were Mr. Welch coming
back," Anson stammered, hoping he didn't sound too stupid.

"I'm Lenore."

(And there it was at last.) "Nice name."

Which sounded *really* stupid, Anson realized immediately, and decided to shut up for a while, completely at a
loss for a follow-up. The standard lines, like "Who are
you?" or "Where are you from?" or "Do you work for
Mr. Welch?" were obviously out of the question.

"Thanks," Lenore whispered, and Anson got the odd
feeling she wasn't accustomed to talking to people—which,
if what he suspected about her was true, was probably actually the case. She was acting nervous too, and apprehensive, and kept picking at her clothes—electric-blue biking
shorts under a loose white shirt-blouse that fell to mid-thigh.
She was also barefoot and the length of leg he saw was slim
and nicely turned. But there was also a sensuality about her
movements—the kind of slow, easy saunter one often saw
in old Tennessee Williams plays, as if she'd just been pre-

sented with this nubile young body and was still trying it on for size.

Which, Anson admitted, he wouldn't mind doing either.

Meanwhile, Lenore seemed to have abandoned all interest in conversation and had narrowed her activities to meandering toward him until there were no more than two yards between them. Her eyes remained drifty and out of focus, as if, new skin or no, she were only living in her body because she had to. And Anson was absolutely not prepared for what happened next.

Before he knew what she was doing, Lenore had reached to her throat and begun unbuttoning her blouse. He caught just enough flash of skin as her hands passed mid-chest for him to note that she wore no bra underneath, and then the stronger realization struck him that this strange, pretty girl he had never met before was taking off her clothes in front of him—and gazing at some unfocused point behind him while she did it. He did not need to wonder why, but he continued to stare as if hypnotized as the girl let the blouse drop to the plush carpet, revealing small, high breasts with little brown nipples. In spite of his shock, Anson could feel his groin tightening, and he swallowed hard and tried not to look embarrassed. He'd had women, of course—lots of them (though never Winnie, which was a major point of contention—*and* of honor, which had been the genesis of last night's quarrel and was one reason he wanted her back)—but it was always *his* call, *his* pursuit of the quarry. He was unaccustomed to being the seducee—and wasn't sure he liked it.

On the other hand . . .

Lenore was peeling down her shorts now, and seconds later she was naked.

"I need you to do it to me," she whispered as she closed the distance between them. But her voice was tinged with regret.

Anson needed no further urging. In a trice his jeans and skivvies were to his knees and he was reaching for the girl.

An instant later she was sitting astride his hips, and before he knew it he had achieved penetration.

There was resistance—which he had certainly not expected, given the girl's direct approach—and then a brief, soft cry that was a cross between a grunt and a yip—and which the girl quickly stifled. There was precious little in the way of lubrication—at first—but Anson had dealt with virgins before (though never ones quite as forward as this) and was proud of his ability, and before very long the two of them were meshing as one. A part of him wondered why this girl had thrown herself at him, and another part mistrusted her motives completely. But did it really matter? She obviously wanted it, he didn't mind, and it was old Matthew's house anyway, so he could doubtlessly pull a string or two and weasel out of responsibility that way. Besides, he still had a couple of aces up his sleeve that he was waiting for the old man's return to play.

And then he had no more time for doubt, for instinct had taken over for both of them. He did not cry out when the itchy, tickly throb in his penis exploded into strong, quick thrusts (though he usually liked to, for the dramatic effect), and Lenore seemed to be making every effort possible to remain silent as well, though she too seemed to be in the throes of climax.

And then Lenore grabbed Anson's hair, stuffed his face into her bosom, gave one final long, sobbing gasp—and it was over.

She stood quickly, still in that dreamy fugue, and commenced putting her clothes on, oblivious to the blood trickling down her legs. Anson cleaned himself up as well as he could with a handkerchief, and did the same. Neither of them spoke, and Anson found himself becoming both embarrassed and concerned. Before he'd been caught up in amazement, then in the urgency of the moment. Now, with his ardor cooled, he had time to consider the event more rationally, and what he was thinking concerned him. Things like why *had* this curious girl acted this way; things like, would there be any repercussions? She was, apparently, a piece of Mr. Welch's property in some weird way, and—Anson could not suppress a chill—he might very well have ruined her. Yeah, that was really scary: suppose his grandfather had had some plan in mind for this peculiar virgin; suppose he'd been saving her for something—some kind of magical rite, perhaps. And now he, Anson, the heir apparent to a title he did not remotely understand except that he wanted it, had stuck his dick where it didn't belong and fouled things up.

For someone who had just been deflowered, however, Lenore seemed oddly at peace. She still hadn't spoken, and was now slowly buttoning her blouse across the breasts Anson realized he had barely even touched. He cleared his throat nervously, whereupon she blinked and stared blankly at him, as if she were awakening from a long sleep. And mixed with that languorous confusion was what Anson could only interpret as elation.

"Thank you," Lenore whispered. "Now I can get out of here. Now I am free." And while Anson stood staring stupidly, wondering if he should reply with anything as inane as "You're welcome," she padded through the hall door and was gone.

And the entire business, Anson decided, as he adjusted his fly and flopped back on the sofa to finish his sherry, was *damned* strange.

Meanwhile, Matthew had finally gotten his London broker off the phone after nearly thirty minutes of haggling over the number of shares of Jaguar stock to buy (there were rumors of yet another shake-up in the new Ford-based management). Which had been followed by another fifteen minutes discussing possible investment in defense industry futures, now that everyone was so hawkish again. They had reached no consensus, but Matthew had concluded his business confident that the morning's reports would show him minutely richer than he'd been when he retired.

And normally he'd have been more than glad to talk a good while longer, had it not been for the fact that he was practically beside himself with curiosity over the intriguing notion that Anson not only held some sort of animosity toward the worrisome Ronny Dillon, but that it was a type he could perhaps manipulate to his advantage. Having two young cocks pecking around the same pretty little hen in the spring of the year was simply *bound* to cause a little trouble—especially when he was in charge of the farmyard.

But all the same, it was not wise to base such potentially crucial decisions on the random gossipings of a randy adolescent, however close kin and deserving. And with that in mind, Matthew decided it was time he investigated a few things for himself. So it was that as soon as he'd laid down the receiver, he locked the library doors, poured himself a drink (port, for a change), and pressed the button under his chair that jingled Lenore's beeper.

The girl was bog-slow in responding; though that was not unusual this time of day, since she was practically addicted to long afternoon naps. Still, four pages thirty seconds apart was a bit *too* much, especially when he had a client waiting, never mind who that client was. He supposed it was time he gave her a talking-to, which was something he'd had little cause for previously, preferring to retain his footholders with kindness, not fear. Still, a little reminder of who was buttering the bread every now and then did no harm. And in any event, he was pretty sure he was going to have to replace her soon anyway.

But if he had to buzz her *again*—

At that exact moment, a key scraped in a lock, and Lenore entered through her private door. She looked tired around the eyes, and Matthew guessed he was correct: that he'd summoned her from a particularly opulent slumber. But he was so preoccupied with his intended Listening that he paid her no further mind when she sank into the familiar pose at his feet and leaned her head against his knee in a devoted, almost worshipful posture she far too infrequently assumed.

As for himself, he intended to do a bit of spying on this Winnie Cowan, since, if he *was* going to help young Anson with his suit (and thus further cement his trust and devotion, as well as creating a bond of obligation), it was important to know which way the sympathies of the lady in question actually lay. Matt knew who she was, of course, but then he knew *everyone* in Welch County, and all of the more interesting ones in the most intimate, albeit nonphysical, way. The younger ones, though—he wasn't much interested in them until they got enough age on them to begin questioning what they had been taught and wanting more ambitious toys than Nintendos. Too, they had a way of lying low and being unremarkable, until—bam—there they were, full-blown adults to be exploited.

Thus it was with a certain feverish and slightly voyeuristic anticipation that Matthew closed his eyes, slid his feet into Lenore's lap, and began to Listen. Unfortunately, he was still appallingly (and disturbingly) drained from his marathon session of the previous night, and much to his chagrin actually *needed* the augmentation his much-faster-recovering footholder provided—that was certainly the last time he'd solo for eight hours straight for a while; he had no idea he'd gotten *that* reliant on borrowed Strength. This time, though, he only had to go a short way under, then tap into Lenore's Strength, and—

—And *couldn't*! There was no gentle, even flow of vitality from the supple girl into his body and thence into the devious channels of his mind. In fact, it was as if he rested his feet in the lap of an *experienced* woman, one who, in her body's urge to circumvent its incompleteness, was draining *him*, which meant . . .

"Somebody's just *fucked* you!" Matthew hissed coldly, the force of his shock alone sufficient to snap him from his trance. He felt like crap, too: tired and drained and old—much worse than even a moment ago—which worried him. Surely he wasn't *that* far gone, even allowing for the unexpected drain.

Lenore blinked up at him, looking hurt and confused—but then her face hardened and she stared at him with a nervous, edgy defiance. "No," she whispered, "I just fucked *somebody*."

And with that she rose and stood staring at Matthew, no longer the compliant girl he had made of her, but the hard-edged proto-bitch queen he had first picked up in Las Vegas.

"You will be gone in a hour," Matthew stated flatly, trying to keep his voice from trembling with weakness. "I will call you a taxi and give you five thousand dollars. That should be sufficient to get you anywhere reasonable you need to go, and to set you up again. But know, my poor, lost Lenore, that should you seek to turn the laws of men against me, the Wind will bring me your Voice. I have lost the service of your Strength, aye, but with it I have *gained* your Voice, and that you cannot hide."

Lenore merely nodded and left.

"Where do *you* get off fucking my servants?" Matthew raged at Anson ten seconds later, so aflame with fury that sparks were almost literally flashing from his glaring eyeballs. The echoes from the parlor door he'd slammed behind him had not yet dissipated.

And, he realized instantly, he had just made a terrible mistake. God knew he scarcely had energy enough for any kind of confrontation at the moment, much less a yelling match; adrenaline was all that was keeping him going at all. *Damn* Lenore for doing this to him now! And damn himself for overreacting like he just had. He *should* have kept it quiet, *should* have gone on like nothing had happened, and kept a low profile until he'd got himself a new footholder. A moment's clear thinking would have done it. But he'd let his emotions get the upper hand and now it was too late. He'd had his own way too long and had grown complacent and sloppy, and now he was paying the price; now he had to brazen it out. "Well," he thundered, and stood up as straight as he could, "what have you got to say for yourself?"

The traitorous Anson, who had been happily lodged between a nondescript dream and a recapitulated sexual fantasy, jumped halfway off the sofa—but came down fighting.

"She fucked *me*!" he countered, and Matt could tell the boy was trying hard to check himself, since, angry or no, his prospective heir had to know he'd violated half a dozen laws of hospitality, and pissed off the most powerful man in the north half of the state in the process. "I was just sittin' in here and . . ."

"You could have resisted."

"I . . ."

"Do you fuck *every* woman who takes her clothes off around you?"

"That's usually *why* they take their clothes off 'round me!"

"Which shows a remarkable lack of discretion on both your parts!" Matthew gave him back more calmly, now that he'd asserted himself and put Anson on the defensive. "Do you have *any* idea what you've done?" the old man continued icily. "Do you have any notion how much I went through to find that girl, how hard it is to keep a girl like that *like* that?"

Anson had somehow managed to recover his cool as well, and also seemed to be reining back his temper, though his hard, wiry body was as tense as a too-taut guitar string. Matthew saw the boy's eyes sparkle with a wiliness he did not like.

"Actually," Anson said in a slow, precise tone that was only a pitch above a whisper, "I *do* know."

"Know what?" Matthew asked carefully. Oblivious to the effort it caused him, he tried once more to Hear the boy—and met the same impenetrable resistance he had encountered when he'd made a similar probe during their earlier interview.

Anson simply smiled sweetly and replied, very calmly, "*Lots* of things."

Matthew was absolutely floored. Not only had the boy already learned how to Silence (though that was probably just the Luck kicking in an automatic reflex it could not have activated until very recently—Anson was eighteen, which meant it was past time for that kind of thing to start happening), but he evidently knew a lot more about *something* than he ought to, otherwise he wouldn't be playing this risky game so confidently. Trouble was, that same Silence prevented Matthew from discovering exactly how much he *did* know, never mind how he had learned it. And since Anson was family, he was pretty much beyond any *other* control, at least without the augmented Strength a footholder provided. Which meant—barely possible, unless the boy were extremely savvy, but still not worth the risk— that Anson *might* be able to contact enough of the right kind of authorities *and* keep Matthew's own influences at bay long enough for things to get really messy, especially if the matter of Lenore came up. Kidnapping *was* against the law, after all. And even the best of Luck would not avail if certain sorts of information became *too* widely known. Even a Welch could not stand against the government, as poor, arrogant Dion had so clearly shown.

Still, Matthew had not played out his hand to this smirking villein-cum-kinsman, not by a long shot. And indeed a part of him was proud to see Anson's response: it meant the boy had courage—backbone—guts enough to use the Strength that was so obviously stirring. And since he still had the lad on the defensive, he might as well take advantage of the situation. "Very well," he said, taking a step backward, and giving himself a mental shake to further calm himself, as he schooled his face into its much more familiar placidity. "I suppose I was a bit peremptory there. I do *not* normally make a habit of verbally assaulting either my guests, or my servants . . . *However*, whichever way you put it, you have interfered with my property, for which you are therefore in my debt. And since you were not an hour hence appealing to me for my intervention in an affair of yours, I think we can strike a deal.'' He paused for a moment to give Anson a chance to reply, but the boy evidently had balls the size of watermelons and was simply leaning back in the sofa with his arms crossed on his chest and a smug smile on his face.

"Therefore," Matthew continued, "if you will find a suitable replacement for what I have lost, a replacement exactly qualified in the particular virtue you have—ahem—rendered inaccessible, I will assist you in your quest for the love of Ms. Cowan."

But if he had expected Anson to breathe a sigh of relief and throw himself at his feet venting paeans of gratitude and mercy, the boy did not. Instead, Anson's response was a flat, even "What about kinfolk?"

Matthew glared at him askance, suddenly troubled. "What do you mean?"

Anson smiled and shrugged, then looked him straight in the eye. "Well . . . you said you didn't make a habit of yelling at clients or servants. I was just wonderin' about kin. *Do* you holler at your kinfolks, Mr. Welch? I'm not sure I would if I was you."

And that did it. Matt froze where he stood, fury and dread so much at war in him that he could do nothing for several seconds but gape. Finally, however, he regained sufficient composure to pour himself a glass of sherry (the boy had taken him up on his previous offer, he noted, which was perhaps the source of the current overwrought, if effective, bravado). When he looked back toward the sofa, Anson had risen.

"Would you like to reconsider our deal, *Grandfather*?" Anson sneered. "I don't think your offer goes nearly far enough."

"And what *does* go far enough?" Matthew managed to choke, feeling his heart starting to pound in vanguard of a blood-pressure attack. He wondered when he had lost control of the situation—and once again cursed the traitorous Lenore who had brought him to such a sorry impasse. Never mind wondering how Anson had managed to discover the secret of his parentage.

"Oh," Anson purred, "I was thinking of another kind of trade."

"Yes?"

Anson folded his arms decisively. "Very well, *Grandfather*, I'll find you another . . . footholder . . . *if* you'll teach me everything you know—right now."

"And what do you think I know?" Matthew asked carefully, seeking confirmation for what no longer needed any proof.

"Luck," Anson stated flatly. "I want you to teach me about the Luck."

"You're not ready yet. It takes time, it takes the right sort of conditioning." Which was not quite true. The boy clearly *was* ready—biologically; it was Matt himself who wasn't . . . and wouldn't be until he could replace Lenore.

"The hell it does!" Anson shot back. "You think I don't know something's goin' on in my head that's makin' me hear voices and all? You think I can't tell when you're lyin' through your teeth? You were eager enough last night, *Grandpa*. What's the matter, don't you like gettin' what you want, or didn't I hear you right when your mom and you were talkin'? Wouldn't you rather I cooperated than had to be manipulated? We really are on the same side, after all."

Matthew did not reply for several seconds, then his ruddy faced cracked in his widest smile. "Well, boy, I guess you are kin sure enough. Welcome to the Clan. Now . . . I suppose we should decide when you get your first lesson."

Anson's only response was a self-satisfied grin.

Matthew grinned back—and hoped he truly had made the best of a bad situation. His mother, he knew, would be furious—and that clinched it.

* * *

Lenore was gone—had been since sometime after supper, which meal she had cooked for him exactly as she usually did, as if nothing were amiss. Except that this time she did not stay around to do the dishes. No words had been spoken between them at all, and Matthew's farewell to her had consisted of ''Taxi's here,'' followed by a quick ''I'm sorry—and thank you for your good and faithful service.''

After that he had gone back into the library to see, as he nearly always did that time of day, what the Winds were saying about county life. Generally, if you Listened to folks after supper you could pretty well catch them with their guards down, especially if there was nothing very incendiary on the news. The thing that concerned him now, though, was how much even the minimal bit of Listening he'd attempted that afternoon had cost him, never mind the unexpected drain. And now, without Lenore to draw on, he'd be forced to rely on his own Strength exclusively, and, since he rarely used it solo anymore, it had grown weak with disuse, with the result that he'd actually had to fix himself a *second* supper to build up any Strength at all, never mind the morning's ongoing headache which he was still combating with Tylenol.

Eventually, though, he managed to scrape together sufficient reserves to attempt a cursory Listening—and learned exactly nothing except that people were still going to see the Road Man, that the Road Man himself was still Silent, as was Anson now, never mind the dome of Silence Erin always had over her offspring. *And* that Winnie Cowan seemed to pretty much have thrown in her lot with Ronny, about whom she had in fact been enjoying a light-duty sexual speculation even as Matt had, so to speak, dropped by. A bit of more intensive Listening there (though not nearly as much as he would have liked, since he was nearly out of Strength by then), had given him a strong, if superficial picture of *how* things stood between her and Anson, if not the *why*—and had done nothing to reinforce any admiration Matthew might have had for his grandson. The bond between them was after all one of blood, not mutual affection: Matthew knew very well he could be raising up a viper. But therein also lay the challenge. It might even be fun: to thwart his mother's high-handed traditionalism, to twist that same tradition to his will and drag it kicking and screaming into the twentieth century, and—not incidentally—to simultaneously raise up and subvert Anson Bowman. It was an ego thing for him, pure and simple. With money and power already at his disposal, one of the very few risks left in Matthew's life was high-stakes gambling.

His mother would have said he was either a fool, or crazy.

Maybe he was—like a fox.

Chapter 9

A Snake in Eden

Cordova Methodist Church
Sunday, April 8—12:05 P.M.

Winnie Cowan had not slept well the previous night. She had been plagued with troubling dreams, born, no doubt, of her subconscious continuing to ponder what her conscious mind had already experienced and reacted to but did not yet understand.

It had begun shortly past sunset. She had stayed at Marilyn Bridges' dam-building party as long as decorum permitted—through supper and into the evening. Marilyn was a good friend and had instantly grasped the implications of Winnie's war wound without being told more than the minimum amount needed for confirmation of the facts—which was just as well, as Winnie had no desire whatever to go into detail about being beaten up by Anson. More to the point, however, Marilyn had been quick to come to her rescue when Winnie had finally admitted that she was still hanging around long after the rest of their friends had split because she still hadn't told her folks what had transpired.

(They'd been at work when she got up, and if she was lucky would be in bed when she returned home.) Unfortunately, Monday was a school day, and she wouldn't be able to avoid facing them any longer. And face was the operative word, too. Sooner or later her mom or—worse—her dad would notice her shiner. They would ask questions and she would tell them the truth because she was that kind of person.

Unless she spent the night at Marilyn's so that the damage would have one more day in which to heal. Then— if she were extremely careful, wore the right makeup (though she didn't usually wear any at all), modified her hairstyle so that her bangs fell into her face, and kept on her shades—it was barely possible no one would be the wiser. At least her damage was nothing like as bad as poor Ronny's had been. No way she could have disguised op art like his.

Blessedly, Marilyn's thoughts had been exactly along those lines, and she'd come through with an unsolicited invitation to sleep over—to which she'd added a few pointed opinions regarding the advisability of reporting the affair to the sheriff—*and* to Anson's mother, who being a woman herself, might have some hope of understanding, and therefore interceding.

So things had looked just dandy, or better at any rate than they had at dawn—especially regarding her rapidly intensifying relationship with Ronny Dillon. Until, somewhere around eight o'clock, she had suddenly felt—there was no other way to describe it—dirty. It was a very strange sensation too: one minute she was sitting on Marilyn's sofa ostensibly watching a *Robin of Sherwood* rerun on Showtime (but mostly dozing on and off when she wasn't thinking about Ronny and how handsome he was or wondering guiltily if his unseen lower part looked as good as the upper half had) when all at once it was as if someone were running slimy fingers through her memories, examining each one with a self-satisfied, triumphant glee, and then replacing it

again. It had actually made her nauseous for a moment—
so much that Marilyn had noticed and immediately risen to
fetch her a Coke. She hadn't explained anything, and Marilyn hadn't asked, but she'd lain awake a long time thinking
about it that night. It was like nothing she'd ever experienced, that was for sure. And she hoped she never had to
undergo it again. Unfortunately, her dreams had had other
plans, and phantom recapitulations of the event had tormented her until almost dawn.

So it was that when she and Marilyn climbed out of the
Bridges' Audi Avant in Cordova Methodist's parking lot on
Sunday morning she was more asleep than awake.

Which was just as well, because the sermon was nothing
special at all. (And hadn't been since the North Georgia
Conference had uprooted Reverend Pasker the year before.)
Still, by the time the collection plate wheeled by and the
last hymn was sung, Winnie was finally beginning to feel
that she could perhaps face the world.

Until she saw Anson.

He was leaning casually against the brick retaining wall
at one side of the parking lot, and gazing up at a single
buzzard floating lazily in an overcast sky, its wings tipping
every now and then as if it sought to keep its balance—
probably in the vanguard of a larger flock that was about
to swoop on a luckless possum some overeager churchgoer
had claimed. Winnie found herself following his line of
sight, but before she knew it, her gaze had drifted back to
her former beau.

He seemed different somehow, more self-confident
maybe; not as wired or show-offish as he usually was—
as if sometime in the thirty-odd hours since she'd seen
him he had come to peace with himself. He also looked
absolutely smashing. Already tall and muscular, if a bit
on the lean side (his muscles were ropy and knotty when
she'd seen him without his shirt, whereas she preferred
firm, smooth ones like Lewis—or Ronny—had), he had
obviously put extra care into his dress this morning. For

a wonder he was not wearing jeans, but neatly pressed
linen pants of light tan, with a plain white shirt and darker
tan jacket over them. He was not wearing a tie, but he
wasn't wearing sneakers either, only a pair of nicely shined
brown loafers. His face had changed too, though at that
distance, Winnie could not say how. And every lock of
dark hair had been blow-dried and moussed into place.
Completely against both her will and her better instincts,
Winnie could not help staring at him. *Something* had
clearly happened, 'cause she'd certainly never seen him
take this much care with his appearance. Maybe he was
feeling contrite or something. And maybe, just possibly,
the outside would be reflected within.

Thus she stood frozen in her tracks, while one part tried
to tell her no, that she was being a fool for even thinking
about seeing Anson again, and the other part was almost
irresistably drawn to him. Probably the best thing to do
would be to snag Marilyn (who'd gotten waylaid by a bunch
of MYFers wanting advice about their next party), and approach her former beau with reinforcements in hand. That
way he'd be on his best behavior (the fact that they were
in a church parking lot with a lot of people still milling
around wouldn't hurt either), *she'd* have a witness to anything he said (one who would also be able to consider his
comments in an objective light), and perhaps they could
start over.

Because, in spite of what she had told Ronny Dillon
yesterday about being through with Anson, she was not
quite sure she was.

She was right on the verge of following up on her decision
and going in quest of Marilyn, when Anson turned his gaze
from the sky to the church door, saw her, and headed her
way with an eager stride. He was grinning too, boyish and
guileless and Winnie simply stood like a hypnotized bird
until he was nearly upon her. That close she realized that
he'd shaved off the ratty mustache. It was the first time
she'd seen him so since he grew it, and its absence made

his face look a lot more finished, which in turn made him even more attractive.

"Mornin'," Anson drawled lightly, eyes a-twinkle with an infectious good humor Winnie found oddly disconcerting.

"Hello," she replied, not meeting his gaze directly. She took a step backward and leaned against the portico railing.

"May rain," Anson opined.

"Probably." Winnie wondered what he was getting at. He was actually making small talk, which was not like him. That, in turn, suggested that he was experiencing a justifiably bad case of the guilts, which was in turn making him almost docile. Nevertheless, she intended to stay on guard until she discovered what exactly he was up to.

"Uh . . . look," Anson managed finally. "I . . . well, I just wanted to say I'm sorry about the other night. I was a real"—he risked a glance at the dispersing crowd, of whom none were within earshot, before continuing—"a real asshole, I guess. No way I should have acted like I did, and I guess the only excuse I have is that I'd been drinkin' a little."

"I know," Winnie stated flatly.

"Well, uh . . . I know what I did, and I'm sorry. And I know what you said about not wantin' to go out with me anymore, and I'm sorry about that too—but I understand, and maybe we can deal with that some other time. But the reason I came over to talk to you this mornin' was . . . well, it was actually to deliver a message."

Winnie looked up sharply and peered intently into Anson's eyes, seeking any sign of teasing or deception, and finding none.

"Who from?"

Anson took a deep breath and shifted his position, as if he were nervous about something. "Uh, well, actually, it's a message from Mr. Welch. He wants to meet you."

Winnie was thunderstruck. "*Me?* Why me? I've only seen

him a couple of times in my life, and he paid exactly no attention to me.''

Anson shrugged. "He didn't say what he wanted, just told me to bring you whenever I could, that he needed to meet you. I told him that you and me'd had some trouble lately, but that I'd try."

Winnie had no idea how to respond. First it was dread at seeing Anson, then a certain guilty stirring of delight that he looked so good, so . . . changed. But then had come the discomfort of actually having to deal with him once more, and then this odd message. Surely he didn't mean it. Surely it had to be a joke.

Except that one did not make jokes about the Welches.

"Did he say *when* he wanted to see me?" Winnie wondered. "Maybe I should call and find out."

"Uh, no," Anson replied smoothly. "But if you want to I could take you over there now. I doubt he'd mind."

"And you really don't know what he wants?"

Anson shook his head innocently. "No idea. All I know is that he wants me to introduce you."

"You? Why you?"

"Because I'm the only person our age he knows that you know—not countin' Lew, of course, since they don't get along."

Winnie puffed her cheeks thoughtfully, then reached a decision. "Okay," she announced. "I'll go. I don't dare risk *not* going. But I won't go today. I've got too much homework. And I absolutely won't go with you."

"But I need to introduce you."

Winnie's expression was firm. "I *won't* go with you, Anson. No way I'm setting foot in a car with you again, much less alone."

"You really don't trust me then?"

"Would you?"

"About the Welches, you should. Nobody dares lie about the Welches."

"Except the Welches themselves."

Anson's eyes narrowed with what Winnie could only interpret as shock. "What's that supposed to mean?"

"It means Mr. Welch could be lying about what he wants you to do."

"Why would he do that?"

"To see if you're reliable. To see if you'll do every little toadie thing he tells you to."

"That doesn't change the fact that he wants to see you."

"Nor does it change the fact that I won't go there with you."

"So where does that leave us?"

Winnie gnawed her lip. "Okay," she said at last. "I'll go. But I can't possibly do it before Thursday. And when I do go, I'm going to Marilyn's first, and I'm going to tell her where I'm going and why. And I'm going to drive myself to Mr. Welch's. If you want to meet me there in plain sight of the house, you can; that way you can still make this introduction you think is so important. But I want you to know I'm perfectly capable of ringing a doorbell for myself—*and* of telling anybody who wants to know who I am. And I *won't* go anywhere with you afterwards."

"I'm not *askin'* you to," Anson shot back defensively. "I only want you hangin' out with me if it's what *you* want to do. And I'm gonna use *all* my strength to make sure that happens," he added in a tone so odd it gave Winnie chills. And then Marilyn swept up, and there was no more time for discussion. "See you sometime Thursday?" Anson said, oblivious to Marilyn's glare as she began easing Winnie toward the wagon.

"Yeah." Winnie sighed. "I guess you will."

The grip on her arm tightened abruptly. "You're not going out with *him* again, are you?" Marilyn hissed in her ear. "After what he did to you? Besides, what about Ronny Dillon?"

Winnie shrugged unhappily. ''I can't help it, Marilyn. This is something I *have* to do. Don't worry about me, I'll be okay—I promise.''

She wondered if she believed that.

Chapter 10

A Modest Proposal

Cordova, Georgia
Sunset

Sometimes, Ronny thought as he scooted his white Ford Escort GT along a certain little-used back road on the south side of Cordova, luck was not so much a matter of circumstance as of *manipulating* circumstance.

Take this errand for instance. All Aunt Erin had *said* was, "Why don't you zip into town and pick us up some ice cream for supper?" That, on the surface, had hardly seemed fortunate at all. In fact, given the trouble he had driving even an automatic like his with his near-rigid right leg, it could have been interpreted as a downright onerous task, and one that Lewis could doubtless have fulfilled far more efficiently, had Ronny's godbrother not been so immersed in a game of Tetris as to have lost all sense of familial responsibility, even to responding to his mother's pleas for *somebody* to go to the store.

Yeah, that was the way it *could* have been. But the way Ronny had *interpreted* that request allowed him complete

leeway as to choice of flavors and place of purchase—with
the result that approximately a minute after he had passed
Cordova's southern boundary, he was turning left onto good
old U.S. 76 East/West. Which meant he had already passed
two grocery stores and a Magic Market. But the Magic
Market *he* wanted was a very particular one: it was where
Winnie Cowan worked.

And there was the Promised Land now, just ahead on the
right, a stone's throw from the western city-limit sign. Ronny's heart leapt as he steered the Escort into the handicapped
parking slot near the door. He didn't know if Winnie was
on shift today or not, but at least this way he could learn
something—about her family and circumstances, if nothing
else. She hadn't been home all last night when he'd tried
to call her, and he'd been too unsure about their relationship
to attempt reaching her at Marilyn's house where her comments might be overheard. But now was the moment of
truth: the time when he met her father—or her mother—or
her kid brother—or somebody—and could size them up
without being subjected to equivalent scrutiny.

It turned out to be the brother—or at least the skinny
thirteenish kid who'd dashed out from behind the counter
to help him with the door (making him feel both grateful
and put-upon) looked a great deal like her, in a gawky,
frizzy-haired way. Mostly it was the eyes, he decided: eyes
and dimples and smile.

Unfortunately, the brother was the one whose approval
mattered least, so that after a quick, muttered "Thanks,"
Ronny immersed himself in the onerous task of deciding
between Mayfield, Coble, and Breyers; and between butter
almond (his favorite), chocolate mint (which Lewis preferred), or good old-fashioned vanilla, which he knew Aunt
Erin, whose money he was spending, would have chosen.
There was not, alas, enough cash to get all three.

After brief consideration, he chose the vanilla (which
could be transformed into other flavors by the addition of
various substances in Erin's well-stocked pantry), and Brey-

ers, because it was *his* favorite and he had made one sacrifice already.

And back in the parking lot two minutes later he had no more idea about Winnie Cowan's family than that they ran a neat, clean, well-stocked store, and that her brother was fidgety but polite.

The sun was brushing the horizon by then, but the ice cream was frozen hard, and he was feeling fey. He had not been out alone very often since he'd moved up—first from attitude, then because Lewis had been very conscientious about keeping him busy and showing him around so that he'd know what people were talking about and not get lost. Still, there were places he hadn't been, and spatial relationships between places that he hadn't worked out yet, and he'd never said he'd come *straight* home—so he decided that he had time to do a bit of exploring.

And the fact that the strip of road he chose to reconnoiter also just *happened* to be the one that ran by the Road Man's camp was only a fortuitous coincidence—except, of course, that Ronny had contrived every bit of it.

So it was that five minutes after leaving the lights of Cordova behind him, Ronny crested a long, curvy grade and entered the mile-long straight that bisected Swanson's Meadow.

—And found himself completely blinded, as even the looming mountains on either side were absorbed by a flaming ruddy glare.

It was exactly sunset, he realized, and good old Sol, in a fit of showmanship worthy of Cecil B. DeMille, was setting precisely at the far end of the straight. Indeed, what he could make out of it from between slitted lids looked like a vast red disk clamped between the two low hills that flanked the road's apparent terminus. Trouble was, his windshield was filmed over inside, so that *most* of what he saw was haze. And there was the small matter of a sun visor that would not flip low enough.

Ronny had no choice but to slow drastically and squint

into the brilliance, shading his eyes with one hand, while shifting his attention to the right-hand side of the road. The result was that he had more time to think as he putted along. Which also gave him more time to yield to temptation.

Before he even realized he had done it, he had passed the ruins of the Swanson place and was easing the Escort onto the opposite shoulder. It was a completely impulsive move, at least as far as his surface mind was concerned; beyond that, he did not dare contemplate, lest his own guilty conscience send him flying. Besides, he had ice cream with him which would melt, so he really couldn't stay long. But ban or no ban, there was no way he was going to get this close and not drop in on the Road Man—especially since there remained the small matter of collecting the tips on technique he had been promised two nights ago.

And, he assured himself, he really would stay only about five minutes.

Seconds later he had stowed the ice cream in the floorboards (and thus out of the sun's direct influence) and very soon after that was making his awkward way across the field toward the looming wagon, his shadow sliding long and dark across the trampled broomsedge. It was strange, he thought, that no one else was around, especially since it was Sunday night—prime time for preachers, as the Road Man was alleged to be. There was also no telltale tink-tink-tink from the forge—no sounds at all, in fact, beyond the occasional odd bleat from an irate goat, or the clink and whizz of a machine.

He had reached the first of the circle of man-high contraptions that in some obscure way seemed to guard the camp. Nor was he surprised to find them different from those he had encountered either time before.

The one on his right, for instance, was another of those elegant, deadly efficient constructs of light-but-strong materials—in this case, lucite, fiber-optic cables, Kevlar, and chrome tubing. Vaguely cylindrical, it was powered—he thought—by a solar collector apparatus on top. Or at least that's what he imagined the three dish-shaped agglutinations of tiny mirrors angled toward the sun were for. What it was supposed to *do*, besides whir, click, and look good, Ronny had no idea. There *was* something inside it, however: a silver latticework sphere that evidently contained something ripely organic—which given the proximity to goats, the forge, and the man's habits in general, didn't necessarily mean anything. What it was *producing*, though, was fiber. Somehow the contraption was extracting thin strands of nearly invisible filaments from the slowly revolving filigree ball and twisting them into a cord that was barely thicker. There was a substantial amount of it already, wound around a spindle poking out of the top like a pearl-white minaret. What the stuff was, or could be used for, Ronny had no idea.

The other machine was of rather more blatant intent. In general, it resembled an iron rebar tripod two yards tall, except that rather than being fixed firmly to the ground, the lower extremities of the three legs were suspended a few inches above the trampled turf by springs which were in turn connected to shorter pegs that *were* driven into the earth, allowing the whole inner construct to move flexibly within a fixed frame. There was a network of hoses, gears, and electric motors halfway up, along with various bits of wiring and electronic equipment including a cassette player and a speaker. And at waist level a large cardboard sign proclaimed ORGASMS: 25 CENTS, with an arrow pointing toward the coin slot from a defunct arcade machine welded to a jutting bit of rebar. Closer examination into the device's darkening entrails revealed, depending from more wires, tubes, and gears—and exactly at Ronny's crotch level—a life-size erect penis cast in brass.

In a fit of madness, Ronny fished a quarter out of his pocket and chunked it into the slot.

The response was amazing. First a circle of erratically flashing red Christmas lights came on immediately above the dangling phallus. Then the machine itself began to bounce gently on its springs. The recorder clicked on, and soft panting sounds began to penetrate the dusk, while a bell-crank apparatus stashed somewhere behind it worked the business end of the penis up and down—or in and out, depending on how you interpreted it. Ronny could not help but smile, and as the machine continued on its lascivious way, the smile widened into an embarrassed, if fascinated grin. Meanwhile, the lights were flashing faster and faster (and several other colors had joined the red now), the machine was bouncing ever more vigorously (Ronny almost feared it would shake itself to pieces), and the pants came harder, faster, and much louder. And then the lights flashed brighter yet, and began to coordinate themselves with the bounces and the pants. Louder/faster/brighter/harder—louder/faster/brighter/harder. At last light and sounds and motion merged into a crescendo—whereupon, with one final satiated sigh, the machine unloaded a spurt of nameless liquid onto the ground.

Two more sighs, and the lights began to blink off. The bounces subsided into quivers.

The show was over.

And Ronny, who'd been standing there gaping, suddenly began to laugh like an idiot.

He was still chuckling—and casting frequent amused glances over his shoulder—when he entered the inner circle of the camp.

The Road Man was nowhere in sight, however, and Ronny would have left then (there was, after all, ice cream at risk in the Escort), had the steady contention of the goats not lulled precisely long enough for him to hear, faint but clear, the sound of singing from somewhere beyond the stand of trees behind the camp.

Once more impulse got the better of discretion and he headed toward the voice. He braved the circle of machines again (noting—and resisting—another one that promised bargain rate orgasms, only this one involved a pink-silk-lined woman's purse framed with rabbit fur), slipped by the increasingly odoriferous goat corral, and found himself on a narrow trail leading downhill through a tangle of pine woods. Once he had entered the forest, the singing became much clearer: a deep male voice bellowing "Shall We Gather at the River" with such volume and enthusiasm that it bordered on the operatic.

Ronny made the best progress he could, though even this close to dusk (the sun had been exactly half visible when he'd left the camp) it was already murky and dim on the forested slope. A moment later, he stumbled out of the woods and onto a shelf of rocks, and for the third time in three days found himself confronting the Road Man.

And once again he had caught him in a compromising position. The first time Ronny had found him shirtless; the second time he had caught him without his pants. This time he had caught him with nothing on at all.

Not that it seemed to bother the Road Man.

The shelf of rocks fronted a shallow pool maybe five yards across, with a stream running in and out on either side. And in the exact center of this pond the Road Man was standing crotch-deep in water, still singing at the top of his lungs, and lathering himself vigorously with a soap so virulent-smelling it made Ronny want to sneeze even where he was. The tinker's eyes were closed, his head thrown back as if in ecstasy, and his mass of red hair was sleeked close to his head. With the sunlight flashing ruddy upon him and his body polished by water, he looked like a god—Vulcan, perhaps, or Thor, or Odin—rendered in frozen flame.

And then his eyes popped open and he saw Ronny.

He did not seem at all concerned by his state of undress, merely grinned broadly and cried, "Welcome, stranger! O ye who are heavy-laden, welcome! These be not the waters of Babylon, but come ye to them anyway and weep away your sorrows! Weep for lost Zion! Be ye Christian or infidel, Turk or Jew, I welcome you. I was just baptizing myself, and I'll be more than glad to baptize you!"

And with that, he swung his arm up and out, and leveled his bar of soap straight at Ronny. Water flashed and sparkled in his wake, and Vulcan became, for an instant, Poseidon.

"No thanks," Ronny called back as cheerfully as he could, though he was mightily put off. "I . . . I've already been done."

"Ah, but were you done *right*?" the Road Man yelled in high good spirits. "No, *of course* you weren't. You ain't been baptized by the Sunset Man."

Ronny rolled his eyes. "No, but I've met the Day Man and the Night Man—and I haven't been baptized by them either."

"Gotta watch them," the Road Man confided, as he slowly lowered himself to a crouch—which had the effect of floating the lather away from his body. "Them boys'll lead you astray. They'll promise you things they can't deliver, and they'll make promises for each other none of 'em plan to keep."

"What about you?" Ronny called uncertainly.

"I keep *everybody's* promises," the man replied instantly. "Oh, and by the way, I'm sure the Day Man'll thank you for the donation."

"Huh?" Ronny stammered, then, remembering the use to which he had put his quarter: "Oh . . ."

"Yeah," the Road Man continued, "he shore does appreciate it. He's troubled, that one is. Can't get no women to cleave to him this time around. Says he must be getting old. Says they just don't come around no more."

Ronny shrugged inconclusively. "Okay . . ."

"I think it's the Night Man's cooking does it. Makes his breath smell bad."

Ronny snorted in disgust and turned to leave, having suddenly had enough, then paused. The fellow was obviously stark raving bonkers. On the other hand, he was also a genius of some rare kind—there was no other way he could make machines out of junk that could accomplish what his did. But even if Ronny *could* somehow pick up a

bit of technique from him, would it be worth the risk?
Suppose the Road Man decided he wanted to cleave to *him*?
He was certainly big and strong enough to accomplish it.
Or suppose the next time the odd food turned out to be
poisoned. Or . . .

A splash behind him made him look around again, to see
the Road Man wading toward the opposite side of the pond.
The water was deeper there, and the bank much steeper and
pocked with clumps of jutting boulders between the rhododendron. Maybe he wanted to swim a lap or two—which
Ronny had no desire whatever to witness. And in any event
the Road Man seemed to have forgotten him entirely, for
he had started singing again: "I will take me a sprig of
laurel and of yew . . ." And with that he reached toward
one of the low-dipping branches of the nearest rhododendron, caught it, and pulled.

The plant did not budge, though, and the Road Man
waded closer and tugged once more, with as little effect.
Closer still, until he was half out of the water—whereupon
he wrapped his arm around a projecting, stove-sized boulder, used it for leverage, and yanked again.

The bush was still too much for him—but the rock, for
some reason, was not. And as Ronny gaped in horror, the
heavy stone slowly oozed out of the muddy riverbank and
slipped into the water—directly atop the Road Man.

"Look out!" Ronny hollered, though already it was too
late, for the Road Man had uttered a *most* sacrilegious ex-
clamation, pinwheeled his arms for a timeless moment of
failing balance, and toppled backward into the water.

Before his head broke surface again, Ronny was moving.
For the tenth time that day he cursed the infirmity that made
any kind of reasonably rapid progress along the wooded
marge of the pond an impossibility. Traversing good ground
was hard enough with the crutch. On rocks and sticks and
uneven, boggy footing, it became a real nightmare.

But he had no choice, because the Road Man was definitely in trouble. He was keeping his head up, yes, but the

rock had clearly pinned his leg somewhere underneath, so that he had to strain to break the surface.

Ronny halted once, halfway around, and called out, ''Are you okay? I can go for help, or—''

To which the Road Man yelled back, ''No time. *You* help me or I die.''

Ronny felt sick to his stomach. Him? Help? How? No way he was strong enough to shift a three-foot-thick boulder. No way he could drag the Road Man free. For either you needed to brace, and for that you needed two strong legs.

But what alternative did he really have?

He had reached the bit of reliable footing nearest the Road Man now, but still could not tell exactly what the problem was. The Road Man was definitely faltering though, obviously having more trouble keeping his head above water.

Ronny wasted no more time. Throwing caution completely aside, he dropped his crutch and leaped into the pond—and gasped, as an unexpected coldness closed around him. How had the Road Man stood it? he wondered. But at least the water buoyed him up, took some of the stress off his weakened leg. Taking a deep breath, he ducked his head under and felt along the curve of boulder until he found where it imprisoned the Road Man's flesh. It was not as bad as it could have been, though bad enough. The Road Man was actually pinned only by his toes, which were trapped between the stone and a sunken log. The trouble lay in the fact that the curve of the rock arched out in such a way that it forced the Road Man's legs to lie almost horizontally, so that he had to essentially curve his torso nearly ninety degrees to get his head high enough to breathe, and had nothing to brace against when he did.

The way Ronny saw it, there were two things he could do. The first was simply to stay there, hold the Road Man's head above water, and squall at the top of his lungs until someone either heard him or they both died of hypothermia.

Or he could try to move either foot or boulder.

Tugging on the leg made no difference, even with what

feeble assistance the thrashing Road Man could give him, so that when he broke surface once more, he had no choice but to attempt the other option.

But first he needed to check on the victim. A floating half step into the chest-deep water to his right, and he was able to grab the Road Man under the arms and hold his head clear long enough for him to get his breath. "Okay," he gasped. "Don't panic, okay? Just relax and listen to me. Your toes're caught, but not by much, and I think I may be able to do something about it."

"And what can *you* do about it, boy?" the Road Man spat and sputtered, with surprising venom. "You who are not even baptized."

"Well, I guess I am now!" Ronny grunted back. "Now, cool it. Take a deep breath and try to float. If you start to go under, holler—and hold your breath as long as you can, and then try to get up and take another, and I'll keep an eye on you. Meanwhile, I'm gonna see what I can do about getting you free."

Which sounded a lot easier than it was. What Ronny needed was something to pry with. The boulder wouldn't yield, but the log might. If he was lucky, there was a bare chance he could shift one or the other enough for the Road Man to drag his foot free.

Except that he had nothing to use for a lever. There were no appropriate sticks anywhere around, and he dared not risk even a quick foray back to the camp where there was surely something appropriate.

Which left his crutch. Ronny wondered if it would work. It was new, was well-made, had taken him where he needed to go, and it was nicely triangulated.

Grimacing in resignation, he reached up to where it lay on the bank, quickly unwound the wirelike sprue that bound the miniature warrior to the top, set it aside, and dragged the rest in. Then, taking a deep breath, he dove down again, located the log, and wedged the pointed end of the crutch into the juncture between log and rock. The Road Man's head broke water just then, and Ronny yelled at him to hang on if he could and listen. When the Road Man grunted his acknowledgment, Ronny told him to yank his foot free the *instant* he felt any loosening, and went to work. His legs might be crippled, true, but there was nothing at all wrong with his upper body; thus, Ronny leaned into the top of the crutch with a vengeance, pushing down with all his might, and rising as far out of the water as he could so that his unbuoyed weight could add to the force.

Nothing happened at first, but then he felt a hint of movement, as if the log had shifted his way an inch or so. But the rock moved as well, and he had to relocate and try again.

He had almost resigned himself to failure and a night spent supporting the Road Man's head, when the log gave an abrupt lurch, the crutch responded with an equally energetic snap-twang—and the Road Man suddenly propelled himself backward in the water.

Two minutes later they were on the lower shoals of the opposite bank, dripping wet and cold, but alive. The crutch was reduced to a abstract construct of bent and twisted tubing interlaced with bits of rubber.

But instead of thanking him, the Road Man merely muttered, ''Must have been something the Day Man did. Must have been his sins comin' home to roost.''

Ronny had nothing to say to that. He was too cold and miserable. And unfortunately he could not yet leave.

The Road Man was little the worse for his experience, however, a quick examination revealing no more damage than a series of scrapes across the top of his large and hairy left foot. He could not walk well on it though, and it took a ludicrous amount of time (and made an equally ludicrous image, given they were both dripping wet, one was naked, and they had two functional legs between them) for them to make it back to the camp.

And as soon as they reached it, Ronny caught the smell of burning.

The Road Man practically vaulted from the awkward half-embrace they'd been tangled in for their mutual support, leaving Ronny to balance desperately until he could regain his equilibrium. Meanwhile, the tinker was hop-limp-running toward a fire pit Ronny hadn't noticed earlier, over which two of the ubiquitous gold-colored pots depended above a bed of coals.

Ronny followed more slowly, and arrived just in time for the Road Man to—with his bare hands, naturally—lift the spit from its props and disengage the nearest pot. Then, without one word of warning, the tinker thrust the container straight into his hands, barked, "Hold this—and *don't* let it spill," and made a grab for the other one.

Ronny's instinct was to refuse, but he'd been taken so far off guard that he found himself accepting the vessel in spite of himself.

It was scorching hot, too, but he found that he *could* stand it—barely. Which was just as well, because the Road Man was limping toward his wagon with the other one by then—resembling nothing so much as a very large and muscular (but no less slimy-wet) Gollum protecting his magic ring. An instant later he was inside.

But *could* Ronny stand the pain? The pot filled both hands, and the shape was just awkward enough, his hold just sufficiently precarious, that he dared not shift his grip an iota or risk spilling whatever was inside. But the more he thought about it, the hotter it seemed to become—except that didn't make sense. Gritting his teeth, he calmly told himself that whatever pain it had cost him, the worst was over, that however hot it had been it really did have to be cooler now, and that the pain wouldn't decrease much faster even if he *did* let go of it, and that by this time tomorrow it would all be over anyway. For the first time in his life, perhaps, he was grateful for the sadistic ninth-grade coach who had gleefully applied those lines to high-school calisthenics.

Fortunately, the curious golden vessel had finally decided

to start cooling in earnest, so that it was actually quite pleasant to the touch by the time the Road Man leapt out of the wagon again (eschewing the steps, never mind that he *should* have had a game leg) and came strolling back quite dry, and dressed in a flaming red jogging suit. Without a word, he held out his hand, and Ronny had to blink at him for an instant before he realized he wanted the pot. Ronny passed it to him and wiped his hands on his sopping thighs, hoping vainly that the Road Man might offer a towel.

Instead, the Road Man looked him up and down and snorted. ''You'll be wantin' a new crutch, I guess, to make up for that 'un you broke back there.''

''It's okay,'' Ronny replied. ''If you can give me something to lean on, I can get home without it. I'll return it tomorrow.''

''I may not *be* here tomorrow,'' the Road Man shot back with a wild look in his eyes. ''I may not be here tonight. I might not even be here *now*, you ever think about that? Or I might be like the Lord Jesus Christ and be here all the time—or not at all.''

Ronny did not reply, but then the Road Man's crazed expression smoothed abruptly (he was actually quite nice-looking, Ronny decided, when he wasn't ranting), and he smiled. ''Ah, but *you'll* be here all the time if I *don't* let you go—and the only way to do that's for me to find you a new crutch—so you just stand there a minute, and I'll see what I can whip up.''

Ronny's heart leapt. Though he was cold, wet, miserable, weirded out, and late, he had also—maybe—been offered a chance to watch the Road Man at work from start to finish. Except that instead of heading toward the forge to bend strips of iron and steel and exotic alloys into the shape Ronny envisioned, the Road Man once more returned to the wagon, leaving Ronny to stand and shiver by the pitiful fire.

Seeing no real point in remaining where he was, for there was precious little warmth, he limped toward the wagon. He was approaching the right-hand side, which he had not had a good look at before, and though it was deep in shadow, enough light remained for him to make out the complexity of shapes there.

And one in particular. At first he thought *it* a crutch, for it certainly had the general configuration of one. Except that the slender wedge of metal was one complex, intricately beveled and angled metal casting. And—Ronny almost cried out at this—it looked almost exactly like the model he had begun for his super-crutch, save that this was of gleaming, if somewhat tarnished, metal; and that it was clamped to the side of the wagon by what looked like bear claws forced into the very wood.

He was still contemplating it when the Road Man returned. Still balancing mostly on one foot (which, with Ronny's similar condition, made them an odd pair), the tinker held out two crutches for Ronny's inspection: one the old-fashioned wooden style, the other a dull gray hospital-type job, rather like the one he had just destroyed. (He still retained the remains—and, of course, the cast silver warrior.) Neither choice set Ronny's heart to racing.

"Choose," the Road Man commanded.

Ronny considered them both for a long moment, then shook his head and pointed toward the side of the wagon. "I want this one," he said, indicating the fine aluminum casting.

And to his surprise, the Road Man smiled. "Ah, then you *are* a lad of taste—for you have chosen the rarest thing I own."

"That?" Ronny replied dubiously, for though interesting in its own way, the object scarcely looked *that* remarkable.

"Oh, aye," the Road Man affirmed. "For that is the cast aluminum traction arm from a 1938 Centauri roadster."

Ronny's eyes narrowed in perplexity. What was a Centauri? Some kind of car maybe? The only thing he knew of that had traction arms were cars, so it must have been. But his foster dad had been a serious auto buff, a fair bit of which had rubbed off on Ronny. And *Ronny* had never heard of a car called a Centauri.

"Oh," he said noncommittally. "Never mind."

"Oh no," the Road Man countered, letting his two lesser offerings fall from either hand. "There's no problem, for there was only one ever made, and it was wrecked, and this is all that survives."

A minute later Ronny was testing the new "crutch" for length (which was perfect). And a minute after that he had affixed the silver warrior to the top.

And a minute after *that*, when he had returned to the front of the wagon, the Road Man took him roughly by both shoulders—and kissed him on each cheek.

Ronny was too shocked to reply, but stiffened automatically and tried to pull away. Whereupon the Road Man released him and simply stood there, looking so thoughtful that Ronny could not resist sticking around.

Finally the Road Man spoke, but it was with a different, more refined voice than Ronny had ever heard him use before. "You are a strong lad," he said, "for you have freed me. And you are a clever lad, for you knew how that could be accomplished. You are a brave lad, for you risked much in so doing, and you are a generous lad, for you gave up your own goods. You are also a lad of strong will, for you withstood pain; and you are a lad of great wit and discernment, for you chose the best crutch on my estate. Therefore, I ask you what the Day Man and the Night Man and the Sunset Man all bid me do, which is that you be my apprentice."

Ronny sat down with a thud—fortunately on the front steps of the wagon, so he did no damage to himself.

And before he knew he was doing it, he replied, in a very low voice, "Then I guess I accept."

And once again he was caught off guard by the Road Man's next remark: "The ice cream is melting."

"But how . . . how did you *know* . . . ?" Ronny stammered.

A grin and a shrug. "Perhaps I read your mind."

And before Ronny could reply: "Or perhaps I saw the receipt that fell out of your pocket at the pond."

And neither changed the fact that Ronny truly did have to leave.

"Come when you can," the Road Man called. And climbed into his wagon and shut the door.

And Ronny stood alone in the dusk in front of a preposterous wagon encircled by a phalanx of perplexing and oversexed machines wondering what in the world he had got himself into.

Chapter 11

Listening 101

Cardalba Hall
Monday, April 9—4:30 P.M.

Matthew had been preparing for Anson's initiation into Listening all day. He was not, however, doing it as he had envisioned in increasingly specific detail the last year or so—ever since he had finally come to the realization that there was no reason *he* could think why his blood was not as suitable a vehicle as his sister's for passing on the Luck. *He* had the benefit of science, after all, as his ancestors had not. *He* could prove paternity with absolute precision—or some folks he knew who dabbled into DNA research could. He therefore saw no sense in continuing the cumbersome matrilinear succession that had been practiced (ofttimes in secret) among his clan of Listeners since time immemorial. Not that there wasn't a potential downside to it, too, of course: freed of the responsibility of providing Heirs, women might begin retaining their virginity and perhaps become Masters in their own right. Certainly there was no biological reason they couldn't—especially since the main

194

objection anyway had less to do with their ability than with the effect they had on footholders.

Still, such change was the way of life, Matt supposed. There were things everyone wanted, wanted so badly they came to be near-obsessions; things one planned in meticulous detail, deciding exactly what would be said or done and when and where. A woman assuming a Mastership might be one of those things. His ongoing fascination with Anson was another.

The first step had been simply to improve the boy's lot in life. Matt had been helping out his mother all along, of course, long before he'd decided to take Anson under his wing: seeing that she had no trouble earning a living, got good bonuses, took maximum advantage of available opportunities. From that, his goals had grown more specific: make the boy's acquaintance. Let him know he was special, be sure it was easy for him to get the things he wanted. And then, by slow degrees, to simultaneously win the lad's confidence and make him beholden to Matt for what no one else could provide. And finally, when Matt was certain the boy would respond to him as his gently contrite grandfather, not as the buoyantly confident Master of Cardalba, to let him know that *he* was the heir.

Unfortunately, Anson's preemptive discovery of his birthright had warped that dream out of all recognition. Still, Matt had to give him credit: he had finessed the revelation well, displaying a talent for wit and savvy and quick thinking that should ensure that the Mastership would be competently served at that distant point when Matthew should pass it on. Oh, the boy still had problems, naturally: a lot of rough edges that needed to be smoothed off. Matthew knew—he hadn't been that different before Uncle Ben began *his* initiation; had been, in fact, nearly as much an arrogant bully as Anson. But thirty-seven years of Listening to the hopes and dreams of others in conjunction with the previous Master, and nine more on his own, had given him a sympathy for the lot of humanity at large. It was hard to remain a bully when you could feel firsthand what the victim of that bullying felt.

There was only one problem. For the first time since his Luck had manifested at a rather early sixteen, he was running out of Strength. As a youth and well into middle age, his own reserves had been more than sufficient, but once he had succeeded to the Mastership, a series of Strong footholders had allowed him to slough to the point where he had grown dependent on them. And now, without Lenore to draw upon, and with no replacement in sight, he was reduced to spending his own resources faster than he could replenish them. It was almost exactly like the situation of a former athlete who had stopped exercising. The potential was still there, but the realization was weak.

Which meant, in the real world, that where a week ago he would have been ready to initiate Anson into the Mystery of Listening with no notice at all, now he had to hoard Strength for nearly a day and hope it would be sufficient. It had better be, for every day he had to Listen without a footholder left him weaker.

He wondered if the strength he had amassed since yesterday would be enough, since once he and Anson began he would have to both guide and retain control. And if, once activated, Anson proved to be as Strong as Matthew imagined he was, that last could be a serious problem. He would have to rely on wiles and wit, not Strength, to keep young Anson in check. It would be a challenge all right. But then, challenge was a large part of what he lived for, these days. And Anson was nothing if not challenging.

Sighing, Matthew poured a glass of his inevitable sherry, settled deeper into his lounger, and Listened for his grandson's approach. He could not Hear him any longer, which he'd expected now that Anson had learned to Silence, but he could locate the Silence that was as clear as a signature. And he was approaching quickly: hurling that slick green car of his along the gravel back road that was the shortest distance between Evelyn Bowman's house and Cardalba

Hall. He could Hear Evelyn, too: proud to have a handsome son who had found favor with Mr. Welch (she knew no more of Anson's lineage than Anson had a few days before, only that his father had been well-heeled, pleasant to look upon, and good to her—before he vanished). But there was also a certain amount of apprehension: doubt about Mr. Welch's motives in so suddenly favoring the boy; fears about Matt's sexual intentions, coupled with confidence that Anson could certainly defend himself against a sixty-two-year-old man; and fear of the repercussions if, by some accident or faux pas, Anson should rouse Mr. Welch's ire. And then there were the *other* concerns: worries about Anson's haughty attitude, about his bullying, about the way he drank and drove fast and womanized. And regret that she had not been able to curb those flaws; regret that the boy had no father.

But a father, of sorts, he was about to acquire.

Matthew had finished exactly half his drink when footsteps sounded on the front porch. The doorbell rang urgently, and he rose. It had sounded once more before he made it to the front hall but there was no evidence of impatience, no over-show of force such as Anson could have used had he so chosen.

In fact, when Matthew finally opened the front door, Anson looked remarkably neat, attentive, and relaxed—and perhaps a touch apprehensive, though he suspected that was an act.

"Come in, my boy," Matthew cried, grinning broadly, careful to mask all trace of his former misgivings with his usual display of expansiveness. He threw his arms wide and ushered Anson into his library.

Five minutes, a pause to pull the drapes and consume a sherry apiece (to help them relax), and they were ready to begin.

Matthew set his now-empty glass down on the floor and peered benignly but directly at his heir—who for his part looked as calm as a rebellious teenager on the verge of a rite of passage *could* look. "All right," he began, "before we commence the actual lesson, there are undoubtedly a few things you're curious about, and several more you should know regardless.—And the *first* question you probably have," he continued, without giving Anson time to reply, "is, why am I doing this in the first place?"

"I *had* wondered," Anson replied dryly.

"I assumed as much, given what you no doubt overheard on my front porch the other day."

"And?"

"You heard me then—in part—and I don't want to discuss it now in any great detail, but suffice it to say that our family is not like most other families in a number of ways, which I *will* discuss in a moment, though I have no intention of revealing everything even then, only the things you need to to know in order to understand what's about to happen. Therefore, I suppose I should start with a basic question: Who am I?"

Anson blinked. "You're Mr. Welch—*the* Mr. Welch. Your name's Matthew. You're my grandfather."

"Anything else?"

Anson shifted listlessly. "I've heard you called Master of Cardalba."

"And what does that mean—to you?"

Anson shrugged. "I . . . I guess it has to do with the Luck, whatever that is."

Matthew nodded. "And so it does—in a way. As Master of Cardalba I am what is called a *Listener*. That's what sets us—the Welches and our like—apart from everyone else. We don't know where the ability to Listen came from or how we discovered how to use it, and so far we've had no scientists in the family qualified to investigate. Also, circumstances are sufficiently, ah, *peculiar* among us that an unsolicited request for research on our, shall we say, parapsychological aberration would not be to our advantage, especially if it led to too deep a probing into our more personal affairs. But to get back to the point I was making, every Listener—everyone with Welch blood, among others—has some degree of talent that sets him or her apart from ordinary people—call it a knack, or whatever you want, but the fact is we've all got it. *We* term the collective accumulation of these knacks *Luck*, though around here that's come to have a specialized meaning having to do with the *application* of those talents to help others—making optimum use of the information those knacks bring us, in other words. Anyway, there are a lot of ways Luck can manifest, and not everyone has the same kind, but there *is* one aspect of Luck *all* of us have—even women, though in their case it's usually limited to their close kin."

"Which is?"

"It's something that used to be called Hearing Voices on the Wind. We call it Listening for short—thus the name for ourselves—but actually it's the ability to enter a trance and hear what other people are thinking."

"*All* people, *everywhere*?"

Matt shook his head. "Theoretically, but it's much easier to focus on those locally—say within about a ten-mile radius of where you are. We'll talk more about that in a minute. For now I need to give you a bit of background on the Mastership, which is basically stewardship of the Luck in a given area. It binds you to that area, but it gives you a lot as well—more if you're clever. It's a big responsibility—but it can also be very rewarding."

"But the Luck itself isn't real? I mean, it's not really *luck* you're talkin' about?"

Matt shook his head. "Not in the usual sense, no."

Anson scowled thoughtfully. "And there're other Listeners, you say?"

"Not many, but enough. We know they're there and they knew we're here, but we stay out of each other's way. There was some kind of ancient agreement, but I've never bothered to find out the particulars—mostly because I don't much agree with it as it's practiced today. Not that there are a *lot* of us, mind you. We tend to generate prosperity where we settle, but we have to be careful because even we have limits. It's a lot easier to provide Luck for ten than for ten thousand—which basically means that there are little pockets of 'Lucky' places all over the world.''

"And the Welches? Where do they come in?''

"Well,'' Matthew replied carefully, "after yesterday I'm afraid I don't trust you enough yet to reveal *everything* about the family yet—who lives where and can do what. For now, let's just say that there are a lot of traditions associated with the Luck that I don't necessarily cotton to. One has to do with the succession to the Mastership. For as long as anyone remembers, inheritance of that position has been passed through the female line because maternity could—until recently—be proven much more easily than paternity. But don't get me started on that or we'll be here all night. For now all you need to know is that under normal circumstances one of my late sister's sons would have been my heir, and affairs were in fact pointing that way until two things happened. The first was that their mother put some newfangled notions in their heads about not wanting to have anything to do with the Mastership, so that they both renounced it and moved away. There's a ritual that accompanies such renunciation, but it has to be done voluntarily, and the upshot of it is that neither can now return here unless they themselves undo it, which they won't. And in the meantime, they've got themselves stuck in jail, so that the Luck, once again, would reject them.''

"Hold on a minute,'' Anson interrupted. "On the one hand you make the Luck sound physical, on the other hand you make it sound . . . magical, or something. Which is it?''

Matthew puffed his cheeks. "Both—and neither. It follows specific rules and evokes specific responses on the one hand, so that it's a lot like instinct in that regard. On the other hand, it sometimes acts capriciously—almost as if it was a separate consciousness that has a will of its own. That *may* be due to the fact that all Listeners are linked to some degree, and the Luck is what forges that linkage. But since it has access to so many minds, it may sometimes become sort of a superintelligence itself.''

"Like collective consciousness?"

"Something like that. Unfortunately, that's a fairly recent concept—and we've had no more psychologists in the Clan than we've had scientists. The Luck *also* has a way of protecting itself.''

"So what about me?"

"I was getting to that. Like I said, my sister Donna's sons had removed themselves from consideration, so the next heir according to tradition should have been her daughter Erin's son: Lewis. Unfortunately, Erin was even more a rebel than her mother and declared absolutely that she would raise her son up to be completely normal, and to prove it she's doing it right under my nose. You may have heard that Erin and I don't get along. That's why.''

"But your mother said Lew should be heir anyway. That implies—"

"—That he doesn't have any choice in the matter? He does, and he doesn't. He has no choice about the Luck manifesting in him, that'll happen regardless if it hasn't already. I imagine he's been having some interesting experiences lately. As to whether or not he ever attempts to assume the Mastership on his own, right now I doubt he's even aware that's a possibility, and even if he did know, the time he'd actually get to assume it's a long way off— as it is for you. Which means there's plenty of time left in which you and I can dissuade him. On the other hand, it would be difficult for him *not* to want it, once he learns of it, so my guess is that Erin is hoping she can somehow keep him ignorant until I die without initiating an heir, whereupon there'll be no more hereditary Master of Cardalba Hall. But she's also an inveterate bet-hedger, so she's kept Lewis eligible, just in case. She, uh, doesn't know about you . . . yet.''

Anson looked confused. "What do you mean about keepin' Lew eligible?"

"That she's kept Lewis physically perfect. Nobody can become a Master who isn't physically perfect—that is, has everything, and I do mean *everything*, they came with. Full teeth, appendix, the whole nine yards."

"You're kiddin'!" Anson snorted. "What's *that* got to do with anything?"

Matthew grimaced in turn. "Again, I don't know—none of us does for sure. What we *do* know is that the Luck isn't with one from birth, it tends to appear in the late teens, rather like puberty, only it happens later. It comes on you of a sudden, but can take a while to completely develop, and sometimes without the right stimulus it *never* completely manifests. It's like the way puberty produces changes that make you able to have sex and reproduce, but doesn't mean you *will* have sex or reproduce. You could have the potential, but never use it. We're not certain exactly how, but it also seems to flow throughout the body in channels sort of like a nonphysical version of the nervous system. And as best we can tell if there's any physical imperfection in the body when the Luck fires up—anything that's not there when it ought to be, like a woman's maidenhead, which is why Listener men make a point of seeing their sisters are deflowered before their Luck appears—then the energy that runs the Luck tends to get tangled up there, as if it were seeking to flow down channels that were clogged up or closed. Usually it simply fades back to a trickle after that, often to the point of disappearing entirely."

"And you really do have to be perfect."

"Within reasonable limits—small scars and things like that don't matter. Why *else* do you suppose that you and Lewis alone of all young men in Welch County High aren't circumcised?"

Anson blushed to the roots of his hair.

"I know a *lot* about you, Anson," Matthew said calmly. "Never doubt it."

"So I gather!" Anson grunted. But then his eyes took on a wily gleam. "Wait a minute. If your problem with

Lewis is just that you don't want him to be heir, why don't you simply disfigure him? That way you'd have no choice but to designate me."

"For two reasons."

Anson merely raised an eyebrow.

"The first is Fixing. It's a thing done to Listener children shortly after birth in order to ensure that when the Luck manifests it'll have an easier time—and that they won't go crazy. They might not anyway, but then again, they might. Even Erin wouldn't take that risk."

"So that means . . ."

"That brings me to the second reason. Like I said, Lewis *was* Fixed to accept the Luck whenever it appeared. I'm almost certain it flows in him now, barely beneath the surface, barely asleep. And if it does, it flows in *all* parts of him—has already set up its paths, in other words, and since it's more nonphysical than physical, it's already been everywhere it needs to go. Thus, even if he lost part of himself now, it wouldn't matter much. The Luck would remember where it was supposed to go and go there anyway. Besides, it's really a moot point, for reasons I won't go into now."

"But . . ."

"If he had *not* been Fixed *and* was . . . incomplete, the Luck would try to go where it *expects* a part of his body to be, find the way blocked, and either start to clot and create back pressures which can literally burn out your mind, or else it may simply find the going so hazardous that it dissipates. Or both."

Anson perked up at this. "So . . . have *I* been Fixed?"

"Not that I'm aware of," Matthew replied carefully. "Your mother was an ordinary woman, so there was no way to Fix you when you were born. Uncle Ben, who *could* also have done it, neither liked your father nor believed in patrilinear succession; and I had no access, being out of the country at the time. You're doing this cold, in other words— which may be one of several reasons why you're so powerful: 'cause this is coming onto you raw. But before you can fully assimilate, you still need me to Fix you.''

"So do it, then, do it now!"

"I can't."

"Why not?"

"Because I'm not strong enough right now for one thing. And because it's dangerous to attempt while the Luck's actually manifesting, for another. It either needs to be done before or after that's complete—and I'll have to admit you're at some risk there. But that's also another tale for another day. If we get into that now, you'll *never* learn anything."

"Yeah, but one thing still puzzles me a lot," Anson said uneasily, shifting in his chair. "If I'm supposed to have all this power, how come it hasn't shown up before? How come I couldn't just do this stuff naturally?"

"Because you didn't know you had it. You were brought up to believe nobody can do the kinds of things Luck entails, so you ignored the signs—and besides, nobody ever taught you *how* to use it, *how* to go into the necessary trance. But as you were growing up, didn't you have dreams that came true, or sometimes know what people were thinking before they actually spoke? Or think somebody *had* spoken when they'd only been *thinking*? That's all part of the same effect, and it should be kicking in really strong right now. It has, too, right?"

Anson nodded. "The last week or so mostly. I've been havin' these really bad headaches and it's like—like my head's full of bees or something—not always, but when I'm in crowds and stuff."

Matt nodded in turn. "That sounds about right. Of course it affects different people in different ways. And the problem is, as soon as you become aware of it and start actually using it, it becomes much stronger. It's like . . . like the first time you masturbate. Initially it only feels good in the place you're actually touching, but the more you do it, the more systems come on line from reflex. They've been there all along, but only when the right stimulus triggers the right reaction do the rest line up and follow."

"So this is like sex?"

"Better in some ways, worse in others. But maybe it's time I showed you. That *is* what you came for, after all."

Anson blinked at Matt nervously, as if he were having trouble taking it all in. Matt didn't blame him. It was a lot to hang on a kid, telling him that there was more to the world than what most folks let on, and that he had a key to its innermost secrets. "Okay," the boy said finally. "I'm ready when you are."

"I'm sure you are," Matt replied dryly. "Well, to begin at the beginning, I suppose it's simplest if you think of the human mind as being like a radio. Every thought or feeling or emotion produces a certain amount of mental energy, and the more powerful those thoughts or feelings or emotions are, the further they can reach. And since every brain cell has a stimulator and a receptor on it, it stands to reason that if someone were stimulating—broadcasting, if you prefer—very powerfully even miles away, a truly sensitive receptor in someone else's brain could receive it—as well as the one that was intended to, of course. At least that's how we think it works. Everybody—that's every single person, even ordinary people—is a tiny mind-radio transmitter, but only us Welches—mostly—can receive those transmissions and make sense out of them."

"Hmmm," Anson murmured curiously. "So how does distance affect it?"

"I was getting to that," Matt continued. "Generally it's like a radio again, with a broadcaster of a given strength becoming harder to receive as distance increases—which naturally means that a very powerful person far away could be *Heard* more easily than someone weak close by."

"By these powerful persons, you mean other Listeners, right?"

Matthew nodded. "But obviously if a person received every single thought in even a small area, he'd go batty; it would be like trying to hear in a football stadium with everyone yelling at once, so either we learn to tune out quickly, or we suppress it by instinct, like people suppress the white noise that goes on around them all the time."

Anson looked perplexed. "Okay . . ."

Matthew rose to pour himself another sherry, then returned. "The *trouble* comes with emotions—and wishes. Those are both very powerful and can boost an otherwise unremarkable thought quite amazingly: if you become angry at somebody you're thinking *everything* a lot more strongly than you are if you're riding along in a car gazing out the window at scenery you've seen every day of your life. Therefore you also broadcast more strongly, therefore you're easier to Hear. Which is fine so far: the information we Welches need is usually the sort that has strong emotions attached to it. But there's also a side effect, which is that just like a person's emotions trigger physical responses in that person, Heard emotions *can*—if we're not careful— trigger the same responses in us. Which is why it's best not to Listen to someone who's angry *while* they're angry— Listen just long enough to recognize the emotional climate, and if it's dangerous, ride the Winds away. Then return and check on them when they're calmer—because that anger *should* leave an imprint a mile wide that anybody like us can key into. Now . . . do you have any questions?"

Anson took a deep breath and shook his head. "Nope. I'm ready."

Matthew regarded him thoughtfully. "Good—but there's one more thing I want to warn you about, in case we encounter it. Nothing dangerous, just something that might surprise you if you don't know what to look out for."

"Which is?"

"Silences. Silences are like domes of resistance in the Wind—think of them as towers around which the Winds blow, or like boulders in a river. But what they *actually* are is people who can Listen, but who don't want to be Listened to—so they build up a barrier around themselves. It takes a certain amount of energy to maintain and nobody I know, with one possible exception, can maintain one indefinitely.

Also, a truly accomplished Listener can extend a Silence to cover or include someone else—especially a relative, since there's already a link there—even without that person knowing they're being shielded. I've been having a certain amount of trouble with that lately.''

Anson did not reply, but he looked even more nervous now, and Matthew, could he have Heard him (and he didn't want Anson to know he couldn't just yet), imagined he was entertaining some doubts about what might occur should he relinquish control of his thought processes to his grandfather—especially when he'd had that grandfather over a barrel less than a day ago.

"So . . . what are you going to do—precisely?"

"I'm going to show you how to go into a trance, and then follow you once we get there. The reason I have to help you is that it's a little like making yourself go to sleep, but it's also a bit like dying, so that most people can't force themselves to go all the way. Think of it as standing on a bridge looking down at deep water. You know the fall's not enough to kill you, and you know the water will cushion you, but it takes a lot of nerve to make the jump. But if somebody goes with you, it's a lot better.''

"So your job . . . ?"

"My job's to push you over the brink, then hold your head above water.''

"If you say so.''

"I do—oh, and there's one *more* thing: once we begin Hearing Voices there's likely to be a good many of them. So it'd help if you had one you could focus on—someone you know well, one of your buddies, perhaps.''

"My mom?"

Matt shook his head. "She doesn't know about you, but she's been close to a lot of Luck over the years without knowing it, so she's gotten so sensitive to it that she's nearly learned how to Silence without it. Besides, it's bad ethics to spy on family.''

Anson scowled thoughtfully for a moment and then said,

very slowly, "Hey . . . how about Winnie Cowan?"

Matthew frowned slightly, though the actual idea did not bother him at all. "Do you have a strong attachment to her? A strong emotional bond?"

"I *hope* so—we used to go out, remember?"

"And she to you?"

"Yeah, I'd say she has strong feelings about me," Anson replied cryptically, but Matthew caught the careful wording.

"Then Winnie Cowan it shall be."

"Fine."

"Oh, and there's one *other* thing," Matthew added after a pause to finish his drink. "Since we're already combining two stages into one here—the trance and the actual Listening—we might as well go ahead and add another. That'll give you an even more complete overview of immediate possibilities, and in the future we can go back and refine, refine, refine. We'll probably be doing *that* for years."

Anson looked at him askance. "So, what do you need?"

"A question: something you want to find out about Winnie. That way you can gain experience Hearing *generally*, Hearing a *specific* Voice, and then Hearing a specific *part* of a specific Voice. So now, what's the question to be? It shouldn't be anything too personal; it's not polite to snoop. Besides, those sort of memories tend to be buried pretty deep. If you dig too far you tend to attract attention to yourself."

"How about just finding out why she wasn't at school today?"

Matthew raised an eyebrow, since he knew perfectly well why Winnie had been absent: her father had finally got a good look at her black eye and forbidden her to leave his house looking that way. He had also learned where the damage had come from. There had been a flurry of angry telephone calls, one to the sheriff who'd said he could do nothing unless Winnie pressed charges, which she didn't want to do. And one to Anson's mother, which a touch of well-placed Luck had prevented getting through.

"Very well." Matt sighed. "Now, let us proceed."

Anson nodded.

"Okay," Matt said. "First thing: Just sit there and relax. Will your body to sink into the chair. Think about nothing except how your body feels, about how *heavy* it feels. Be aware of all the little tensions of muscles pulling at other muscles when they don't need to, and release them. Begin at your feet and work up, and while you're doing it, notice your breathing. Inhale slowly through your nose and then exhale through your mouth, and begin counting while you're doing it. And all the while, feel your body getting heavier and heavier as it settles against the seat, getting so heavy that the weight becomes part of the cushion and your whole consciousness begins to collapse into your head. Focus on your eyes now, see what's inside your eyelids, see those little hazy squares and circles that gradually appear and then recede. Watch them, and feel yourself drifting away."

Anson did as instructed, and Matt could tell from experience when the boy had reached the crucial juncture, whereupon he entered a trance of his own. From that point on, Anson still heard his words, but now they were inside his head. He did not notice. They never did.

Once he was Within, Matt Listened for Anson's Voice, and—since he was alert for a possible reflexive Silence—adroitly slipped around it when the Sound of Anson's mind reached his own. He'd been correct too: Anson was right on the brink, Matthew could feel his eyes poised to roll back, his breathing on the verge of becoming deep and automatic. And then he pushed.

Anson did not scream with his mouth, though he *did* scream. But then the wonder of it all thrust upon him, and Matthew simply sat back and enjoyed his protégé's rebirth.

It was like swimming in sound, and Matthew, who was used to going it alone, was nearly as caught up in wonder as Anson—for the boy was Singing at the top of his nonexistent lungs. Singing—that's what they called it when one Spoke among the Winds—was something of a reflex, too:

it helped maintain one's identity amid the onrush of Sound.

For a while they drifted there, with Matthew keeping close to Anson, letting the Winds of Welch County blow around them and bring them news. It was delicate, tiring work, for Matt had to maintain the fiction that he had infinite resources to draw upon, when actually he had no more than exactly enough to accomplish what he had planned.

Eventually, however, he sensed Anson growing impatient with battling the steady barrage of Voices, and began showing him how he could catch one as the Wind blew it by and follow it until it dissipated (which also meant he was Hearing the same thing over and over), then trace its backtrail to its source. That proved diverting for quite a while, though Matthew took care that the boy discovered nothing of any consequence—their most scandalous revelation was that the music teacher at the high school was lusting in his heart for a girl Anson had done more than lust after.

Okay, Matthew said, and though they spoke directly mind to mind, it was still in sentences. *Now we will Listen for Winnie. Since you know her so well, simply think about her, imagine you hear her voice—her* real *voice—speaking to you. Before long that voice will become a Voice, and when that happens, do as we have done already and follow the Wind to its source. And don't worry, I'll keep you from getting lost.*

Anson did as instructed, though Matt was surprised at the negative as well as positive feelings toward the girl that contact with the boy's Voice revealed. But an instant later, Anson had found Winnie's Voice, and—careful not to reveal more than a passing familiarity with it—Matt joined him in following it to its source. He also felt a glow of almost sexual anticipation as Anson realized where he was, and along with it sensed the inevitable desire on Anson's part to delve deeper. Matt did not permit him to, though it took care not to betray that circumvention. At least the technique was straightforward enough: he basically inserted a bit of his own Silence between Anson's Singing and those parts of Winnie's mind Matt did not want him to Hear. New to this strange, unseen country, Anson could not tell the difference, and ascribed his failure to his own ineptitude.

See? Matthew noted. *Before it was like you were standing ear-deep in a vast river of Voices, and each Voice belonged to a different person. Then we rode a current back to one Voice—and now that we have found that single Voice. Listen again: is it not like before? Are there not a thousand thousand smaller voices Singing? All are Winnie, but each is different. But if you think of what you seek, the right Wind will find you.*

Once again Anson succeeded admirably, though Matt was aware he was having a hard time maintaining his discipline and not snooping. And he also knew Anson *would* do exactly that, as soon as he tried this again unsupervised. That, alas, was one of the perils of the trade.

Still, he allowed Anson to find the answer to his question. But while the boy was busy there (it was a complex situation, actually), Matt violated his own prohibition and allowed himself a bit of deeper browsing. His earlier delvings into the workings of Winnie Cowan's mind had proven quite interesting in their own right, though he had found it necessary to curtail them. But what he was curious about now was what had attracted Anson, who was not known for either his discretion or his moral fortitude, to seek out such a relative paragon of virtue as the Cowan girl. And then he *discovered* why—and could have kicked himself for not noticing earlier what lay so near the surface.

The girl was a virgin. Oh, she had lustful thoughts all right, and some of them about his grandson and both nephews, but they were all hypothetical, all speculative. And more intensive prowling revealed the interesting tidbit that it was an assault of Anson's against that same virtue that had triggered their recent blowup. A hasty check of Anson's Voice (for this closely linked, there was no way the boy could Silence) showed that Anson had been misinformed by one of his buddies about Winnie's condition, which was why he had not immediately nominated her for replacement footholder when Matt had intimated that he was in dire need of one.

Well. Matt laughed in that secret part of himself Anson could not access. *I've certainly learned a number of interesting things this evening—and I'm afraid young Master Anson may have to learn that two can play the deception game. After all, willing girls are a dime a dozen, but prospective footholders are very rare indeed.*

Chapter 12

Smithing 101

Erin Welch's house
8:30 P.M.

"*Will* you sit down?" Lewis grumbled, looking up from a calculus problem he'd been puzzling over for the last fifteen minutes. He snagged a handful of popcorn from the clear plastic bowl on the den coffee table and glared at Ronny meaningfully.

Ronny glared back—and continued pacing, as he had been doing ever since Aunt Erin had departed for a school board meeting half an hour before.

"Ronny! Stop it, okay? I can't concentrate when you do that."

Ronny flopped down in the nearest chair—a black-and-white pinto skin strung within a metal frame—and folded his arms irritably. "Okay, so I've stopped."

"Fine!"

"You'd pace too if there were two important things you had to do and you couldn't do either of 'em!"

Lewis laid his notebook on the sofa beside him and grabbed another handful of popcorn.

"Mom thinks it's for your own good."

"Bullshit." Ronny snorted. "I mean, what the hell is she *afraid* of, anyway? Boo-coos of folks are dropping by to see the Road Man all the time, and there's not been an iota of trouble I've heard about. But let *me* go, and all of a sudden it's bells and whistles and alarms. I mean it's like she's afraid he's gonna carry me off or something . . ."

"Did you tell her about his offer?"

"What offer?"

"To make you his apprentice."

"How'd you know about that?"

"You told me."

"I *did*?"

"Didn't you? Last night when you came in all dripping wet and soggy? I've never seen anybody flyin' so high and draggin' so low at the same time. The apprentice business was part of the high stuff," Lewis added.

Ronny's brow wrinkled thoughtfully. "If you say so. Frankly, I don't remember a whole lot beyond Aunt Erin informing me, very coldly, to please leave my wet clothes in the laundry room. Jeeze, I wish she wouldn't do that— I'd a lot rather she yelled."

"Ice cream came out okay anyway."

"I'm glad *something* did."

Silence. And then: "Lew, tell me something, okay— buddy to buddy—do *you* have any idea what Aunt Erin's got against the Road Man?"

Lewis shook his head. "Nope, and that's the truth. I mean the guy's weird and all. And he gives me enough of the willies that I really *don't* want to hang around him. But I can certainly see why he fascinates you."

"Think she'd be pissed if I went back to see him?"

"You mean tonight?"

"Yeah, while she's gone. You could tell her I went out

for calculator batteries or something. Shoot, I'll even buy some so you won't have to lie.''

''You *are* grounded, you know.''

''Words. I mean, what's the worst she can do? She can't physically restrain me—I'm bigger than she is. And I doubt even she'd go to the trouble of getting the law on either of us. Shoot, if it comes to it, she can come and watch. I don't know what the Road Man'd do, but at least me and her wouldn't have to be worried about each other.''

Lewis shrugged. ''You could always ask.''

''*You* could always go with me. Maybe that'd make her chill out.''

''No thanks.''

''When's she coming back, anyway?''

''I really don't know. They're supposed to be discussing new teachers for next year and voting on financing. It may run a while.''

''Didn't she *say* something about it lasting past midnight?''

''Maybe.''

Ronny's face broke into a grin. ''Okay, then. If I go now, I can be back before then. If I'm lucky, she'll never know.''

''And if you're not?''

Ronny shrugged in turn. ''Well, I'll still have had at least one lesson, which she can't take away from me. Otherwise I'll have had none.''

''She'll be pissed.''

''She'll get over it. Besides, it's easier to get forgiveness than permission.''

''What about Winnie?''

''What about her?''

''Thought you were gonna call her.''

''I did, but only got her brother. He said she was working.''

''He say anything about why she wasn't in school today?''

''I didn't think it was cool to ask. Though from what she told me when I talked to her last night, I had a pretty good idea already. Mostly I was covering bases—not that I wouldn't have loved to talk to her, but if I can't, I at least want her to know I tried."

Lewis checked his watch and picked up his calculus again. "Well," he sighed. "If you're gonna go, you better be at it."

Somewhat to Ronny's surprise, he discovered that he was becoming quite a master of stealth. Since his was the only white Escort GT in the county, so far as he could tell, it wouldn't do to leave it too blatantly in sight near the Road Man's camp. And since Aunt Erin had her radar up now, and Ronny wouldn't put it past her to decide to return home by that route, he decided that the smartest alternative was to hide it—which he did, by the simple expedient of tucking it in behind the derelict Swanson place.

And somewhere around 9:15 he wandered into the torchlit glare of the Road Man's camp. Ronny's brow wrinkled in perplexity as he passed the rampart of machines (yet a different batch from yesterday, or perhaps it was merely a different arrangement; the only common denominator was that they were the glittering, delicate night machines, not the raw, vulgar ones he had come to identify with the day). Never had he seen the place like this, for the Road Man had set torches (mostly made of pine knots stuck on chrome steel poles) at ten-foot intervals around the entire fifty-foot circumference of the inner camp, and the flare and flicker of their light imparted an aura of unreality to the entire area.

The Road Man was waiting for him—or appeared to be, for he was sitting on the middle step of his wagon with his arms folded across his chest and his face turned toward the prickly darkness of the meadow. He was bare-legged once more, but Ronny saw the lower fringe of a pair of cutoffs peeking out from beneath the red sweatshirt of the day before. His left leg was bandaged to the knee.

"No need to make faces, it's only Fire's child, Light," the Road Man said calmly, while Ronny continued to blink and squint. "Your eyes should drink it in like a sponge drinks in water."

"Yeah," Ronny replied uneasily, as he drew closer.

"Sit," the Road Man continued, motioning Ronny in the general direction of a substantial, three-foot-tall tree stump by the corner of the wagon—which, Ronny suspected from the indentations pockmarking the top of it, did double duty as yet another sort of an anvil.

Ronny obeyed.

"Drink," the Road Man went on, reaching across himself to hand Ronny a quart-sized pottery jug on a leather cord.

Ronny accepted it—hesitantly—recognizing the smell as that of the minty liquid that had quenched his fire three nights before.

"That woman who looks after you: she didn't want you to come, did she?"

Ronny took a draught and shook his head, feeling both refreshed and oddly at peace. "How'd you know that?"

"I see a lot of folks in the space of day. And I've known how to ask the right questions for a long, long time."

"Yeah."

"Like answers, too."

"Huh?"

"I said I like answers. I asked you a question, and I'd like an answer. I asked you if your aunt-woman didn't want you to come."

"But you know the answer to that—so you said."

"It's still my question. Poor little thing's gonna be hangin' out there forever just waitin' for an answer that'll never come if you don't give it one."

Ronny puffed his cheeks in exasperation. "No," he said shortly.

"No, what?"

"No, she didn't want me to come."

"She doesn't like me."

"She doesn't even *know* you."

"Yes she does."

Ronny jerked his head around and regarded the Road Man incredulously. "She does?"

"Everybody knows the Road Man."

"Oh."

"But *I* know her, too—or the Day Man does."

Ronny rolled his eyes in despair. So it was back to that again, huh? The Day Man/Night Man/Sunset Man stuff. Was there a Sunrise Man too, he wondered. And an Easter Man, and a Labor Day Man, and—

"The Day Man, he's got a problem," the Road Man confided. "He's got the most religion of any of us, which makes him better than the rest of us—or makes him think he is. But he's got a heap more sin on his conscience too, and that makes him the *worst* of us. He leads us into temptation a lot, but he don't always deliver us from evil."

"Yeah," Ronny grunted, so the Road Man would know he was listening. He took another sip of—whatever it was— and returned it. If it was wine, he wanted to be *real* careful.

"The Day Man, he knew your aunt-person. He wanted to cleave to her one time but she wouldn't let him."

"*Oh?*" Ronny realized too late that he didn't really want an answer to that question. But what he knew already told him a lot. Suddenly a piece of a so-far largely unseen puzzle clicked into place.

"It's his trouble, though, not mine."

Ronny cleared his throat. "Uh, look . . . I can't stay long . . . I kind of had to sneak out to even get here at all, and Aunt Erin's gonna be really pissed at me. So I figured that . . ."

"Well?"

"I thought that we could maybe talk about what you promised."

"I didn't promise nothing."

"You asked me to be your apprentice."

"That wasn't a promise."

"Okay, but . . . well, whatever it was, I sure would like to learn something."

"Like what?"

"Like . . . like . . ." Ronny's gaze swept the fiery circle of the camp. "Like how those machines of yours put out more energy than they take in."

"*Lots* of folks'd like to know that."

"You gonna tell me?"

"I might let you find out sometime."

"Are you gonna teach me anything at all?"

"What do you think I've been doing?"

"Talking . . . and beatin' around the bush."

"No," the Road Man said calmly. "I have been teaching you smithing."

"Bullshit."

"It's goat shit around here, and you can dry it and burn it, by the way. And their milk makes an excellent cheese."

"All right, goat shit."

"That's much better."

"Go on."

"With what?"

"With what we were talking about! You said you were teaching me smithing, and I said we were just talking."

"You didn't say that."

"I said the same thing."

"But what are you doing when you talk?"

Ronny looked puzzled. "You . . . you're verbalizing ideas."

"And what is an idea?"

"It's . . . it's a thing that you just think, I guess."

"But where does it come from?"

"I don't know, they just are. You get a stimulus, or a response, or an idea."

"*Not* an idea, that's a circular argument."

"Gimme a break."

"I'll give you nothing until you tell me what an idea is."

Ronny closed his eyes and concentrated, torn between the desire to bolt once and for all and be done with nights spent in endless foolishness, and the almost obsessive need to somehow, some way, make some sense out of the enigmatic Road Man. One thing was certain—he bet nobody else had conversations like this with him.

"I'm waiting," the Road Man prompted, but not unkindly.

"Okay . . ." Ronny ventured after a long pause. "How about this: an idea's a thing you make with your mind."

"Very good!" the Road Man roared, clapping him across the shoulders so hard he nearly toppled off the stump.

"Uh, thanks."

"Yes, my boy, yes indeed. An idea is a thing made with the mind. *Anything* that is made exists first in the mind. But remember this too, and keep it holy"—and Ronny thought he'd shifted a little into his Day Man voice there, and could practically hear the capital letters and the red ink and the underlining—"Yea, verily I say unto you: The world is full of things that are made, and all men, be they smiths or no, are makers. But of these things that are made, there are five kinds: there are the things you make with your hands, and there are the things you make with your head; there are the things you make with your heart, things you make with your soul, and the things you make with your dreams. Each is as real as the other, and none is more important than its kin."

"I . . . I'll have to think about that for a while," Ronny conceded after a moment's silence. "Maybe I'll go home and write it down."

"Do that," the Road Man said. "A thing of the head made into a thing of the hand for the sake of the heart and the soul and the dream."

"Tell me about it," Ronny replied glumly.

"I *am* telling you about it."

"No, I meant dreams."

"What about them?"

"I don't have any. Not anymore."

"You lost them, or you gave them away?"

Ronny stretched out his damaged leg and thumped it with

the crutch for emphasis. "They were taken from me!"

"There'll be others."

"Not as good."

"Who can say?"

"I can."

"No you can't."

"Oh, just . . . *fuck* it!" Ronny spat, feeling a good ten minutes' worth of frustration meld with the simmering, resentful anger that always lay close to the surface. "You don't know what you're talking about, anyway!"

"I know *everything* I'm talking about."

"Well, you don't know what it's like to have your life exactly like you want it and then lose it. You don't know what it's like to have a neat house and groovy parents who love you and support you, and a great girlfriend, and good buddies, and something you're really *really* good at to do, and then have the whole thing vanish 'cause you had a bad dream and got freaked and fell off a goddamn diving board!"

"You're really good at metalwork."

"Bullshit." Ronny snorted. "I'm *good* at water sports, I'm only better than everybody else at school in metalwork."

"You're also better than everybody else at school at feeling sorry for yourself."

Ronny slid off the stump and glared at the Road Man. "Who in the *hell* do you think you are, man? You don't know me, you don't know my school! You're not even from around here!"

"Do you *know* that, or are you once more assuming?"

"I . . . oh, fuck it; I'm leaving, man."

"Then you plan to abandon your bliss?"

"My what?"

"Your bliss. It's what Joseph Campbell talked about in *The Power of Myth*."

"The *what*?"

"And you thought *I* was an ignorant vagabond of the road."

"I didn't . . ."

"You did, but then so does everybody, and so—sometimes—I am. But I can read books and think same as anybody."

"Get to the point."

"The point is, my young apprentice—and yes, I know where that line comes from too—that for everybody there is, ideally, one thing, one act or hobby or craft or undertaking that makes them happier than everything else. One thing they'd do even if they didn't have to. One thing they'd do for free: that's their bliss."

"Well, then I've had my bliss—and lost it."

"When?"

"Diving was my bliss."

"You liked diving better than anything you ever did? Better than sleeping late on Saturday or having sex or building models?"

"How'd you know I built models?"

"Most boys build models."

"Okay, but . . . yeah—I did."

"Did you? Was there never a time when you didn't drag yourself out of bed and say, 'I wish I didn't have to go to practice today,' or feel sore muscles and wonder if it was worthwhile?"

"Yeah, sure, but—"

"But is there ever a time when you're making something with your hands—that little warrior, say—that you're wishing you were doing anything else? Can't you lose hours that way and not know where they've gone? Can't you set yourself a goal and finish it, but not be able to wait even a day to get on to the next stage?"

"I . . ."

"*Can't* you?"

"No," Ronny said in a small voice. "I . . . guess you're right . . . *maybe*. At least you're right about losing track of time when you're making something. But I did that when I was diving too. I *loved* that.''

"Loved the act? Or loved the recognition? Loved falling through the air and knowing you were good at it? Or loved it when people clapped, and you got the medals and people told you how good you were, and the girls wanted to go out with you 'cause you were on the team, and you got to show off your nice body in front of everybody 'cause you knew it really *was* a nice body and folks would be jealous, and that even the guys on your team were jealous of you and you liked them better 'cause they made *you* feel good 'cause you were better than them, which really meant you *didn't* like them, 'cause no good person ever wants people he likes to feel bad.''

Ronny was too overwhelmed to react. He sat absolutely still and tried very hard not to admit that a good bit of what the Road Man had told him was true. And he tried *very* hard not to start crying.

"Well,'' the Road Man said, a moment later. "So what do you think we should make?''

"I don't know,'' Ronny replied, after a very long pause. "What do *you* think I should make?''

"What would you *like* to make? I will only be here a short while, only be able to teach you very little. What one thing can we make in a little while that would embody the maximum number of the smithly arts?''

"Well, I'm working on a design for a new crutch—''

"You can do that at school. Besides, I've already given you a crutch.''

"What about more little warriors?''

"Those you have already done. I can teach you little there your heart does not already know.''

"A walking stick?''

"Too easy.''

"A . . . a suit of armor?''

"Better, for your heart was in that one. But it would be too much to finish in the time we have.''

"A helmet then?"

"Possibly, but I would rather it were something you could actually use. There's nothing like using something you have made, and the using will tell you how future things can be made better. I doubt you'd have much call to use a helm."

"Or . . . I've got it, how about something really useful, then, like a knife—yeah, that's it: how 'bout some kind of hunting knife?"

The Road Man looked thoughtful. "Not a bad idea," he acknowledged. "I will see what I can find by way of materials. And meanwhile, you stay there and think very hard about what you consider to be the absolutely ideal knife." And with that, the Road Man ducked into his wagon.

Ronny found himself staring out at the darkness, at the circle of strange, complex machines. Did he want to do this? Did he want to commit himself to sneaking away from home night after night, or day after day, or whenever it became possible for him to do such things? Was he prepared for the escalation of tensions between himself and his godmother that would inevitably result from such constant defiance? He much preferred being honest, getting his way by setting a good example and being rewarded for it, not from threat or rebellion or coercion.

But he also wanted to learn the secrets the Road Man alone could impart to him. And if he could pick up even a thousandth part of the Road Man's wit or savvy or skill, he would be ahead of the game. For if he had had any doubts before, he no longer entertained them. The Road Man *was* a genius—and Ronny wasn't. But where Ronny could succeed was in the fact that Ronny also knew how to function in the real world, and he doubted very much that the Road Man could. *He* was all dream and fire and talk. If Ronny could keep his own creative flame alive, but harness it to a viable purpose—why, there was nowhere he couldn't go.

Or would that corrupt the dream? Wasn't it the dream itself that was the most important thing? What was it he had heard on TV one time? That most people spent all their time doing things they didn't like in order to make money to buy things to make them happy, when they *should* simply be doing the things that made them happy in the first place. It didn't quite work for Ronny, especially if what one needed to satisfy one's soul required money. But he thought he had the gist of it anyway.

And . . . God, he was tired of philosophy.

Where was the Road Man? he wondered. He could hear him rummaging around inside the wagon, and considered joining him there—until good sense got the better of him. With his luck there'd be an Inside Man and an Outside Man as well, and he truly wasn't up for any more verbal fencing that evening. So he set himself to sipping on the Road Man's wine and trying to picture in his mind's eye the perfect knife.

And he was still limning spectral weaponry against the vault of sky when the Road Man emerged from his wagon with a large square bundle under his arm. "Took me a while to find this," he said. "I don't usually bother with stuff like this now, 'cause the Day Man, he can just close his eyes and remember. But you ain't that good yet. So here—"

Ronny took the bundle—which proved to be a drawing board, an assortment of stubby but serviceably pointed pencils, and half a pad of two-ply bristol board. He could not suppress a sigh. "Let me guess, you want me to draw what I want to make."

"I do. You won't always have to. But I want you to do it now."

Ronny bit his lip and dived in. And for the next two hours (hours which sure enough seemed to compress into mere minutes) he sketched blade after blade and hilt after hilt, then began combining the two in every combination he could think of. The Road Man didn't put forth a lot in the way of advice either, at first, but as Ronny's sketches grew bolder and more imaginative, and he began to flirt with decoration, the enigmatic tinker began to offer insights into potential problems or nuances of construction. "That would be a weak spot if you did it like that," he would say. "A good blow—or even if you pressed too hard, if it were the wrong type of material or poorly tempered—and it would snap. Do you want that?" Or, "In order to execute that design properly it would really need to be etched, and that would destroy the temper of the blade." Or, "Now *that's* an interesting concept: I would never have thought of blurring the distinction between blade and hilt like that."

It was close to midnight when they finished.

Ronny blinked tired eyes at the last sheet of paper in the pad, and only then realized it *was* the last sheet. The Road Man was right, he supposed: he'd become so engrossed in the creative process he'd lost all track of everything else, even of husbanding resources that were not truly his to squander. But the design looked right. He'd made the final sketch pretty much life-sized: a basic hunting knife, but with a couple of subtle curves and one secondary cutting edge that made it a little special. As for the hilt—he hadn't decided if it would be cast, etched, inlaid metal, or only carven bone. But it would be in the shape of a dragon.

"A good night's work," the Road Man acknowledged, after Ronny had shown him his final suggestion. "I think this will be more than sufficient a challenge, and if we're lucky, the Day Man will agree. Now be off with you, before the Sunrise Man finds you."

Ronny grunted and rolled his eyes, but slipped off his stump. "You wanta keep this, or shall I—"

"I will," the Road Man said. "I will need to show it to the others."

Ronny managed a wry, if somewhat confused smile. When he had collected his crutch, he glanced up at the Road Man again.

The Road Man was gazing at the sky.

Ronny followed his gaze, but saw nothing but the same familiar, unblinking stars. "What're you looking at?" he asked curiously.

"I'm not looking at anything," the Road Man murmured offhandedly. "I'm listening to the Sounds of Silence."

"Like in Simon and Garfunkel?"

The Road Man shook his head curtly. "These are far older than that—and something tells me they are about to be disturbed."

But for once, Ronny was too elated to ask more questions.

PART II

FORGE

Chapter 13

Whirlwind

Anson Bowman's house
Tuesday, April 10—12:30 A.M.

Anson felt so much different from when he'd left school nine hours earlier that he half-suspected he had somehow died and been reincarnated. So much had altered during that time, so many revelations had been made, so many doors opened or closed or relocated or simply *exposed* that he had completely lost count of them all—just like he had lost track of the time he had spent at Matthew Welch's house earlier that evening.

Had it only *been* eight hours since he'd commenced his Listening lesson? It seemed longer—and no time at all. As for the hours the session itself had consumed, he had no recollection of them as a continuum, for time did not exist as a linear concept when one Listened to the Voices on the Wind, and Matthew had already intimated that one could even ride those Winds into the future or past—though to spy on one's own fate was to risk one's sanity.

As for what had transpired *after* Matthew had closed off

the Winds from him so that they only heard each other's
Voices, and then only their own, Anson had little recollection. It had been dark when his eyes had slitted open, with
the only illumination coming from four lighted candles. And
he'd been so tired, so sleepy (Matthew had warned him that
Listening could be as taxing as physical labor, especially if
one engaged in it actively, as they had been doing), that
he'd accepted the old man's inevitable offer of sherry and
dozed off again where he sat.

When he'd awakened once more, Matthew was gone and
the candles had lost half their length. There was, however,
a note in Matt's hand telling him he was welcome to spend
the night if he needed to, but that if he wanted to return
home, to let himself out the front door, which would automatically lock behind him.

This Anson had done, to sneak into his mother's modest
ranch house somewhere after 11:00 P.M.—fortunately to
discover her still away at some school board meeting or
other. Finding himself to be absolutely ravenous (his grandfather had also warned him about that), he'd microwaved
half a frozen pizza and—impulsively, for he liked to maintain a positive image at home—had raided his mother's stash
of Coors. Thus fortified, he'd retired to his room, where he
wolfed down the pizza, stripped to his skivvies, and threw
himself down on his bed, with his half-empty beer in his
hand.

That was when the full weight of the day's events had
fallen upon him. That was when he had realized that his
old ambitions had been far too limited; that, when armed
with the new abilities he was already amassing, he could
accomplish almost anything. Anything that involved information and manipulation, at any rate. All he needed to learn
was control—and subtlety.

And how to get Matthew to teach him the maximum
amount in the least time, and then get him out of the way.
His grandfather was no fool, after all, even if Anson had
managed to seize the upper ground the day before. The old

geezer had been tired then, burned out for no reason Anson had been able to ferret out; today he'd seemed better, if not absolutely well. And Anson had sense enough to realize that Mr. Welch was not a person to be trifled with *or* made a fool of, both of which he had flirted with. He wondered, not for the first time, what exactly Matt saw in him—and could reach no viable conclusion. He certainly had no delusions about *himself*: he *was* a bully and liked it that way; and if he couldn't be loved or admired like his former friend Lewis was, why, then, by God, at least he could be feared. As for what bound him and his grandfather now that they'd had their little altercation—perhaps it was a common ruthlessness, a mutual sense that both were treading on dangerous ground. Anson *liked* danger, liked pushing the limits, and he had a pretty good suspicion that the Master of Cardalba enjoyed it too. Cobra and mongoose: that's what they were. Which was which did not matter: either could destroy the other. And if Anson lost, at least he'd have made the attempt, and wouldn't be out much in the long run—life was a crock anyway: ethics and law and decorum masking the older, stronger instincts that assured survival of the fittest. Frankly he was tired of maintaining that facade.

And in any event he doubted that would be the case. He was stronger than Matthew, both physically and—he was certain—Luckwise (though how he knew the latter he could not say). All he had to do was keep the old guy from regaining his full strength by promising to deliver a footholder he felt no urgency to seek, and he'd be okay. And if he was lucky—that word again—he'd have all the power he wanted in short order. Then people would love him. Or fear him. It made no difference in the last analysis. But in order to have free rein, Matthew would have to be disposed of—and to effect that in a way that would neither implicate him nor deny him his rightful place afterwards, he needed to learn a lot more.

He already had some idea about things Matt had *not* shown him, too, for with their minds so close and the old man so weak (though he'd been trying very hard to mask the fact), it had been no trouble at all to peer further ahead in the workbook, so to speak, when the teacher wasn't looking.

And one of the things he had discovered there was that one could not only Listen, but that one could also send messages on the Wind.

And now, with his energy levels rising again, and his mind so overflowing with its own potential he could scarcely contain his glee, he'd decided he might just attempt exactly that.

He had no footholder to draw on, of course—nor had Matt suggested why or when he would need one. But he suspected that the essential act could be carried out alone. What was he risking, after all? If he had the skill and ability, he could do it; if not, he couldn't. But if he didn't at least make the attempt he already knew that speculating about it would plague him the rest of the night—and since his whole system was overloaded with adrenaline already, which negated any real hope of sleeping, that was not an appealing notion.

But who should he Speak to? His friends? He had nothing to say to them, and the small amount of Listening he and Matthew had done in their direction had shown him how tenuous the bonds between them actually were. Winnie? She was a possibility, but Matt had warned him about riding one Wind too long, lest it turn on you and ensnare you.

So who then? Maybe someone he could learn something from *and* do something to.

Somebody like Ronny Dillon.

Smiling, Anson took a final sip of beer, leaned back on his pillow, and closed his eyes.

It was the first time he had attempted the trance by himself and only the second time at all, and he was naturally apprehensive. But as soon as he initiated the ritual, the reflexes began to kick in, almost as if they had been preprogrammed. He wondered if they had, if old man Welch had somehow fooled with his mind to facilitate such activities. But then he had to focus on his breathing, and *then* his eyes rolled back.

Before he knew it, he was Listening alone. The Winds were different too, for this late at night most people were abed, so that their Voices were quiet, save for the whispering breezes that were their dreamings. And the few Voices he *could* Hear were mostly faint: vague interest in this late movie or that, mild amusement at Johnny Carson or Arsenio Hall, a few worries about the next day's tasks or regrets over things unfinished from the day just ended, or of things said and wished unsaid. There was a fair bit of sexual energy too—anticipated or dreaded or speculated about—but he avoided those, remembering what Matt had told him about keeping clear of strong emotions lest they resonate in turn. Besides, he had to save *something* for the future.

For now, he wanted to find Ronny Dillon. What he would say—what doubts or fears he would insinuate into his troublesome rival's head—he had no idea. He'd cross that bridge when the time came. Perhaps he would simply suggest, very gently, that Ronny's Luck had finally run out.

But he could not *locate* Ronny, and he somehow did not think it was purely because of the Silence Erin Welch kept around him. *That* he *had* found: an edifice of unshaking calm within the ever-blowing Winds, with the smaller, connected dome that was Lewis when she was apart from him. Ronny should have been yet another adjunct dome, and the framework of such a structure *was* present, tenuously but firmly attached to Erin's—but as best Anson could determine from Outside, it was empty. Which meant . . . what? That Ronny's Voice should be easy enough to find, or failing that, his own personal Silence—in the unlikely event he knew how to do that? How many Silences *could* there be in Welch County, anyway? Not many, he'd wager. And yet there was no sign of Ronny.

But what difference did that make? He could always deal with Ronny another day. What he wanted now was to find someone to whom he could Speak—or, more properly, shout "*Boo*," and then sneak back into the Winds and hide.

Why not Lewis, then? Lew was a rival too, though of a different—and ultimately more threatening—kind. So maybe he ought to try Speaking to good old Lew instead. It *would* be difficult—because of Erin's Silence. Indeed, according to what Matt had told him, it might not be possible. But he would have to confront Silences sooner or later, and the quicker he dealt with one, the better. Besides, there was the perplexing matter of the half-dissolved Silence that should have/might have held Ronny. Perhaps, if he were careful, he could slip in there and come at Lewis that way—through the back door, as it were. He checked Erin's Silences again—and confirmed that though Ronny's was tenuous, it was still too strong to breach. *But* Erin had stretched her own Silence thin in order to accommodate Ronny's, with the result that there were now a few tears where the two joined, into which a clever Wind could blow an inquisitive Voice.

Anson located one such access point, crept inside—and found Lew.

He was asleep—or at least his Voice was drifty and unfocused: images more than ideas. And that, Anson realized, made him vulnerable.

So what should he do? Should he simply wake old Lew up with a psychic "Boo!" and ride the Wind away and hide? Or should he leave him with something more lasting, and more subtle? A dream, perhaps—or a nightmare? But what was Lewis afraid of? Anson had no idea—indeed, knew very little about Lewis at all anymore, except that he was bright, good-looking, accomplished, and popular—and had done nothing to earn any of those things. So what if he *lost* them? What if Lew dreamed he was hideous and sickly and stupid and poor? What if he dreamed he had leprosy, dreamed he awoke on a Middle Eastern street to the sound of his fingers falling off into his tin begging pan, dreamed he tried to pick them up and put them on and found the other hand bore only stumps. Suppose he was hungry, but had nothing to eat *except* those stumps. And then suppose someone dropped by with a mirror and showed him his face, and that he was bald and his scalp was a mess of sores and his smooth skin was hanging in tatters, and his strong firm muscles were flabby and decayed. And then he could have children come by and laugh at him, and tell him how far he'd fallen. And then he could send flies down to bite him and rats to gnaw on him.

And *then* . . . why, he could use those images he'd noticed in Matt's mind: the ones about being dead that he thought Matt might have used before, though the reasons for that were hidden. Still, they were pretty bizarre: images of not *being*, of dissolution, of falling away to dust and not returning, of utter, complete obliteration, of . . .

Before Anson knew what he was doing, he was Screaming.

And in his bed in his mother's empty house, Lewis Welch also screamed, but did not awaken.

Erin heard him as soon as she walked in the front door, knew immediately what was causing it, and cursed herself for the drink she had shared with a friend after the school board meeting. She was getting sloppy lately—or tired—or old. Or all of the above. And now when her sons were most vulnerable—when she needed to maintain her Silence most—she was letting it slip more and more frequently. Just like she had let it slip when Eddie Banner had eased his hand onto her knee over at the Riverside Bar. She would not let it happen again, either—even if it meant denying a large part of what made her human.

Closing her eyes, she drew into herself and reinforced her Silence, feeling her way through it until she found every weak place and chink in what once had been impenetrable armor—shocked to discover the condition she had somehow allowed it to sink into during the last few hours. Immediately she began to rebuild it, strengthening it with her will and banishing the random Winds that had found their way inside until it was once more a towering edifice of protection.

Never again, she told herself. If she had to stay awake the rest of her life, she would keep the Silence strong.

Except, she realized, as she slammed Lewis's bedroom door open, that Ronny was still Outside.

But she didn't have time to worry about him now, because Lewis was curled up on his side tearing and brushing at his arms and legs as if he were trying to divest himself of some unseen but persistent tormentors. And all the while he was screaming at the top of his lungs—incoherently, except that every now and then the words coalesced into a horrified "No" or "Leave me alone" or "Goawaygoawaygoaway."

"Lewis," she shrieked, throwing herself down beside him on the bed and cradling him in her arms, as she tried to shake him back aware, to call him back to consciousness.

But he would not wake up. Whatever Voice assailed him was much stronger than the one she had lately sensed poking around her Silence. In fact, it had much the feel of a full-blown Listener—which meant it might be too strong for her.

But she *would* find whoever was torturing her son. He was still there, hiding somewhere *Inside*. She could feel him, sense his Wind slipping past hers when she tried to catch it and cast it out. And then she had it—and recognized it.

Anson! Her Voice rang loud in the netherworld.

Erin! Anson replied. *Or should I say 'Aunt Erin'?*

You should say nothing! You should not even be here!

Ah, but I am *here!*

Not for long!

And with that, Erin did instinctively what she had heretofore never had to do, which was by sheer force of will to drive someone completely out of her Silence. Always before when she had found someone snooping around—Uncle Matt, usually, or else the distant and randomly curious—she had simply slammed the Silence down and shut them out that way. But that would not work with this one, for he was too far Inside, and with the link he had somehow established with Lewis, he was likely to remain that way.

So she pushed—and met resistance and an explosion of derisive, soundless laughter. And sensed, somehow, that Anson, however he had come into such power, was already and innately remarkably strong.

For as soon as she set her Wind against his, he set his against hers. Hers blew harder, so did his, and for a long time her Silence resounded with the sounds of contending Voices. And then, to her horror, he began to master her, to drive her back, to erode the edifice of her Silence.

That she could not allow. She thrust back, pushed harder, and felt him yield; pushed harder yet, forced him to release his hold on Lewis—and pushed with the last effort of her will and found the rent through which he had entered. He resisted there, made a last stand, and it took all the Strength she had to fling him through and slam her Silence shut. Only when she was once more alone with her son in her Silence did she realize that something was not the same.

She had rebuilt her Silence *too* well, with the result that she had inadvertently trapped herself inside—unable to re-establish the link between mind and body.

Ronny knew something was wrong as soon as he walked through the front door. It was subtle, but there was a . . . wrongness in the house, as if the air itself were charged with some heavy, oppressive tension. It felt like the nervous calm before a lightning storm, but Ronny did not have to go far at all to discover whence that tension came.

It was Lewis's room, for he could hear sounds from there: low-pitched moanings coupled with gasps and groans and snatches of inarticulate language.

"Lew!" he yelled. "Aunt Erin!" And by that time he was making what haste he could toward the bedroom.

An image from hell greeted him when he came to the open door.

Lew was lying in his bed curled into a tight, shivering ball like a tanned and muscular fetus. Ronny could not see his face, for it was jammed down between his kneecaps, but he could hear Lew's teeth chattering, hear him mumbling to himself, "No . . . no . . . no . . ."

And Aunt Erin, still in her dressy go-to-meeting clothes, was sprawled on the floor beside him, one arm wrapped protectively around his head. Her eyes were closed, and she was breathing but shallowly, her face so contorted with what Ronny could only assume was utter concentration, that she scarcely looked human. She was talking too, or mumbling through gritted teeth, and from the snatches he could make out, her voice sounded at once full of anger, fear, and hate. Very little was clear, except that she seemed to be carrying on a conversation with someone. But one word he *was* able to make out: *Anson*.

"Son of a bitch," Ronny growled under his breath. As best he could tell, Aunt Erin was caught in some kind of trance. And he had no idea how to get her out of one—had no experience with such things at all. But he *had* to do something to protect his best friend.

His crutch snagged the corner of the doorjamb as he flung himself past. It was wrenched from his hand, but he made it halfway across the bedroom before his injured leg gave out on him, sending him sprawling on his face atop Lewis's abandoned school clothes. He was up on hands and knees in an instant, though, and scrambling on. Somehow he reached his aunt, took her by the shoulders, and began to shake her, calling out to her over and over, "Aunt Erin, Aunt Erin, hey, come out of it, Aunt Erin; it's me, Ronny—snap *out* of it!" But his words had no effect.

What then? He hated to resort to desperate measures, but perhaps that was his only recourse. And if it were not, then he'd have no choice but to call the police—or an ambulance—and hope whoever showed up could accomplish something.

Steeling himself, he drew back his hand and slapped Erin Welch sharply across both cheeks.

—To no avail.

—Not the first time. But by the time he had repeated the action twice more, she had stopped mumbling, and her face had begun to relax.

The fourth assault consisted of only a gentle tap.

And then—blessedly—Erin opened her eyes.

"Ronny?" she gasped, her voice weak and distant, as if she had been forced awake from a deep, drugged sleep. Her eyes were out of focus, her body limp and swaying. "R-ronny . . . what are *you* doing here? I—"

"We'll talk about that later," Ronny replied tersely. He scrambled around to snag his crutch, then stood and helped his guardian to his bed, where she sagged against the headboard, breathing heavily.

"Ronny . . . ?" Erin murmured. "I . . . I'll be okay in a minute, just give me a second . . . I . . . ."

"Fine," Ronny interrupted. "You stay there and try to get your act together. *I've* got to tend to Lew."

Oblivious to the agony in his over-stressed leg, Ronny crossed the room again and flopped down on the bed beside his friend. He grabbed Lew by the shoulders and shook him gently, noting how cold Lew was, how shallow his breathing had become—how every inch of his body was covered with sweat.

"Wake up, Lew!" he called. "Lew, can you hear me? Wake up!"

But Lew merely continued to shake, to curl ever tighter into himself. Ronny could feel the iron-hard tension of his friend's shoulders, see the knots of muscles springing out along his back and arms, as if every fiber strained to draw its fellows in.

"*Lew?*"

And then: "Aunt Erin! Get over here—*now!*"

And with those words, Lew calmed. His muscles relaxed, his teeth stopped chattering.

And by the time Ronny was making a tentative attempt at unrolling him far enough to see if he was still breathing, Aunt Erin was beside him again. She was much calmer, much more in control.

Ronny made room for her and let her take over. "Lewis, Lewis—can you hear me?" she called softly, as she gently eased Lew's arms from around his knees (leaving Ronny to finish unfolding his legs and fling a corner of blanket across his barely clothed hips). "Lewis, it's okay, child, it's your mother. I won't let anything hurt you, I promise. I never have and I never will."

Lew was on his back now, face pale as Ronny had ever seen one, but he *was* breathing, and ever more deeply. And then his eyelids flickered open and he raised his head a fraction and blinked up at them.

"M . . . Mom?"

"It's me, hon," Erin crooned. "You're gonna be okay. You just had a nightmare, a really bad nightmare."

Lew's eyes shifted downward. "And Ronny? Wh . . . what did I *do*, anyway?"

"You screamed in the night, and I heard you. Good thing, too."

Lewis closed his eyes and collapsed against his pillow. "Oh, *Jesus*, what a dream!" he moaned. "Oh, dear Lordy Jesus!"

"What *did* you dream, Lewis?" Erin asked urgently, smoothing the hair out of his eyes with a gentle brush of her hand.

"I don't know . . . I don't even want to think about it. It was too awful . . . too real!"

Ronny's breath caught. For he had himself said those exact same words not two months ago, to his lost best friend Aaron in a Florida locker room, right before—never mind.

"I need to know, son," Erin persisted. "I truly do. I know you're scared, but you need to tell me. That way I can make sure things are okay."

Ronny shot Erin a peculiar glance at that, but then Lew

took a deep breath and drew his attention that way.

"It was like I was sick, Mom," Lewis whispered. "And . . . and then I had leprosy or something and I was rotting—and then . . . then I was *dead*! It was awful! . . . Like what being dead really must be like! It was . . ." But then he was sobbing.

Ronny felt as if someone had slammed a fist into his solar plexus. For perhaps five seconds he sat completely frozen. If his heart was even beating, it was a miracle.

Whatever had found its way to Florida to torture him had now made its way here and attacked Lew. And since he, Ronny Dillon, appeared to be the common denominator, he could only conclude one of two things. Either it was after him and had snared Lew by mistake—or Lew had been its intended focus all along.

But if so, why?

For, as best he could tell, Lew had never *had* bad dreams before, at least not of this magnitude. And there was the small matter of Friday night, when Ronny had awakened from what he'd thought was a reprise of one. And then there were the rather pointed questions Aunt Erin had asked him Saturday morning over breakfast.

But what it all meant, he hadn't a clue. And he doubted one o'clock in the morning was a good time to start putting anything together.

A touch on his arm jerked him from his brief indulgence in reverie. He blinked, met Erin's eyes. "Go run him a tub of water, Ron. Hot enough to steam but not to scald. He's tensed himself up so much that he's gonna cramp for the rest of the night and tear something if we don't give him a chance to loosen up gradually."

Ronny did, limping across the room, with frequent hand-holds on furniture for balance. Once in the bathroom, he set the tap from experience (for he liked hot baths too): at a point just below unbearable. Lew would tense as the water touched him, but as it took him in, it would begin to soak the tension free.

A moment later, Ronny was back in the bedroom.

"You watch him a minute," Erin whispered, rising. "He'll be okay, but I need to go get something."

Ronny nodded. "Sure." As Erin left the room, he resumed her place beside his godbrother. Lew was breathing evenly now, was not sweating so much, and his face was no longer panic-stricken. But he took Ron's hand in a tight, desperate grip. "It was scary, man. Oh, God, Ronny, it was so real, so *goddamned* real!"

"I know it was," Ronny whispered. "Trust me, bro. I know."

Lewis shook his head. "No way, man, no way *anybody* could know what a nightmare like that was like."

"Unless you've had them too," Ronny replied, in an even softer voice, as he raised his head in urgent anticipation toward the doorway. "Oh Lord, Lew, I . . . I wonder what's going on here with me and you?"

"You mean . . . ?"

But Lewis was not allowed to finish, because Erin had returned with a small fabric pouch in her hand. "Is he okay?" she asked quickly, and when Ronny assured her that he was, she nodded grimly and disappeared inside the bathroom. An instant later, she had returned sans pouch, but even in the bedroom Ronny could detect a sharp, spicy odor in the air.

"I've put something in the bathwater to help him relax," she announced briskly, as she once more displaced Ronny by her son's side. "Now help me get him in there—come on . . ."

"I can walk," Lewis grumbled. "I had a dream, not a seizure."

"No," Erin countered quickly. "What you had was *not* a dream."

"Then what was it?" Ronny asked pointedly, seizing the opportunity to catch Aunt Erin with her guard down. For as soon as she had finished her sentence, her eyes had grown large, as if she had suddenly realized what exactly it was she had let slip.

Erin fixed him with a steely glare. "Never mind," she replied in a low, no-nonsense voice. "I've said too much already. Now go and stay with Lew until he's done. He needs to stay immersed up to his neck for fifteen minutes, and further than that as long as can be managed. Then get him into some clothes and back into bed. The fumes from the bath'll ease his mind—yours too, if you're lucky. You think you're up to it?"

"I'm up to it," Ronny gritted, slapping Lew gently on the back. "Long as I don't actually have to carry him."

"I'm *not* sick," Lewis pleaded, now fully if groggily awake. "It was only a dream. No big deal, not really."

"Well, okay then, if you're sure?" Erin conceded dubiously. "*And*," she added in a voice so low Ronny was certain it was for his ears only, "We will *not*, repeat, *not* discuss this in the morning. The matter had better not even come up."

Ronny wondered why. But by the time Erin had left and he had followed her instructions involving Lew's peculiar bath, he was feeling sleepy himself. Perhaps it was the thick-scented vapors that did it, for they did seem to have a remarkably calming effect.

Except that he didn't exactly like the way his memories appeared to be deadening, as if everything that had happened was already taking on the texture of a dream. Thus, as soon as he was certain Lewis was safely squared away, he stuck his head back in the bedroom and took a deep breath. The fresh air cleared his thoughts immediately, and he spent the next half hour alternately keeping an eye on Lew until he felt his memories growing dim, and then refreshing himself outside. He wished he could do the same for his friend—but then again, perhaps there were some things better *not* remembered.

So it was, then, that he was more or less lucid, if still a trifle muddleheaded, when Aunt Erin returned to the bedroom a short while later. Ronny was watching a bleary-eyed Lew climb out of the tub when he heard her knock on the bathroom door.

"Just a sec," Ronny called, handing Lew a towel.

Lew took it gratefully. "I'm okay, I think—'cept I can't seem to think very clearly . . . like why am I in here and all—and what are *you* doing in here?"

Ronny scowled thoughtfully, then opened the window to let the warm night air in. He inhaled deeply and, satisfied Lew was in no danger of hurting himself, slipped through the doorway and entered the bedroom.

Erin was sitting on his bed, now in her green bathrobe. "How is he?" she asked tiredly.

"Fine."

"Where'd you go tonight?"

"We'll talk about that later," Ronny told her—amazed at his presumption. "Right now I think you owe *me* some explanations."

Erin stared at him woodenly, and he could tell that whatever had lately transpired had cost her a huge amount of effort. She shook her head. "I *can't* tell you," she whispered. "Truly there's a big part of me that would love to—but I dare not. Right now you're safe—relatively. But the more you know, the more at risk you'll be. As it stands I can protect you—you and Lewis both. But if you—if *either* of you knows what's going on, you're bound to start acting unilaterally—and I can't allow that."

"But if it's something we *ought* to know . . ."

Erin shook her head. "I've protected you all these years, I can keep on protecting you. Otherwise . . . otherwise you'll get involved, and I've put too much work into preventing that very thing to let it happen now. I want you to just forget this has happened, okay? I've put an end to the threat, I think—I've sealed it off from you. And even if I haven't, I'd rather confront it than have you boys do it. I may already be lost, but you can still be saved, if we can just make it through the next year or so. Then you boys'll go off to college and we can all live normal lives.''

Ronny gaped at her incredulously. "What are you *talking* about? What's *happening*? Do you think I'll be able to live a normal life when I'm spending every free minute wondering why you were sitting in a heap in Lew's bedroom with your eyes rolled back in your head and speaking in tongues?''

"I can *make* you forget," Erin told him dully. "That's what I ought to do.''

"The hell you will!" Ronny raged. "You've tried that already, haven't you? You put something in the bathwater!''

"And I will again. You're not as strong as me, Ronny; you don't have my strength of will. *You'll* have to sleep sometime, but *I* never will again. And when you do, I'll make you forget.''

"Oh no you won't! I'll leave this house now and take Lew with me if I have to. But I'm not going to stay around when something *this* weird's going on.''

"It's for your own good, Ronny," Erin pleaded desperately. "I swear to you nothing I've done for you was *ever* done to hurt you. Everything—and there have been a thousand things neither you nor Lewis will ever know about—was done for your own good, so you could grow up happy and well-adjusted and—''

"*Normal?*" Ronny interrupted. "But we're *not* normal, are we? There's something screwy about all three of us, isn't there?—and I'm going to find out what it is if it kills me!''

"It might! Especially if you become involved in it.''

"Then you *really* have to tell me.''

"No.''

"I'll leave!''

"And where will you go? Back to Florida? You're still a minor, you can't touch any of the stuff down there.''

"I . . . I'll go off with the Road Man!''

"Is that where you were tonight, with him?''

"I was."

Erin bit her upper lip pensively, her expression suddenly softer. "Well," she whispered, "that may very well be what saved you."

"Saved me from *what*?"

"Ronny, did the Road Man say anything about me?"

"He said . . . well, I guess the best way to put it is that he used to have a thing for you."

"I know."

"Want to tell me about it?"

"No."

"Aunt Erin! For God's sakes, isn't there *anything* you can tell me?"

"No."

"You've got to promise me one thing then, or I swear I'll leave, I swear I'll run off with the Road Man."

"What's that?"

"That you won't play games with my memory. If something *is* going on that affects me, at least let me confront it with my memory intact. If I'm *going* to have to fight something, let me fight with a full deck—I've already got a physical handicap, I don't need a mental one."

Erin looked at him curiously. "No," she said, very softly. "Maybe you don't."

"Thanks."

"Two things, Ronny, before I think better of it."

"I'm listening."

"Very well. The first is that I've never seen you so content as when you're talking about metalwork, and never so unhappy as when you're cut off from it, so that if you *really* think some good can come from working with the Road Man, you can visit with him—but only after school and before sunset. No more of this sneaking off in the night business."

"And the other thing?"

"The other thing is . . . Ronny, be very, very careful about Anson Bowman."

"Anything else?"

"I'm sorry, but no. Now I need to get to bed, and you better turn in too. I can give you something to make you sleep."

"Not a chance."

"You'll lie awake and worry all night."

"At least they'll be *my* worries."

"One last thing—and this I truly do beg you."

"Yes?"

"Please, oh please, Ronny, don't say a word about this to Lewis."

"I can't promise that. Especially not without a reason."

"And I can't give you one. Suffice to say that if I *did* tell you, and he found out and played his cards wrong, it could kill him."

Chapter 14

Sound and Fury

Welch County High School
Tuesday, April 10—lunchtime

"But what if we get caught?" Winnie protested nervously, as a tired-looking Ronny eased his head around the corner of Welch County High's upper building that lay nearest the industrial arts annex.

The coast was clear, more or less—or at least neither the few students nor the single teacher he could spy ambling around in the midday sun down by the breezeway were looking their way at the moment. Ronny flopped back against the dull-red brick and flashed Winnie a conspiratorial grin that belied the trauma he and Lew had undergone the previous night. "Then *we'll* apologize profusely, *you'll* dazzle them with your blazing smile, and *I'll* proceed to confound them utterly by asking when was the last time they caught somebody cutting lunch to work on a class."

"Fine for you." Winnie sighed. "What about me? What's my excuse?"

"I'm teaching you stuff—which is what I really will be

doing. I mean, what's the worst that can happen?''

"That folks'll get the wrong idea, of course."

Ronny smirked mischievously. "Ah, but would that really be so awful? Would it hurt *either* of our reputations?''

Winnie rolled her eyes in resignation. "I got enough grief when I started going out with Anson. I don't need—''

Ronny was too impatient to let her continue. "Then if nothing else, it'll show everyone your taste has improved.''

"Stuck on yourself, are you?" Winnie teased more lightly.

"Somebody has to be,'' Ronny chuckled back, then ran a final surveillance check, grabbed Winnie's hand, and yanked. "Come on!'' he hissed. "Just act like you know what you're doing—don't run or look around or anything. And if anybody asks us what we're up to, let me do the talking. I'll say Wiley wanted to see me about a casting project—which is true, he just didn't say now.''

And with that, Ronny and Winnie sauntered calmly and purposefully (if a tad awkwardly because of Ronny's crutch) across the asphalt pavement between the two buildings and entered the industrial arts annex by the front door. With a third of the student body at lunch and the rest in class, the central hall was deserted. A moment later they were in the metalworking shop.

Ronny had the drill down to near perfection by now, and threaded his way expertly between the benches, tables, and racks of supplies. The room was not in use that hour—it was in service only three of the seven periods anyway—and he was surprised at the calm that pervaded it when not filled with the clamor of voices. The light was excellent, too: clear but slightly diffused. And without further ado, Ronny crossed to his locker, opened it, and lifted out a cardboard shoe box.

Smiling secretively, he carried it over to his worktable and set it down.

"You *can* open it if you want to,'' he noted pointedly, when Winnie showed no sign of taking the hint.

Winnie removed the Ray-Bans she'd been wearing to mask her shiner and shot him a dubious glare that said she didn't trust him not to be pulling one on her, then lifted the lid and folded back the tissue paper inside so she could see.

From her expression Ronny knew she was pleased before she said a word.

"Wow!" she gasped. "Did you make *all* these?"

Ronny nodded proudly, easing around for a better view—which coincidentally brought him closer to Winnie as well. "Worked on 'em all day in class yesterday, an hour after school, and most of my free time Sunday."

And with that, he removed seven small warriors, perfectly scaled to match the one that already glowered from atop his new crutch—except that these were sculpted of purplish-red wax. One at a time he arrayed them across his work space, then reached for his crutch and began to fit them around the baroque curves and angles of the one-time Centauri suspension arm. In less than a minute the whole upper front corner was transformed from a dully gleaming, triangulated fretwork into a quasi-battlefield, as the tiny warriors followed their commander (the guy he had already completed and cast in silver, whom he had come to think of as Elon) in a mad upward rush to rival his lofty perch. One merely climbed, two glanced back and struck blows lower down at targets Ronny had not yet contrived. A fourth hung on for dear life, and another (his first sculpted Amazon) helped a smaller male friend along. There was only one of the enemy, so far: a near-naked savage clad only in a skimpy fur loincloth and cap helm. He carried a trident instead of sword (with which he was poking at the feet of the defender immediately above him), and his shield bore an intricately wrought device.

When he had affixed the last figure, Ronny held the crutch out for Winnie's inspection. "Welcome to the battle at the end of time," he intoned theatrically. "You too can watch in awe as the forces of Law make a final glorious stand against the insidious encroachment of Chaos."

Winnie bent closer, allowing the light to flicker across the miniature warriors so that they took on the appearance of an army that had fought so long and hard they had become covered with blood, which had then congealed into the tableau at hand. She paid particular attention to the lone savage.

"Notice anything special about him?" Ronny inquired eagerly.

Winnie squinted at the figure more closely. "He looks . . . familiar."

"He's supposed to."

Winnie studied the tiny warrior a moment longer. "I still can't quite . . ."

"Check out the device on his shield. It's symbolic."

"It's a bird," she stated flatly.

"What *kind* of bird?"

"*I* don't know—some kind of heraldic bird, maybe?"

Ronny couldn't resist a giggle. "Yeah, well, you're right there—but I copied that design from something else. It's real close too—so try to think where you've seen an emblem like that before."

Winnie's brow wrinkled in thought. "It's that great big decal on the hood of Anson's car . . ."

Ronny nodded emphatically and punched her gently on the shoulder. "Right you are . . . so now who does that drooling savage look like?"

Winnie regarded the figure's face for several seconds, and then her smile widened. "Oh Jesus, it's . . . it's *Anson!*"

"Perfect casting, don't you think?" Ronny crowed excitedly, hoping she caught his inadvertent pun, which she didn't. "Making him a soldier of Chaos and all! He'll be defeated, naturally—'course I haven't had time to make the folks who'll do him in yet. He'll be attacking those above him, but I'll make three more little fellows to sneak around to either side and stab him from behind. And one guess who they'll be . . . I'll even give you a hint: one'll be a girl."

Winnie stared at him shyly, but with a flattered twinkle

in her eye. "You . . . and Lew, and . . . me, maybe?"

"You got it! I'm gonna make the molds for these little guys in class today, cast four of 'em tomorrow, three the next day, and then begin on the next batch and have them ready to go on Monday. What I *may* try is to do all the sculpting at home, so I can make maximum use of class time for the casting, since Aunt Erin doesn't have a torch that'll melt silver."

"Gosh . . ."

"Yeah, neat, isn't it?"

"You *could* say that," Winnie replied. "So do you have a master plan?" she continued more seriously. "How do you *make* this stuff? Do you draw it out, or—"

"Not anymore," Ronny interrupted once again, too caught up in his enthusiasm to let her finish. "Not since yesterday. Nowadays I just put on some good heroic music—*Conan* or Jethro Tull's *Broadsword* or something, and let it flow."

Winnie raised a dark eyebrow. "What changed yesterday?"

Ronny propped the crutch against his desk and began removing the figures, making minute adjustments to their poses as he repacked them. "A *lot* of things."

"Like what?"

"Like I had a long talk with the Road Man."

"*Ronny!*"

"No, don't freak," he countered quickly, putting the lid on the box. "He's really okay, if about as weird as they come. But I've learned a lot from him already . . . lots of philosophy. I thought it was B.S. at first, but I've been thinking about it some since, and I've decided to give it a try."

"Try what?"

"Just letting go and making what I feel, instead of having a plan all the time. It's what the Road Man calls letting heart and dream and soul rule head and hands. I made little Anson here by design, and he works fine, but I think the

guy and girl helping each other along work a lot better—
and would you believe I made them this morning before
breakfast? Took me 'bout half an hour.''

"You're kidding!"

Ronny's expression darkened. "I . . . well, I had kind of
a bad night last night . . . couldn't sleep and all, and—"

"I *thought* you looked kinda fried."

"Very observant."

Winnie slipped an arm around his waist and snuggled
close. "So what was the problem?"

Ronny shrugged listlessly and would not meet her eyes.
"I can't tell you."

"Ronny!"

"No, I'm sorry, but I really can't. All I can say is that
something really screwy's going on with Aunt Erin and Lew,
and I don't know what it is."

"What do you mean?"

Another helpless shrug. "I honestly don't know. All I
know is that there's something really weird about Aunt Erin,
and that something funny's going on between Lew and
Anson."

Winnie frowned. "Oh, *really*?"

"Uh, yeah, and . . . well, actually, I was hoping you
might be able to shed some light there. You've known 'em
both longer than I have—or Anson, anyway; I guess I've
sort of known Lew since Aunt Erin started bringing him
down for a couple of weeks every summer when we were
kids. So do you know about anything bad going on between
them? I mean most folks up here really like Lew, and those
who don't just leave him alone—though sometimes I wonder
how much of that is really friendship and how much is
brown-nosing 'cause he's a Welch."

"A lot of it really is friendship," Winnie replied instantly.
"He truly is a nice guy."

"But what about Anson?"

Winnie grimaced. "*That's* a real good question. When I
moved up here him and Lew were pretty good friends—

kind of natural allies, in a way, since they lived fairly close together and neither of 'em had fathers.''

''Anson doesn't have a dad?''

''Nope.''

Ronny bit his lip. ''Gee, that's a very . . . a very Welch sort of thing.''

Winnie nodded thoughtfully. ''Yeah, maybe it is at that. But like I was saying, Anson and Lew were friends, and then somewhere around sixth grade we started finding out about sex and all, and suddenly Anson—he was a year older anyway—started getting a *lot* of grief over . . . being what he was, that Lew *didn't* get because he's a Welch. So anyway, Anson went to high school the next year, and got in with a really rough bunch from the north part of the county where the Welches don't have as much influence as they do down here, and they started hanging out together. By the time Lew and me got to high school, the war was on. Lew's mom raised a big stink about it and got a bunch of folks transferred to other schools, so it's not as obvious now, but it's still going on.''

''So Anson was kinda head of a rival clique, huh?''

''Sort of, except Lew never tried to make his gang a clique. He never *tried* to do anything at all; it just happened—I mean like Coach asked him to be on the wrestling team, at which he promptly became a star; teachers asked him to do stuff, folks invited him to parties.''

''So there's nothing specific?''

''Not really—I guess it's mostly resentment that they were friends, and then people started putting Anson down for something they overlooked in Lew.''

''What about lately? Anything gone on in the last few days, say, that'd make Anson have it in for Lew?''

Winnie shook her head. ''Not that I can think of. Anson was really grouchy the last week or so before we broke up—said he'd had headaches and all, like his head was full of static or something—but something must have happened over the weekend 'cause he looked like a new man on Sunday. He smiles a lot, and . . .''

Ronny regarded her askance. "You're not getting interested in him again are you?"

Another shake of head. "No . . . but I have to admit that as big a butthole as he is, I can't help but find him attractive."

"But I . . . well, what does that do to us?" Ronny asked apprehensively.

"I . . . don't know." Winnie sighed. "I like you a lot, Ronny. I like you a whole lot better than Anson. But I think maybe we're still finding out about us."

"Oh . . ."

Her face broke into a beautiful smile. "I also think it's gonna to be a whole lot of fun to learn."

Ronny's expression brightened immediately.

And brightened further when Winnie pecked him on the cheek. He returned the assault. And the next try lasted longer.

Ronny was still flying high from his promising encounter with Winnie when he headed down the breezeway to his English class. They had parted surreptitiously, by the simple expedient of merging with the students who erupted from the classrooms across from the metalwork shop when the change-of-periods bell sounded. And the seal on . . . whatever *had* happened/*was* happening between them had been no more than a brush of fingers and an exchange of wistful, knowing smiles. Which had been enough.

Ronny was feeling as good as he had in months. Even his knee was giving him less grief than usual, and the new, baroque crutch, he had discovered, was simplicity itself to maneuver with. For the first time since he'd transferred to Welch County High, he was actually making eye contact with other students, and—occasionally—even saying "Hi" and getting "Hi'd" back.

Thus, he was in absolutely no mood whatever for what

he encountered shortly after he ducked into the men's room for a quick resculpting of coif and check for residual lipstick—which he couldn't decide whether to keep or remove.

Lewis was there ahead of him, appropriately engaged at one of the line of urinals that marched across the opposite wall from the bank of mirrors and sinks where Ronny was primping. Lew hadn't seen him, however, and the unspoken etiquette of such places (and his own reserve) prevented Ronny from hailing his friend, though right now he'd have given a lot to get Lew alone so he could enthuse a bit about Winnie.

And, too, he wouldn't have minded a follow-up check concerning last night's events, which Lew had scarcely seemed to recall at all over breakfast—not that he remembered them that clearly himself, which he also thought odd.

Unfortunately, etiquette did *not* appear to be of concern to Anson, who sauntered in just as Lew was zipping up and turning around. Ronny witnessed it all in the mirror, and heard everything as well.

The two former friends saw each other at exactly the same time, and Ronny realized this was their first face-to-face encounter since that ill-starred near-altercation in Matthew Welch's yard on Friday. It was also their first contact since Lew had found out about *Ronny's* encounter with Anson later that night. Ronny was therefore prepared for fireworks.

What he was *not* prepared for was the fact that both boys froze, that Lew looked vaguely puzzled, almost frightened, and that Anson simply stared at him with an expression of drippingly mock concern on his face and inquired loudly, "What's the *matter*, Lewis? You don't look well. Been sleepin' okay lately?"

Lewis gave him back glare for glare, his shoulders tense and his fists clenched. "No, I haven't," he replied calmly, "as a matter of fact. Thank you for your concern."

And with that he stepped aside and walked neatly past the triumphantly smiling Anson and into the hall.

"You got a *problem*, Welch?" Anson spat to his back. "Luck runnin' out on you, maybe?"

The door swung closed behind Lewis without even a whisper of sound.

And the rest room rang with Anson's laughter. The few remaining boys inside glanced around nervously, and Ronny, who knew he was caught in the open, tried not to react at all. Oh, he was torn with indecision, granted: what he *wanted* to do was flail the crap out of Anson with his crutch—or better, with his fists. But something told him that would not be wise, that it would do Lew no good. Lew was a wrestler, after all, and perfectly capable of defending himself—as Anson no doubt knew. Anson was no fool, either, and was certainly aware that any altercation with even a black-sheep Welch would be unlikely to bring the school authorities down on his side, never mind the right or wrong of the situation. And in any event, he had already scored a moral victory of sorts, because, in a way, he had made a Welch back down from a fight.

But then Ronny remembered Winnie and what Anson had done to her and the threat he might yet pose, and he thought of his still livid and tender cheek. And with those firmly in mind, he eased around and thwacked Anson, who was now standing immediately inside the doorway gloating like a fool, on the butt with the heel of his crutch.

Anson spun around like a cornered fox, and for the first time acknowledged Ronny's presence.

"That was a shitty thing to say," Ronny said softly, but with as much malice as he could muster.

"*What* was?" Anson retorted with an air of mock innocence that made Ronny want to puke. "Oh, that little business with Lew? But I was only *sayin'* what's true. Surely *you* don't mind if I express my concern about the health of Welch County's finest."

"You don't give a damn about him, and you know it!"

Anson's eyebrows shot up. "I don't? And how do *you*

know so much? I've known Lew a lot longer than you have—asshole.''

''Then you know he doesn't deserve grief, and certainly not the kind you're laying on him!''

''I was givin' him grief?''

''You have been.''

Anson frowned dangerously. ''And exactly what do you mean by that?''

It took all the self-control Ronny possessed to keep from leaping atop the leering bully. ''You know very well what I mean! I don't know how you're doing it, or why you're doing it—but you're pulling some kinda weird crap with Lew's dreams.''

A self-deprecating shrug. ''And how am I supposed to be doin' that, Dillon? I'm just a plain little old nobody, remember? How am I supposed to get at a goddamned Welch, with all their goddamned luck?''

''I don't *know* how,'' Ronny shot back, ''but I'll tell you this much: it's gonna stop!''

Anson took a step closer and regarded Ronny contemptuously. ''And how do you plan to accomplish that? You snotty little cripple.''

Ronny had to resist the urge to back up, but managed to stand his ground. ''I . . . I don't know,'' he stammered, suddenly at a loss for words. ''But you can be damned sure I'll do something.''

''What if I get to you *first*.''

''Try it!''

''I've *already* tried it. You're still wearin' the scar.''

''That was an accident. I was trying to act civilized.''

''You sayin' I'm not civilized?''

''Why *should* I, when you just said it for me?''

Anson glared at him and took another step closer, and Ronny knew he was being consciously subjected to physical intimidation. For the millionth time he cursed the infirmity that kept him from Anson's throat.

''You little son of a bitch,'' Anson snarled, practically

in Ronny's face. "You're just hidin' behind that crutch, aren't you? If you didn't have that I'd beat the everlastin' shit out of you!"

"That didn't stop you before," Ronny challenged. "Besides, you beat up women, you beat up guys when they're sleeping."

"And I also have my pride."

"Which means you won't do it where anybody can see you."

"Which means I'm gonna ram your teeth down your throat if you don't shut the fuck up."

Ronny had no reply.

"See, see?" Anson crowed, spinning around to address the room at large. "Push him to the wall and he clams up tighter'n a nun's cunt."

"Bullshit!"

He whirled on Ronny again, face reddening with rage. "*Okay*, Dillon," he warned. "One day we're gonna have it out. One day you're gonna step out from behind that crutch, and I'm not gonna pull any punches!"

"And when that happens," Ronny shot back, "I'm not gonna pull any either!"

Somewhere a bell sounded.

"Better run," Anson chortled, easing just far enough aside to clear a path for the door. "Wouldn't want you to be late for class.

"But don't worry too much about Lew," he added, as Ronny thrust into the hall. "He's got his luck to protect him—but I suppose you don't understand about that, not bein' a Welch and all."

But Ronny suddenly had the oddest feeling that Anson was wrong.

Chapter 15

Smithing 102

Welch County High School
Thursday, April 12—3:00 P.M.

A burst of steam around his hand, and Ronny caught the first glint of silver as two more tiny metal warriors emerged into the light of day. Not counting one that he was going to try casting in bronze, they were the last of the seven he had shown Winnie two days before, and he already had eight more ready to pour plaster around as soon as he got the time: ones he'd sculpted mostly by sneaking wads of wax into study hall or lunch or into particularly dull and undemanding classes. Nights were for studying, watching TV, or playing Nintendo, and afternoons after school were reserved for the Road Man. And meanwhile, Project Crutch was moving along just dandy, though how far he would carry his augmentations, he had not yet decided. There was still one more week to be spent on casting in class, and he suspected he might be able to persuade Mr. Wiley to grant him some extracurricular access to the torches if he asked nicely—perhaps he might even lend him one. But as far as having an actual *goal* in mind at which point he would consider the project "finished," he didn't. Presumably when the crutch became so encrusted with battling warriors it could accommodate no more. And at the rate he was going that would not be long at all.

He had only made one change since his initial design: given that the whole thing was supposed to represent a climactic battle between Law and Chaos, he'd decided to cast the forces of Chaos—of whom the already-sculpted Anson clone was one—from brass and bronze, not silver. They were the adversaries, after all, the base metals that could never be transmuted into gold. Besides, it would give him an opportunity to work with materials he had no previous experience with. In fact, if he had time in the remaining week, he might try casting even more metals, or *maybe* attempt to create some exotic alloys of his own, possibly even *mixing* different metals in one mold—to make a sword or shield or cloak of a different material from the body to which it was attached.

And those were only a *few* of the projects he had lined up. Meanwhile he poked the dripping mass of crumbling plaster with a pencil until he had freed the boy and girl who had been helping each other evade the threatening metallic Anson. He'd even considered making them look like himself and Winnie, but had decided that since he already had plans for their miniature analogs, it would be vain to include himself/themselves twice. But since he liked the idea of incorporating his friends into his works, he had reshaped the faces to resemble his old girlfriend, Anita, and his lost best friend, Aaron. It was the least he could do, though he wondered why he even bothered. He'd gotten exactly one letter apiece from them, from which he had divined from between the lines that they were dating.

Fine.

The very idea made him stab the male figure a shade too hard, so that he feared for a moment he had damaged it, but fortunately he was wrong, and an instant later he held two more completed warriors in his hand. Wiley obligingly checked by, but only nodded wearily and muttered, "Call me if there's something you *can't* do, and I'll see if I can muck it up further," and left. As for the rest of the class, they no longer clustered around, but neither did he detect the envious hostility that had heretofore been the norm. Was it possible, he dared to wonder, that he was actually on his way to being *accepted*?

Something had certainly changed in the last couple of days, though its exact nature was far too subtle for Ronny to divine. Maybe it was because he had paired up with Winnie and that her friends were therefore including him in their circle, even as Lewis's chums (though he had relatively few really close ones, in spite of his general popularity) were likewise including him in theirs. Or perhaps it was merely the fact that word had gotten out about how he had stood up to Anson.

There *had* been witnesses to their verbal altercation in the rest room, after all, and by no means all had been Anson's partisans. As for Anson himself, Ronny had had no more trouble from him, though whether that was because of Ronny's intimations that he knew more about whatever Anson was up to than he was telling, or merely circumstance, he had no idea. He *hoped* the former but was also a little nervous about it, for fear Anson would call his bluff. He *did* know something was up, he strongly suspected it was something very weird indeed, and he hadn't a clue what it was.

Probably, Ronny thought as he scooped the plaster detritus into a convenient trash can before carrying his latest trophies to his worktable for a final inspection, de-flashing, and polishing, he should simply ask Lew; they talked about everything else, after all. But something—besides Aunt Erin's warning—told him that would not be wise. Even if Lew *did* remember anything (and so far he'd shown no sign of it), Ronny suspected that he probably wouldn't be able to reveal much more than he already knew. And if Lew did *not* remember, Ronny doubted he'd be doing his friend a service by reminding him of suppressed unpleasantnesses.

Except that *nobody* should be able to erase several hours of a very traumatic night from someone's mind simply by exposing them to fumes. What Aunt Erin had been up to there, he absolutely could not fathom. And how she had learned such esoterica he did not want to imagine.

And in any event, what *ought* to concern him now was figuring out precisely where these latest two figures should go.

He was still trying various arrangements, still gently adjusting limbs and torsos and heads, when the dismissal bell sounded.

Which meant that in less than two minutes he would get to see Winnie.

She was the other good thing in his life that had not been present a week ago, and they were getting along famously, though a part of him still distrusted both his motivations and hers. After all, there was always the chance she was hanging out with him because she felt sorry for him, though if that was true she was doing a first-rate job of concealing it. And there *was* the fact that, as twin victims of Anson's malice, they shared a certain mutual suffering which made them natural allies. And finally, to be perfectly honest, he suspected she was still in awe of his Welch connections and might be seeking subconscious security from that association—especially since he and Lewis were among the few willing to stand up to Anson.

That she might also, as she had intimated two days before, still carry a small torch for the troublesome bully, he did not want to contemplate at all, any more than he wanted to imagine what sort of intimacies might have transpired between Winnie and Anson during the almost-two months they had dated. He was too much of a gentleman to ask, and all she had volunteered was that she'd certainly never given Anson as much as he wanted. Ronny had to make do with that.

Still, he was not exactly comforted by what passed between them when they met on the steps above the parking
lot a few minutes later, preparatory to collecting their cars
and departing. Ronny had asked, as he'd asked every day
since Tuesday, if Winnie would accompany him to the Road
Man's camp, adding before Winnie could reply, "There's
really no *reason* for you to be afraid—besides, I'll protect
you, I promise."

And, as always, she'd shaken her head and given him
the same excuse. "Sorry, but he just gives me the shivers.
Besides, I've got a *really* busy schedule after school today."

"Like what?"

There was the merest shadow of discomfort in Winnie's
reply, a brief, downturned twitching of her lips that stopped
just short of grimace, as if something were gnawing at her
she did not want to reveal. "Well, first, I'm going over to
Marilyn's to do some homework, and after that I have an
important errand, and after that I have to—"

"What *kind* of errand?" Ronny interrupted, more forcefully than he'd intended.

The incipient grimace manifested. "Sorry, but I can't tell
you. It's no big deal. Just something I was asked to do."

"Well, *that's* mighty cryptic."

Winnie would not meet his eyes. "I have a meeting."

"With who?"

"With—Ronny, won't you just trust me with this?"

"When you don't trust *me* enough to tell me who you're
going to see? Why should I?"

Anger flashed in Winnie's eyes, and Ronny realized he'd
let his own disappointment rouse ire of an entirely different
kind. "Sorry," he whispered, risking a shy smile. "I had
no right to say that."

"Yes," Winnie replied slowly, "you did. I'd have said
the same thing in the same circumstances."

"Which leaves us where we were."

"Yeah."

"How 'bout if I said 'please'?"

"Okay, okay . . . it's not that big a deal anyway. I'm going over to Mr. Welch's, *okay*?"

"Mr. Welch's! What does *he* want with you?"

Winnie shrugged uncomfortably. "Heck if I know. I got word—via Anson, but don't get pissed, 'cause it was his doing, not mine—that Mr. Welch *needed* to see me. But I really couldn't go until today."

Ronny gaped incredulously, torn between amusement and indignation. "You mean you . . . ?"

Winnie chuckled in spite of herself. "I kept a Welch waiting."

Ronny sighed glumly. "Well, at least that means you're not gonna be seeing anybody else, I guess."

"No danger," Winnie assured him. Ronny thought he detected a trace of nervousness there, as if there really *was* something she wasn't saying.

"I hope not!" Ronny forced himself to laugh. And with that they exchanged a quick hug and a brief but passionate kiss that did not go unobserved by either classmates or the looming Ms. Shepherd.

And then Winnie sprinted across the parking lot, climbed into her four-year-old black Mustang, and followed Marilyn Bridges (who had been none-too-patiently waiting in her mother's Audi) out of the parking lot.

A short while later, Ronny was back at the Road Man's camp.

That his sometime-mentor had visitors should not have struck Ronny as odd, given what he knew about the tinker's supposed avocation as itinerant preacher and jack-of-all-trades—and given that there had been at least a dozen other cars besides his parked along the north side of Swanson's Meadow. But he was still taken aback to thread his way through the circle of machines (rustic ones again, though of less risqué configuration than he *had* seen) and find himself confronting what to all intents and purposes was a revival.

The Road Man's congregation numbered roughly twenty people, mostly middle-aged farmer types (of which Welch County boasted not as many as one might have expected from a rural area), at least two of whom were, to judge by the license plates Ronny had noted on his way in, from neighboring Union and Fannin counties. Still flush from his latest success in shop class, and still a bit flushed in a different way from his even more recent encounter with Winnie, Ronny was not exactly in a mood to either receive the Holy Ghost or accept the Sweet Love of Jesus. On the other hand, he *was* working with the Road Man now, so he supposed anything he could learn about his mentor might be of some service. And since it was a still a couple of hours until sundown and he obviously wasn't going to be able to get to work immediately, he folded himself down as well as his leg would allow behind the last row of on-lookers.

And enjoyed the show.

The Road Man was standing behind his stump-and-anvil. He was in his Day Man manifestation, which meant he was unkempt, more than a little dirty, and brawnily shirtless. He also had a Bible in one hand and a ten-pound sledge-hammer in the other, and he was in full rant.

He had taken as his primary text the business in Isaiah 2:4 about beating swords into plowshares—and was actually engaged in approximately that activity as he spoke. Or at least Ronny suspected that the mangled mess of metal the sledgehammer was descending upon to emphasize points in the sermon had once been a sword—doubtlessly one of the cheap Spanish replicas he'd noticed affixed low down to the same side of the wagon that had produced his crutch.

As for his delivery—well, it was what Ronny thought of as old-time religion, given to short staccato bursts and bellows and frequent inquiries as to whether or not the congregation believed.

"What do you *see* when you *look* at me?" the Road Man shouted. "You see a man! You see a common man and a

strange man and a strong man. You see a man with no shirt
on because I'm a workin' man and God gave me this body
to do my work and I work best when I can use that body
freely, so that when I preach to you like this, I'm doin'
God's will better than if I was wearin' a silk necktie and
standin' in the pulpit—do you *believe* me?''

And the congregation rather bewilderedly replied with
variations on a theme of ''Amen'' and ''I believe'' and
''What you said.''

''And what did the Lord say?'' the Road Man went on.
''He said, 'Believe in me and I will make you fishers of
men.' He said, 'I will *make* you fishers of men.' Not 'you
will become,' but 'I will *make*'! And that's the most important thing a man can do in his life—to make. You make
a family and you make children and through them you make
a future. But most folks don't make much else. But what
did *God* do? What's the *first* thing that happens in the Bible,
what's the *first* verb you find in there? It's *made*! 'In the
beginnin' God *made* heaven and earth.' And that's what
we've got to do, brothers and sisters. That's the one way
we're like God! We can *make* things. Oh, you may not be
able to make much, but maybe you do a little embroidery,
or you paint pictures, or you do bodywork on your car, or
you build houses. But all those things are like worship,
'cause when you're makin', when you're usin' that great
and wonderful brain of yours to bring some new thing into
the world, that's when you're bein' most like God. He gave
you a gift, he gave all of you gifts. He gave me more gifts
and stranger ones than most. But what he's gonna judge
you by is what you do with those gifts. If you *can* play the
piano and you *don't* play the piano, and you don't let nobody
know you can play the piano, you're denyin' what God gave
you, and you know why that is? Because you're denyin'
yourself the pleasure you could have from that, and God
wants us to be happy and feel pleasure. And you're denyin'
your fellow man the pleasure of hearin' you and maybe
feelin' better than he did, and maybe knowin' you a little

better 'cause he can feel your feelin' in what and how you play. And you may be denyin' somebody else their future 'cause somewhere there might be a little child who'd never heard nobody play piano before and once he hears you, he never wants nothin' stronger in his life than to be like you, and to do something like that. And it may be the one thing that makes him happy, only if you don't do it, he'll never know—so that when you're denyin' your gifts, you're denyin' God—but not just to you, but to everybody—'cause you're keepin' one little spark of God asleep in somebody that might otherwise be awake! Say Amen!''

And they all, even Ronny, shouted ''Amen.''

''And now we shall talk once more about the sword and the plowshare,'' the Road Man went on, frequently pounding the unfortunate Toledo replica for emphasis. ''For there's a second side of makin', and that's makin' something good out of something bad.'' He went on from there for easily another fifteen minutes, extolling arguments of ever more convoluted complexity and doubtful spiritual veracity that Ronny was reasonably sure went right over the heads of most of his congregation, though they continued to voice their approval with appropriate responses from time to time. A certain amount of it was over Ronny's head as well, but a fair bit also meshed rather nicely with some of the tidbits of philosophy the Road Man had pummeled him with on Monday night. In fact, some of them meshed so closely that Ronny suspected the Road Man was laying them out here for his specific benefit.

But he absolutely was not prepared when, just as he was fairly certain the Road Man was winding things down to a conclusion that he had no doubt would involve the passing of a collection plate, the Road Man suddenly stared straight at him and shouted, ''Come here, young man, and testify!''

Ronny's first impulse was to bolt, his second to shake his head in denial, his third to say, very clearly, ''No thanks.'' But what he actually *did* was freeze and blush, and—without knowing why—make his way awkwardly to his feet and limp up beside the Road Man.

The Road Man looked him up and down, roughly, but not unkindly.

"You didn't *want* to testify, did you, boy?"

Ronny was still too shocked to reply, but managed to shake his head.

"*See*," the Road Man roared gleefully. "Here we have an example. This boy does not *want* to testify, yet he *knows* what I say is true, for he has *felt* the joy of makin'. But there is another kind of joy of makin', and that is of makin' things from oneself, and that is a lesson he is still learnin'—right, boy?"

Ronny forced himself to meet his eyes. "Right—I guess."

The Road Man grabbed him by the upper arm and shook him so hard he nearly fell down, and meanwhile he was grinning at the congregation and gesticulating broadly with his hammer-wielding hand.

"Aye, this boy is not here to speak to you, for that is not his art. What I have called him here for is to ask him questions, and those he only has to answer *yes* or *no*."

Ronny did not know how to respond, but the Road Man had so completely overawed him by then he was ready to do anything if only this trial would end.

"You enjoy makin', do you, boy: *yes* or *no*?"

"Yeah," Ronny managed.

"You enjoy makin' things with metal, *yes* or *no*?"

"Yeah."

"And you're good at it, or you think you're good at it, or people *tell* you you're good at it, *yes* or *no*?"

"Yeah, sure."

"And you never knew you had this art until you lost something else, did you?"

"Yeah, right." Ronny did not like where this was leading.

"And what did you lose?"

"That's not a *yes* or *no*," Ronny flared, releasing his suppressed anger.

"Okay, I'll change my question." The Road Man laughed. "You lost your leg—lost the ability to use it as a normal leg, *yes* or *no*?"

"You know I did."

"*Yes* or *no*?"

"*Yes*, dammit, *yes*!"

"All right, boy, you're gettin' *passionate* now, and I can just *feel* your soul wantin' to do some speakin', only it's afraid to talk in front of strangers and I won't make it do that today. But I gotta ask you anyhow: Were you happy then?"

"Yes! Yes, I was happy!" Ronny yelled angrily.

"But what *made* you happy? Yeah, I know that's not a *yes* or *no*, so I'll ask it another way. Was it the *swimmin'* that you did that made you happy? Or was it the *recognition* that made you happy? Was it the result or the act itself? If it was the result say *yes*."

"Yes," Ronny replied dully.

"And if it was the act as well, say that too."

Ronny froze. And before he quite knew he had done it, whispered, "*No*."

"And what do you like better now, swimmin' or makin'? If it's swimmin' say *yes*."

Ronny did not answer.

"And if it's makin' things, say *no*."

"No," Ronny gritted. "No, wait, *yes*. I like making things."

"And by that your soul is filled. *Yes* or *no*?"

"*Yes*," Ronny replied heavily.

"And so is mine," the Road Man said beaming, "for I have made of this boy a new thing!"

The congregation heartily 'Amened.'

"But in order to keep makin' these new things," the Road Man went on, "why, the old Road Man, he needs money, so if those of you who are so minded could kindly drop a dollar or two or ten or a hundred in my old iron wash pot''—and Ronny noticed a handsome kettle for the first time, conveniently placed near the right side of the congregation—"I'd be mightily appreciative. And those of you who do, I'll bless, and those of you who don't, I'll wonder why you had the money to buy gas to come get religion, but don't have money to keep that religion alive."

Sensing that he was no longer the center of the spotlight, Ronny slunk behind the nearest of the machines (which was vigorously kneading some kind of foul-smelling dough), and tried to become invisible. And meanwhile, the clearing resounded with the low buzz of voices and the sounds of coins and bills being pitched into the pot.

And then the crowd was ambling away and he and the Road Man were once more alone. Almost an hour had passed him by, an hour in which he had hoped to be working on his knife.

"Ready to begin?" the Road Man asked, as soon as he had hung the kettle (apparently with its contents still intact) under the wagon.

Ronny nodded eagerly. If he had planned right, today should just about finish the rough work on the blade. They had chosen material on Tuesday, and the Road Man had spent most of the session talking about the qualities of various metals, but had allowed Ronny his own choice among the various bits of bar stock he had to hand.

And yesterday, he had learned about heating and folding. That had been by far the most physically demanding bit of metalwork he had attempted so far, but the tinker had made him do every bit of it alone, merely demonstrating on a piece of scrap. Still, once Ronny had got the hang of it, it had actually seemed fairly easy: first you heated the bar in the forge while pumping its bellows vigorously with your foot, then you flattened it with a hammer, then you heated it once more and folded it upon itself, then repeated the process over and over. "You can fold it as often as you like," the Road Man had told him. "Some fine Japanese swords have two hundred folds. But you don't need that many to make the knife you want, and once you know how to fold, the rest is your own choice. Now let me show you a bit about how to hold your hammer, and where and how hard to hit.''

And Ronny had watched, and imitated, and had had absolutely no trouble at all matching the Road Man's technique exactly. It felt completely natural, as if it was something he had been doing all his life.

Today he had hoped to spend half the time folding, and the rest tempering and quenching. Then would come days of shaping and grinding and polishing and re-tempering, and edging, and Lord knew how many other steps; and between times he would work on the molds for the hilt, which he planned to cast in gold if he could somehow prompt Aunt Erin to come up with something expendable made of that metal.

Thus, it was to his very great surprise that the Road Man did *not* bring out the implements he had used the days before, or the cardboard box that contained both Ronny's drawings and the incipient blade itself.

Instead, he presented Ronny with a box containing miscellaneous bits of junk metal, including a fair bit of costume jewelry; though there was also a pair of broken candlesticks, one silver, one brass; a set of unmatched spoons rather like the ones he was rendering down into warriors; a few bits of bar stock; and three old watchcases as well.

"I thought we were going to work on the knife," Ronny muttered, at once confused and irate, since he'd already wasted what was to him a precious hour.

But the Road Man shook his head. "This is not the time for that," he said. "There will be time for that along and along, but this is time for another thing."

"But I need to finish the knife before . . . before you leave. You've got to show me how."

"I *will* show you how, too—or one of us will. But the

Night Man said to tell you that today was not a good day for you to work on the knife.''

"So what am I supposed to work on then?" Ronny snapped. "Or should I just leave?"

"Go or stay as pleases you," the Road Man replied promptly. "You will learn nothing if you leave; you will certainly learn something if you stay."

Ronny rolled his eyes and bit his lip in exasperation.

"It's your choice, though."

"Okay, okay," Ronny gritted. "I'll stay, I'll stay. So, uh, what's the deal with all that stuff?"

"The Night Man said to give it to you," the Road Man informed him. "He says he never sees you anymore, so I'm to give it to you. And I'm to tell you to make something out of it."

Ronny peered dubiously at the junk. "But *what*?"

The Road Man shrugged. "He didn't say. All he said was that while I was teachin' you how to make stuff with your hands and head, you ought also to be makin' something with your heart and soul."

Ronny inclined his head toward the crutch. "I thought that's what *this* is."

The Road Man shrugged once more. "Mr. Night Man says that's not enough. He says you should make something for somebody else, something you can fill up with love."

"Love?"

"You've got a girlfriend, don't you? Good-lookin' boy like you oughta have lots of girlfriends. Oughta *cleave* to 'em as much as he can, if you know what I mean. Boy like you is *ripe* for cleavin', got them man-juices flowin' stronger than they ever will again. Got a hundred million little wigglers a day just a-*dyin'* for a chance to do some cleavin' . . .''

Ronny wished the Road Man would change the subject. He liked him fine—when they were talking about metalwork. But when the Road Man brought up his other fixations . . . well, Ronny wasn't so sure about them.

"Well, answer me, boy," the Road Man bellowed. "You

got a girlfriend, don't you? 'Cause if you don't, I'd sure like to know who's been puttin' perfume on you and smearin' your face with lipstick like the Whore of Babylon.''

"Yeah," Ronny admitted. "I guess I do. Or anyway, I'm interested in one, and I think she kinda likes me."

"Then you ought to make her something. Make her something special."

"Like what?"

"You decide—but let your heart decide, not your head."

"But how do I do that?"

The Road Man held out the box. "Just prowl around in here and choose whatever you fancy. Not something you can use for any purpose, just what draws your eye. Don't worry if it's old, it can be made new; don't worry if it's flimsy, it can be made strong. Just find those objects that speak to you."

Ronny shrugged and peered into the box once more.

The first piece that caught his eyes was one of the empty watchcases—probably nineteenth-century gold and worth a bundle. The second was a spool of copper wire so red it was almost auburn. The third was a piece of costume jewelry encrusted with what he supposed were bogus pearls. And the fourth was the pedestal that had once supported a silver candlestick.

Without asking, he removed them and set them aside.

"Interestin'," the Road Man mused. "You ain't proud to take the best, are you? But that's okay, 'cause a man ought to use the best when he's makin' something for his woman."

Ronny eyed the material—it comprised barely a double handful—dubiously. "I don't have a clue what to do with this stuff."

"Your heart'll know. Just start foolin' around with 'em. I've got a jeweler's kit if you wanta use something like that."

Ronny puffed his cheeks thoughtfully and wondered when

exactly he had decided to make Winnie a piece of jewelry. In fact, now he considered it, sometime in the last minute or so he had settled on a bracelet. A silver and copper and gold and pearl bracelet.

"Got a pencil and paper so I can do some designing?" he asked shyly.

The Road glared at him. "That'd get your head into the act, and I'm not supposed to let you do that."

"Oh, for heaven's sake!"

"Heaven has nothing to do with it. This is between you and your lady and a pile of junk."

"Great!" Ronny grunted with heavy sarcasm.

"If you need any specific help, about melting or forming or anything, let me know," the Road Man told him. "Now, I gotta go wake up the Sunset Man. He gets pissed if he don't get his daily baptizin'—takes him about an hour to get goin' good."

Ronny ignored him and began examining the bits of metal. He hadn't a clue as to what to do with them, except that he had somehow conjured a vague image that involved melting the silver down into a U-shaped strip, cutting slots in it, and then weaving the copper through them. He'd inlay a design in gold over *that*, and then stick pearls here and there across the whole thing. Mostly what he did, however, was simply fondle the objects, feel how they hefted, how their surfaces were worked. And almost, he discovered, he could tell silver from gold merely by how they felt, by how they held his body heat and reflected it back. He wondered if it was just him, or if everybody had that knack.

Before he knew it, he was softly singing: Neil Young's "Down By the River," of all unlikely tunes.

He had just come to the second verse when a heavy hand thumped onto his shoulder. He started so violently he nearly fell, and whirled around angrily to confront a grim-faced Road Man, now in the red jogging suit, and with a towel flung over his arm.

"Jesus, man, don't *do* that!" he cried. "You scared the everlasting crap outta me."

"Crap *is* everlasting, isn't it?" the Road Man mused, looking remarkably serious. "I'd never thought of that. That's the third thing that's inevitable besides death and taxes—'cept I don't pay no taxes. But even I crap, and—"

"Just don't do that again!"

"I won't if you won't."

"I don't plan to."

"That's not what I meant."

"Then what *did* you mean?"

"I won't scare you again if you won't sing."

"Well, I'm sorry it bugs you, but I know it's not *that* bad!"

"It's not bad at all—quality-wise. But you need to be careful about things like that."

"Why?"

"Because songs have power. And if you sing while you make something, you might accidentally give it power."

"Give me a break!"

"I am, and I have before; several, in fact."

"Jesus!"

"—Has nothing to do with it. What it *does* have to do with is the fact that things have power because you give them power, and if you're going to give them power, you'd better be careful what kind of power it is that you're passin' 'round."

Ronny could not reply.

And the Road Man, in his incarnation as the Sunset Man, gazed toward the western horizon and announced, "It must be 'bout time for you to be gettin' home."

"Yeah," Ronny replied, feeling an odd sense of relief, "I guess it is."

"Oh, by the way," the Road Man added, as Ronny packed up the proto-bracelet. "Come back the same time tomorrow—earlier if you can."

"I'd planned to."

"And one *other* thing."

"What?"

"Tell your aunt she needs to take better care of her Silence."

Which left Ronny completely flabbergasted.

Chapter 16

The Lady and the Tiger

Cardalba Hall
Thursday, April 12—4:00 P.M.

Winnie did not like lying to Ronny. She did not, in fact, *like* lying to anyone. Nor did she enjoy being duplicitous or telling half-truths—like the one she had foisted off on the poor boy when they had parted after school. And she *had* told him all she could: that she was going to see Mr. Welch and that the Man Himself had sent word to that effect. What she had *not* added was that she still considered herself bound by her agreement with Anson, which was that she would go to Cardalba under her own power, but that Anson would make the introductions.

Now, as she wheeled her Mustang along the tree-lined back road that curved along the Talooga toward Cardalba Hall, she wondered about the wisdom of agreeing to even that much. Oh, she wasn't worried about herself in particular, or at least not about the sanctity of her person. She'd told Marilyn everything, after all, and had stressed, in no uncertain terms, that if she hadn't returned by six o'clock,

Marilyn was to come looking for her. She'd also informed Anson of the same thing by phone the night before. He'd had no problem with it, to the point of being nonchalant about the whole affair, as if whatever hostility he'd formerly held toward her had completely dissipated.

As for her family, she'd likewise felt honor-bound to level with them. They certainly hadn't *suffered* from Welch patronage, and Mr. Welch had been instrumental in finding her father a job when they'd moved to Cordova in the early eighties. Indeed, in many ways her folks held the Welch Clan in more superstitious awe than many of the natives— if for no other reason than because they, having lived in places where Luck was not a purchasable commodity, had a standard of comparison. And it was a fact that Welch County was prosperous, that everyone was employed and fairly well, and that nobody really lacked for money. That it was all owed in some mysterious way to the Welches she did not doubt. How that was actually effected, she had no idea.

But the fact was that when a Welch, especially *the* Welch, snapped his fingers in your direction, you jumped. And if anybody *knew* he'd snapped them in your direction, you made doubly sure to jump real far, high, and fast, 'cause if you didn't *everybody* would know you were a fool and entitled to whatever misfortune came your way.

Winnie wondered if she was in for good luck or bad.

Whichever it was, she'd find out in about five minutes. She could already see the roofs and gables of Cardalba Hall looming above the surrounding trees on its knoll less than a mile away on the left. And she was coming up fast on the intersection where the gravel road that led right to Anson's place entered this one, which was where he was supposed to meet her.

Sure enough, there he was: she could see the shark-nose of his Trans Am poking out from behind the stand of trees that screened the road until one was nearly upon it. He had pulled onto the shoulder and was idling. She slowed as well and eased right. Anson had seen her now, for he flashed her a grin and salute. She replied with a terse nod and waved him out ahead of her. He grimaced but complied, and turned out onto the gravel. Winnie gave her mirrors a quick check and fell in behind him, though she held rather far back for fear of the stones the Pontiac's big tires constantly flung up from the loose gravel.

So it was, then, that little more than a minute after she'd entered Anson's wake, his left turn signal blinked on, followed almost instantly by the flash of brake lights as he swung hard left over the ancient stone bridge that marked the nearer entrance to Cardalba Plantation. Winnie felt every cobble filter up through the Mustang's stiff suspension, and discovered to her dismay that she was very soon going to have to go to the bathroom—probably a function of nerves as much as anything else. As for Anson, he was now trundling along at a virtual snail's pace while he waited for her to catch up. She did, and followed him along another stretch of smoothly paved road, then left again into the wide paved turnaround at the foot of the avenue of boxwoods that led up to Cardalba's front door.

In spite of the fact that she had lived in Welch County for years, Winnie had never been this close to the Welches' seat of power and was both impressed and disappointed. The house itself was large and imposing, in excellent repair, and perfectly situated for effect. But it was also rather lackluster in design. It was made of wood, for one thing, not the stone or brick she associated with the palatial estates of Druid Hills in her native Atlanta. And the two-story porch that graced three-fourths of the front (the other fourth was projecting bay window) was plain and unadorned, free of the ornate carving and frivolous bric-a-brac that were trademarks of the high Victorian style that had been popular a few years before the current Cardalba Hall was built.

But what the Welch family seat lacked in actual presence, it more than made up in reputation, and though the day was clear, the sun bright, and the yard dotted with dandelions and daffodils, Winnie was almost physically ill with apprehension.

Still, she had no choice but to soldier on, so she steeled herself, stopped the car directly behind Anson's, turned off the ignition, and climbed out, pausing only to hit the power door-lock switch.

And blinked at the sudden change of atmosphere. For here, outside the Mustang's solar-filmed environment, the sunlight was almost too bright to bear—so cheery, in fact, that she fished in her purse, pulled out her sunglasses, and put them on. And thus fortified with new clean jeans, white blouse, and sleeveless emerald-green sweater, she waited for Anson, who was still fiddling with something inside his car, to join her. When he finally did a moment later, she was struck anew with how much better he looked when he wasn't being sullen. In truth, he looked—there was no other way to describe it—lighthearted. But she nevertheless gave him a cool reception when he strolled over to her and gazed curiously at her an uncomfortably long time before speaking.

"So you really did make it?" he drawled at last. "I was afraid you'd stand me up."

"I don't lie, Anson," she replied shortly. "Not unless I absolutely have to. Besides, there's half a dozen people who know where I am."

Anson chuckled obligingly (and phonily, Winnie thought). "I like a woman who's cautious."

"You didn't like me being cautious last Friday night," she shot back before she could stop herself.

Anson merely shrugged and grinned. "We all make mistakes. That 'un was my biggest—but I guess you're gonna go on remindin' me about it for the rest of my life."

"I hope I never have to remind you about it again," Winnie snapped. "Now, can we get this show on the road?"

"On the walk, actually," Anson countered with another chuckle Winnie suspected was intended to put her at ease but did not. He offered her his arm, but she pointedly ignored it and slipped in front of him to precede him up the walk.

The closer she got, the more impressive Cardalba Hall became, and numerous details she hadn't noticed earlier began to catch her eye. Like the way every windowpane was perfectly clean, without a trace of paint overlap, like the fact that the grounds were exquisitely tended (except for the odd dandelions), like the way that even at a distance she could tell that all the exterior hardware was polished to within an inch of its life, and that there were no stray leaves or twigs or loose shingles on the jutting gables. Even the four ornate brick chimney tops visible from this side were clean—they all worked, too: she'd seen smoke drifting up from them the previous winter.

Still, she was not prepared when she found herself walking up the steps, or when Anson eased her gently aside so he could rap smartly on the massive oak front door.

Nor did she expect to be greeted by Matthew Welch himself. Somehow she'd assumed that a man living alone with his mother (though she'd heard the rarely-seen Miss Martha Welch was out of town right now) in such an enormous house would of necessity have servants. On the other hand, she'd never actually *heard* of any permanent ones. Matthew spread his trade around a lot and never quibbled about price, and she knew plenty of people—mostly boys— who had earned a fair income doing odd jobs in or about Cardalba. Presumably Matthew himself, or perhaps his mother, was up to housecleaning chores. Or maybe he brought in help from outside, since she'd also heard reports of cars with out-of-state tags sitting at the turnaround for days at a time.

But it *was* Matthew who opened the door, and Matthew who peered out and smiled like a carnival showman when he discovered that it was Anson, and that he'd brought company. A sideways glance included her in his largess, and before she knew what was happening, Winnie found herself following Anson into the comfortable, sun-dusted warmth of Cardalba's front hall.

"Come in, Anson, come in," Matthew was enthusing, as he steered them toward the first door to the left. "And this must be Winnie—long time no see, my girl. You look a lot like your mother, by the way, which is by no means an insult."

Winnie was rather taken aback by the old man's easy manner and, in spite of herself, began to relax. For whatever else he was, the Master of Cardalba was certainly neither an egomaniac, nor the imperious, crotchety old man she'd expected. He was also somewhat shorter than she'd been led to believe—roughly Lew's height—which helped put her at ease. Never mind that there was a sort of hopeful tiredness around his eyes that at once made him seem more accessible and hinted at ill health. Even the house, though full of priceless antiques of every description, exuded a homey quality that Winnie found remarkably soothing.

"Thank you," she said abruptly, blushing when she realized she had been too busy staring around to reply to Matthew's compliment.

"You're welcome," Matthew replied easily, ushering them into the front parlor. "The pleasure is mine, since I'm the one who gets to look at you."

Winnie's hackles rose immediately, for it had sounded suspiciously like the prelude to a come-on. For the briefest moment her eyes sought left for the scanty security afforded by Anson's presence. But Anson wasn't paying attention at all; he was merely meandering restlessly around, pausing at this objet d'art or that, as if he were in a museum he had explored too frequently.

Winnie remained where she was until an expansive wave of Matt's hand indicated she should take her choice among burgundy velvet chairs and sofas. She chose one of the former—with high arms for added security—sat, placed her purse in her lap, and folded her hands primly atop it.

Meanwhile, Matt had crossed to a lace-doilied table by

the door and was filling two grayish-red earthenware mugs from a matching pitcher. He retained one and offered the other to Winnie. "It's a mint julep," he informed her smoothly. "Your favorite, isn't it?" he added with a wink. "Though you don't want your mother or father to know, correct?"

Winnie started at that. She'd hoped she'd been sufficiently discreet about her brief experiments with alcohol to keep such information under wraps. Not even Anson knew, for heaven's sake, or at least she'd never told him. On the other hand, if *anybody* would know, she supposed it would be Mr. Welch.

"Thanks," Winnie said softly, accepting the mug but ignoring the rest of the question.

"My pleasure," Matthew replied, eyeing her keenly. "Now, if you'll excuse me, I must say farewell to your young . . . associate. It was I who asked him to bring you here, you know. But I have no intention whatever of conducting this meeting under his auspices."

And *that* was certainly a perplexing remark. The *tone* had been cordial enough, but the words contained just enough implicit threat and hostility to make her wonder if perhaps there was some unseen strain or contention between them.

Still, a glance at Anson seemed to indicate that if he had been clandestinely insulted, it had slipped right past him. For Anson simply grinned again, shrugged, set down the matte-porcelain Venus de Milo he'd been molesting, and sauntered toward the door Matthew had already opened for him.

"Thanks," Matthew murmured, as Anson slipped by. "I'll be in touch about future services."

"No problem," Anson called from the hall. "If you need anything, just holler."

And Winnie found herself alone with the Master of Cardalba.

He sat down opposite her and allowed himself a healthy

swig from his julep—whereupon Winnie realized she hadn't even tasted hers. She did, and found it excellent.

"They're a little hokey, I'll admit," Matthew told her, wiping his mouth delicately on a silk handkerchief. "Maybe a touch too Old South. On the other hand, there's something to be said for the Old South. Just because something's old doesn't mean it's bad, after all. It merely means you ought to reexamine it once in a while to see if its validity still holds."

"Yeah, I can see that, I guess," Winnie replied carefully, trying to mask her uneasiness with another sip of drink.

"And I can see that you're a very nervous young lady," Matthew went on. "And I want to tell you right now you've no need to be. I want exactly nothing out of you right now. My primary interest in you at the moment is academic."

"What do you mean?" Winnie managed in a low voice, having noticed the use of "right now" and "at the moment."

Matt's left eyebrow lifted delicately. "Well . . ." he began, taking another swig, "as you are no doubt aware, I enjoy keeping up on current affairs. Specifically, I like to keep my eyes and ears open regarding the life of this county. I like to know who's doing what with whom, how often and how well. And if I begin getting either very good reports or very bad reports about certain people, well . . . let's just say I sometimes give that person a look-see for myself. I like things to run smoothly, Winnie, and if something is upsetting affairs, I like to know."

"But I . . . haven't done anything."

Matthew rolled his eyes in self-effacing exasperation, then smiled reassuringly. "No, of course you haven't. I wasn't implying that at all. What I've heard about *you* is all good. Of course I'll admit I hadn't heard much concerning you at all until the last year or so. Then again, that's often the way with young people, and to be perfectly honest, I don't really *care* much for young people—they're too changeable, too flighty in their passions—though their passions *are* quite grand ones, don't you think?''

"I suppose so," Winnie ventured. She faked another swallow, not wishing to lose whatever edge sobriety might afford her. She also wished Mr. Welch would get to his point, whatever it was.

"Quite right," Matthew affirmed offhandedly. "But the point I was making is that I've been hearing a *lot* of good things about you. Very good things—and not all from Anson, let me hasten to add, not by any means. And since I know you're wondering what those things might be but are too polite to ask, let me tell you that I've heard you've been helping your parents out in their store even when you didn't want to, even at the expense of as full a social life as some of your friends. And I've heard that everybody you've waited on thinks you're marvelously helpful and excruciatingly polite. I've heard you get along fine with your brother, and I've heard you're in the top five percent of your class and climbing. You don't swear unless you're angry, don't do drugs under any circumstances, and you drink only a little under very safe and controlled circumstances. Oh, and I've heard you are, shall we say, an uncommonly virtuous young lady when it comes to *traditional* virtue. Am I correct?''

Winnie did not know how to respond. To give Mr. Welch an affirmative would sound far too egotistical, and though she supposed his observations were mostly true, she was not really conscious of them as *good* things; they were simply the way she was. She did good things because those were the sorts of things she did, not because there were rewards for being good or punishments for being bad.

So the best she could manage by way of reply was a careful ''Well, that's very flattering, but I don't know if I can quite live up to *that* sterling a reputation.''

"A reputation *is* a hard thing to live up to, isn't it?"

Matthew chuckled. "I know . . . I've had to live with one all my life."

"I suppose you have," Winnie replied.

Matthew finished his drink and shifted in his chair. "So tell me about yourself."

Winnie's brow wrinkled in perplexity. "What do you want to know? Seems like you know a lot already."

"Only what I've heard, but I want to know more—what do you do for entertainment, what're your favorite foods, who's your favorite actor, what kind of music do you enjoy?"

That took Winnie off guard. Those were much more the sort of questions she was accustomed to from guidance counselors than from patrician Southern gentlemen. But something about Mr. Welch's manner told her he really was interested in what she had to say, so that in spite of herself she found herself responding.

They talked until she had drained her julep and the sun was westering. A glance at her watch told her it was nearing six, which was when she had promised herself she would leave. But in the surprisingly brief hour her interview had lasted, she'd found herself confessing that she liked Joust but hated Mario Brothers; that she thought New Kids were cute but their music was bland, that U2 was good but pretentious, as was Kate Bush; that R.E.M. were fine, but preachy; that she'd started watching "Ninja Turtles" in spite of herself; and that she was certain Fords were better than Chevys. She'd also confessed to a fondness for the color green, slim guys as opposed to muscular ones, Sandman comics, fast dancing, and Italian food; and admitted to missing the zoo in Atlanta and cruising the malls with her mom—to which she had added that she *also* liked being by herself and long walks in the country. Additionally, she had somehow confided that she did want to get married but wanted no more than two children, that she hoped to attend college outside the South, and that in spite of the fact that she had numerous friends in Welch

County, she had no desire whatever to spend the rest of her life in north Georgia.

And finally, she'd found herself admitting to having a crush on Ronny Dillon and a serious dislike for Anson Bowman (for which she'd apologized profusely), whom she insisted had used her badly. Matthew had frowned at this last revelation, but his tut-tutting had been directed at Anson, not at her. His only actual comment had been something to the effect that Anson was not a happy boy, he didn't think, and probably with good reason, given the way children tended to treat the un-fathered. And that a lot of his show-offishness was insecurity. As for Anson's tendency toward violence, well, Matt hoped he would grow out of that. *He* had, he admitted. "All he needs is to feel good about himself," Matthew confided. "The rest will take care of itself."

"You must really like him," Winnie replied, more sympathetically than she intended. She'd *planned* to keep this interview short and the conversation remote and controlled—and had failed utterly, unable to resist Matthew Welch's very real, if somewhat superficial and affected, charm. The man was phony as a three-dollar bill—and as fascinating.

Matthew shrugged. "There's much to like and much to dislike about Anson. But I also think there's more to young Mr. Bowman than most folks suspect. Mark me, he'll go far when he gets a little mellowness on him. Twenty years from now you'll return to Cordova and see that he's changed remarkably."

"You think he'll *stay* in Cordova?" Winnie asked in surprise. "I kind of figured somebody as wild as he is would split as soon as he could and go to Atlanta or somewhere."

Matthew shook his head emphatically. "No, that boy's roots are here, and here he'll stay—mark my words."

Winnie checked her watch again.

Matthew saw her, as she'd hoped he would. He sighed

and rose to his feet. "Ah, but you have to be going, don't you?"

Winnie nodded. "I promised a friend I'd drop by for supper."

"Wisely," Matthew replied cryptically. "Well, I won't detain you—but I *would* like to entertain you again sometime."

"Thanks," Winnie told him noncommittally, and rose as well.

Matthew saw her to the door.

"Thank *you*," he said. "You have graced my house as it has not been graced in a long time. And I look forward to you gracing it again. After all, I have a virtually *infinite* supply of mint juleps."

"That was good too," Winnie acknowledged. "Thanks again."

"Good-bye."

And with that Winnie stepped out into the late afternoon light, feeling uncannily light, as if she had been relieved of some terrible burden. Probably it was the alcohol, she told herself. Probably that was it—and being free of any further obligation to Anson.

But she hoped it would be a long time before she once more set foot in Cardalba Hall.

Matthew, however, hoped it would not be long at all. Winnie was a *wonderful* girl, he'd decided at once. Very bright and a potentially fine conversationalist, as the departed Lenore was not. That one had known which side her bread was buttered on and had been content with being materially pampered and the security life at Cardalba brought her. Winnie would be a bigger risk, but the rewards would be greater as well. Besides, she had a huge amount of Strength to offer—much more than Lenore. And it was Strength of which he was very much in need.

Working with Anson was keeping him drained, and though he worked hard to retain the illusion of normalcy, he suspected Anson knew he now had the upper hand, both physically and in the realm of the Winds, where the boy was displaying remarkable flexibility, range, and staying power. He also knew that his grandson was an amazingly quick study (which would have borne out years of arguments with his mother about the viability of the male line as well as confirming certain *other* suspicions), and that Anson was without a doubt augmenting his ''studies'' with experiments of his own. What the boy would be able to achieve when he had a footholder to draw on, Matthew could not imagine. Nor did he intend to let Anson find out anytime soon.

What he *had* wanted to determine he now had, which was that Winnie Cowan would make a first-class replacement for Lenore. True, he wouldn't be able to keep her very long; she had too much real-world potential for him to hold her back, and unlike Lenore, he intended for her to remain in school. But since Anson had been waffling for a week on procuring him a footholder on his own, he felt he had no other choice if he was ever going to regain the ascendancy in the high-stakes but entertaining game he was playing.

Oh, he still planned to make Anson his heir, but he'd also make damned sure the boy knew who the Master was. His grandson would resent it, too, but the promise of eventual rewards far greater than any his peer group could aspire to would triumph in the end.

All of which assumed that neither Erin, Lewis, nor Ronny did anything stupid. Which, given the additional stubborn immobility he'd sensed the last time he'd tested Erin's Silence, he doubted.

Meanwhile, he had one thing left to do.

Sighing, he poured himself another julep (his fourth of the day) and crossed to the chair Winnie had occupied. It required but a few seconds' inspection of the velvet-upholstered backrest to procure what he wanted: four long, dark hairs that could belong to no one else but Winnie Cowan.

With them, when midnight rolled around, he would perform certain rituals which would awaken her Strength at the expense of her Voice. And in the meantime, he supposed he should compose a letter to her father. Ernest Cowan had prospered a lot in the last few years. It was time Matthew called in his marker.

Chapter 17

Finishing Up

The Road Man's camp
Saturday, April 14—4:30 P.M.

Ronny couldn't believe the difference two days could make when you did virtually nothing with the free time in both of them except work on two projects.

And that was in spite of the fact that he'd lost most of yesterday afternoon checking up on Winnie, who had stayed home from school sick.

It had been the first time he'd actually been to her house (a nicely restored nineteenth-century farmhouse, he discovered), but her brother, Kelly, had cornered him between first and second period and told him how she'd awakened in the night with a fever, and had been throwing up about once an hour ever since, never mind that she was also exchanging chills for sweats with roughly the same rapidity. The doctor claimed it was flu, but Kelly had other ideas, though he wouldn't say what they were—and in any event, the point of the conversation was that Winnie had left a couple of books at school and he wondered if Ronny would mind running them by afterwards, since he, like Lew, would be off at a wrestling meet in Dahlonega that night. Ronny had not needed to be asked twice.

But poor Winnie had looked like death, lying on the sofa, with blankets up to her chin and the odor of chicken soup filling the air. She'd smiled weakly at him and thanked him with a bit more enthusiasm, all the while apologizing for having to break the date they'd made that evening to catch the newest Bond film at the Cordova Triple. And he in turn had apologized for the fact that he couldn't stick around because the Road Man was expecting him and he was already late. He made no mention of the bracelet, since it was not his policy to discuss gift-type projects until they were completed. But he did intimate that it wouldn't be long before she'd know why he was in such a hurry to rendezvous with the perplexing tinker, and that he thought she'd approve.

And he'd then hied himself to the Road Man's camp and spent half the remaining time until sunset putting an edge on the knife and doing a preliminary wax rough of the dragon sculpture he was going to use for the hilt.

The other half of the time had been expended on the bracelet, and he'd basically succeeded in rendering the silver down into a series of equal strips, and in melting the gold watchcase into an oblong ingot with a blowtorch.

And while Lewis was off somewhere forty miles south, fumbling around on a padded mat with a bunch of guys in singlets, Ronny stayed home Friday night and worked some more on the wax mold for the handle.

And, as soon as the sun had risen on Saturday, had been back at the Road Man's camp.

It was the Day Man he met there, though a part of him had hoped to drag himself up early enough to see if there was, indeed, also a Sunrise Man. He was lucky to make it there at all, he supposed, for Aunt Erin had expressed considerable alarm when he'd announced his intention. Ronny's argument had been that she'd told him he could be there

until sunset, and she hadn't specified how much *before* that
he could start, to which he'd added that he suspected the
Road Man might be about ready to move on, so that he
doubted he'd have the chance to work with him much longer
anyway. She'd asked if he was actually learning anything
besides sedition and abstract philosophy and he'd tried to
tell her, but hadn't the vocabulary. Much of what he'd
learned of technique was simply feel: how one held one's
tools, how one let them fall, how the different metals were
supposed to sound if you hit them right or wrong. And all
of that was lost on Aunt Erin, whose art was much more
literal.

But somehow, in spite of that, it eventually got to be
three o'clock.

Work on the bracelet had gone famously all day, and
Ronny was now beginning to suspect he might actually get
it finished before dark, in which case he knew he would
not be able to resist delivering it to its intended recipient
that very same evening. Already the basic work was completed: the half-inch-wide silver channel into which he'd
cut slots through which he had woven lengths of braided
copper wire in an interlace pattern. That was set in turn in
a slightly larger channel of the same material, so as to
confine the woven wire from behind, and the two had been
soldered together. That had taken most of the morning, and
for the last several hours he'd been engaged in alternately
cutting, filing, etching, and engraving a design from a strip
of gold, which was supposed to illustrate the climactic battle
from Winnie's favorite book, *Watership Down*. His eyes
were starting to hurt from all the fine work, though, in spite
of the goggles and jeweler's loupe he'd alternately been
using. And he had a headache from the constant pound-
pounding of the Road Man's hammer against his larger anvil
a few yards off to the right. What the tinker was contriving,
Ronny could not tell, except that it was a further modifi-
cation of Thursday's aborted plowshare, to which the Road
Man was attaching a veritable nightmare of gears, ratchets,

and pulleys, while a red-plaid golf bag full of rebar stood conveniently by.

Sweat was running into Ronny's eyes, too, despite the red bandanna he'd knotted around his head. And his bare torso—for it was a warm day and he had a role model to emulate—was slick with sweat. In fact, it was getting to be quite a nuisance, the way it was starting to trickle down the small of his back and pool between his buttocks so that he had to scratch his bottom about every other minute—usually to a rude comment from the Road Man. Sighing, Ronny laid down his handiwork and took a swig of the strange, minty wine the tinker always seemed to have about.

"Tired already, are you?" the Road Man asked roughly. "I figured a young feller like you'd just be goin' good by now."

"Not tired," Ronny countered, taking another swig. "Well, not tired like beating on an anvil's tiring, but tiring enough, I guess. My eyes are gettin' real burny."

"Put clover on 'em," the Road Man told him. "It'll help you see more clearly."

"Clover? Give me a break."

"I—"

"Yeah, I know," Ronny chimed in before his mentor could finish: "You have, over and over."

"I still know things you don't. I still have my wonderful machines that can do things no other machines can. Do you therefore doubt me when I tell you that clover will cure what ails you?"

"I suppose not," Ronny grumbled. "Know where any is?"

"This is a meadow," the Road Man stated flatly. "You should be able to figure out the rest."

Ronny spent the next ten minutes searching for four-leafed clovers (on the theory that if any clover was good, lucky clover would be even . . . luckier). And he spent another five mixing it with a little of the green wine and grinding it into a paste with a marble mortar and pestle the

Road Man dragged out of a burlap potato bag.

And when he smeared some of the resulting green goop under his eyes (per instructions) the resulting vapors did indeed banish all the pain and strain and fatigue from his eyes.

They also, somehow, sharpened his brain and set him off again on his creative endeavor.

By four o'clock he had the gold band ready. By four-fifteen it had been set in the place provided for it in the silver band, where its yellow contrasted nicely with the ruddiness of the woven copper wire visible through the piecework behind it. By four-twenty-five a thin layer of solder held it in place, and by five o'clock, he'd drilled the twelve holes into which he would set the bogus pearls. At five-thirty, he had bent the whole thing into a circle, and was soldering a pearl-embellished hook to either end. And at six-fifteen, he set the last of the pearls, and began a final polish with what the Road Man claimed was jeweler's rouge, but smelled to him like a mixture of ground-up rust and powdered goat shit. And long before the sun began to flirt with the horizon, he had it finished.

He held it up for the Road Man's inspection, saw the sunlight gleaming ruddily over the three metals, then gather in the strategically placed pearls.

The Road Man spent easily five minutes examining the bracelet, peering at it from every angle, and turning it every which way so that the sun flashed and glimmered from the surface. He said nothing at all as he returned it to Ronny, and for an instant Ronny feared that he had not done well at all, in spite of what his instinct told him otherwise.

And then the Road Man clamped his arms around him and lifted him into the air in a startling, and rather slippery hug. "Good job," the tinker roared. "I knew you could do it if you'd just let your soul do the hard part."

Ronny found his chest too confined by brawny arms to reply, but managed to hang on to the bracelet without crushing it.

And eventually the Road Man set him down again, whereupon Ronny took several deep breaths and croaked, "I gather that means you liked it?"

"I don't *have* to like it," the Road Man told him. "All that matters is that you took pleasure from its making and that your lady takes pleasure from wearing it—though frankly, I'd be careful if I was her—that's a mighty fine piece of work, but I did catch you singin' a time or two while you made it."

"That was accidental," Ronny replied. "Besides, mostly I was humming or whistling."

" 'Flowers in the Forest' and 'Scotland the Brave,' if I caught you right. And both of those are songs with a fair bit of feelin' behind 'em. Still, we'll see what happens."

"But you really do like it?" Ronny ventured again. For in spite of the fact that he had only finished the bracelet a few minutes before, it already seemed an alien thing, an entity completely remote from him. And already he was planning how he would make another that was in all ways superior.

"Fishing for compliments, are we?" the Road Man rumbled, lifting an eyebrow.

"Uh, not really," Ronny stammered, blushing. "I guess I'm just real insecure."

"Well—and this is only my opinion; you might hear something completely different from the Sunset Man or the Night Man—*I* think it's a damned fine piece of work, almost *too* fine."

"What do you mean?"

"Well," the Road Man said in a low voice, "if I hadn't been there when you commenced it, and if I hadn't watched you every step of the way, I'd swear you had help on that thing. You did nothing wrong, absolutely nothin'. Once I'd shown you what to do, you did it, and if you didn't know how to do something—why, it took you about five seconds to pick it up once I'd explained it, and even then, you figured out ramifications and applications I've never even imagined.

And I'm not even gonna mention the design work. *That's* worthy of the Scythians. Remind me, though," he added pointedly, "to show you a thing or two about granulation."

"Gee," Ronny whispered. "And I thought it was only a bracelet."

"Nothing is ever *only* anything. And anything made with love is very special indeed."

Ronny checked his watch. "Uh . . . there's still time to work on the knife . . . Could I . . . ?"

The Road Man shook his head. "You have done enough and more than enough for one day." And with that, he vanished into the wagon.

Ronny sighed and laid the bracelet beside the small jeweler's anvil he'd been working on. What the Road Man was about now, he didn't know, though he rather suspected he was shifting from his Day Man persona to his Sunset Man incarnation—which basically involved a costume change and combing his hair. *And* the ritual baptism that took place every evening, and which Ronny had, so far, declined.

That day, however, he was feeling fey, and he was hot and sweaty and dirty, and he decided that both the optimum and most immediate remedy would be to take a dip in the pond back in the woods. In fact, if he hurried, he could beat the Road Man there and be out before the Sunset Man arrived.

And with that in mind and the precious bracelet in his hand, Ronny came as close to prancing into the woods as his bum leg would permit him.

A moment later he was relaxing in the chill of the waters.

"Baptizin' yourself, are you?" the Sunset Man hollered cheerily, just as Ronny realized he had nearly fallen asleep with his body completely submerged and his head precariously pillowed on a projecting root. And before Ronny could scramble out, the Road Man had doffed his clothes and was wading in beside him.

"I say, are you baptizin' yourself there?"

"Uh, no," Ronny stammered. "I guess I must have dozed off. I was just leaving."

"Not without bein' baptized, you're not!" the Sunset Man bellowed. "You're *this* close, you're gonna be baptized. A man ought to always be baptized when he brings a new thing into the world, 'cause every new thing in the world makes it that much greater, and that makes God that much greater too."

And with that the Road Man grabbed Ronny around the chest (effectively pinning his arms), and thrust him underwater.

And, Ronny discovered, as he felt his lungs begin to plead for air and saw bubbles start to rise from his mouth, the Road Man was showing no signs of letting him up again. He began to struggle—but still the tinker held him firm. He tried to strike out, tried to find purchase, but could only reach the rock-hard solidity of the Road Man's legs. And those he could not budge.

Longer and longer the Road Man held him down, and his lungs began to pain him something fierce. He could also feel his heart beating fit to burst, and there was a buzzing in his ears, a troubling hint of red at the outskirts of his vision.

And then, abruptly, there was no constriction about his chest at all—and he flung himself up and into the air.

And as soon as his lungs were working again, began to rail at his mentor.

"What the fuck were you *doin'* there?" he yelled. "You could have drowned me! You came *that* close to drowning me!"

"I wouldn't have drowned you," the Road Man replied impassively. "I know exactly how much temper to put into those I forge."

"Forge *hell*! I'm tempted to call the law on you."

"What for?"

Ronny glanced down at his nakedness. "For . . . for making improper advances."

"You were here first. You were naked first. I merely joined you."

"Okay, for . . . for *assault* then."

"Can you prove it?"

Ronny examined his sleek sides. There was no trace of a bruise.

"See," the Road Man answered for him. "You can't prove anything. Besides," he added cheerfully, "I won't have to baptize you again until you finish that knife."

"If the Day Man ever lets me." Ronny sighed. Then: "I guess I owe you an apology—but that was *really* scary there."

"It was intended to be."

"And what was I supposed to learn from that—since I assume there's some lesson implied?"

"You were supposed to learn to trust nobody, and you were supposed to learn what it feels like to be a dozen heartbeats from death."

Ronny regarded him curiously. "And I bet it would have been *exactly* a dozen too, wouldn't it?"

"It would," the Road Man agreed solemnly. "Now go away, I need to meditate alone."

An hour later Ronny was dry, showered, shaved, dry again, fed, and dressed in clean jeans and a gray-and-red sweater over a plain black T-shirt. And he had on his Sunday Reeboks.

As he headed for the front door Erin intercepted him, pallet knife in hand. There were dark circles under her eyes, and her face was grim. "Where're you off to now?"

"Oh," Ronny replied in some surprise, having been seriously preoccupied for the last several hours, "I thought I told you."

"You didn't."

"Oh," Ronny repeated dumbly. "I'm going over to Winnie's."

Erin fixed him with a dubious stare. "You have a date, then?"

Ronny shrugged impatiently. "Not a date, exactly. She's been sick, and I made her something. I'm hoping that giving it to her'll make her feel better."

"Can I see?"

For no good reason he could think of, Ronny held back. "I made it at the Road Man's place."

"So what difference does that make?" Erin replied with a sly smile that made her look a lot more relaxed than she'd been lately. "If I see it and I like it, I'm more likely to let you keep going over there than otherwise, aren't I?"

"Yeah, but . . . uh, doesn't that mean the opposite is true as well?"

An eyebrow lifted delicately. "I guess you're gonna have to trust me then—besides, from the way you've been grinning since you got home, I don't think I'm going to be disappointed."

Ronny grimaced and reached into his pocket where the bracelet was nestled atop a square of cotton in a white cardboard box that had once contained one of Lew's Christmas wallets.

He handed it to his guardian without a word.

Erin opened it carefully, and Ronny had the rare and unexpected pleasure of hearing her gasp.

For perhaps a minute she gazed at it without touching it. "Oh, Ronny, this is *wonderful*!" she cried at last. "I've seen those little warriors you've been making and I think they're really well done. But I had no idea you could do something like this."

"I didn't either," Ronny replied, beaming. "It just sort of happened."

"Well," Erin said softly, as she handed bracelet and box back to Ronny, "maybe some good will come of you hanging out with the Road Man after all."

* * *

Ronny was still flying high as he flung the Escort around the last few curves below Winnie's house. She lived in town, on the northern of the two long ridges that together with the valley between them comprised greater Cordova. In fact, the Cowans had quite a spectacular view—though Ronny was beginning to suspect that most folks in Cordova had pretty good views, just like they had pretty good everything else. There wasn't a scuzzily dressed kid in school, and he still hadn't seen a car in the whole town that was more than six years old, except for restored jobs from the fifties and sixties and a few (mostly Mark III, IV, and V Lincolns) from the seventies.

Winnie's car was nowhere in sight when he parked at the edge of the drive, but that didn't necessarily mean anything. The Cowans had a two-car garage, after all, so her Mustang was probably stashed in there. It occurred to him then that perhaps he should have called ahead just to be sure. But the notion of simply appearing on Winnie's doorstep (especially if she was still as sick as she had been yesterday) and presenting his gift without portfolio was too much to resist. He liked surprising people, and a surprise such as he had might be exactly the thing to cheer up his—he dared hope—girlfriend.

But she wasn't the only one who needed cheering up, he realized instantly, when three presses of the doorbell finally brought her father—whom he had only met twice before— to the door, for Winnie's dad looked like he had aged years in the day since Ronny last had seen him. He was stooped, where before he had stood straight, and his eyes were hollow and shadowed, his mouth thin. He was wearing an undershirt above khaki trousers, which Ronny thought made him look decidedly old as well as old-fashioned, and he didn't appear to have shaved for several days.

Still, folks *did* have their off days, and it *was* Saturday, which Winnie had told him was the day her mother worked at the store, so that Ronny supposed Mr. Cowan had a right

to let himself go once a week. Nevertheless, it was a lot
more change than he had expected.

"Hi!" he said, when Winnie's dad showed no sign of
initiating conversation. "I'm Ronny Dillon, remember? I
met you at the store a couple of nights ago, and then I was
by yesterday to bring some school stuff to Winnie."

"I know who you are," Mr. Cowan replied in a dull,
lifeless voice. He did *not* offer Ronny a chance to go inside.
"Winnie speaks very highly of you."

"Is she here then?" Ronny asked eagerly, craning his
neck to peer into the gloom beyond the screen.

"No."

"Oh . . ." Ronny gaped. "Uh, well, when do you expect
her back?"

"When she comes back."

Ronny's heart went cold as stone. "When she . . . Mr.
Cowan, is . . . is something *wrong* with Winnie?"

"No."

"But she's not here?"

"That's correct."

"Well, can I leave something for her then?"

"I don't know when she'll get it."

Ronny swallowed a scathing retort. This wasn't going at
all well, and his excellent mood was rapidly evaporating.
"Uh, look, I don't want to be nosy, but Winnie really *is* a
good friend of mine and I really *do* care about her, so if
you could tell me what's going on . . ."

"Winnie's gone, son," Cowan said heavily.

"Gone? Where?"

"Gone to keep house for Mr. Welch. He sent a letter to
me special delivery this morning saying he needed her over
at Cardalba."

"And you *let* her go?"

"I had to. Mr. Welch has done a lot for me, a lot for
the whole family. And he said he needed her."

"For what?"

A shrug. "Said he needed her to keep up the luck."

"Gimme a break!" Ronny gritted, then remembered who he was addressing, and that Mr. Cowan didn't seem any happier about things than he was.

"So is she just working over there, or living over there, or what? And what about school, we've got exams next—"

"I know all that, boy," Cowan interrupted, still staring dazedly into space. "He says she can still go to school, long as she stays nights at his house. Says he's only gonna need her for a year."

"That son of a bitch!" Ronny snarled.

"It ain't like you think, boy," Cowan said.

"The hell it's not!" And then Ronny could stand it no longer and turned and fled. By the time he got the car started his eyes were awash with tears.

Chapter 18

The Worm Turns Again

Cardalba Hall
8:00 P.M.

Anson wondered where his Saturday had gone. Being unemployed except for the inconsequential but well-paying chores he performed for Matthew Welch, and equipped with an unusually indulgent if high-strung mother whose position at the local newspaper required she work weekends, he tended to sleep very late those two days. *Not*, however, three hours past noon, as he had done today; *that* was very atypical. Still, he *had* been a little run-down lately—and had found himself snoozing more than common as a result.

He had a pretty good idea why, too. Though he hated to admit it, Matthew had been right: Listening took it out of a body—especially if there was no footholder to draw on to restore the Strength expended. He wondered if he should start seeking one of those elusive creatures for himself—after he secured one for his patron, of course, for which he was still, officially, on quest. God knew there was little cause for optimism on that *front*, even allowing for the fact that he wasn't putting much effort into his search. And what pickings he had been able to ferret out were proving to be remarkably slim—much more so than he'd expected when he'd made the agreement. Most girls the Winds told him were qualified (including Winnie, whom he did *not* intend to put forward as a candidate since she was part of a separate deal) wouldn't give him the time of day (unless, perhaps, he fiddled with their minds—but he didn't know how to do that properly yet). Or else they had boyfriends who could complicate matters. Or *else* they simply didn't seem like the type to have good chemistry with Matthew Welch, and Anson *did* want to say on Mr. Welch's rather ill-defined good side as much and as long as possible.

But sooner or later he would *have* to come up with something. Perhaps he should zip down to Atlanta tomorrow and see if he could lay hands on a suitable runaway there. That was what Lenore had been, though he imagined qualified female vagabonds were as scarce as snowflakes in Saudi Arabia. And he hadn't a clue what the policy, so to speak, was on male virgins—not that he had access to many of them either.

He hoped something would jell soon, though, because it galled him to admit that Listening as frequently as he had been of late wore him to a frazzle. And even strong as he was (and he was *very* strong, as he had discovered when Matthew had let his Silence slip enough for him to peek through the night before), he could not Listen indefinitely. He knew: he'd practiced for a couple of hours that afternoon and Heard almost nothing. Which worried him, because he had wanted to appear fresh and alert when he showed up for today's instruction session, otherwise he feared good old Matthew would either detect his fatigue and know what he'd been up to, or simply read past his weakened Silence and discover his overextension that way—and in either case would give him a talking-to he neither desired nor (he felt) deserved.

Not that it really mattered. Give him a few more weeks

and it wouldn't matter much *what* Matthew Welch said or did.

Sighing, Anson tumbled out of his bed; showered; dressed in jeans, sneakers, and sweatshirt; and sauntered into the kitchen to nuke his third pizza of the day, which he washed down with two cans of Jolt Cola.

Twenty minutes later, he was ringing his grandfather's doorbell. And instantly knew something had changed.

Matthew, who had been showing obvious signs of failing since the defection of Lenore, looked better than Anson had seen him in the week of their de facto partnership. His carriage was more erect, and his color was much, much healthier. His white hair had a new gloss to it, too, and was neatly trimmed and combed so that it reminded Anson of an Arctic snowfield; and his eyes held a sharp, feral glitter behind their silver-framed lenses. He had also dressed with more care than normal, in a burgundy corduroy suit and crimson silk shirt that he wore without a tie. His feet, Anson noted with a scowl, were stuffed into red leather slippers, but were otherwise quite bare.

"Ah, Anson, I was *wondering* when you were going to arrive," Matthew cried boisterously, flinging his arms wide to usher his protégé into the bowels of his mansion. "I feel very good today. In fact, I think this is going to be a *very* productive session."

"I hope so," Anson replied, more sullenly than he meant to, for his intention was to act as if he too was in the full flower of youthful vigor. Fortunately, he knew enough to Silence now, and though that was also rather shaky at the moment, he assumed Matthew was sufficiently savvy not to try to Listen in his direction—especially if he kept the surface layer hard and unyielding so that the underlying softness did not show through.

"I'm sure you'll be surprised," Matthew continued with a strange little smile that Anson found vaguely disconcerting.

"I'm sure I will." Anson was already heading toward

the library door, though he knew from past experience that it was usually locked and that Matthew alone held the key. He hoped he didn't seem *too* impatient—no sense showing the old geezer another quirk to give him grief about.

But Matthew did not seem perturbed. "Ah, but we *are* in a hurry, aren't we?" He laughed easily, insinuating himself ahead of Anson and inserting his key into the shiny brass lock. "Perhaps that's just as well."

Something about his patron's tone struck Anson as odd. He shot the old man a speculative glare. "Why?" he asked carefully.

"Because," Matthew replied slyly, turning the knob while continuing to block access, "in case you haven't noticed, I haven't been quite up to snuff lately. But in the *last* day, however, circumstances have, let us say, improved considerably, and I'm feeling much, *much* better."

And with that he thrust open the door and strode into his library, leaving a bewildered Anson to follow in his wake.

The Master of Cardalba was nowhere in sight when Anson would have joined him—but someone else was, and he felt his heart skip a beat with anger and resentment as it slowly dawned on him that he'd been had. For, sitting with her back to him at the foot of the chair Matthew used for Listening, was, unmistakably, a teenage girl.

He heard the door thump shut behind him, caught the faint, sharp clicks that fixed the lock.

"Anson, my lad," Matthew laughed cheerfully from the shadows to his right, "I'd like you to meet my new footholder. I'd introduce you, but I believe you've already met."

Anson's heart skipped again. For the girl who had turned wide, dazed eyes in his direction was none other than Winnie Cowan.

"You bastard son of a bitch!" Anson snarled, whirling around to confront his grandfather, who was leaning nonchalantly against a waist-high bookcase. "You goddam double-crosser!"

"Right on all three counts." Matthew chuckled softly, whereupon he pushed past Anson and strolled confidently toward the sideboard that supported his sherry service, leaving Anson to gape at his back. "Sherry? Or maybe port?"

Anson's mind was so awash with competing floods of anger, betrayal, and hatred that he could not reply. What did this old asshole think he was doing, anyway? Playing games like this! Anson hated him, wanted him gone, wanted him . . . *dead*.

"That won't work," Matthew murmured calmly, turning around with a half-full glass in either hand. "You're not strong enough to think anyone dead in the first place, and even if you could you'd be in over your head, because you'd have no one to continue your lessons, *or* Fix you—both of which I still plan on doing—presuming you continue to cooperate."

Anson had not moved from his place by the door, nor had his eyes left Winnie. "Asshole!" he spat from between gritted teeth. "You lying asshole. You were gonna do this all along, weren't you?"

Matthew regarded him seriously and stepped toward his Listening chair. "No, I was not," he said evenly. "In fact, if *you* hadn't suggested Miss Cowan here as the subject for your little eavesdropping session, I might *never* have found out what a remarkably talented person she is. Her presence here is as much *your* fault as mine."

"Liar!"

"Oh, Anson, just sit *down*." Matthew sighed, indicating the chair to his left. "You're making me nervous mouthing and foaming that way. Affairs have altered since last we met, but not necessarily for the worse, at least as far as you're concerned—though now that I have a footholder again, I suppose we'll need to renegotiate our bargain."

"Bargain, *hell*!" Anson shouted. And could contain his rage no longer.

He lunged across the few yards between himself and his grandfather, and before Matthew had time to respond, Anson's strong hands had clamped the old man's shoulders, wrenched him from his feet, and flung him backward toward the sideboard. He hit hard—*too* hard. With a stomach-wrenching crack, the back of his head slammed into a projecting corner molding. His eyes went wide with pain and shock, then dimmed abruptly as he slumped to the floor. His breath trickled out with a dull rattle. The glasses had slipped from his hands and shattered on the polished oak. Sherry slid under the edge of the rug, mingling with blood from a wound Anson could not see. A frantic thumping was a half-dazed Winnie scrambling out of the way.

"*Dammit!*" Anson said into the air, his voice full of shocked frustration. "I didn't *want* to hurt you, old man!"

And then the full realization of what he had done fell upon him. He swallowed, gagged—and before he knew it, was kneeling beside the inert body of his former patron. Matthew wasn't breathing, he could tell that immediately, and he had no pulse when Anson felt for one. He gagged again. Less than a minute ago he had been a student of arcane sciences. Now he was a murderer—a quasi-patricide!

"Mr. Welch!" he cried, lifting the old man's body into his arms and cradling his head as he smoothed back the snowy hair. "Mr. Welch, I didn't *mean* to! Come on, wake up. Tell me you're okay!"

But Mr. Welch did not wake up, and when Anson finally worked up sufficient nerve to ease a hand around to the back of the old man's head he knew why. There was a depression at the base of the skull two fingers deep and four fingers wide, and he could feel broken bones wiggle and grind as he probed the surrounding flesh.

—And then, unbelievably, Matthew Welch shuddered and gasped and opened his eyes.

"Goddamn shit *fuck!*" Anson screamed before he could stop himself.

"Get *off* me!" Matthew grunted, as soon as he had dragged sufficient air into his lungs to speak. "Dammit, boy, do what I say!"

Anson was too shocked to respond.

"Get off me, I say," Matthew repeated, pushing feebly at Anson's arms.

Anson did—woodenly; his emotions so jumbled, his senses so confused he could barely move. Somehow, though, he managed to flop against a bookcase and stood there panting, eyes wide and blankly staring.

"Are . . . are you okay?" he gasped finally, not moving as his grandfather made his way to his feet, leaving a plate-sized pool of blood on the floor.

Matthew shot him a scathing glare and shuffled toward his chair. "Of course I'm okay," the old man growled irritably. "Except that I've now got a headache that won't quit and have a hole in my skull that'll take six months to grow over."

Anson simply stared and swallowed—and got yet another shock when he caught a glimpse of the back of his grandfather's head. His fingers had told him no lie. There was a dent there—a blood-filled depression full of matted hair and clotted gore. And the entire back of Matthew's jacket was dark with blood. He did not, however, appear to be bleeding now.

"Do you need a doctor?" Anson gasped dumbly. "Or . . ."

Matthew eased into his chair and arranged his feet in Winnie's lap. He sighed contentedly, then: "I'd rather you didn't. I doubt he'd be able to make heads or tails about what he'd find."

Anson swallowed hard—again. "And what might that be?"

"Well," Matthew replied, "he'd probably say that I should be dead."

Another gulp, as a disquieting suspicion began to dawn. "And . . . and . . ."

"Was I?" Matthew finished for him. He tried to shrug—and winced. "I suppose I was. I really didn't want you to find out about that part yet. It tends to incite overly rash behavior among the young.''

Anson managed to recover sufficient composure to make his way to the sideboard. Six glasses still remained and he somehow filled two to the rim, though his hands were shaking so badly he feared he would drop the decanter. "Find out about w-what?" he stammered, and polished off half of one glass.

Matthew grimaced and twisted around in his chair to gaze at him. "Well, I guess you might as *well* know," he grumbled. "Now bring that over here, boy; it's time for us to do some hard talking."

Anson nodded and made his way to Matthew's side. He passed him the full glass and sank down in the chair opposite and tried very hard not to let his teeth chatter.

Matthew took a long draught of wine and savored it expressively—though Anson noticed his head wasn't moving quite right, as if he had a crick in his neck. And *wished* it was as simple as that.

"I'm sorry," Anson managed finally. "I got pissed and just—overreacted."

Matthew regarded him levelly, then shook his head. "This from the boy who not a minute ago was wishing me dead? Well, you almost *got* your wish, so let's just leave it at that, at least for the moment. We may as well be *honest* with each other, Anson. I'm enjoying these little sparring matches a lot, and I knew when I took you on that I was taking a risk. On the other hand, when you can have or do practically anything, taking risks is all the fun that's left in life, or at least that's the way it is with me. But let's not fool ourselves. You really *did* want me dead, and you really *were* sorry—but *not* because you thought you'd killed me. You were sorry because you were afraid you'd get into trouble with the law on the one hand, because you hadn't learned everything from me you wanted to yet on the other—and now because you're afraid you're in trouble with *me* on the third. You're scared that now that you've screwed up I won't teach you any more.''

Anson's eyebrows lifted slightly, as he began to regain his composure and rise to the implicit challenge. ''You've got my number, don't you—or you think you do.''

Matthew inclined his head slightly—and winced again. ''Oh, I do—but for my part, I was careless too: *I* forgot to allow for the fact that anyone who has access to Strength would ever resort to mere fisticuffs—so I suppose that makes us even. We've both underestimated the other, we've both been rash, and we've both been stupid, and now we're the better for it. But you had better *not* let it happen again!''

''I'll try not to . . . sir,'' Anson whispered.

''Very good. And now that we've got the cards on the table, answer me one question. What is it, exactly, that you *do* want?''

Anson took a deep breath and puffed his cheeks. ''What do *you* want?'' he asked carefully.

''Very good,'' Matthew repeated, lifting an eyebrow. ''We both want to determine the other's bargaining position first. Fine, I'll begin: I want two things, Anson. I want Winnie as my footholder until she graduates from high school. And I want your word you won't seek to interfere with her in any way. The woods are full of girls, after all, but very few are like this one. It's only for a year anyway; I don't think that's asking very much.''

''And if I promise that, what do *I* get?''

''This is a *bargaining* session, Anson; I'm open to suggestions—or does the idea of dealing with a dead man disturb you?''

Anson swallowed hard. ''Okay, then,'' he said hesitantly. ''Since you asked, and since we're layin' it on the line here, *I* also want two things : I want my own footholder . . . and I want to be Master of Cardalba—now.''

Matthew started. ''I'm sorry,'' he whispered. ''Both those things are impossible.''

Anson could not suppress a surge of anger; after all, the

old guy had started it. "What do you *mean*, impossible?" he gritted.

"Well," Matthew replied calmly, "to start with, only a Master can properly *use* a footholder; if anyone else tried without the proper safeguards, it would burn out his Luck—and probably his mind in the bargain. If you don't believe me, you're welcome to try."

Anson scowled, but his brain was quickly emerging from its shock and starting to tick again. "So make me Master of Cardalba, then, like I asked."

Matthew smiled condescendingly. "I *can't*, lad, for a *number* of very good reasons. You may think you're strong enough and clever enough to be Master, and maybe you are from a purely quantitative point of view. But the Winds can be far more dangerous than you imagine, and you'll need somebody to show you around the pitfalls. You also need to learn a *lot* more about the world at large, learn the businesses, learn contacts, learn how to cover your tracks."

"So show me!"

"I *can't*, not all at once. It takes time, Anson. Honest to God, it takes a huge amount of time, years even. I could no more show you even a thousandth part of what you need to know in one session than I could teach you calculus that way."

"So show me in your mind! Let go your Voice and let it blow directly into mine."

Matthew chuckled grimly. "I *ought* to do it: I really should open up to you and give my Voice free rein to blow until you're so full of Wind you have no Voice of your own left—until it blows your very *self* away. I could do it, too."

"Then why don't you?"

"Because I still have hope for you. But that's beside the point. There are other reasons you can't be Master before I'm good and ready. One of which is the fact that, as I've told you, I'm by no means the only Master in the world. And if I *stop* Listening suddenly—before it's expected or before I alert the others, which would be the case should I cease being Master of Cardalba anytime soon—especially against my will—some of those others will wonder why and come to investigate. And I doubt that even you could stand against a whole phalanx of trained Listeners—especially if they were already on guard about you, which they would be. Therefore, if you assume the Mastership in your own good time, with my approval, things will go much more smoothly for you.''

''I don't believe you. Besides, I don't feel like waiting until I'm ninety.''

''Why not? I was fifty-three when I took over, but I worked with Uncle Ben for years before that. Haven't you figured out yet that learning's a lot more interesting than doing? That becoming is more interesting than being?''

''I still don't believe you. You're still holding something back.''

''Feel free to Listen to my Voice, then—but don't forget what I just told you. I might just take that as an invitation to fill you up!''

''Anything else?'' Anson growled sarcastically. He hated being toyed with and made to look the fool, but he also knew Matthew admired folks with balls.

''Well, there's the small matter of my mother to contend with sooner or later. She's not in your camp, after all.''

''I can handle her!''

''I'd like to see you try!''

''I'll worry about her when the time comes.''

''If you do, you'll have waited far too long.''

''I—''

''Wasn't there something else you were curious about?'' Matthew inserted casually. ''Or are you so easily distracted by delusions of grandeur that you forget the more basic mysteries at hand?''

Anson blanched at that, for he knew what Matthew was hinting at and both did and did not want to broach the subject. He took a deep breath. ''Okay,'' he began. ''A while ago . . . were you *really* . . .''

"Dead?" Matt supplied for him again. "Don't be scared of it, boy, it's only a word."

"But *were* you?"

"Probably, or so close as makes no difference."

Anson stared at him incredulously. "What do you *mean*?"

"I mean," Matthew replied, sliding a hand behind his head to rub his neck, "that I can't *be* killed. Not by you, not by anyone, at least not today."

"You're *shittin'* me!"

Matthew shook his head—which made a soft grinding sound. "No," he whispered. "I absolutely am not."

"But you're not tellin' me everything, are you?"

"Of course not."

Anson looked puzzled for a moment, but then his eyes narrowed suspiciously. "This has something to do with the Luck, doesn't it?"

"Of course it does," Matthew snapped. "Once it's fully manifested—which it hasn't finished doing in you yet, by the way, so don't take any chances—the Luck remembers what you're supposed to be like and rebuilds you—as long as you *want* to remain alive. Which I most certainly did at the point when I lost consciousness."

"And you *really* can't be killed?"

Matthew grimaced. "Persistent little devil, aren't you? But inattentive—which will cost you when or if you become Master. I didn't say that, not in those words. What I *said* was that I couldn't be killed by you today. Not by normal means, at any rate."

Anson eyed the old man warily. "What about *abnormal* means?"

A sip of sherry. "Ah, so you caught that, did you? Then you're getting better. As for the *exact* means . . . well, it's different for every Listener. Nobody knows what it is except the ones who Fix them and the one they hide it in, and they're sworn to secrecy."

"You mean . . . ?"

Matthew nodded. "The only people who know how I can be killed before my time are my mother and the two people who assisted her, one of whom is dead, and the other I do not know. It's basically a fail-safe—there are *lots* of fail-safes in this business. My mother's mother *used* to know, but she's dead. And Mother certainly never told *me*; it's generally safer that way. Even Erin, who hates Listening so much she tried to raise her son away from it, dared not deviate from the Law *that* much."

"But I don't understand," Anson interrupted, so intrigued he was forgetting to be frightened. "If you can't *be* killed, why would your *mother* want to come up with a way to do it anyway?"

Matthew started to shrug but caught himself. "Again, that's how it's always been done. That's how the Law of the Listeners works. It's so that if someone goes renegade there can be a way of stopping them, but it can't be a way that could ever, *ever* happen accidentally."

"Hey, but wait a minute," Anson said slowly. "If *you* can't be killed, what about the others? What about Lew . . . or me. Can *we* be killed?"

Matthew reached to the floor and picked up a three-inch sliver of shattered crystal. "Drag this across your wrist and see."

"I'll pass," Anson replied dryly. "What about Lew?"

"Lewis is in the same gray area you are just now, depending on how far along the Luck's got with him—which is pretty far, I imagine. So things could go either way with him. And in any event, his mother knows his Flaw, I don't. One obviously doesn't spread that sort of information around. And Erin and I haven't been on good terms since he was born. It's a miracle he was even Fixed, and she probably wouldn't have even done that had she not feared the alternative."

"Which is?"

"Madness—possibly."

"And do I have to worry about that?"

"Hopefully not. It *should* have shown up by now. Let's just say you've got good genes in that regard and let it rest, okay? In fact, I can only think of one problem, and that one was a special case."

Anson closed his eyes for an instant. This close one did not need to go into trance to hear the other's Voice—or Silence. "You're lyin' about Lew, though," he said silkily. "I can tell."

"*Am* I?"

"Your Silence quivers every time you don't tell all the truth, did you know that? It's like the rest of the story is tryin' to push its way out and you won't let it."

"Thank you—I *didn't* know that," Matthew replied, smiling. "I'll certainly be more careful in the future."

Anson glared at him. "You want Lew out of the way as much as I do, don't you? As long as he's alive, he's a threat to both of us. So why are you so hung up on protecting him all of a sudden?"

Matthew raised an eyebrow ever so slightly. "Maybe I've changed my mind about my heir."

Anson bit back a bitter retort, though he was certain Matt knew he had nearly lost it—and probably enjoyed seeing him squirm.

"Okay," Anson said steadily, though his eyes flashed warning. "But if you want Lew alive so bad, and he can't be killed, what was all that business with his dreams?"

"You Heard that, did you?"

"You let your Silence slip."

"I'll also have to watch that in the future."

"The dreams," Anson prompted.

Matthew sighed dramatically. "Do I really *have* to spell it out for you? You want to be Master of Cardalba and yet you overlook the obvious."

"I thought we were being straight here: I asked you a straight question."

"Very well, it's actually quite simple. Excepting old age itself, which causes the Luck to leak away, no adult Listener can be killed by physical means, not by disease, not by weapons, at least by not by any that leave his body mostly intact. And of course I don't need to tell you what they call physical attacks that occur *before* the Luck manifests. Murder is murder, in other words—and most murderers leave evidence behind. *However*, the fact that someone is effectively immortal in his flesh *doesn't* mean he can't be destroyed by his own mind in one of three ways. Either by dreams that frighten him so much he actually *wills* himself dead from fright; or he goes insane, because it renders him an unfit vessel for the Luck; or . . .''

"So is *that* what you were doing when you were sending him all those dreams?"

"*Trying* to do," Matthew corrected. "Unfortunately, the boy's mother has erected the most amazing Silence around him I've ever seen, as I'm sure you've noticed. Therefore, I have not, so far, been able to send him dreams strong enough or frequently enough to either kill him outright from fear, or drive him mad—which is what I would prefer to do, but only for as long as it takes to confirm you as my heir. I'm no longer pursuing *either* avenue at the moment."

"So is there another way, then?"

"I already said there was—but I'm not pursuing it either."

"I'm listenin', though."

"Fine, I hope you are, because all of this *could* apply to you. The other thing is quite simply that Lewis could conceivably take his own life—either to escape the dreams, or to escape the madness they portend."

"And no weapon can kill him? What about what you said about the Fixing ritual, or whatever it was?"

Matthew glared at him. "My, but we're sharp today. I *knew* I shouldn't have told you about that. Still, I suppose that's what comes of talking esoteric philosophy too soon after being killed."

"Well I *didn't* forget, so can we just cut the crap and get on with it?"

"Very well," Matthew said. "The means by which Lewis could be killed *against his will* was determined at his Fixing ritual, though it's not officially part of it and has nothing to do with when or how the Luck manifests. My mother was there, *his* mother was there, and *her* mother, my sister Donna was there. They determined it."

"So what is it?"

"A weapon, I suppose. It usually is."

"But you don't know? You've been Master all these years and you haven't been able to find out?"

Matthew shook his head. "It's . . . a little embarrassing," he admitted. "I know . . . but I *don't* know."

Anson's eyes narrowed. "What do you mean? Didn't you say something about 'the one they hide it in'? Is *that* what you're talking about?"

Matthew frowned. "Yes, actually. That's the final fail-safe. Since the whole thing concerns the succession to Mastership, it only makes sense that the Master know. But since there's always a chance the Master might try to extend his tenure beyond his appointed time by destroying his heir, the information is hidden in his mind so deeply he can only get at it when all the other Fixers are dead *and* the Luck determines he has need of it."

"So you really don't know?"

Matthew shook his head. "I do not."

"But *I* want to know."

"Why, so you can kill Lewis?"

"So I can hedge my bets," Anson shot back. "I'd prefer not to have to kill him. But I'd also like to have as many options open as I can—I'm more secure that way."

"It's still pointless to discuss it, since I don't know myself."

Anson frowned. "But if it's in your brain, you ought to be able to get it out."

"I can't, though."

The frown deepened. "No," Anson said slowly. "But maybe I can."

"You *what*!" Matthew cried incredulously. "Boy, I have met *some* egos in my life, some cocky little sons of bitches, but you take the cake, the plate, the napkins, and the silverware all."

Anson shrugged. "Do we have anything to lose?"

"Beyond my peace of mind, you mean? Haven't you put that in enough jeopardy for one day?"

"Sorry." Anson sighed, suppressing a yawn.

—And the instant he closed his eyes he felt Matthew's Silence slip. And in that moment, he acted.

Before Matthew could stop him, Anson was deep among the old man's memories. There was pain there: a lot of it, and along with it a terrible swirling pit of *nothingness* he dared not venture near. He felt a start, a mental cry of alarm as Matthew realized what he had done, but it did not avail him. The Winds of Matthew's thoughts roared after him, but Anson was quick and clever, even if he was not, at the moment, as strong. But he had found what he wanted now, for by the simple act of thinking about the thing he could *not* think about, Matthew had in effect opened most of the way *to* that thing. Anson Heard it there: the chant endlessly intoned by three women: an old one, a middle-aged one, and a young one. And he remembered it.

An instant later he opened his eyes to stare smugly into Matthew's wild, incredulous ones.

"A knife," Anson said. "A knife made of iron, silver, and gold. One worked on only in the light of the sun and the light of the moon, and folded in the light of each once a day for seven days. One made by someone who can Listen but has no Voice."

Matthew continued to blink at him, his face pale with a mixture of awe and fear. "What *are* you?" he whispered. "I know you're special in ways I haven't told you, but *no one* should be able to do that!"

Anson grinned fiendishly. "I guess we're both still learnin' things. I won't underestimate you like I did a while ago, and you don't underestimate me."

"But . . ."

"About that knife . . . Is it possible?"

"Oh yes," Matthew affirmed, his voice still thin and shaky. "It *has* to be possible in the material world, however improbable. The Luck has to have an out."

"Could *you* make a knife like that?"

"No."

"Do you know anybody who could?"

"Maybe."

"Well then," Anson said sweetly, leaning forward and clasping his hand on Matthew's knee, "I think you should have a knife like this made, okay? You'll start now, and when it's done you'll give it to me, and I'll take care of young Mr. Lewis."

Matthew's face was still a mask of shock. "You actually want to do this?"

Anson shrugged again. "Like I said, I like to keep my options open."

"What about the law?" Matthew whispered. "What about Lewis's mother?"

"I'm sure you've had *years* of experience circumventing them both." And with that, Anson leaned back and fell silent.

Matthew stroked Winnie's hair absently. He looked tired, Anson realized, no longer the dapper, ebullient gentleman who had answered the door not so long ago.

"Suppose I refuse," Matthew said at last.

"Why, then," Anson replied, glancing at Winnie, "I *suppose* I would have to make that footholder as useless as the other one was—since we never did make that bargain."

"Then where would I get the power to Fix you?"

Anson yawned dramatically. "Okay, you win—for now." He sighed, starting to rise. "Maybe we both win. We both know more than we did when I got here. I don't suppose there'll be a lesson tonight?" he added as an after-thought.

Matthew shook his head. "Not tonight. I have a head-ache," he added sarcastically.

"Tomorrow then?"

"It's possible."

"And in the meantime, you'll see about that knife?"

"I'll . . . take it under consideration."

Matthew started to rise, but Anson pushed him gently but firmly back into his chair. "Oh no, Grandfather," he said. "*You* stay there and rest! I'll let myself out."

But as soon as Anson's back was turned, Matthew could not resist a secret smile. For the quiverings of lies behind Silences could themselves mask other lies.

And besides, he hated to waste an opportunity.

Chapter 19

Bargains Made and Broken

Cardalba Hall
Saturday, April 14—mid-evening

Something far more precious to Matthew Welch than the back of his head was smarting as he strode from Cardalba Hall's dining room into its kitchen two minutes after he had watched Anson roar away in his Trans Am: what most pained the Master of Cardalba now was his pride. He had failed. Somehow or other, in spite of his efforts, in spite of his schemes, he still could not regain the upper hand with his grandson. The best he could hope for anytime soon, he suspected, as he pushed through the door that let onto the back hallway and thence to the garage, was to maintain an uneasy peace. He would give Anson *almost* all he asked for, but never quite everything—keep one more carrot (even if it was a phantom one) dangling before him, and hope that as he continued initiating his protégé into the mysteries of Luck, some sense of responsibility would sink into him. He knew how the boy felt, after all: he had been much the same when Uncle Ben had initiated him—except that Matthew was a child of a gentler, more ethical, if also more socially stratified, age: a time when everyone knew their place and did not aspire to more than they were born to, and certainly did not question the idiosyncrasies of the local gentry.

And now, Matthew thought wryly as he stepped into the echoing warmth of his vaulted, three-car garage, he was about to do something idiosyncratic even for him. Somewhat to his surprise, he began to hum softly—the march from *Aïda* as it happened. A moment later he had chosen his mount—not the brand-new burgundy Lincoln Town Car he used for official occasions, nor the red '63 Thunderbird Sports Roadster he drove when he wanted to go sporting around, but the beat-up black 1981 Ford F-100 pickup he took when he wanted to be incognito. He didn't drive the truck often, so it took a couple of twists on the key and a vigorous pounding on the gas pedal to get the engine to catch—which was just as well because it gave the automatic garage-door opener time to clank and rattle into the concrete arches above. But less than a minute later he was backing into the drive. A deft bit of fingerwork with a selection of buttons on the dash, and the same march he had been humming began to thrum and thunder through the truck's interior, courtesy of an aftermarket in-dash CD player. Matthew hummed louder as he hurled the pickup into the stillness of the Welch County night. At some point he began to whistle.

It did not take long to reach his destination, but, like his grandnephews Ronny and Lewis, Matthew was not one to want his nocturnal activities noted, so like them too, he chose to make his approach as unobtrusively as possible. Thus it was that he also knew of the shadowed place behind the derelict Swanson house and proceeded to ease the pickup in there.

Three minutes later, clad in a long canvas coat and a wide-brimmed hat, Matthew glanced furtively to left and right, and, seeing nothing, marched purposefully across the highway and straight toward the Road Man's camp.

The way was well-traveled by now—over a week of curious rubberneckers had seen to that, so that he did not have
to brave the advances of upstart broomsedge. It was also
late enough that the camp seemed unoccupied. He could
see it up ahead already, for the wagon that comprised heart
and center was completely ringed with flaming torches
within a larger, dimmer ring of bizarre metallic contraptions
Matthew could not quite make out beyond random gleams
and glitters, but could hear clicking and muttering and whir-
ring to themselves as he approached. When he came to
within two yards of the closest one, though—a near-sphere
of curved glass rods and chrome tubing, laced with fiber-
optic cable, all suspended within a simple man-high cubical
framework of square copper rods—it stopped its soft whine
and fell silent. And as soon as he passed the bounds of the
circle itself, the machine to its left clicked to a stop as well.
They started up again when he had gone another pair of
paces, but he scarcely noticed, for by then he had seen the
Road Man himself.

The tinker was sleeping—or appeared to be, though how
anyone could rest lying face down on a combination of
muddy ground and the spiky stubble of shorn broomsedge,
he could not imagine—especially when that person was stark
naked. Almost Matthew turned and left, for as he had driven
the few miles between Cardalba Hall and Swanson's
Meadow he had become increasingly less certain that the
Road Man would be able to deliver what he wanted. Still,
he *was* a tinker and something of a smith—and, more importantly, he could definitely *silence*, which meant he could
probably listen as well: a suspicion given credence by a
number of things he'd read between the lines of his recent
patrons' Voices. Too, he was about as weird as they came
on the one hand, and of rather dubious reputation on the
other, and so would be less likely than most to ask awkward
questions when confronted with a project as peculiar as
Matthew was about to propose. He also wasn't local, and

Matthew was certain that would provide an additional level of circumspection.

Finally, he was available and Matthew was in a hurry. Except that he wasn't at all sure he wanted to confront somebody twice his size who had no qualms at all about stretching out naked in the moonlight. Yeah, maybe he *was* making a mistake—a big one. Better he got what he wanted from some of his Atlanta contacts or from old Mr. Rakestraw down in Jackson County. Grimacing sourly, he turned to go.

And at that moment, the Road Man spoke.

"Don't bother. The machines won't let you out 'less I tell 'em to. Better you state your business like an honest man—or did you just come here to gaze in awe and wonder at my naked bum?"

Matthew blushed—whether from embarrassment or fury he didn't know. To cover, he cleared his throat. "Well, seeing that you *are* awake," he said in his most businesslike tone, "I believe I'd rather talk to your face than to what I'm looking at."

In reply the Road Man farted explosively, then languidly heaved himself to a squatting position facing Matt. He made no move to cover himself. At all. "Well, what is it, Mr. Welch?" He yawned, scratching his backside luxuriously. "In spite of my vanity, I doubt you came here either to admire the beauty of *my* moon or to interrupt my basking in the waning glow of the one in the sky—so how about if you tell me what you want, and then leave. My machines have work to do, and they won't do it as long as you're around."

Matthew raised a bemused eyebrow but said nothing. And very cautiously drew on his slender mental reserves and began to Listen.

"That won't do any good," the Road Man said promptly, plucking a handful of straw from the ground, which he proceeded to braid into the most intricate piece of knot work

Matthew had ever seen. "My Voice rides stronger Winds than any you're accustomed to Hearing."

"Who are you?" Matthew whispered.

"Is *that* why you came? You know I won't answer that."

"Yet you knew who I was without asking, and you know about Listening and Voices . . ."

"I know *many* people without asking, especially if they're moderately famous—or infamous. And surely *you* must know that more folk than you know about Voices."

Matthew frowned. "I repeat, who are you?"

The Road Man matched his frown in spades. "Someone who's losing patience with unfounded arrogance. Someone who can do you a service if you'll swallow your pride."

"Then you know why I came?"

The Road Man shook his head. "Not specifically. But I've got a pretty good idea you wouldn't have come yourself unless you wanted something you dared not tell anyone else about. And if you didn't want to do that, it stands to reason it's something you're worried about, and since I doubt you're much concerned about threats to your person, I'd imagine it's something that threatens the other things dearest to you, *which*—you being a rich and powerful man with good connections—I'd bet you twenty dollars is your pride."

"Ah, you're a psychologist then?"

"I'm many things. Mostly I'm just the Road Man—the Night Man, presently. But then again, there are an *awful* lot of Roads."

"Well," Matthew said decisively, though a part of him discovered he was actually enjoying this verbal sparring match, "did any of those roads happen to lead to a place where you learned anything about making knives?"

"They could have."

Matthew scowled. "It would have taken considerably less energy to say *yes* or *no* than to continue to be obtuse."

"Yeah," the Road Man replied, standing and casually catching up a long-tailed shirt which, it still being mostly buttoned, he proceeded to slip over his head. "But by making you say that, I've cost you energy you wouldn't otherwise have spent. I have, in effect, wasted a moment of Mr. Matthew Welch's precious time."

"And by thus responding," Matthew shot back acidly, "you've also wasted yours. We could be discussing a commission by now."

"True—but if I'm to sacrifice my time for something I may not believe in, doesn't it stand to reason you should waste a little of yours the same way? My life is at least as important to me as yours is to you."

"Your life won't be worth a hill of beans, if you don't talk sense."

"Very well." The Road Man sighed. "We'll *talk* sense—and if I'm lucky, dollars too—lots of them, since I'm sure you have them to spare. And having said that: what can I do for you?"

Matthew heaved a deep breath. "Well, to make a long story short, I need a knife."

The Road Man shrugged. "The stores are full of knives. What's wrong with them?"

"They're not what I need."

"What *do* you need?"

"I need a . . . a custom knife."

"The Atlanta phone book is full of people who make custom knives."

"I need a very particular custom knife, and I need it in a hurry."

"How big a hurry? I'm leaving shortly."

"As soon as you can do it. You don't have any other commissions pending, do you? If so, I'll pay you off and them too. They can wait, I can't."

"And why are *you* so important?"

"Because I can give you enough money to make you happier than you are right now, and if necessary, I can give your patrons enough money to ease whatever pain doing without your services would entail."

The Road Man eyed him warily. "We're talking greatest good for greatest number, then?"

Matthew nodded.

Whereupon the Road Man frowned again. "It isn't common that knives ever do anyone much good—except those who get to sew up the wounds they inflict—and so I repeat, how big a hurry?"

"When are you leaving?"

"When I get ready."

"Hmmm. That won't do."

"And why not? It's not hard to make a knife. I could make you any one you wanted by tomorrow morning if I started now."

"Except that it *wouldn't* be the knife I want."

The Road Man's eyes narrowed suspiciously. "And just what kind of knife *do* you want, Mr. Welch? A long knife, a short knife? A sharp knife, or a dull knife? A hunting knife, or a pocketknife?"

"I don't care," Matthew gritted. "You've got free rein on design and execution within certain basic parameters. Where you *don't* have free rein is on how you work on it—and when."

The Road Man's eyebrows shot up. "Yes? And what might these conditions be?"

"It needs to be made of gold and silver and iron. It needs to be worked on in light of sun and light of moon. And it needs to be folded seven times under the influence of each."

The Road Man stroked his chin thoughtfully. "Those are *very* peculiar conditions," he said at last. "But I've heard stranger—though not on this side of the ocean, or along this particular Road."

"But you can do it?" Matthew asked hopefully.

"I can."

"And will you?"

"If you meet my terms."

"I'll do my best."

"Are you sure?"

"Well, I *can't* say for sure until I hear 'em, can I?"

"Okay," the Road Man replied. "It will cost you seven thousand dollars. One thousand big ones for every sleepless night."

Matthew blanched at that, then nodded. He'd probably need the damned thing someday anyway, and God knew when he'd find as likely a maker again. "Done," he said.

"And one other thing."

"Which is?"

"A seed."

"What *kind* of seed?"

"A seed that will grow in fertile ground. It will be no trouble for you to provide, I promise; for you already have it in your possession—in a way. I will say no more."

"And when do *I* collect?"

The Road Man shrugged again. "Well, you've said it needs to be folded seven times under the light of the sun, and a like number under the light of the moon. So if you're lucky—by which I mean, if the weather holds—that would mean exactly a week—not counting working on the hilt, sharpening, or polishing; that'd add another day, so let's say next Saturday. How much of an edge did you want on it, by the way?"

It was Matthew's turn to shrug—which he did, stiffly. "Whatever you feel like doing. It's mostly for . . . insurance. I have no intention whatever of using it unless I have to."

"I hope not," the Road Man replied cryptically. "For such a knife could cut some very unusual things indeed. Some very *strong* things, too."

"It could," Matthew acknowledged, with his own secret smile.

"It *could*, perhaps, even carve its way through Silence."

"Ah, but *all* knives can do that." Matthew chuckled. "They do that anytime you slash one through the air."

"Well said!" the Road Man roared. "And now, unless

you have something *else* that needs to be said, you can be on your way.''

Matthew glared at him, not liking, or being accustomed to, being dismissed.

''I have no intention of beginning work with you around,'' the Road Man informed him shortly. ''You may as well leave.''

''But how will I know you're working on this right?''

''Because I don't lie. It's a *sin* to tell a lie.''

And as Matthew stood there gaping, the Road Man added, ''Besides, you seem to be in a remarkable hurry. It therefore stands to reason that if I can begin tonight, while the moon is out, that'll save you a moon later on.''

''True.'' Matthew grinned. ''Which means I get it half a day sooner—and that's probably good. In my business half a day can make a lot of difference.''

''Exactly what *is* your business?'' the Road Man asked pointedly.

''Let's just say I make things too—only the thing I make most of is Luck.''

''And I,'' the Road Man replied promptly, ''have always found that one makes one's *own* luck. All you really need to do is to listen to your heart. Your heart always knows what you ought to do. Trouble is, head keeps overruling.''

''Yes, but . . .''

The Road Man glanced at his wrist as if consulting a watch Matthew could not for the life of him see. ''Don't you have somewhere else you need to be?''

Matthew puffed his cheeks in exasperation, and rose. He extended his hand toward the tinker. ''Shake on the bargain?''

The Road Man shook his head. ''Let us rather shake when it is fulfilled. You need new plug wires by the way; that truck'll crank a lot easier with a new set. '81, isn't it? By the sound?''

Matthew grimaced irritably and retraced his path across the field. The Road Man obviously knew more than he was saying—about a great many things. But all Matthew could hear, when he once more tried to Listen in his direction an hour or so later, was the Road Man's Silence.

Ronny did not expect the Road Man to be occupied when he stumped through the ring of machines somewhere between nine and ten o'clock, several hours after he'd left Winnie's father standing forlornly on his front steps. To be perfectly honest, he didn't know if he expected much of *anything* anymore, given that the last *umpteen* things he'd expected, most of which had had to do with Winnie, had not gone at all as he had planned—and he hadn't a clue what to do about it, either.

The fact was that Winnie had somehow managed to get herself in thrall to Lew's mysterious uncle, with the result that Ronny had suddenly found himself even more curious than heretofore about who Matthew Welch was, and how, exactly, he exercised such invisible but iron-fisted control over the citizenry hereabout. In fact, right now, Ronny was so curious about the illustrious Master of Cardalba he could easily have enjoyed finding out how long it took him to bleed to death from a slash in his jugular, how loudly he would scream if flayed alive, or how many beats his heart could manage after Ronny ripped it out of his chest. Yeah, all those things he had *considered* several times over during the last few hours, but what he had actually been *doing* was running the roads. Once, even, he had actually found himself pointing the Escort toward Cardalba Hall, but good sense had interceded there—mostly the fact that nobody would know he *was* there. As for those from whom he could have taken solace, Lew was still at his wrestling meet, and he had no desire whatever to confide in Aunt Erin, who was, he imagined, still painting away in her studio.

Which left the Road Man, who, he hoped, would still be up, but who also—as Ronny discovered when his eyes finally adjusted to the torchlit glare around the wagon—seemed disinclined to talk to him.

Ronny had been standing not two yards behind his mentor for at least a minute—watching him poke and prod through a nail keg full of the same lengths of metal bar stock that had produced the raw materials for his nearly completed knife—before the Road Man gave any sign at all of noticing him. And at that, his only acknowledgment was a low, grunted " 'Lo," whereupon he continued rummaging.

Ronny cleared his throat. "Is . . . is this a bad time?" His voice came out hoarse and shaky—legacy of the tears that still occasionally trickled from his eyes. The last few words were muffled by a sob born partly of anger, partly of despair at finding yet another source of comfort forestalled.

"It *could* be a bad time," the Road Man replied finally. "It depends on who you're talking to and about."

Ronny had to bite back a scathing remark. Surely the guy could tell by looking at him, by the tone of his voice, by the way his lips were shaking that he was upset. Surely even the Road Man was not insensitive to pain when he saw it so clearly manifested. It took Ronny a moment to recover enough from his disappointment to reply.

"Look," he said slowly. "I . . . I really don't want to bother you if you're busy, but . . . well, I've got a really bad problem, and I *really* need somebody to talk to."

"I have a really bad problem, too," the Road Man grumbled. "I've already given you a shitload of time today."

"But this is really important."

"So is this."

"It's a matter of—"

"Life and death? I doubt it. But what I have to do, on the other hand, *is* a matter of life and death—or could be."

"Oh . . . never *mind*!" Ronny shouted abruptly. "Just *never* mind!" He was aware that his control had snapped and cared not the slightest whit. "Never mind!" he repeated, for emphasis, whereupon he whirled around and stumped toward the ring of machines. He had not gone two yards, however, before his eyes fell on the small jeweler's anvil he had utilized all day, first to fine-tune the knife, then to work on Winnie's bracelet. He still had the bracelet too; the box was in his shirt pocket.

But he sure as hell didn't need it any longer, not with the pain having it around would cause. So what more fitting end could there be for it than to cast it back into the fires of its first making?

Except that would be too easy, too remote. Ronny wanted to effect the destruction himself. And with that in mind, he made his way to the enormous anvil that stood beside the Road Man's forge. An instant later, he had centered the bracelet on the darkly gleaming iron, dropped his crutch, and was hefting above his head the largest sledgehammer he could find.

But just as he started to tense his shoulders in order to slam the hammer down atop the bracelet—just as he felt his damaged leg start to buckle beneath too much unaccustomed weight—just at that *exact* moment, he felt the wooden handle snatched from his fingers as easily as he could have snatched a toy from a week-old kitten.

And spun around to come chest to chest with the Road Man.

"I wouldn't do that if I were you," the Road Man whispered, and Ronny saw that his face was as grim as he had ever seen it. "Pain is fleeting, pleasure is not."

"Bullshit. What do *you* know about pain?"

The Road Man ran his hands across his bare forearms and exposed thighs, and Ronny could not help noticing the vast webwork of scars laced among the brighter tattoos and wiry hair. "I know a great *deal* about it."

"Not the kind I'm talking about."

"And how do you know? Do you want me to drag out my heart so you can see the scars Cupid's apocryphal arrow has left there? I like women, yeah; but I'm not like the Day Man; *I* cleave to 'em a lot more with my heart than with my peter."

"Fuck you!" Ronny raged, his eyes once more a-brim. "Just spare me your fucking philosophy already! You wouldn't talk to me when I wanted to, so don't you dare try to talk to me now!''

The Road Man's eyes flashed dangerously. ''Grow *up*, boy!''

''I'm fucking *trying* to!'' Ronny shouted back. ''If I wasn't, I'd have killed my fucking self two hours ago!''

''And the world would be much poorer.''

''*Fuck* the world!''

''I have,'' the Road Man replied calmly. ''In about every way, both literally and figuratively, I can.''

Ronny could only blink at him through his tears.

And the Road Man reached past him to recover the undamaged bracelet. He peered at it curiously for a moment, polished it against his shirttail, then returned it to Ronny. ''Things made with so much love should not be destroyed so capriciously,'' he said simply. ''Nor should you think that the love you have made with your lady can be destroyed by anything as small as a man.''

''But . . .''

''I have a job to do, Ronny. I have a very important commission.''

''But . . .''

''You have a job to do too, as soon as you are man enough to face it.''

''And what does that mean?''

''If I have to *tell* you,'' the Road Man snorted derisively, ''I surely have taught you nothing.''

And with that he resumed sorting through the keg of bar stock.

And Ronny trudged back through the meadow.

PART III

TEMPERING

Chapter 20

Love and War

Erin Welch's house
Saturday, April 21—midnight

Ronny couldn't sleep—though that was scarcely a novelty anymore. He *hadn't* caught more than a couple of hours of shut-eye at a hit for a week now: not since last Saturday evening, in fact, which he had taken to calling Hell Night. Come to think of it, when he got right down to it, the only thing that differentiated tonight's insomnia from the last six bouts was that he had decided to replace the literal tossing and turning he'd been doing in bed with a slightly more figurative sort outdoors.

And for no clear reason, he had chosen as the locale for his nocturnal reverie the sturdy granite railing of the stone bridge that arched across the Talooga and linked Aunt Erin's property to Cardalba Plantation. It was a kind of no-man's-land, he supposed: earth-above-air-above-water, connecting the homey world he knew with that far more mysterious one he both hated and (he was embarrassed to admit) feared. And here, at midnight with the night breeze blowing unseasonably warm and the waning moon beating down upon him and turning the cobbles to blue and the water to rippling silver, it was easy to suspend disbelief and pretend he was on the fringe of another, more magical realm. He wished he was, too; wished a beautiful lady in grass-green silk would ride out of a hollow hill and carry him away. That way he wouldn't have to confront the images that haunted his every waking hour.

Like Winnie slumping around school with that horrible, empty, lost expression on her once-animated face; speaking to him only in minimal, sorrow-laden monosyllables when she could no longer actually avoid him, and then merely about the most inconsequential of matters—which was *not* what they needed to discuss. All Ronny had to do was *mention* Matthew Welch, and she closed up—completely. She was like a fire that had gone out, he thought; a candle bereft of the flames that gave purpose to its being.

Her grades were slipping too, he'd heard her teachers say; and she was only going through the sketchiest motions of doing homework and taking tests. And naturally the other kids were talking about her as well, though he wasn't certain *what* they were whispering about behind their hands, since folks tended to clam up as soon as he came within earshot. Which was just his luck—to use a word he was *also* hearing all too frequently: right when it was beginning to look like he was finally going to get somewhere with somebody and maybe be on the way to making a few friends in the bargain, suddenly bang-thud-swoosh, and he was an outsider again— though whether it was misplaced sympathy that made Winnie and Lew's buddies too uncomfortable to speak to him, or merely a case of ostracism by association, he didn't know.

One thing he *did* know was that Anson was even wilder and more unpredictable than usual. True, he generally *looked* like death on a stick until about 10:00 in the morning—and had a disposition to match—but by the time afternoon rolled around some mysterious source of energy had kicked in and he was practically bouncing off the walls, so full of himself he was almost giddy. He had been sent to the principal's office three times, and put on detention once. In fact, the change in him was so marked that, had Ronny even halfway considered him a friend, he would have been concerned. Such radical mood swings weren't normal, nor was such surfeit of energy, nor the fey, mad sparkle in his eyes. Was he on drugs, perhaps? Downers and uppers, or some such? If this had been Tampa, that would have been a pretty good guess. But Ronny had seen no sign of such goings-on in Welch County, so the only other explanation he could think of was something to do with Matthew Welch—with whom, if the virtually continuous presence of Anson's car at Cardalba Hall was any indication, he was keeping pretty much constant company. Ronny did not even want to consider what that implied about Anson and Winnie, who was now officially Matthew's house guest.

And speaking of Welches, neither Lew nor Aunt Erin were any great shakes either. His guardian looked more worn and frazzled every day, which Ronny knew was due to a lack of sleep even more pervasive than his own—though in her case it represented a conscious choice aimed at staving off the nightmares Lew was still, in spite of her best efforts, having. It was too much for anyone to do, Ronny knew: too much to stay awake all night and keep . . . whatever it was at bay. If she slept at all, it was in the relatively secure daytime hours, and he had doubts about even that. He hated himself for that, too: despised the fact that he was so weirded out by his godmother he did not dare ask her the questions he knew he should. Like what, exactly, had gone on that awful Tuesday night? Like how was Anson involved? Like what was the extent of her—he supposed—paranormal powers, and what, precisely, did she do behind the closed door of her bedroom in those long, dark vigils between midnight and dawn? And, most importantly, why was she increasingly failing to shield—if that was the right word—Lew from the tormenting nightmares? The only *useful* information Ronny had been able to ferret out of her in a solid week of trying was that she knew more about the dreams he'd had back in Florida than she was willing to talk about, except that Anson had *not* been involved, and that they had probably not been intended for him. *Everything* else was taboo—including, in particular, any mention of the rift between her side of the family and Matthew Welch. All she would say about *that* affair was that Matthew had not approved of the way she had chosen to raise Lew. The rest—her unusual abilities and odd flashes of prescience—she either sidestepped completely or obscured by mumbo jumbo about artists' temperament, mind-expanding drugs she'd taken in college, or having once studied with a controversial psychologist. She would not discuss Matthew or Anson at all—which gave Ronny all the fuel he needed to suspect their involvement even more.

As for poor Lew . . . Like the rest of Erin's household, he hadn't had a solid night's sleep since his return from the wrestling meet a week ago. He had won the 135-pound class (which had surprised no one except him), but since then not a night had gone by when Ronny was not jarred awake by his godbrother shouting in his sleep. There had been no more catatonic episodes, however; and Lew had either quieted on his own, or—as was the case on three occasions—merely stayed awake long enough to drift off again with Ronny sitting beside him.

The puzzling thing was that Lew didn't seem to remember those interludes, or so Ronny assumed after he'd twice put out discreet early-morning feelers, to which his friend had only mumbled something about not sleeping well and having nightmares that he couldn't recall. And while Lew tried to shrug it off, Ronny knew the accumulating tension was taking its toll. He was growing more irritable and jumpy by the day, and displayed only a shadow of his normal good-humored energy. So things were definitely rotten in his personal Denmark as well.

And finally there was the Road Man, who was likewise

becoming increasingly unpredictable—though that was rather a hard call in his case, Ronny had to admit. Still, *something* was definitely up with him, something he did not want Ronny to discover. But Ronny *did* know, or at least he knew that four times in the last seven days he had shown up for his daily smithing sessions at some time other than the expected hour only to have his mentor glare at him and spirit something small and shiny into the perilous bowels of his wagon.

As for his metalworking efforts themselves, *they* were progressing nicely (and were about the only things that were). The knife was finished except for filing down a bit of silver inlay Ronny had set into the golden dragon handle. And the crutch now boasted so many prickly augmentations it was becoming hazardous to stump around on. Ronny imagined the time was fast approaching when he would either have to abandon it in favor of some more functional, if mundane, alternative or begin another. There was simply too much dollar value hanging off it to risk it now, in silver and other metals, never mind its worth as art. Mr. Wiley's wife, who ran a small jewelry studio on the outskirts of town, and who had studied Celtic, Norse, and Scythian metalwork all, had taken a gander at it after class one day and stated flatly that it needed to be in a museum somewhere, insured for a couple of million bucks. Ronny doubted that, as he doubted all things to do with his craft—for try as he would, no artifact he produced bore more than the most shadowy relationship to the image burning in his head. But he also had to admit that praise such as Ms. Wiley had heaped on him felt mighty good. Almost it was a viable surrogate to the applause of the crowds in that lost other life in Florida.

Almost.

And that was the key word for his whole life now. *Almost* a smith, *almost* Winnie's boyfriend—*almost* able to figure out what the heck was going on. There were a good many pieces on the table now, but he didn't know how to sort them out. Or didn't want to, given the blatantly irrational direction many of them were tending. The fact that he'd had four major exams the previous week hadn't helped either.

And so he sat on the railing of the bridge and worried and fretted and pondered until at some point he drifted off long enough for the moon to have tangibly moved when he awakened again. He blinked, rubbed his eyes, and shivered, for a chill wind had crept in among the warmer breezes of the last few days as a reminder that it had been known to snow in Georgia in April. And that cold reminded him of his warm bed at home. Which, unfortunately, was a thing he also dreaded.

Lewis was snoring softly when Ronny returned to their bedroom twenty minutes later. He paused for a moment to stare down at his friend where he lay in a pool of moonlight. Lew looked almost like a child, he thought: the gentle curves of his lips complementing the smooth planes of a face that had not yet firmed into the crisper angles of adulthood. It was a beautiful face too, Ronny conceded, acknowledging a fact that had nothing to do with sexual attraction. And it was also a face that did not deserve to contort with the anguish that had afflicted it of late. But poor Lew, poor suffering Lew, still would not admit that the dreams bugged him. In fact, he did not even seem to remember the first one any longer, the one that had necessitated the strange, vaporous bath Ronny himself had a hard time fixing on. And naturally Aunt Erin wouldn't talk about that either, except for a few cryptic comments about having minored in botany.

But as far as Ronny could tell, the coast looked clear this evening, and he hoped it would stay that way. It *was* late, after all; and it was also Saturday night, which was classic tomcatting time for randy lads like Anson. So maybe—just possibly—the troublesome Mr. Bowman would be too sated with any number of more immediate vices to resort to petty torture from afar.

Lew was still sleeping peacefully when Ronny padded out of the bathroom five minutes later, clad only in red bikini briefs. And his breathing remained calm and regular when Ronny felt himself drifting off amid plans for the next day's smithing.

But two minutes later it was nightmare time again.

Lewis's scream brought Ronny bolt upright and sent him out of bed and scrambling across the room before the first long, drawn-out cry had faded. He wrenched the hall door open as he passed, hollered "Aunt Erin!" into the half-light beyond, then turned his full attention to his foster brother. Lew was sitting straight up in bed, eyes wide open and mouth stretched wider still. He wasn't *looking* at anything, as far as Ronny could tell, but he was definitely still screaming, and the muscles were already cramping into hard tight bundles across his chest and neck and arms.

"Lew!" he cried, throwing his arms around his friend, trying at once to shake him awake and to massage the worst of the knotting muscles loose, and all the time waiting for Aunt Erin to arrive, while the screaming went on without letup except for strained gasps for breath.

But Aunt Erin did *not* come, and Ronny knew, after more than a minute of shaking and hollering and a frantic trip into the bathroom for a hot towel to wrap around Lew's knotting shoulders, that there was nothing more he could accomplish without her. Biting his lip apprehensively, for he hated to leave Lew for even a second when he was like this, Ronny grabbed his crutch and stumped up the hall to his guardian's room.

"*Aunt Erin!*" he shouted again, pounding on her door with his fist. "Aunt Erin, you've got to come quick!" But when that brought no response, he turned the knob and — to his surprise, for his aunt usually kept it locked—pushed his way inside. It was not a thing he did lightly, either, because Erin valued her privacy almost more than anything in the world, and since that fateful Tuesday night, both he and Lew were under strict orders never to enter her room after she had retired without her express permission. Since she was generally easy to get along with otherwise—indeed, almost like a girl their own age in some regards—they both cut her slack on that relatively minor idiosyncrasy.

But not now.

Fortunately.

Erin was not in bed at all; nor did the bed—a huge four-poster affair directly opposite the door—look as if it had been slept in recently. Ronny squinted into the half-light, waiting for his eyes to adjust from the relative glare of the hall to the bluish moonlight here. And then he saw her.

His aunt was sitting stiffly in a large, rust-velvet recliner. She was fully dressed—which for her at home meant jeans, a rock-band sweatshirt, and sneakers. A wineglass glittered balefully on the floor beside her and Ronny could barely make out the transparent shimmer of her favorite Château Elan Chablis therein. But what drew him like a fascinated moth to the dazzling peril of flame was the fact that, like Lew, her eyes were wide open and she was staring into space.

But she was not screaming—not audibly—though there was an eerie *tightness* in the air that made Ronny want to clamp his hands over his ears, as if he was picking up some kind of supersonic. And his brain suddenly felt both dull and alert, as though every single neuron was trying to interpret several sets of orders simultaneously and either overloading or shutting down. He blinked, staggered, and—in spite of the crutch—fell. "Aunt Erin!" he yelled again, but she did not move, did not change her expression. An awkward scramble closer showed him that her lips were moving slowly in silent supplication. "*Aunt Erin!*" he cried once more, not three feet from her, but still she showed no more reaction than a single blink that might have been mere reflex. Impulsively, Ronny reached up to touch her left hand, which was clamped hard across the end of the chair.

But as soon as his flesh brushed hers, the world changed.

He no longer *had* a body—was in a colorless void filled with nothing but sounds—except that they were also like winds because they all seemed to have a point of origin and all appeared to lead somewhere specific, so that they possessed a quasi-physical dimension as well. They also tended to Doppler in and out of clarity as they blew past him, and without meaning to, he found himself following one—and discovered to his surprise that if he stayed with it, it was not so much a sound as something between a thought and a word, and that there was even a ghostly personality attached to it that seemed vaguely familiar, and would be more so if he could somehow make his way back to its origin.

But just as he began that quest in earnest, he became aware of two *particular* sounds—shrieking and shrilling at each other with a fury like a pair of tornados full of angry cats whirling into each other. And as he drew closer and followed those sounds along, they gradually clarified into what he could only call voices—and then he recognized both those titanic winds: one was Anson, and the other, nearer one was Aunt Erin.

Something brushed his consciousness then, and he cringed for the barest instant at the awful alienness, the utter vulnerability of his innermost secrets being laid bare.

Ronny? And with that he realized that in some uncanny way Aunt Erin had called his name. She had seemed full of awe, too: and wonder and relief—and then, for no reason Ronny could fathom, an astonishing amount of fear.

Ronny? What are you *doing here?* Then: *Oh my God— I forgot to lock the door, and you . . . you're touching me, aren't you! But you have to stop, you have to! I—*

You what? the Voice that was also Wind that was also Anson taunted, rising to a crescendo of force. *You have to defend another weakling against me? One who's not even kin?*

You can't keep this up indefinitely, Anson! Erin responded, with a cyclonic shriek. *Uncle Matt may have in-dulged you this far, but mark me, it will go no further! He and I may disagree about* many *things, but I'm quite sure we'll be in agreement on this!*

Much good it'll do him!

I could Call him now!

Do it, then! But can you be sure he'll be on your side?

Of course he will! You're a much bigger threat to him than I am.

Ah, but suppose he has no choice!

One always *has a choice.*

He *doesn't*! With a trace of smugness. Then: *If you'll 'scuse me, I believe I'll play with my cousin a little while longer.*

Like hell you will!

But Anson did not reply. Ronny felt a surge as the Wind that carried Anson's voice swished away with a force like the strongest hurricane he'd ever huddled through. And he heard—almost—Lewis's screams of terror redoubling. This time, however, he caught images as well: Lew lying naked in the middle of a swamp, while blood poured endlessly from open wounds that cracked wider by the minute . . . insects feasting on that blood, laying eggs in the festering sores that surrounded those horrible gashes . . . maggots stirring beneath the skin of his lips and eyelids and erupting forth in grainy white cascades . . .

Stop it!

That had been Erin again, but somehow, Ronny knew, his own unheard shout had joined her.

Anson paused—but only long enough to lash out at Erin more fearsomely than before.

Don't you know anything, bitch? he screamed. *You're too weak now; I've hurt you already and you can't be repaired. I know: I can feel the doubt in your mind.*

Ah, Erin gave him back, *but there are things I still know that you don't! I may have denied my Luck but that doesn't mean I don't have it!*

Ha! Anson scoffed. *Matt says it's like your real body; you don't exercise it, you lose it. 'Sides, you're a woman, you've had a kid; the* best *you can do is Silence and Listen to kin—and it doesn't look like you're much good at either of them.*

Yes, but a physical body can do remarkable things if properly motivated—by fear, say, or by anger. And I can assure *you that my anger is greater than yours.*

Bullshit!

It can also do remarkable things when it has other Strength to augment it.

What Strength?

Ronny's.

Ronny? You mean that limping little asshole?

No, I mean Ronny who now sits at my feet . . . Ronny who is my son!

Your . . . son?

Yes!

Had Ronny been standing, he would have collapsed, had he been conscious he would have swooned. But he was floating free among the Winds now, and had nowhere to hide—for the instant he tried, Erin was there, holding him firm, reassuring him, drawing on him in some strange way, digging deep into his soul, yet leaving the source of his Strength intact. His Strength! He could feel it, like a cool fire circulating around and around in that distant, heavy thing that was his body—and the more he became aware of it, the more intense it became. Yet, unlike his physical body, there was no weakening, no odd numbness around his shattered knee. This body—this *form*—at least was whole. And it was the Strength of that completeness which Erin was drawing into herself then forcing into him again, so that the two of them became in effect one being. Ronny had felt that closeness once before, he realized, with his new, expanded consciousness; for his Strength was one with his mother's now as their blood had been in the months before his birth.

And it was too much, the union *too* complete. He had lost himself completely, and the drawing was getting fiercer as well. There was no return of Strength now, he discovered to his horror: he was being sucked dry faster than he was being replenished—being utterly drained of that strange fluid *nothing* that was all the self he had in this world of sounds and voices and winds.

And then, for a long empty moment, Erin simply *wasn't*. Panic-stricken, he reached out for her, but she had returned by then—and felt different in some way: more energized, stronger, more . . . powerful. And, Ronny knew, it had taken no real time at all.

So what if he's your kid? Anson shrilled furiously. *Old Ronny can't do nothin' 'cause he's incomplete—'course I guess I'll have to off him sooner or later, anyway, just to be safe.*

But is he incomplete, Anson? Could I draw on him like this if he were? Matt was too late, boy. The Luck was already kicking in when Ronny fell; all it needed was a little encouragement to set it straight.

So what? He doesn't know how to use what he's got. He's as crippled that way as his body is.

Ah, but I know another *secret, Anson*, Erin's Voice replied sweetly, though Ronny could sense she was deeply troubled—as, indeed, was he, since that was Lew's life—and his—they were discussing. *Would you like to know what that secret is?*

I can't lie to you now, can I? Anson gave her back. *So I have to say yes. On the other hand, maybe I'll just Blow into the gaping screaming holes I've cut in your Silence and find out for myself.*

And maybe I'll lure *you there and lose you.*

You don't have the nerve! It'd kill you.

I have to die anyway; that would be a very useful way. Without you to torment my sons, who would I be concerned about?

Good old Grandpa Matty, of course.

Oh? But with you gone, I'm sure he'd see the error of his ways. Did you ever think about that? He can't approve of what you're doing; he's that much of traditionalist.

Is he? I know for a fact that he's ordered a knife to be made—a very particular knife.

How . . . *particular?* (And Ronny could sense so much apprehension filtering into him from Erin that it would have made him sick had he been more closely linked to his corporeal self.)

Particular enough to kill someone. Say . . . Lewis, maybe.

And how particular is that?

Made of iron and silver and gold, folded seven times by sunlight and seven times in the light of the moon. Is that particular enough?

He wouldn't dare! He's not even supposed to know that! I locked that memory myself. It was—

He'd dare anything to keep on my good side right now— and so would I. And I'd certainly dare enough to make poor trustin' old Matt have a knife commissioned that could rid us both of a potential enemy. Now . . . you were sayin' something about secrets?

Oh, you still want to hear them? I expected that someone as Strong as you—

You know I do.

Do we have a bargain, then?

I don't remember sayin' anything about bargains.

I don't want the Mastership for Lewis, Anson, Erin told him flatly. *Nor, I'm sure, does Lew—and I think I can say the same for Ronny. I only want peace for both my children. If I tell you, will you leave them alone forever? On your honor as a Listener?*

That would be a pretty stupid thing for me to agree to, wouldn't it?

It's also stupid to refuse knowledge that might help you, and I'm sure you know already that one such as you—as we—are eats and sleeps and breathes knowledge.

I doubt there's anything you can tell me old Matt can't.

Don't be so certain. Suppose it's a secret that could make you very powerful indeed—something Matt himself does not know.

I found out about the knife, didn't I? I'm sure I could find that out too.

And you could prowl through Matt's mind a thousand years and not find it, too. It helps to know what you're looking for, and you wouldn't. But I promise you, he doesn't know this. I only just found it out myself.

So why would you want to tell me something like that, anyway?

Because it could also completely destroy you, and I think you like to gamble. So do I: it runs in the family.

You drive a hard bargain.

I meant to.

Very well.

You mean you agree.

Oh, why the hell not? It's only a promise, and there's no way you could hold me to it—and even if there was, you can't bind Matt by it—or keep me from workin' through him.

Tsk, Anson, do you always tip your hand like that?

Sometimes—if I'm the dealer. Now, you were sayin' . . . ?

Okay, then: Anson . . . have you ever wondered who your father was?

Sure—but that's no secret anymore: he was Matt's son. His name was Paul.

And where is he now?

Away, livin' rich and famous in California under an assumed name. That's what all the extra sons and by-blows do—except us designated heirs—so I'm told.

Well, you're right about the California part, and Matthew was his father. But he's not rich and famous—he's insane. They Fixed him, but it happened anyway.

You're lyin'.

I can't lie this way, remember? A tongue can lie but not

a Voice. Besides, that's not what I wanted to tell you.

So lay it on me, then—or shut up.

Anson . . . have you ever wondered who Paul's mother was?

Some local slut, I guess. Some bitch Grandpa got into trouble and paid off. Probably one of his footholders.

Wrong!

Wrong?

Well, partly right. She was local, and a footholder—of a sort—for a time; but she wasn't a slut, not by any conventional definition.

Who was she, then?

Matt's sister—and my mother.

A pause; then: *So dear old Dad's a child of incest? Well, that's sure not a big enough deal to save your sons.*

Ah, but that's not the whole story.

So lay it on me!

My pleasure! Erin replied with so much satisfaction Ronny could feel it himself, and wondered if Anson was likewise sensing it. *Have you ever wondered who your mother is?*

Evelyn Bowman, of course. Paul Welch knocked her up and wouldn't marry her—or the Welches wouldn't let him.

Wrong again! You're adopted—more or less.

Ronny felt the Wind that was Anson shift and eddy uncertainly, then recover.

Bullshit!

Erin pressed her advantage. *Actually, Evelyn was pregnant by Paul about the time you were born, so that much is true. But that child died at a very convenient time in a very convenient and unrecorded way, so it was arranged for her to bring up another child of Paul's who was born at the same time without ever realizing it was not her own.*

Another . . . ?

By Paul's mother!

No!

Ronny felt the force of Anson's will waver once more, and then collapse. An instant later, he—there was no other word for it—blew away.

But Erin would not leave him in peace. *What's the matter?* she jeered, as she hurled her own Wind after him. *Can't stand knowing that you're not only a bastard yourself, but that you're a child of double incest by a crazy man as well? It does strange things to one, don't you think? Makes all those recessive genes come out. Sometimes it even makes you crazy.*

Nooooooo! Anson cried. And was gone.

And Ronny was alone in a tattered Silence full of the unheard sobbings of his mother.

Chapter 21

Love and Death

"Aunt Erin?" Ronny called urgently. "Aunt . . . M-mom—wake up!"

He had been back his his own proper world less than a minute—barely long enough to make his way into the adjoining bathroom for the cold, wet towel with which he was so frantically massaging Erin's face and hands and arms. She was burning up; Ronny had known that the instant he had returned to himself and felt her hand in his own. In fact, never in his life had he felt a human being so consumed with fever.

"Oh, please, Mom," he pleaded, his voice cracking with desperation. "Please come out of it and talk to me."

He patted Erin's cheeks dry with the other end of the towel, appalled to see sweat bead out on them again as soon as he had finished. But then, to his vast relief, she blinked and he did his best to smile reassurance at her.

"Aunt Erin?" he asked hopefully, reaching for her arm.

"Don't touch me!" Erin cried, wrenching her hand away. "Oh, Ronny, Ronny, my poor foolish son, please don't touch me!"

"Why not?" Ronny asked, his face a mask of confusion, though he complied.

"Because I can't stand it! Because you have awakened that in me which cannot now be controlled."

Ronny flopped backwards on the thick carpet and stared at her. "What're you *talking* about? I mean, I *know* you're my mom and all, now—I guess' I suspected that anyway. But I know about Anson too, now—sort of . . . but there's so much I *don't* know, and—"

"There's no time to tell you now, either," Erin interrupted sadly. "But maybe I can begin."

"What? I don't understand . . . I mean you've . . . defeated Anson, you've got all the time in the world. Oh sure, you've got a fever, but that's no big deal. We'll start getting you cooled down, and then I'll call the doctor, and—"

Erin shook her head. "Anson is not defeated, I don't think, though if I'm extremely fortunate I *may* have bought you and Lewis some time. As for calling a doctor, don't bother. When I cool down I will . . . die."

"Die?" Ronny gaped incredulously. "*Die?*"

"Die," Erin affirmed sadly. "Because, oh my beautiful, dutiful, foolish son. I did something very forbidden and very foolish just now. Anson was too strong for me—far too strong, as a result of his double Welch blood. But he was acting unilaterally and without a footholder, and . . ."

"What's a footholder?"

"What that girl you like so much has become, I'm afraid. Oh, Ronny, there's so little time, and so much of it is strange, so much is hard to believe."

"So how 'bout letting me sort out the believing part for myself!"

"Said like a Welch!" Erin chuckled grimly. "Which is something I thought *I* would never say—but I'm wasting time. A footholder is someone whom a Master—one of us Listeners who's been specially trained—can draw on to augment his Strength—like a battery, sort of. They're always of the opposite sex from the Master because there are parts of our inner selves that only mental communion with the other sex can access—which in practice means they're always female. It also means they have to be virgins; otherwise they're imperfect and the Strength—that's sort of what powers what you've heard called Luck—will back up where it shouldn't and cause problems—either that, or they'll instinctively try to complete themselves with the Listener's power and drain him dry. Unfortunately—for me, at least—female Listeners have the same problem—in spades. It's too complicated to go into now, but basically it's traditional that male Listeners always see to it that their sisters are deflowered before their Luck activates—generally in their late teens. That's so we can never be as strong as they are. The Luck *is* still there, of course—though usually severely curtailed—but instead of dissipating or driving you mad like it often does in men if they're not Fixed before it activates, it just sits and festers—*unless* a male touches you *while* it's being used, whereupon it'll drain him of Strength in an instant trying to finish itself. But *you're* a boy *and* my son *and* a Listener all, so when you touched me while I was already using my Luck, all your power rushed into me of its own accord, and . . . Ronny, I *can't* tell you this.''

''But you *have* to! How else will I know?''

Erin bit her lip, then nodded decisively. ''Yeah, okay, maybe you *should* know, though only because I know you're strong: but . . . well, you *overloaded* me. In effect, you burned me out. You gave me enough Strength to stand against Anson until I could force him to retreat. And, more importantly, you gave me Strength enough to Listen to the past and Hear there the thing that would defeat him, the thing even I did not know until I Heard it, for it was a dark secret my own mother never told me.''

''And by doing that I've killed you.'' Ronny groaned dully. ''Lew will never forgive me. Nor,'' he added, ''will I.''

''You're wrong there—about both of us. I've done everything I can to protect you, but I see now it wasn't to be.

Matt isn't the only one to suffer by going against tradition.''

"What are you talking about?''

"Oh Ronny, Ronny, Ronny." Erin sighed, easing the towel from her fingers and wiping her brow with it. "There's no way to make you understand.''

"So tell me about being my mother, then; about why you *wouldn't* tell me you were my mother.''

Erin took a deep, shuddering breath and nodded. "Well, you must know now that you *are* my son. You and Lewis are twins—or at least you were born at one birth. But you are only half brothers—I hope.''

"Huh? We don't have the same birthdays or anything.''

"Oh yes you do. Don't forget birthdays are matters of record, and records can easily be revised—especially if you have influence with Luck.''

"But why . . . ?''

"It was pure idealistic self-indulgence, I can see that now, but I promise you my intentions were good at the time. I was just out of college when I had you, Ronny. I came of age at a time when all the old standards and institutions and traditions were being questioned and many thrown away. Well, naturally I started looking at the traditions of the Listeners the same way, and decided that it was a pretty sorry system that ritually deflowered women before their Luck manifested, and forced men into roles that required them to trade their Luck for goods, thereby subjecting them to all kinds of preposterous temptations. Unfortunately, I also knew I couldn't *completely* defy the family traditions, but at the same time I wanted desperately for at least one of my children to be free to seek his own destiny—which brings us to your begetting. I—are you *sure* you want to hear this, Ronny?''

"Of course I am!''

Erin grimaced, then nodded. "So anyway, my brother, Dion—you'd recognize him as your adopted parents' lawyer, but he was still in law school then—agreed with me about the need to try to circumvent the traditions. But my grandmother, who is *also* Matthew Welch's mother—wouldn't let me rest until I had children to carry on the line. And so I did—but Dion and I set it up so that I lay with two men one night—his college roommate and . . . and himself. I know that sounds awful, Ronny, but I really did love him, he was *so* beautiful. Now one of the few things Listener women *can* do is control their fertility, so naturally I got pregnant—with twins. But because one of them was also Dion's child, and because I was going to school in Florida then, we were able to shield knowledge of the second child from everyone until time came for the birth. We put one over on them on that too, and set it up so that only Dion and Gil were present when the twins were born. I hadn't been able to completely hide my pregnancy, though, and thus Dion and I decided that one child—you—would be secretly Fixed and then hidden away, while the other would be acknowledged as a Welch and Fixed with full Clan panoply, thus satisfying the tradition, but that I would *still* do my dead-level best to see that he grew up as normal as he could anyway.''

"Lew?" Ronny whispered.

Erin nodded. "But now I'm afraid our plan was too dangerous and stupid to ever work, because *now* you both need the Luck you're heir to—and don't know how to use it.''

"So Lew's your and . . . and Dion's son?"

Erin shrugged, then grimaced as if even that simple act sent paroxysms of agony coursing through her. "I don't know. Dion and his roommate looked much alike, and they both had fair-haired mothers. Either of them could have fathered you *or* Lew.''

"Or both of us?"

Erin shook her head. "There were *two* ova; I knew when each was quickened. And now I also wish I'd Heard the Winds that began to blow then, but at the time I chose not to. I didn't *want* to know which child was also my brother's.''

''But . . . do you . . . now?'' Ronny asked slowly.

Erin shook her head once more. ''No, and I wish I did—because whoever it is would have Listener blood on both sides, like Anson. Someone double-blooded like that would be able to defeat him and restore the proper order.''

''But is that necessary?'' Ronny asked, scowling. ''I don't understand half of this.''

''And there isn't time to tell you half of what you need to know, either.''

Ronny puffed his cheeks thoughtfully. ''Maybe not—but you've *got* to try. Right now I know a little of everything and not all of anything, and I've *got* to know!''

''Then listen, for I must tell you quickly,'' Erin replied. ''In fact, if you'll open your mind to me, I can tell you with my Voice much more efficiently.''

''S-sure,'' Ronny replied.

He closed his eyes—and felt what could best be described as a gentle breeze brush through his memories, and an instant later, he *knew* things. Knew about the Mastership and about footholders, knew whole reams of family history, knew centuries of speculation about Luck and Winds and Voices and Silence. And then, abruptly, images began to replace ideas. They moved too fast for him to really focus on but a few stood out clearly.

One showed a very young woman, almost a girl, lying in a bed in a richly furnished room he somehow knew was in Atlanta. Her name was Donna, and she was obviously in labor. Two other women stood by, one the tall, stern-faced lady whom he knew from photographs was Matthew Welch's mother, Martha. And as Ronny watched, a child was pulled from under the sheets that swathed Donna's lower body. And he knew who that child was: it was Matthew's son, Paul.

And then he saw that same woman, Donna, a few days later, and she was standing in front of the middle-sized boy/

man who was Matthew Welch as a teenager. She held her
baby in her arms and was screaming at him. And then he
had grabbed her and was flourishing a knife in his hand and
seizing the child while still holding her and nicking the
baby's arm so that blood flowed and then slitting his own
arm and Donna's and forcing their blood into the rift in the
baby's flesh. And then he saw Donna screaming again, as
Matthew took the child away, whereupon he looked at her
and said, "You have done your part of the Fixing of our
child, I will do the rest."

Abruptly, he saw Donna again—now a woman of middle
years. Once again she was in childbed—though rather too
old for it—but the setting was anonymously cold and sterile.
The only attendant this time was someone who looked like
his family's lawyer, Dion, only much, much younger. The
child came, Donna fainted, and Dion held her child in his
arms and looked at it speculatively.

And then more images, moving quickly:

Once again he was witness to childbirth, but unlike the
scene he had just observed *he*/Erin was in the bed and those
who stood attendance were two men: Dion once more—
looking only slightly older—and someone who resembled
him who was called Gil. And there was pain like he couldn't
believe—twice: him and Lewis.

This was followed by a pair of mirrored scenes that were
each more placid renditions of the violent Fixing scene he
had earlier witnessed. In one, done in Cardalba Hall, the
participants were Martha, Donna, and Erin; while in the
other, set somewhere much further south, the celebrants
were Erin, Dion, and Gil.

And thus Ronny Dillon learned the recent history of the
Welches of Cardalba.

As best he could piece things together, Matthew Welch
had been a rather rash and rebellious youth, and even in his
teens had tended to push the limits of tradition. Thus, when
in his late teens—just when he was beginning to come into
his power—he became infatuated with his pretty young sis-

ter, Donna, who also had a tendency toward taking risks;
the two of them dared what should not have *been* dared,
and Donna allowed herself to become Matt's footholder.
This was extremely dangerous, even allowing for the fact
that both had been Fixed, but by exercising careful control,
they managed it. Unfortunately, the two became so fascinated with each other by virtue of the close spiritual communion that act sometimes afforded, that they became
lovers—and Donna, who was only in her mid-teens, became
pregnant. Anson's father, Paul, had been the fruit of that
union, but both Matt and Donna had managed to hide the
truth from Matthew's mother, Martha, until the pregnancy
was well along—*and* from the then-Master, Ben, for a good
while longer.

Matthew, however, had already begun to harbor a fondness for the notion of passing on the Mastership to *his* seed,
so he decided to once again violate tradition and have Paul
Fixed (it not being common to Fix the offspring of male
Welches, since they could not inherit—and Paul, as the
child of incest, being something of an abomination anyway).
But Donna, who was beginning to have flashes of the prescience the women of the family sometimes possessed in
regard to their children, saw something in the future of the
child she did not like and refused to have anything to do
with his Fixing—which she was, by tradition, *supposed* to
be involved in. Matt was stronger than she, though, and
forced her to join him in a jury-rigged Fixing of Paul. Paul
was then adopted as usual by a family who had no idea he
was a Welch by-blow.

Unfortunately too, shortly after the Luck had awakened
in Paul, but before he was sent away to seek his own fortune
elsewhere, he discovered the true tale of his conception.
Furious (and somewhat unstable because of his double Listener blood—in spite of his Fixing) he confronted his
mother/aunt (who by then had three approved children,
Dion, Gilbert, and Erin, all of whom were away at college)
and raped her. Paul then moved to California and went

insane, though this fact was not widely known.

Meanwhile, Donna managed to hide her pregnancy from the entire clan except Dion—*including* Matt, who was out of the country at the time—and, since tradition forbade abortion, had her child: Anson. Dion, however, being rather dispassionate in the way of male Welches, wanted to see what the results of double Listener incest might be. He therefore arranged for the child to be raised so it could be watched by either himself or Donna. Donna, who was herself growing rather unstable as a result of so much stress, reluctantly agreed, and a substitution was made for another bastard of Paul's by one Evelyn Bowman, whom the Clan *did* know about. That child died under mysterious circumstances without his mother being the wiser. Thus, the only people who knew of the rape were Paul, Donna, and Dion. And even Paul did not know of the resulting pregnancy. The child was not, however, Fixed—as far as anyone knew.

Finally, Dion had arranged a fail-safe in the event Anson should discover his true heritage and claim what he had no right to—especially since the boy was already too much the apple of his grandfather's eye (and in spite of the fact that Matthew did not know of the lad's true heritage). A double-blooded Listener brought up under tighter control than was likely for Donna's son would be just the thing. And since this plan dovetailed nicely with Erin's desire to raise at least one of her children away from the family tradition, Dion contrived the conception of Ronny and Lewis.

Meanwhile, Donna had been slipping further and further into depression and, when Erin was at last delivered of her (so it was thought) single son, assisted in his Fixing ritual—then killed herself. As for Ronny, he had been spirited away, *his* Fixing ritual being performed clandestinely by his mother and his uncles Dion and Gilbert.

"The only problem," Erin said, when they had both returned to themselves, "was that Dion didn't count on being jailed; otherwise he could have perhaps kept Anson under control. Still, I suppose things could have been worse. At least this way I was able to learn the true tale of my mother's death. I never knew what happened to her before, only that she was depressed and eventually killed herself.''

"And now I've killed *you*," Ronny whispered dully.

"And been forgiven already," Erin replied. "I know it will be hard to bear, but you've borne the hardest part of it already. Besides, I think I know enough of Winds and Voices to know that one is never really dead. In fact, I think this sordid tale we are somehow engaged in has been played out countless times before.''

"So what do you want me to do?"

Erin took a long slow breath and gazed at him wistfully. "I don't quite know. Obviously my brother had a plan for you I didn't know about: to raise up a second child with double Welch blood in the event Anson learned the truth—which he obviously has done—and became unruly. As a check on him, in other words. So with *that* in mind, I would say that since either you or Lewis *is* of double blood, that one must stand against Anson and defeat him—assuming Anson gains Mastery over Matt, which I'm sure he'll do before long. And—''

She paused, coughed, tried for breath and almost failed. Ronny thought she was gone already, but then she steeled herself and continued.

"Yes, part of me wants either you or Lewis to defeat Anson because one or the other of you is the only one who can. But *now* I've learned that Matt has commissioned the knife that should not have been made and may very well use it, and so there is now a twofold threat to you. Thus, the part of me that is your mother and a rebel *still* wants to do as I have always done: shield you both from all this madness, so that you can grow up without the curse of Luck that will surely fall upon you if you succeed. *That* part—my heart, I suppose—says for you to take Lewis and go far, far away—now: tonight.''

"But which one *should* I do?" Ronny asked helplessly.

But Erin did not answer. And it took Ronny over a minute to realize she was not breathing, and never would again.

Chapter 22

Thirty Pieces of Silver

Erin Welch's house
Sunday, April 22—1:00 A.M.

Lewis—Winnie; Lewis—Winnie; Lewis—Winnie . . .
Those were the names flashing through the tattered remnants of Ronny's self-possession like the light bar on a state patrol car as he stumbled frantically down the hallway toward his and Lewis's room, with the thumps and scrapes and attenuated shouted "Leeeew!" of his progress acting surrogate for sirens. Lew was no longer screaming, but that wasn't necessarily good—not in light of what Ronny had just witnessed. Not when silence could very well mean death. Already the house was filling up with a different sort of quiet—one so vast and empty and terrifying Ronny could never have imagined it until now that Erin was gone.

Gone.
Dead.
Departed.
He had lost her before he had truly known he had her.

And, he realized dully, he had also now lost two sets of parents in three months.

Three months! He was an orphan again.

He was—

No! he told himself firmly. He was *not* going to dwell on that now. Not when the remaining two people in the world he loved most were both in direst danger.

How he had divined that theat he could not explain, but he knew as certainly as if he had followed the Winds in Anson's wake that sooner or later his maniacal cousin would come sniffing around again. And *this* time there would be no Erin to shield them with her Silence. *This* time they would be on their own.

Which meant that three things had to be accomplished very quickly. The first, and most imminently important, was to check on, and preferably rouse Lew; the second was to somehow stop Anson; and the third was to rescue Winnie. For if what Erin had hinted at was true, it would only be a matter of time before Anson completely subjugated Matt and claimed Winnie for himself. And then . . . the whole damned world had better look out, 'cause there'd be a first-class megalomaniac on the loose.

Ronny had reached his room by then, but slipped as he swung through the door and for the second time that night sprawled forward, the heavy encrustations on the crutch poking and prodding (and in one case cutting) him cruelly. But he picked himself up again and scrambled awkwardly to Lew's bedside.

For a moment he thought Lew was as dead as Erin, for though his godbrother was lying on his back once more and was no longer screaming, neither could Ronny detect any sign of life. "Lew?" he called tentatively from the floor. "Lewis? Can you hear me?"

But Lew did not respond, and only when Ronny held his hand close to his friend's mouth could he feel the moist warmth of breath. As for Lew's chest—well, Ronny *thought* he saw it rise and fall, but so subtle was the movement he could not be certain.

So here he was: in a house with one dead person, one maybe dying person, and with a lunatic cousin undoubtedly plotting more mischief somewhere nearby.

What should he do?

His first impulse was to call the cops. But they'd be bound to ask questions, and most of those queries would be damned hard to answer, and he did *not* want to be subjected to *any* sort of interrogation, intensive or otherwise, in the middle of this crisis. Besides, if he could trust what Erin had revealed to him about Matt and Anson, the local constabulary would either choose not to cooperate once they discovered who they were up against, or might very well find themselves in over their heads instead. And if there was *anything* Ronny wanted to avoid, it was involving more innocent lives in his family weirdness.

His second impulse, therefore, was to take matters into his own hands—but *that*, he knew, would *really* be the height of stupidity. What could *he* do, after all? March into Cardalba Hall and lay it on the line to Matt—and Anson too, if he was there? Matt was a trained . . . *whatever* he was. And if Anson was as strong as both he and Erin had intimated, his native talent made Matt's look like small potatoes. So what could he, Ronny Dillon, who could not even walk unaided, hope to accomplish against Anson, who was young and strong and certainly more practiced in the ways of the family Luck than he? Oh, Ronny had Luck too, he supposed: he could feel it now, in some almost incomprehensible way. And Lew likewise had it, and was probably subconsciously aware of its blossoming. But Ronny hadn't the first notion what to do with it, how to use it, what its strengths and limitations were. And he knew enough already to know that a weapon incorrectly used was always more dangerous than one not used at all.

But he *had* to get help somewhere, or at least find someone he could appeal to for advice. Except that there *was* no one. He had no real friends at school to start with, and *absolutely* none who were not scared shitless of the Welches; and ditto for Welch County High's faculty, including Mr. Wiley. Which left . . . who?

And then Ronny knew.

He aimed one final apprehensive glance at Lewis and decided not to wake him just yet on the dubious premise that Anson was probably still licking his war wounds, that one hysterical person in the house at a time was enough, and that he should at least grant his friend—his *brother*— a few more hours of peace before the shit really hit the fan. Lew was invulnerable anyway, he'd discovered—at least to any physical threat—so he was surely as safe here as any- where. And in the meantime, he'd chase down the Road Man and see what *he* suggested.

Ten minutes later, Ronny was halfway to the Road Man's camp—and would have reached that point even sooner had he not detoured past Cardalba Hall in order to ascertain whether or not Anson was, in fact, there. He was, Ronny thought, though he couldn't tell for certain if the low, dark car half-hidden by the willows across the creek was Anson's Trans Am or not.

He was still puzzling over that, and still cursing himself for not snatching one of Aunt Erin's numerous guns and simply striding into Cardalba with barrels blazing and put- ting an end to matters that way, when he topped a rise and found himself within sight of the old Swanson house. Not wishing to be seen, in spite of his need for haste, he braked hard and swung the Escort into its accustomed hiding place in the dark lane behind the derelict dwelling.

And got a shock, for another vehicle was there ahead of him—a pickup truck he did not recognize save that it was roughly ten years old, a Ford, and black.

Ronny cursed, crammed the car into reverse, and backed up frantically, feeling the rear end start to fishtail at such a maneuver executed with so little finesse. Five seconds later he was roaring down the straight again—but only as far as the eastern end of the meadow where the forest grew close to both road and field. A quick wrench of the steering wheel hard left, and he had executed a smart U-turn in the middle of the highway—whereupon he urged the Escort off the shoulder and into the semi-cover of the nearest of the overhanging trees.

And set off overland, skirting forest and field alike, until he reached the finger of woodland beyond which he had first seen the Road Man's camp. He paused there, to catch his breath and get his bearings.

He already knew that the Road Man was not alone, but what Ronny had *not* expected was that his mentor's mysterious visitor was none other than the person who had caused all this trouble in the first place—the man whom Ronny had first seen in grainy photographs in the county paper, then in glossy blowups and portraits in half the public buildings in Cordova, and most recently in the shared memories of his mother: the one and only Matthew Welch.

But what in the world could Mr. Welch want with the Road Man *this* time of night?

Ronny had no idea. That Matthew was here at all was both intriguing and disturbing, and the fact that he had arrived in a ratty pickup rather than his flashy T-bird or formal Town Car seemed to indicate that he was on some sort of clandestine business—especially when his appearance implied the same: long dark coat, dark shirt and trousers, topped by a wide-brimmed hat snugged down hard to mask his snowy hair.

As best he could tell, Matt hadn't been there long, though obviously he'd had sufficient time to stash the car and wade across the field before Ronny arrived on the scene. But the look on the old man's face—impatience mixed with ill-disguised apprehension, all conflicting with the air of patrician nonchalance Ronny had more or less expected—seemed to hint that the Road Man intended to grant Welch

County's premier citizen an audience only when he was good and ready.

As a point of fact, from his vantage point between the last of the trees and the first of the moonlight-powered machines, Ronny couldn't see the Road Man at all: the wagon was directly between him and the tinker's work area, and to shift to either side would risk betraying his presence. Still, he could definitely hear the clear tones of his mentor's voice, coupled with the steady, low-pitched rasping sound of something being filed or sharpened—which fact, in light of Anson's recent revelation, gave him the granddaddy of all great chills.

But then, abruptly, the rasping stopped, and the Road Man strode into view to the left of the wagon. Something small and shiny caught the glare of one of the surrounding torches and glinted brightly in his hand—something the tinker quickly shrouded in a red bandanna chosen from the five braided through slashes in his left pant leg. It was certainly of vast interest to Matthew Welch, too, for his face took on an eager, almost hungry luck as he reached toward the object.

And Ronny could contain himself no longer. Flinging caution to the winds—for he scarcely had anything more to lose now—he angled right (thereby temporarily imposing the wagon between himself and the two men), then scurried as quietly as he could across the short distance between the arc of machines and the caravan. A goat bleated, and he held his breath in alarm, but was unobserved when he peered cautiously around the wagon's back left corner.

He was less than four yards from the two men now, and the night was quiet, the air still. So it was that he was able to make out every word that passed between the two.

The Road Man had still not relinquished his bundle, and Matt's eyes looked as if they were ready to pop out of his head from anticipation.

"So that's *it*?" Matt asked finally.

"It's not an *it*," the Road Man replied promptly. "It's a knife."

Matthew ignored his sarcasm and continued to stare at the object—which, Ronny thought by the little bit he could make out, *was* a knife of some kind.

"And it fulfills all the conditions of the agreement?" Matthew asked, after a moment.

The Road Man looked puzzled. "There was an agreement?"

"There was."

A shrug. "Then it must fulfill the conditions."

"And I have your word on that?"

"If it will do you any good."

"It was constructed exactly as required?"

"Aye."

"And will accomplish exactly what it needs to?"

The Road Man shrugged. "I've never been told what that is," he noted pointedly. "But I have no doubt that it will perform admirably."

"If it will kill what cannot otherwise be killed, that will be sufficient."

Another shrug. "*All* things that live—and some that do not—can be killed," the Road Man muttered, raising his wrist and staring at it as if he consulted a watch Ronny knew was not there—unless one was secreted among the intricate tattoos. "I would be *interested* in meeting that which can't."

"You wouldn't be impressed."

"Ah," said the Road Man. "So you won't tell me—but you won't lie about it either! I find that very interesting."

Matthew's eyes narrowed, but his lips curled in a sly grin. "Let's just say this is insurance," he murmured. "I promised someone I would have it made, and I have—mostly because it was *convenient* to have it made right now. But I have no intention whatever of letting them use it."

"Nor have I—until I've seen the color of your money, smelled its ink, and felt its texture."

"Ah," Matthew replied, smiling. "I was *wondering* when you'd get to that." He reached into his coat pocket and withdrew a large, unfolded wallet on a thin gold chain, from which he extracted a fat sheaf of bills. Ronny couldn't make out the denominations, but he imagined that since they were obviously well secured they were also quite large. The Road Man snatched them without them being offered, flipped them past his eye with the thumb of his opposite hand, then nodded, pocketed the wad, and handed the bandanna and its contents to Matthew. The old man hefted the bundle for for a moment, then nodded in turn. "Well," he muttered, "I can't tell a damned thing by feel, but if this is what you say it is, I reckon I'll know sooner or later. And if it's not—well, it'll probably be too late to make any difference to me anyway."

"And how will you find me if it is *not* what you wanted?" The Road Man chuckled. "I have ways of making myself scarce."

"I'll listen for the Sound of your Silence," Matt replied, and turned away.

"Ah," the Road Man said to his back. "But suppose my Silence itself makes no Sound."

"Cryptic double-talk bullshit," Matt spat, then paused and looked back over his shoulder. "Oh, by the way—didn't you also say something about wanting a seed?"

Once again the Road Man looked befuddled—but then realization spread across his face. "Oh . . . a *seed*." He laughed. "As to that . . . I'll collect it when it comes planting season."

"It already is." Matt snorted and stalked away.

And Ronny, who had been thinking at least as hard as he'd been listening, and with as few encouraging results, made his way back into the night as well, though he retreated only far enough beyond the circle of machines to watch a dark vehicle ease out from behind the Swanson place and veer left onto the highway. Only then did it turn its lights on.

But Ronny scarcely cared—for unless he had wildly misread things, he now knew that the Road Man, who moments before he had supposed to be his friend and last source of aid, was a traitor.

After all, what knife *could* that have been but the very one Anson had mentioned that could kill Lew? The fact that Matthew was buying it at night—in disguise—from a person of dubious character—*and* for a large sum of money—gave about as much proof to that assumption as anyone could need.

Which meant he *really* had to hurry.

Chapter 23

Awakenings

Erin Welch's house
Sunday, April 22—The wee hours

Ronny's head was considerably clearer when he braked the Escort to a crunching halt in Erin's driveway a few minutes after leaving the Road Man's camp. Unfortunately, though, that only made it easier for him to recall what he did not *want* to recall, which was that his aunt—his *mother* (he had learned it so recently the reality of it still had not sunk in)—was dead. Yet it was *Erin's* house he was looking at: *her* exposed beams and stucco and tile roofs; *her* silver Lincoln Continental gleaming behind the garage doors, *her* furniture inside, *her* appliances, *her* clothes . . .

Her son.

Her *self* growing cold and stiff where she sat unattended in her bedroom.

Fortunately, the frantic madness that had first driven him from home and later been redoubled by his discovery of the Road Man's betrayal had finally given way to a more focused sense of purpose during the high-speed dash back here. And he'd been lucky as well, because he'd been so full of anger and frustration when he'd left the tinker's clearing he had abandoned all concern for circumspection and simply run as best he could across the meadow toward his car, not thinking until it was too late that either the Road Man, Matthew, or both could easily have seen him. Since then, he'd ignored three stop signs and gone sideways on loose gravel twice—the second of which occurrences being when he'd forced himself to calm down enough to lower both side windows, on the theory that if he didn't make *some* effort to get his act together, he was going to trash himself before he did *anyone* any good.

And, wonder of wonders, that flood of cold, clean air had helped tremendously. Trouble was, like his mother before him, he now found himself with conflicting options regarding course of action. The logical part of him knew that whatever he did needed to happen tonight, before the authorities got involved—as they would eventually have to, given there was a body not a hundred feet away. Too, there was the fact that Anson was off balance now and might therefore be more vulnerable. And of course there was the underlying fear that if Ronny did *not* act quickly, they might lose their momentum utterly and thereby grant Anson victory.

And with Winnie also a prize in that lottery . . . well, he *really* didn't want to think about that!

On the other hand, there *was* the small matter of Erin's heart's desire, which was for both him and Lew to abandon everything and get as far away from Matt and Anson and their machinations as possible. That was certainly the most attractive option in the short term, but he wondered how it would play a few days—shoot, a few *hours*—down the road, when practicality caught up with them in forms as diverse as police or poverty. Oh, Ronny could *get* Lew away, of that he was fairly certain. If nothing else he could simply pack a couple of suitcases and stuff them—and his brother—into his car and drive off. And if Lew awakened in the meantime, why, he'd just fill him full of sleeping pills and keep going. After all, he had a fair number of credit cards, courtesy of Erin, and could probably get a good long way before the money ran out entirely. And there *were* other Listeners, after all; maybe he could enlist their aid. If not . . . well, Mexico wasn't *that* far, and there was always South America—preferably some place without extradition treaties. What they would *do* once they got to whatever *there* they wound up at, given they were both underage, he had no idea. Cut their hair and grow mustaches, he supposed, since such a precipitous departure would certainly point the long accusing finger of the law in their direction if they skipped out without leaving word.

All that—and a great deal more—was fighting for ascendancy in Ronny's head as he slid his security card through the front-door lock. But the choice was not actually *made* until, two minutes later, he found himself once more gazing down at his brother.

Lew was still asleep, his face so placidly at rest that he resembled an angel from a Renaissance painting. And that worked a change in Ronny. For Lew was too good, too beautiful, too vulnerable to have to confront the sort of sordidness that underlay both their family and the whole frigging county they lived in. And while he knew that his brother was aware of his position in town, of the hinted secrets of the Luck, he likewise knew that Lew didn't care a fig about such things, that he had absolutely no ego investment in them at all. Therefore, there could be no confrontation, at least not with his brother involved.

And since Ronny also knew that *he* was in no way qualified to combat Anson, there was only one alternative. Which meant he had to follow Erin's heart instead of her head, and somehow, some way convince Lew to go away with him.

Except that he knew in *his* heart of hearts that shirking responsibility like that was a cop-out of the worst degree.

Still, that was the direction he was tending toward when

he dragged a pair of suitcases out of the closet and commenced stuffing them with his and Lew's clothes.

And that continued to be his intention when overwrought nerves made him yank a drawer so hard that both its contents and the alarm clock whose cord had been in the way spilled noisily to the floor, prompting a grimace, a short harsh gasp, and a quick glance at Lew out of the corner of his eye.

Nor had that plan altered when his brother's eyes popped open while Ronny was still looking at him, for he knew then that he would do anything in the world to spare him pain.

But he was not ready for Lew's first words.

Lew blinked, rubbed his eyes, sat up on his elbow, then blinked again and peered perplexedly at Ronny. "Something's . . . gone." He yawned. "There's no . . . *energy* in the air."

Ronny sat down beside him. "You're just dreaming, Lew," he whispered. "It's just one of those bad dreams you've been having."

Lew rubbed his eyes and stared down at his bare, watchless wrist, then glanced around in quest of the clock Ronny had so noisily displaced. "What time is it?"

Ronny checked his own watch. "A little past one-thirty."

Lew yawned once more and fell back onto his pillow. "Air feels funny," he mumbled sleepily, rolling over and clutching his pillow to his chest while drawing his knees up like a child. "Something's gone. There's no sound . . ."

And then, abruptly, his eyes opened again. "Mom! She's . . . she's not there!"

Before Ronny knew what was happening, Lew had grabbed him around the shoulders. He was shaking. "What's going on, Ronny?" he gasped. "Something's not right. I didn't know, and then . . . and then I just *did*!"

Ronny had no choice but to hold his brother close, to try to still the sourceless, empty horror that now gripped him. "Everything's fine," he murmured. "You just had another bad dream. That's what it was. That's what you said it was.''

"But the emptiness . . . ?''

"Part of the dream.''

Lew stiffened. "No," he whispered in a stronger voice. "It's not—'cause I still feel it. And I . . . I can *hear* what's in your head and I know you're lying, though you don't want to, and that something bad's going on you don't want to tell me about except that you know you're gonna have to!''

Ronny did not reply, but in some way he did not understand he raised a barrier around his mind, so that his thoughts were once more his alone. And only then did he realize that by so doing he was also shutting out a virtual cacophony of sounds—or thoughts—or . . . or *Winds* that completely without him being aware of them had come to pervade his consciousness. One of them had been Lew, too, he recognized; and so, very carefully, he eased part of his Silence—if that's what this desire to keep Lew's thoughts away was—apart so that he could reach out to his brother with his feelings but keep Lew from responding in kind.

"Ronny?" Lew asked fearfully, not releasing his hold. "What did you just *do*? You . . . you were here . . . but then you weren't . . . *there*! But it wasn't the same way Mom isn't there, and . . . .'' He shook his head as if to clear it.

"No, I'm here for you always," Ronny whispered. "But Lew, I . . . I have to tell you something. Something bad, something that's *really* gonna upset you.''

Lew loosened his grip and stared back at Ronny. "What?''

Their gazes met, Lew trusting and afraid, and Ronny trying very hard to be compassionate and honest but determined.

"I . . . Oh, crap, I *can't* tell you now," Ronny cried, "I just *can't*! I can only say that we've *got* to get out of here tonight. Aunt Erin says we have to leave now, before anything else bad happens.''

"Mom? But . . . she's not here! When did she tell you this?"

"Before . . . before she left," Ronny replied carefully.

Lewis wiped his nose. "Okay . . . but you're not telling me everything are you?"

Ronny was suddenly aware of the intensity of Lew's curiosity forcing his thoughts against his. And this time he relaxed and let his brother in.

—And saw anew as Lew saw for the first time how Erin Welch had died.

Almost he couldn't stand it, for in some unfathomable way his brother was reliving the entire last several hours of Ronny's life, and as he did, Ronny had no choice but to go along. Something told him that this was a natural, if unpleasant, adjunct to whatever they were doing: that when whatever it was that energized Lew's thoughts touched his own brain cells they had no choice but to fire, and once they did, Ronny could not help but experience whatever had first stimulated them simultaneously with Lew.

Yet at the same time, a part of him was in Lew's mind, and for a while they were almost one soul in two bodies. Ronny did not dare snoop among his brother's memories, though, for he was too concerned with guarding his own— and with making sure that Lew did not go too far too fast in reliving the events of the last hour. Still, Ronny knew that whatever was happening between them was certainly a more direct, more forceful, and, he hoped, more convincing form of communication than any number of words would have been. Which meant that maybe, just possibly, Lew would see the wisdom of Erin's plans for them and act accordingly.

Except that when Lew withdrew from Ronny's mind and they found themselves once more staring at each other, Ronny knew that his brother had chosen a different course of action.

Lew's mouth was firm, his jaw set, his whole face hardened into a mask of grim resolve Ronny did not like. And there was a fire of determination burning in his eyes. For maybe a minute they remained on Lew's bed, scarcely breathing, not daring to speak lest that poor communication profane the perfect one they had so lately shared. Finally, though, Lew cleared his throat and said, very softly. "I forgive you, too."

Ronny felt himself relax and did not know until then how tense he had been. "Are you sure?"

Lew nodded. "I'm sure. I was there, remember—for all practical purposes. And I know absolutely that everything you did was out of concern for me. As for the rest—there's no way you could have known—though I have to say it would've been nice if Mom had trusted us more."

"Wouldn't it?" Ronny agreed, standing and reaching for his crutch. "God, I wish I'd had a chance to get to know her better—*really* get to know her, and by that I mean the *real* her, the self she always kept hidden."

"She must have really loved us, to go to so much trouble to see that we lived normal lives. She was caught between the Devil and the deep blue sea, I guess."

"Which is why we have to abide by her wishes now and leave."

Lew shook his head, rose, and snatched his jeans from the pile on the floor. "Which is why I have to go have it out with Anson."

"*You?* But why?" Ronny cried. "You know Erin didn't want it."

"I also know it's what I was made for!"

"No, it's not! She wanted you to be normal! And the only way either of us can be normal is to get away from here!"

Lew zipped his fly and grabbed a black T-shirt. "You think it's *normal* to be on the run? You think pulling up roots is normal? You think pretending there's nothing odd about the fact that you have no parents but are trying to get into school somewhere else is normal? Shoot! We've both seen *Running on Empty* and you know how much trouble that was—and this is a thousand times worse because wherever we go Matt or Anson can follow us.''

"But there are other Listeners," Ronny pleaded. "Aunt Erin—Mom—told me. Maybe they can help."

"How? All we know is a little about what we can *do*. We don't have a clue about how it *works*."

"Instinct seems to point the way pretty well—at least it did just now."

Lewis had found socks and sneakers. "Instinct also tells me that if we *don't* act tonight we'll have lost our best opportunity."

Ronny shook his head, but somehow managed a wry chuckle. "I just convinced myself of the same thing a little while ago—and then unconvinced myself again."

Lew looked at him hopefully. "So . . . does that mean you're with me?"

"*Me?*" Ronny snorted, glaring at him as sudden anger welled up in him. "Ha! Fat lot of good *I'd* do. I'm imperfect, don't forget. I'm the one Anson doesn't even care enough about to want to kill!"

Lew's face tensed as he brushed past Ronny to search in his closet for a sweater. "Be glad. Besides, you *are* perfect—inside. The Luck's there, I can feel it!"

"But I can't *use* it! I don't know how!"

"You couldn't swim either—once. Or make cast-silver barbarians."

"*Lew!*" Ronny cried, standing. "Be reasonable. You don't know crap about this stuff! All you know is what you read in my mind which is what *I* read in *Aunt Erin's* mind, and at that, there was so much I don't have a clue what I know or don't know right now. All that's clear is that you and I have some kind of power to play with thoughts, but we don't know how to work it, or the limitations—'cause Aunt Erin said everyone was different, everyone has his or her own talents. And even worse, we *don't* know what Matt and Anson can do—beyond the fact that Matt's been teaching Anson all this stuff, and that Matt wants you dead—or did. And let's not forget that Anson appears to have no qualms at all about torturing you with dreams—*or* with offing you entirely.''

Lew turned around and looked at him. ''I have no choice.''

''Sure you do. You can pack your bags and walk out that door with me.''

''And leave a mess for somebody else to clean up? I was brought up better than that, Ronny. And I think you were too.''

''But . . .''

Lew folded his arms defiantly. ''Think about responsibility, man; think about why we're here. Dion went to a lot of trouble to prepare us as weapons against Anson. Think how he'd feel if we didn't do something now.''

''Think how *I* feel knowing my whole life was a lie and a cop-out and a setup!'' Ronny shot back acidly.

Lew stiffened. ''Well, think how *I* feel, having run of my own life for seventeen years and then having to share my space with some poor schmuck my mom felt sorry for!''

''Well, *excuse* me!'' Ronny shouted back, too much emotional trauma having destroyed his self-control. ''*Next* time any nightmares sneak up on me I'll be sure to tell 'em they've got the wrong guy. Next time I'll arrange it so my *head* hits the concrete when I fall, not my knee. Next time I'll be sure to die so you won't have me to inconvenience you!''

Lewis was dressed now, and spun around to glare at Ronny in turn.

''There'll *be* no next time,'' Lew gritted. ''Don't you see that? If we don't act, if we don't stop Anson, there's no telling what'll happen.''

''*Lew . . . !*''

But Lewis was already halfway to the door. ''Think about other people sometime, why don't you,'' he said quietly. ''Think about how some asshole cousin of ours killed our mother and is bullying our uncle and is holding your girlfriend hostage—or have you gotten so wrapped up in self-pity you've forgotten about her too? And then think about the fact that nobody can stop him *except* you or me.''

''There's always Matt—or Martha. Hey, maybe we could get hold of Martha . . .''

Lew shook his head again. ''You know as well as I do that it's got to be me—and it has to be tonight, while they're not expecting it. Now—are you for me or against me? Because if you're against me, I can't wait any longer.''

Ronny stared at him incredulously. ''I can't,'' he whispered miserably. ''I know I ought to, but I *can't*. It's just too dangerous. We've seen what they can do just with dreams—think what they must be like in person. And if . . . if they hit me with dreams again . . . I don't think I could stand up to 'em.''

''Coward.''

''Yeah, sure—but the thing I'm *really* afraid of has nothing to do with looking out for myself.''

Lew simply stared at him, aloof and dispassionate.

''I don't want to see you die, Lew,'' Ronny told him flatly, his eyes awash with tears. ''And if I did, I can almost guarantee it would kill me.''

''If not me, who?'' Lew repeated, and left.

Chapter 24

One More Double Cross

A dirt road near Cardalba Hall

As he urged his misfiring pickup past the intersection with the road to Evelyn Bowman's house, Matthew Welch wondered for the millionth time in the last twenty-four hours when, exactly, he had lost control of his life. Certainly as recently as three months ago things had seemed just dandy: He'd provided Luck where it was needed, folks had brought him goods and services in return—and his pet advancement project for Anson had been no more than a fondly tended dream in the back of his mind. Why, when you got down to it, even two months ago the only alteration in that scheme was that somewhere in the previous fourteen days he had decided that he *would* defy the traditions and make Anson, the true fruit of his own loins, his heir, and so he had begun his dream assault on Lewis. And just fifteen *days* ago— when he had finally revealed his intention to his mother— he had *still* been supremely confident that he would be able to control the lad in spite of the questionable taint of his father's double blood. Now, however, he knew he had been mistaken.

Oh, the Luck had activated like it was supposed to and manifested in spades as soon as Anson had become aware of its existence. Trouble was, no one had a lot of experience with the offspring of double-blooded Listeners beyond the knowledge that they, like their sires, tended to be unstable; so that Matthew had suddenly found himself fighting an uphill battle on unfamiliar ground. Still, he suspected he could have managed had it not been for Lenore's defection. *That* had put a major crimp in his plans, and it had taken all his diplomatic skill *and* savvy *and* acting acumen to conceal the extent of his weakness from his accomplice during their tutorial sessions.

But then he'd chanced on Winnie and thereby—he thought—regained the upper hand. Only he still hadn't reckoned on the extent of Anson's ruthlessness, or on the fact that his grandson was stronger without a footholder than *he* was with one. And when the boy gained control to go *with* that strength—well, a good chunk of the world could very well be in trouble.

And nobody would ever know how much it galled him either, how much Matthew hated having to defer to anyone, much less a cocky adolescent. Why he didn't simply kill the lad himself—assuming he *could* be killed, unFixed as he was—he didn't know. He supposed it was because in spite of Anson's bullying he still had a warm place in his heart for the boy. Blood is thicker than water, he'd often heard. And like it or not, that was true. Even alligators took care of their young.

Why else would a particular knife made in a particular way be gleaming on the seat beside him?

Perhaps as a sign of good faith? he thought. Perhaps to lull Anson into a sense of false security? Maybe to keep the boy happy until he could figure out something else to do? Or perhaps as a bargaining chip.

He had reached the bridge now, the one that arched across

the Talooga and led into the road that fronted Cardalba Plantation. He slowed obligingly, felt the truck buck and threaten to stall again, as it all too frequently had since leaving the Road Man's camp. "C'mon," he grunted, and tickled the accelerator enough to placate whatever gremlin was fouling things up. First thing Monday morning, he vowed, *first* thing, he was gonna march old Black Betsy here right on over to the Ford place in Cordova for a complete tune-up and (if need be) overhaul.

For some reason that notion cheered him, if only because it was so *ordinary*. Oh, managing the Luck was entertaining, he supposed, was challenging and fulfilling, was an absolute joy sometimes—as was the power it provided. But it was tainted joy because you had to keep the pleasure to yourself. Getting your car fixed was something *everyone* could identify with. And if he, Matthew Welch, the Master of Cardabla himself, showed up in person at the service department, folks would know he was just a regular Joe too. That was how you did it if you worked it right: that was how you maintained the balance between familiar and remote that kept the mystery of the Mastership alive.

But for now the mystery he *ought* to be concerned with was how to somehow regain the upper hand with Anson without destroying either the boy's spirit or his *self*; and how to instill the lad with a little responsibility—and humility—in the bargain.

Matthew had no idea how either of those formidable goals could be accomplished—and was still evaluating possible solutions when he swung around the final curve below the mansion and aimed the automatic garage-door opener at its receptor on the nearest gable. A moment later, he eased the pickup inside, whereupon it obligingly sputtered to a stop and would crank no more, forcing him to manhandle its suddenly non–power-steered bulk into its final resting place.

He was not surprised to find Anson at the house ahead of him, either; for he had passed the boy's car down at the visitor's turnaround. Nor was he much taken aback to dis-

cover the lad actually inside—it required very little Luck,
after all, to figure out where Matt hid his emergency key.
What *did* alarm him, though, was the look on his grandson's
face when Matthew finally located him in the front parlor.

Anson looked like death—or at least like someone who
had stared hard *at* death and barely come away with his
life. He was sprawling on the same red velvet sofa that had
hosted the deflowering of Lenore (a fact not lost on Matthew, who scowled when he saw him there). And though
the boy wore clean jeans, a fresh purple-and-gold paisley
shirt, and new white Reeboks, he somehow managed to
look as though he'd run through the woods and fields in
them for about a month. His face was pale—*very* pale, his
hair completely uncombed and unkempt, and he sported
what was easily a day's worth of stubble. But his eyes were
worse: ringed by dark circles that seemed determined to
suck the orbs back into his head, they glittered with a distant
hauntedness no amount of dissembling could disguise.

And Matthew, who moments before would have relished
seeing this troublesome lad laid so low, suddenly found
himself awash with sympathy instead.

"Anson?" he called tentatively, for the boy had not
moved when Matthew had entered the room. "Anson . . .
are you all right? What're you *doing* here this time of
night?"

Anson raised his head a fraction of an inch and vented a
long, slow breath. "I'm . . . tired," he groaned. "I am so
goddamned tired of bein' shit on!"

Matthew's eyes narrowed suspiciously, but he recovered
quickly and claimed the chair opposite his heir. "Would
you like to tell me about it?" he asked sympathetically.

Anson shook his head so slowly Matthew thought even
that effort cost him. "You *know* about it," he gritted. "Or
you ought to, since you're the cause of most of it."

"Of *what*?" Matthew asked sharply, abruptly on guard
and in no mood to bandy words. "Talk *sense*, boy! If you

need my help, ask. But don't come into my house with
accusations unless you can back them up."

Anson merely blinked tiredly at him. "I wish to *God* you
could have kept your goddamned pecker under control!"
he spat. "I wish to God I had never been born."

Matt had a sudden chill. "What . . . do you mean?"

"You *know* what I mean!" Anson shot back with unexpected fury. "About my dad and all. And about *his* mom,
and you and . . ."

"Is *that* all?" Matthew interrupted. "I was a *child* then,
son. I was younger than you are now. And *you* know what
that's like, even when you're normal, never mind that a lot
of times the Luck makes it ten times worse 'cause you start
running hot in your head as well as your body. Shoot, it
can make you as randy as a whorehouse tomcat."

"But why did it have to be *her*?"

A cold, sick feeling twitched Matthew's heart. "*Which*
her?" he asked carefully.

"You *know* which!" Anson snarled. "Your sister!"

Matthew's eyes flashed warning. "Who *told* you that?
Where'd you ever hear such a preposterous thing?"

"Your niece."

"*Erin?* She told you *that*?"

Anson nodded dully. "I made her—more or less."

"And then . . . she did *this* to you?"

Another nod. "More or less."

"And . . . Anson, what did you do to *her*?"

Anson shrugged in the manner of one who was beyond
caring. "I *hope* to hell I killed her—*something's* sure as
hell got to her."

Before he could stop himself Matthew Listened to Anson's Voice—and found a Silence so vast and impermeable
it was like a mountain of stone. "Goddamn it, boy, answer
me! What the hell did you *do*?"

Anson would not meet his eyes. "I don't want to talk
about it."

"What did you *do*, Anson? What the hell *happened*?"

"Don't ask," Anson replied wretchedly. "I don't want to have to lie."

Matthew shot out a hand and grabbed his grandson's leg, digging his nails in hard enough to make him wince. "Well, by God, you better tell the *truth*, then; because I swear I'll beat it out of you if you don't! And if *that* doesn't work, I'll rip the knowledge out of your fucking naked brain!"

Anson smiled weakly but triumphantly. "You and who else, old man? I may feel like shit right now—but I'm still a hell of a lot stronger than you are!"

Matthew did not reply.

"Try it!" Anson challenged. "Go ahead, try!"

"I'd like to," Matthew gritted. "Trouble is, it might kill you."

Anson shrugged. "So see for yourself then. Listen in her direction, and then you tell *me* what you find."

"I'd rather not."

Anson chuckled grimly. "And why *not*, Grandpa? Even *you* oughta be able to Hear a Silence as strong as Erin's."

Matthew glared at him, but rose abruptly. "You stay right there!" he snapped. "I'll be back in a minute."

And with that he rose and strode for the door. "You know where the liquor is," he added from the hall, then let the door swing to. That had been the *perfect* closing touch, he thought with some satisfaction: exactly the right sort of clincher to prove he was still in command.

And as soon as the latch clicked shut behind him, Matthew hurried to the library and buzzed for Winnie. She was slow in responding, though; and when she did appear, clad in black sweatpants and an oversized University of Georgia sweatshirt, she looked profoundly sleepy. But at least there was *some* sparkle in her eyes now, *some* bounce in her step, which meant that the ritual he had performed in order to Bind her to him was beginning to sink in, once more freeing her intellect for the sort of scintillating conversation he knew she could provide. And in the meantime, he would use her to check on the veracity of Anson's troubling intimations.

The boy knew *something*, that was for sure. And unfortunately he was also correct in assuming that without a footholder's Strength to augment him, Matthew had become so drained by the training sessions that he could not even manage a simple Listening unaided.

And something told him he needed to do some heavy-duty Listening.

Winnie was merely staring at him, blinking dumbly and rubbing her eyes from time to time. He nodded to her, tried to smile reassurance, and murmured, "I'm sorry to wake you, child, but this is important. It will only take a little while, and then I'll send you back to bed."

Winnie shrugged listlessly and flopped down in a graceful heap at Matthew's feet. He closed his eyes, felt the blessed pulse of her Strength flow into him, and began to draw the closest, strongest Voices his way.

—And had just recognized with some surprise whose they were and what they were about, when he was ripped from his trance by two heavy thumps on the door, followed by the sound of splintering wood. He looked up groggily, senses still dull with the heavy drag of altering perceptions, like a fully clothed swimmer fighting his way up through deep water.

—And saw the hall door fly open and a wild-eyed Anson standing just outside. The remnants of latch plate and lock alike tinkled to the hardwood floor as Anson strode into the room and, without sparing Matthew more than a cursory glance, grabbed Winnie by the arm and yanked her to her feet, then spun the half-conscious girl around so that he could stare into her eyes. Matthew, who was still too woozy to react with any speed or strength, saw her stiffen, then heard her utter a soft, kittenish cry. At the same time he felt something snap in his mind—as if some bond had been severed. Which was exactly what had happened. And which was also something Anson should not know how to do unless—chilling thought—he'd somehow found a way to prowl further among Matthew's memories than he'd ever dreamed possible.

As for Anson, he looked immensely better already. In fact, he was smiling wolfishly. Without asking permission, he sat down in the sofa opposite Matthew's and pulled Winnie down beside him. "I was hoping you'd do that," he laughed. "I was just *sure* that if I played my cards right I could get you to come in here and drag out good old Winnie so *I* could claim her. You just have *no* idea how hard virgins are to come by in this county."

"But you *can't* use her!" Matthew protested. "She'll burn you out—you haven't been Fixed, remember?"

"Ah," Anson replied, "but Fixing doesn't *really* matter when you're double-blooded, does it? At least that was Erin's opinion—though I'm sure she wouldn't appreciate how I learned that. It really is amazin' what you can find in people's memories while they're dyin'—especially when *they* think you've gone, when really you're just watchin'."

"But you're *not* double-blooded; that was your father."

Anson smiled grimly. "Oh yes I am—but I forgot, you didn't know about your son and your sister, did you?"

Matthew had to fight to maintain composure in the light of that revelation that suddenly explained a great many things. "Well," he replied carefully, "I'll give you credit for one thing: you're a damned fine actor. You had me convinced you were wasted as hell."

"I am," Anson replied smugly. "Though I'm still stronger than you are right now. And fortunately—Luckily, let's say—I know how to turn a liability into an asset. Not that I'll have to worry about it anymore, now that Winnie's mine. Just think of it, Grandpa: double-blooded *and* with a footholder. That oughta make me just about the Luckiest guy on this side of the pond."

"Or the biggest fool," Matthew shot back. "Luck's fine, boy. But it's like anything else: if it gets too big, it becomes hard to control. Besides—what are you going to *do* with all that Luck? There's already money enough for you to have anything you could reasonably want. Beyond that, what is there?''

''The same stuff you've said there is: matching wits with folks. Only I think I'm gonna spend most of my time matching wits with other Listeners.''

''They'll kill you, too.''

Anson shrugged. ''Not if they don't know what I'm really doing. See, what I'm gonna *do*, Grandpa, is that I'm gonna be exactly what you want me to be—on the surface. But you're gonna teach me *everything* you know. You're gonna tell me all the hidden shit about Listeners, and when you're done, I'm gonna be real sneaky, but I'm gonna go after them all one by one. And then one day the last one will wake up and see me grinning at him, and then I'll be the only one.''

''You're not ambitious, are you? Just your basic master of the world, huh? I guess I was wrong about you not being crazy.''

Anson shrugged again. ''Well, you *do* want your heir to do well, don't you? You do want me to do better than you did, right?''

Matthew smiled in turn. ''Well, if I were you right now, I'd spend my energy some way besides threatening powerless old men.''

Anson's eyes narrowed. ''What do you mean?''

''Don't *know*? But I thought you were all-powerful.''

''Watch it, old man.''

''No, *you* watch it! If you were as strong as you claim you are, you'd know already.''

''Know what?''

''That they're coming to get you—or one of them is.''

''Who is?'' Then: ''Oh, you mean Erin's brats? They're no problem. One's a cripple and the other doesn't know what he is.''

''He does now.''

''So what? You've got the knife, don't you? That *is* where

you went, isn't it? So what better chance to see if it works than right now?''

''I wouldn't if I were you, Anson,'' Matthew said softly. ''Those things are mostly fail-safes. And the Luck has a way of knowing if it's being used rightly or wrongly. If you kill either boy with that thing—and it *could* kill them both, since whatever else it is, it's still a knife and can do what any ordinary knife can do—well . . . let's just say the Luck may turn on you.''

''I'll take that risk.''

''It's your neck, then.''

''So where is it?''

''Wouldn't you like to know?''

''Go get it.''

''No.''

''I said, go *get* it!''

''And I said *no*.''

Anson did not reply, and Matthew briefly thought he had won that clash of wills. But then, before he knew it was happening, Anson had grabbed him by the throat. The boy was strong too, much more so than Matthew had expected. And there was no way he could prevent Anson from forcing his head up so that they were facing each other eye to eye. Matthew Heard Anson's Voice strike his and tried to Silence, but Anson was too quick for him and ducked behind that barrier and was waiting for him there inside his own mind. He tried to close his eyes then, tried to break that horrible gaze that was already forcing him down into himself, but Anson merely brought his other hand into play and dragged Matthew's eyelids open.

And Matthew knew he was lost, knew Anson had finally won. The last thing he saw before his own will went spinning downward into an abyss filled with the howling Winds of madness was Anson's clear blue gaze.

And then all he heard were the Voices of the damned.

Chapter 25

In Deep

Erin Welch's house

"If not me, who . . . ?"

The chandelier in the foyer was still tinkling nervously from the force of the slam Lewis had given the front door when he'd rushed through it bare seconds before. But all Ronny could hear as he stared at the dark rectangle of carved oak were his brother's departing words.

"*If not me, who?*"

Who indeed?

Ronny already knew, though he vainly wished he did *not* know, that there wasn't *any* other choice than the one he had already made. It had to be *him* that stood up to Anson, if only because *he* had started the whole sorry affair. Had he been able to resist the dreams, he would never have fallen from the diving platform. Had *that* not occurred, he would not have had to move to Welch County. And without that relocation, he would never have met Winnie Cowan and thereby incited the jealous rage that had led Anson to mistreat the poor girl—which in turn had driven her closer to Ronny, causing Anson to practically go apeshit in his desperation to win her back at any price—up to and including (according to what he had just learned from his mother) co-opting the Luck of the Welches. And in order for Anson to cement his claim to that dubious prize, Lewis had to die.

Yeah, it was definitely Ronny's fault, because all the what-ifs depended on choices he had made—even the business with the knife that was supposed to kill his brother, since as best he could determine, it was mostly because of him that the Road Man had hung around long enough for Matthew to have commissioned that weapon from the tinker in the first place. Of course the mysterious Mr. Welch *could* have tried other sources, but Ronny doubted he'd have gotten anything like the Road Man's discreet cooperation.

And none of those speculations even *considered* the fact that neither he nor Lew knew for certain which of them carried the double blood which was the key to defeating Anson. Erin either hadn't known or had not chosen—or been able—to tell him. And though she *had* told him the Luck was now awake in him, and had probably begun to take root before the injury so that it was possible it now flowed in its proper channels—albeit phantom versions; and though he could definitely feel *something* pulsing through him this very minute, he still feared the Luck might yet reject him—or backfire in some way and kill him. On the other hand, if *one* of them had to die, it might as *well* be him. After all, Lew had a perfectly good life already up and running, whereas Ronny was still reassembling his from shattered bits. And it was always preferable to preserve something good than something of equal original value that was ruined.

And, in any event, there was no more time for delay.

Roughly two minutes later, but rather more fully dressed than the bikini briefs that had been his only garment, Ronny was pushing through the front door.

The question now was, how did he catch up with Lew?

And a great deal of the answer depended on the route his brother had taken to Cardalba Hall. Probably the shortest, he decided. And with that in mind, Ronny climbed into his Escort, cranked it, and roared away.

He found Lew's car less than half a mile down the road, maybe thirty yards past a short concrete bridge that scanned a major tributary of the Talooga. A dark mass of National Forest grew close on the left, while a wide pasture sloped steeply down to the right, terminating in the line of willows that marked the Talooga proper. The Probe was parked on the right-hand shoulder, but catty-cornered, as if it had suffered some sudden malfunction and been abandoned there—except that he didn't think that was the case because there was also a fine set of skid marks behind it, which seemed to indicate that Lew had had to brake abruptly and swerve off the road. Probably to avoid something, he decided. Perhaps a deer, since the whole county was crawling with them, and there *were* woods right across the way.

Or, given Anson's fondness for playing with illusions, maybe something worse.

And in any event, a quick cruise-by showed that Lew was no longer in the car—though he had pretty much known that already.

So where *was* his brother, then? Ronny parked the Escort in front of the Probe, climbed awkwardly out, and scanned the surrounding countryside. Fortunately, the waning moon was still shining brightly, casting a sheen of blue across the looming pines behind him and laying a patina of pale silver across the stubbly field.

And there, on the near bank of the river, he caught a hint of movement which a closer inspection proved to be a human figure. Lew? he dared hope, and without really thinking about it, shut his eyes and opened himself to the Luck— and instantly felt a resumption of that communion he and his brother had so recently shared.

—And something else: something dark and insidious and foul that had cast a pall across his brother's mind.

'No! Ronny recoiled in terror, for it had reminded him too much of the dreams. Reflexively, he returned to himself, opened his eyes, and breathed a sigh of relief—which quickly became a gasp of alarm.

Lew was still there, poised uncertainly on the bank of the Talooga, but as Ronny watched in horror, his brother very calmly and methodically stepped straight off the bank—and instantly disappeared from view.

A quick recast of the Luck—there was no other choice— brought Ronny only impressions of cold and fear and choking.

—Which meant he had to act right now.

But what the hell could he *do*?

Well, it was at least a quarter mile to the river, and there was no possible way he could cover that much distance over uneven terrain with a bum leg quickly enough.

But . . . there *was* a potentially faster alternative less than forty yards to his right. Which, *if* he was lucky, *if* he truly busted ass, *might* get him where he needed to in time.

Ronny made his way to the Talooga tributary in what amounted to a series of crutch-assisted vaults, pausing on the bank above only long enough to skin out of his sweater and pry off his shoes. An instant later, he was up to his neck in fast-moving water.

It was icy cold, too, for in spite of the unseasonable warmth Welch County had enjoyed lately, it was still April, and most of the watercourses hereabout were born in the chill hearts of mountains. Ronny gasped and flailed out, tensing at the sudden shock until trained reflexes took over and set him swimming with long clean strokes along the direction of flow. But even at that he feared he was already too late—that his progress was still too slow.

The crutch was a major encumbrance, for one thing, as were his leg and waterlogged clothes—but fortunately the streambed was even steeper than it had first appeared, and he made excellent speed in spite of them, adding his own momentum to that of the rushing waters. Thus, in far less time than he could have run across the field, he found himself swept into the larger body of the Talooga no more than a hundred yards from the place he had last seen Lew.

But where was his brother now? Ronny couldn't tell, and here in the river itself the moonlight was largely diffused by the overhanging willows, so that many false lumps and empty shadows appeared and disappeared along the surface of the water.

Only one thing was clear: Lew certainly hadn't been in control of himself when he entered the river; thus, it was unlikely he was swimming now. Which meant that—alive or dead (if that was possible, given he was supposed to be invulnerable)—he was probably being swept along with the current. *Unless* the shock of the cold had snapped him out of Anson's—or Matt's—control. Or unless simple self-preservation instinct had taken over and was *making* him fight to keep his head above water.

But Ronny could hear no splashes save his own, and when he finally managed to find bottom firm enough to provide sufficient leverage for a leap above the surface so that he could scan further down the shadowy length, he could still see nothing.

"Lew!" he called softly, then realized such caution was stupid, given that either Anson or Matthew knew at least one of them was there anyway. "Lew! *Lewis!*" he yelled, putting all his force into one long, throat-straining bellow.

And got no answer.

Not daring to wait any longer, he pushed off again, and swam as fast as he could downstream.

Less than ten seconds later, the current whipped him around a sandbar and he found himself literally slammed against Lew's head. He saw stars and almost dropped the crutch, but at the last instant before the waters could whirl them apart again, he managed to snag his brother with his free hand. Fortunately, Lew, though seemingly unconscious, had been floating along on his back, and Ronny could tell as soon as he touched him that he was still alive—

another function of those newfound mental powers, he supposed.

But as he shifted his grip to gain a more secure hold, his movements brought his bare arm in direct contact with the skin of Lew's face and neck—and nearly made him let go again. For at that touch, the whole world had *changed* so that he and his brother were no longer struggling against the treacherous currents of a cold north Georgia river, but boiling alive in a stream of molten, glowing lava. He screamed—he thought—but no sound came out, and then he cared no more because he was completely overpowered by his brother's terror. He was mostly in the realm of the Winds now, and that gave him comfort the same way he knew that, in spite of what his senses told him, none of what he was experiencing was real. What *was* real, though, were the two Voices he could now Hear, as if at a great distance: Anson, who was so busy contriving agonies for Lew almost all trace of self was obscured, and, much more faintly, Matt, who seemed to be mostly—and unhappily—along for the ride.

"Stop it!" Ronny yelled, shifting his grip on Lew to a more secure one before stroking off as best he could toward the Cardalba side of the river. Keeping his eyes open helped, for it weakened the image of the incandescent stone. And breathing as often as possible proved useful as well, for it mixed real scents with the odor of phantom brimstone that had threatened to stifle him.

Still, it took far more effort, far more time, and far more concentration than he ever imagined swimming a dozen yards could require for him to drag Lew to the shore.

The illusion—dream—whatever it was—left them as soon as he hauled Lew up on dry land, and Ronny was grateful for that brief respite and simply sat for a long moment panting, coughing, shivering, and generally recovering his equilibrium. Lew was panting and coughing too, the latter copiously, which were both good signs because they meant he was conscious, and as soon as Ronny was reasonably functional himself, he twisted around to pound his brother on the back.

Lew coughed even more forcefully, expelling a fair quantity of water, then shuddered and looked around at him, a slightly dazed expression on his face. "I was on the crystal bridge," he whispered slowly, his eyes still refusing to focus. "I was trying to cross the lake of fire, only the bridge wouldn't hold, and I fell, and . . ."

"I rescued you," Ronny finished. "Yeah, I know. But we've got to get going again, got to get down to Cardalba."

"Cardalba?" Lew murmured absently, his brow furrowing into a scowl Ronny did not like. "That's right! I was going to Cardalba to . . . to have it out with Matt and Anson!" These last words were pronounced with far more conviction than the others, Ronny noted, and with a great deal more vehemence, but even so, he was not prepared when Lew rose to his feet in one smooth, fluid motion, and commenced clambering up the slope toward the riverside path they had taken that fateful day two weeks ago when they had first encountered the Road Man.

Ronny had no choice but to follow, though the combination of wet clothes, crutch, and bad leg made it a frustratingly time-consuming proposition, with the result that Lew was already striding purposefully down the lane before Ronny even made the top of the bank. Ronny had to execute another one of his hop-limp-hop-style sprints to catch up with him.

"Lew?" he called softly, as he once more came even with his brother, but Lew wasn't listening, or if he was, he was choosing to ignore him. Ronny poked him in the side, but only provoked a grunt. A quick jog ahead of him so that Ronny could get a glimpse of his eyes showed him that Lew's vision *seemed* to be clear—or at least his eyes were once more in focus.

But what was he *doing*? Why wasn't he answering?

Impulsively, Ronny cupped his free hand around the bare skin at the base of his brother's skull.

—And found himself surrounded by bones.

Oh, it was still the fenced fields, ominous forests, and derelict weathered buildings typical of the rural South. Except that *every single object* had somehow been rendered into bones: *millions* upon *millions* of bones.

Collections of laminated ribs replaced fence rails; clumps of skulls made boulders large as cars; and the very earth itself was white and dry and crunched beneath their tread, as if it too were made of ground-up bone. Even the trees— well, they could not really *be* trees, though they maintained that general form; were elaborate conglomerations of long bones and scapulae, not all of them human. For Ronny, it was a place of absolute dread, for the thing he feared most in the world was death: the transformation from living flesh into bones that could then be desecrated. And this place was the ultimate desecration, for all the graveyards in the world put together could never yield up bones enough to comprise this charnel plain.

And there was no end to it, though the terrain rose and fell and revealed unexpected vistas as he and Lew continued to trudge along with the bone dust rising around them and the crutch gleaming eerily in the unsourced yellowish-blue light that was the only illumination. And all the while he kicked pebbles which were also toes or heels or knuckle-bones out of the way ahead of him.

Something was nagging at him, though: trying to remind him of something he was supposed to do. But he couldn't get it to focus, couldn't think of *anything*—not when he was completely surrounded by bones.

And then, abruptly, he saw the skeleton.

Only it was not a skeleton, though the log projecting from the oily waters of a pond a few yards off to the left certainly *was* made of bones. And of all the strange things Ronny had seen here, this was the most peculiar, for in a world comprised entirely of osseous material, this skeleton alone was not. Indeed it was not a proper skeleton at all, he now saw, though it had certainly looked like one initially. Rather, it was a probably accidental assemblage of driftwood that had somehow become entangled with a coil of barbed wire (which was the only *metal* he had seen so far) and lodged in such a way that the hidden sun had warped and gnarled and dried the twisted limbs into the exact semblance of a desiccated human form. In other words, he thought dully, the only thing that *ought* to be made out of bones here wasn't.

Lew hadn't noticed it either, as he had noticed nothing since they had found themselves there. But Ronny continued to stare first beside him, then behind as they staggered past.

And so it was that he did not see the skull half-buried in the . . . sand? until he stumbled over it.

Which probably saved him. For with that movement, he released his hold on Lew's neck, staggered a few awkward steps, and slammed to the ground.

—And tasted cool damp air and felt soft grass beneath his fingers, even as he saw from the corner of his eye Lew weaving blindly on toward Cardalba Hall, which now loomed ominously at the top of the hill to his right. They had made it all the way to the visitors' driveway.

And then something smashed against his consciousness with force enough to keep him pinned to the ground: Anson, without a doubt—for it Sounded exactly like him. And though Ronny *knew* it was an intangible threat, those centers of his brain in charge of responding to external stimuli weren't buying it. And so, in spite of himself, he felt himself trapped inside his own body and could only watch in grim horror as his brother continued on his slow plodding way up the company driveway and thence into the avenue of boxwoods that led to Cardalba Hall's front door. A dog came out to sniff him there: a white dog with blood-red ears, its limbs so thin they more properly belonged to the landscape Ronny had just evaded. The last thing he saw was the worst, though; for as he lay helpless on the ground, he saw Lew trudge up the steps to Cardalba Hall, open the door, and disappear inside.

The Winds brought him a ghost of satisfied laughter—and then the bones reclaimed him.

Chapter 26

Cut to the Quick

Cardalba Plantation

White—in the merest blink of an eye: white and cold. But what now surrounded Ronny where he lay spread-eagled on the ground was *not* the crunchy white of arctic snow-fields, but the dusty dry pallor of an endless desert of crumbling bone eroded by perpetual icy winds. Grit clung to him when he made to rise, crept under his eyelids when he tried to blink, clogged his nose with a dustiness that made him at once want to gasp and sniff and sneeze. It even found its way into his mouth so that he had to spit and gag to rid himself of the tasteless residue of countless unseen deaths. And all the while he shivered.

For a long time he simply lay there, the only thing alive in that barren world of bones, helpless against the relentless assault of osseous wind-borne powder that was slowly scouring his numbing flesh away. Yet in spite of the threat posed by that constant abrasion, the effect was somehow soothing—like being gently scratched all over; and before he knew it, his eyes closed and he drifted down to sleep.

And as he lay there, the words came back to him that he had once so dreaded: *You* will *die . . . sooner or later you will. You will be* nothing *. . . your flesh will wither and your bones will be naked to the world. Your mind will shrivel and your senses fade; and then even your bones will flake away, one molecule at a time and you will become one with the universe: one with everything that ever lived. You will be everywhere, and you will be nowhere at* all *. . .*

Ronny believed it too, as he had not before; for who could doubt such a soft caressing voice? And this time he wanted desperately to comply, to turn himself off and will his own dissolution.

He was still lying mostly on his face amid drifts of dry white powder, but as the wind continued to blow, it uncovered some bones—skulls mostly: piles of them—and obscured others. That was when the bones began to speak to him, murmuring in wispy, hissing voices he could not quite understand. But then one bone rose above the rest and remained within his line of sight. It was a small bone: a rough triangle three or four inches long and maybe two-thirds as wide. And as he squinted at it, words began to form in his head, and this time they made sense.

I am your right patella, it said. *Once I marked the juncture of your shin and your thigh. Your femur was my friend, as were your tibia and fibula. And then the dreams came and I was wrenched out of place and shattered, and so you abandoned me. Now I am here, in this place of bones, for this is what I and all my kin come to at last. But you are more than this: bones hold you up, give you shape. But they are not what make you human. For that you only need will, and as long as you have will, you can stay alive. And as long as you are alive, you do not belong here.*

But I don't want *to be alive,* Ronny protested, only then aware that he'd actually been thinking that. *It's only pain and trouble and hassle. You spend your whole life working toward a goal and then something stupid happens and suddenly you lose it all.*

And is that what you've been learning lately? You've changed a lot since you and I parted company, Ronny. Surely you have learned something worthwhile along the way.

Well . . . I have *learned how to make things,* Ronny replied. *How to do metalwork and all.*

And is that not a thing worth living for? To make things, to continue to make things, to leave solid proof you have existed?

Who are you really? Ronny wondered, ignoring the previous statement. *This isn't real, I know that; but I don't want to go back to the world of pain either. But who are you? Why're you bugging me?*

I'm exactly what I appear to be. I'm that part of yourself that frightens you because you ought *to be afraid to be as different from other people as you are. But I'm also that part that's proud to know you are unique. More to the point, I'm a part of you from your old life looking at the you of now and wondering if you're going to lie here and talk philosophy until your brother dies.*

Are you the Road Man, sneaking into my dream? This is starting to sound like stuff he'd say.

Some of it is. He is part of you now, you know—but then so is Anson, so is Matt, so is Lew. Sometimes it's hard to tell where one begins and another ends.

But you really sound *like him.*

Ah, but do I look *like him?*

You look like my kneecap.

Then there you are.

But . . .

If you have *to give me a label, you could say I'm your conscience. Or you could say I'm the bliss the Road Man talked about that you'll never follow if you give up now. Or I'm the hollow at the center of your soul that nobody ever finds on this side of the grave unless they're so absolutely reduced by terror they're a dozen breaths shy of death. Or you might think of me as the place where the blood of your mother and the blood of your father, who were blood of one mother in turn, come together and mix and mingle; that place your father programmed into you when you were born, when he did the forbidden thing and looked into your future—which even your mother did not know. I am your fail-safe, for while Matthew knew he could drive you mad with dreams, the double-blooded require two kinds of weapons to kill. One must slay the body and one must slay the soul.*

You're telling me this so I can use it to defeat Anson, aren't you?

It's your choice. But it would be wise to act quickly.

And none of this is real?

Everything you see, everything you feel and smell and taste and hear Anson has planted in your mind. But he is distant, you are stronger. It is your mind—take control of it.

But what about you? How do I know you're not Anson's doing, too?

I am what Anson awoke and can neither hear nor keep silent. When you awaken, I will be no more.

But . . .

Awaken—and let me die.

But how . . . ?

The opposite of the way you came here.

And what was that? Ronny wondered. If he opened his eyes, it would be to once more confront the place of the dead. Which could only mean that he was to search *inside*.

Once more he closed his eyes, obeying at least overtly that whispering voice that still suggested he drop his awarenesses one by one and let go and die. Except that when he finally *did* let go, he found himself with a new and stronger center where he had no body at all, but where the Winds blew strong and clear. And he opened himself to them, let those phantom breezes flow into him and give him Strength. And he began to think of making, only instead of creating something tangible, he crafted with his mind alone. He thought of it as a sphere—one of those weird fiber-optic jobs like the Road Man had, only with cutting edges all over it. And he imagined that sphere expanding outward, slicing away the connections Anson had made with him, the ones that carried the Winds that held him thrall.

And opened his eyes onto the Georgia night.

Anson knew it too, for Ronny could sense his rival's Voice howling around the Silence he raised the instant he was back in control. Trouble was that while it was true nobody could Hear you when you were inside a Silence, you couldn't Hear anybody either. Which meant that he was still acting blind, as far as fathoming Anson's intentions was concerned.

But that didn't stop him from squaring his shoulders and sticking out his chin and making his way with as much haste as he could muster straight up the steps of Cardalba Hall.

Two of the white hounds met him on the porch and bared their teeth at him, but a firm touch of his Voice sent them slinking away with their tails between their legs. The front door was not locked, and Ronny didn't bother to knock, but simply twisted the knob and went inside. The hallway beyond was dimly lit by a brace of candles in gold candelabra set before a matching pair of mirrors. And four yards down on the right a large oak door gaped wide, the frame beside the lock splintered. Beyond that opening, Ronny could hear someone sobbing.

Not bothering with more than minimal stealth, he made his way there and peered inside.

And for the first time gazed upon Matthew Welch's library.

—And upon Anson lounging in the center of the candlelit room in what he somehow knew from its size and situation should have been Matthew's Listening chair. He looked remarkably well, too, and cut quite an impressive figure in his new jeans and purple-and-gold paisley shirt. Nor did he react when Ronny entered; simply went on smiling in a vacuous, drugged-out way, offering neither threat nor pro-

test—perhaps because he was also resting his bare feet—
black-haired toes and all—in Winnie Cowan's lap.

Winnie!

Ronny's first impulse was to run to her, to fling Anson
aside and grab her and hug her and never let her go—until
he saw her uncomprehending expression and noticed the
small shiny object in Anson's right hand that hovered per-
ilously near her throat.

The sobbing was louder, too, and did not come from
Winnie. But *then* he glimpsed what had been obscured by
the high backs of two chairs—and could not suppress a cry
of dismay. For there, cringing on all fours in the middle of
the floor, was a wild-eyed and soaking-wet Lew.

Anson's gaze shifted toward the cowering figure and intensified abruptly. Ronny's heart flip-flopped as his brother
crawled a few feet in his direction, then collapsed onto the
rug and commenced writhing and clawing at himself like
an animal being consumed alive by fleas, all the while
moaning and gibbering in incomprehensible anguish. Ronny
got two paces into the room before a warning twitch of
Anson's blade made him freeze—and that was when he
finally saw Matthew.

The Master of Cardalba rose from the chair across from
Anson's and Ronny caught the bright metallic gleam of a
knife in *his* hand as well. But even worse than Winnie's
and Lew's, the old man's eyes were completely void of
inner fire: were in truth, the eyes of a man who for all
practical purposes had already surrendered his life.

Ronny had to fight to retain his composure. Anson might
be strong, but he doubted he could control three people
while a serviceable set of fingers were clamped around his
neck. Or maybe he should simply stake it all on one mad
rush, smash his crutch into his cousin's head and destroy
his rival that way. Or—

"You'd be a fool either way," Anson chuckled. "You
need to watch your emotions if you don't want 'em to push
your Voice beyond your Silence like they did just now. And

don't forget this little knife in my hand. It's an ordinary blade—but it should do just fine on your lady if you even *think* about messin' with me.''

''You wouldn't dare! I thought she was why you were doing this.''

''Oh I don't have to *kill* her,'' Anson grinned back. ''There's a lot I can do without killin' her. She might even enjoy some of it.''

''Fuck you!''

The air grew abruptly tenser. Ronny saw his cousin's eyes brighten with fury, then seek to lock with his, and Heard his Voice shouting around the Silence he was still trying hard to maintain.

They strove there for a moment, neither speaking, neither giving ground. Until suddenly Anson broke eye contact, shrugged, and turned his gaze back toward his grandfather. Though no words were spoken, Ronny felt that tension intensify so that it was like a fine wire stretching taut within his consciousness.

—Whereupon Matthew stiffened, then calmly walked over and crouched beside the cowering, cringing Lewis, who did not even seem aware of his presence. Metal flashed as he raised his blade high, brought it down—and froze inches from the hysterical boy's spine.

''Nooooo!'' Ronny screamed, and only the knowledge that however quick he was, one of those knives would surely be faster kept him from abandoning all caution.

''You're right,'' Anson laughed loudly, once more sparing him a glance. ''I could kill Winnie—*or* Grandpa could kill Lew—before you could stop the other. And I'm sure you know all about that knife Grandpa's got. I'm sure you know *everything* now, since poor Lew here learned all *he* knows from you—or did, before I scared his humanity clean out of him. But I'm not gonna do *anything* to good old Lew yet. Not while I can still make you squirm a while.''

Ronny bit his lip, forcing himself to be calm. ''We don't *want* your damned power. You can have it for all we care.

Just leave us alone until we can finish school and go away. We won't be back, I can promise you that.''

Anson reached down and ran the back of his hand gently along Winnie's cheek. "And what about little Winnie here? Don't you want to include her in the bargain?''

It was all Ronny could do to keep his cool. "Of course I do," he shot back acidly. "She walks out of here with me and Lew tonight. The woods must be full of virgins who'd do just fine—since I'm sure you're not as picky as Matthew is—assuming he still *has* a mind.''

"You're bluffing, cuz," Anson snorted. "Everything you've said is bullshit and you know it. I don't even have to *listen* to you if I don't want to. And I sure as hell don't have to sit here while you try to bargain with me in my own library.''

"It's Matthew's library, Anson; don't forget that. I doubt your name's on either the will or the deed.''

"It *will* be—on both—soon enough." He reached down to fondle Winnie again, and slid his hand further to cup her right breast. She did not so much as flinch.

"I'm afraid I may have damaged her." Anson sighed with mock wistfulness. "I had to retune her to suit me without an instruction manual.''

"Bastard!''

"Poor word choice, cuz." He looked down at Winnie again. "You *could* free her, of course—if you were quick and knew what you were doin'. You could do it the same way I freed her predecessor—except, of course, *you* don't have the balls.''

"Anson—''

"Oh, shut up!" Anson snapped. "I've got you by the dick and you know it. One move and I off good old Lew here before your eyes. Another, and this knife could do a fine job on your gal. And all because you're too slow, all 'cause you can't cover ten feet on your own without fallin' down. So you might as well just sit down and watch the show, you goddamned faggot cripple!''

Ronny hated himself. Anson was right; they had reached an impasse. He could do exactly nothing but stand helplessly by.

Anson knew it, too, for though he periodically glanced toward Ronny and kept his blade within striking distance of Winnie's neck, he had turned most of his attention toward Matt.

"It's time," he whispered to the old man who still crouched stiffly by his nephew. "Let's put this piece of soggy trash out of its misery."

Matthew did not reply—nor had he spoken since Ronny had arrived—but Ronny saw Anson's eyes narrow and felt the air grow so tense it practically hummed, which he now knew indicated one will being brought to bear on another. And as Ronny looked helplessly on, Matthew raised his arm once more.

"Now!" Anson cried.

But Matthew did not obey—not immediately. He remained frozen where he was, his hand trembling violently while poor Lew sobbed and groaned before him, fists pressed over his eyes.

"*Now, you son of a bitch!*" Anson repeated even more vehemently.

The tension reached a crescendo, Anson's brow broke into a sweat—and this time Matthew complied. Ronny saw the tendons in his wrist tense. And then the knife was flashing toward Lewis's unprotected back.

Blood flew, splattering onto Matthew's face. A second blow flung a line of it across Winnie's snowy sweatshirt.

And on the third stab, Ronny reached the breaking point. In spite of Anson and the knife at Winnie's throat, he hurled himself forward—lashing out with the crutch so that its sturdy metal foot slammed into Matthew's wrist before the blade could complete a fourth arc. The blow connected with so much force the old man reeled sideways into Anson, his knife flying out of sight somewhere beyond his grandson's chair. And so strong was Ronny's swing that the crutch continued on into Anson's hand, knocking his knife away as well.

Anson shrieked in pain—and Ronny had just time to grab a breath and feel the first brief rush of elation when, with far more speed than any normal person should ever have been able to muster, Anson grabbed the foot of the crutch with both hands and wrenched it out of his grasp. Ronny yelled, flailed, then lost his balance and toppled heavily to the floor. He tried to rise immediately, hoping to reach one of the knives, or at least to somehow maneuver Winnie out of the way, but before he could even get up on his elbows Anson had kicked his footholder aside and was looming before him, the crutch raised over his head. Ronny saw it flash in the dim light, caught the glitter of the bronze and silver warriors—and saw them all merge into a shimmering metallic blur as Anson swung the crutch's heavily encrusted head straight into his temple.

The whole universe exploded into pain. White light filled his eyes, then went colorless. And then Ronny's head hit the floor.

But he did not quite lose consciousness, though a part of him badly wanted to in order to escape the agony pounding through his skull. And neither did he move, though he expected every instant to feel a second blow, and then a third and fourth, by which time he was sure his brains would be puddling across the rug. But so far Anson was only staring at him (he could somehow sense that without actually seeing him) as if his assailant could not quite believe what he had just done. And then Ronny felt something brush against his Silence, presumably Anson trying to ascertain whether or not he still lived. He obligingly eased back that barrier just enough to expose his surface consciousness where lay the addled incoherence he hoped was all his cousin expected to find. Evidently it was, and a moment later, Anson withdrew.

"Fuck you too," Anson spat, and then something heavy thudded to the floor beside his head—undoubtedly the crutch. And since Ronny was lying on his left side with his left hand close to his heart and his right arm flung over his head thereby obscuring his face, he was able to crack open the eye farthest from the floor just enough to see Anson turn away and commence fumbling noisily around in the shadows by the opposite door, evidently in search of one or the other knives.

Which meant he was ignoring Winnie, who had scooted out of the way during his counterattack and was now cowering in confusion beside Anson's vacant throne. Her expression looked clearer, though, as if she had just awakened from a long, troubling sleep; and Ronny felt vastly relieved—until her eyes found him. "Ronny!" she groaned in despair and started toward him. Anson apparently heard her, glanced her way, frowned, then shrugged and drawled, "Oh, go ahead! Son of a bitch'll be dead in a few minutes anyway—one way or another."

Winnie stifled a sob, and her eyes filled with tears, but she kept on moving—which almost certainly implied that Anson had relaxed whatever deep control he'd maintained over her.

Not that it would do *Ronny* much good now, not when the agony in his head was growing worse by the instant, not when he could feel his awareness ebbing and flowing in waves that brought with them unspeakable nausea. Not when he no longer even cared what happened to him or Winnie or Lew. Not when all he wanted to do was continue down the road that would bring him at last to death. At least now he knew what was waiting.

But then Winnie touched him, and that touch sent one final spark of pleasure, of joy, of regret that it was almost certainly the last coursing through him. That was when he remembered that there was one final thing he wanted to do for her. He still had the bracelet in his shirt pocket—had kept it there ever since the night he had nearly smashed it. And now, feebly, with agony sparking through his head at every movement of his shoulders and neck, he fumbled his left hand into the pocket. Darkness lapped toward him, and he could already hear the distant hiss and burr of the bones talking. "Here," he whispered with the last bit of will he could muster. "I made this for you."

He heard the soft thump of the box hitting the rug, and caught one final glimpse of Winnie's hand closing over it. And then he could hold out no longer.

He shut his eye and let the darkness flow over him as he drifted down and down, abandoning his body completely, and only distantly aware that his Silence was slipping away as well and that he no longer had will enough to sustain it. Which meant that his mind was open to other Winds.

One of which was blowing toward him from Winnie. But . . . but footholders should not *have* Voices! Or perhaps it was merely the fact that she was so near him and awash with emotion herself—for her Voice carried far more feeling and instinct than conscious thought. She had put on the bracelet, it told him, and then thrown herself sobbing across his body. She also believed he was dead, and the horror of that despair washed out of her and into him.

—And awoke a part of himself that knew that however much pain he felt, he had no right to cause someone he cared about even worse when he didn't have to.

And so he breathed—once, twice, and then more deeply—and sensed Winnie's unbounded relief when she found that he still lived. Her joy reinforced her Voice; and since she was now in physical contact with him, he could pick up her thoughts quite clearly. And though she was far too overwrought to think in sentences, he could tell from her confusion, anger, and fear that he'd guessed correctly: whatever bindings Anson and Matt had laid on her no longer held—and she was beyond furious at both of them, but had not yet decided exactly what to do.

Ronny, in short, had a new ally—if only he could figure out how to use her. And if only he could find a way to save Lew.

Lew! He had almost forgotten about his brother and wondered distantly how much time had passed, and whether his twin was even still alive. He was—he thought—for surely he would have known it otherwise; surely there would have been a swirling among the Winds if the one that carried Lew's Voice had ceased to blow.

Which meant that he might still have time—*if* he was careful, *if* Anson kept his attention focused elsewhere and did not recover his weapon too soon.

With that in mind, Ronny gritted his teeth against the pain and the hovering blackness and dragged his eyes open again. He saw Winnie's knees mostly, for she was still kneeling over him, her hands resting on his side, with her thoughts sparking fast and thick as she assessed her situation. But by peering beyond her, Ronny could just make out Lew still on the floor, still breathing heavily and twitching from time to time. Anson was nowhere in sight, but Ronny could hear him cursing under his breath and scrabbling around on the floor behind his chair, where he had evidently finally located Matthew's knife. As for Mr. Welch himself, *he* was standing again, gaping down at the body of his grandnephew, while that same kinsman's blood trickled down his chin. His eyes looked more alive they had, however, and Ronny wondered if maybe Anson had inadvertently relaxed his control on him as well.

"Ah ha!" Anson crowed triumphantly, and rose. And Lew also evidently saw—or felt—or Heard—his torturer approach, for, beyond all hope, he too roused himself from his stupor and scrambled frantically across the floor in Ronny's direction.

"Oh no you don't!" Anson hissed, and flung himself atop his cousin, the knife glittering in his hand as he drove it down.

—And missed, as by some miracle Lewis anticipated him and managed to twist far enough aside that the blade only ripped his shirt and pinned it to the floor—where it remained, stuck between two boards. And then practically out of nowhere a clear-eyed Matthew was charging toward his now-defenseless protégé. Anson saw him at the last instant and kicked, knocking the old man flying—then snatched up the crutch from where it lay midway between the brothers and leapt to his feet.

Ronny tried to rise to stop him, tried to yell, tried to do anything he could think of to distract his cousin . . . but to no avail. For the second time in as many minutes, Anson swung the crutch, only this time his aim was better or his intentions more malign—for when he smashed the glittering mass down atop the incredulously gaping Matt's head, he struck true. Ronny heard the bone shatter, saw the mix of brain and blood that oozed out from a broad gash in the middle of the old man's skull before the former Master of Cardalba toppled forward and smashed his brow against the heavy carved corner of a nearby table—and rose no more. Ronny Heard the Wind that had once carried his Voice sigh away.

Meanwhile, Anson was staring stupidly at the crutch, at the tiny silver warrior on its frontmost horn whose equally tiny—and now crumpled—silver sword had led the thrust that had destroyed all that had ever made Matthew Welch human.

"You . . . you're *dead*! . . . you bastard," the new Master of Cardalba gasped, flinging the crutch away as if it had burned him. "But . . . but you can't *be* killed! But I've *killed* you . . . but . . . Why didn't you tell me that was how you'd die, you son of a bitch? *Why?* I didn't want to *kill* you, I only wanted to—"

Lew, unfortunately for himself, picked that moment to groan.

Anson's gaze darted instantly from his grandfather's corpse to his still-prone cousin. "And what are *you* doin' alive?" he shouted, leaping toward him, though he sounded (to Ronny's surprise) close to tears. "You're the fucker who's *supposed* to be dead, not Grandpa!"

Ronny wanted desperately to go to his brother's aid, but even as he tried to rise, the darkness swept in again and it was all he could do to stifle a gasp, as his stomach twisted violently and poured sour liquid into his mouth. He coughed—he couldn't help it—though Anson did not seem to notice. But when he was finally able to open his eyes again a moment later, it was to gaze once more on horror.

Anson was actually crouching astride Lew now, and before Ronny could gather his strength for one last frantic lunge, his cousin commenced driving the knife up and down into Lew's ribcage, all the while screaming at the top of his lungs, "Die, damn you; why won't you die? Die, damn you! Die! Die! Die!"

But though Lew cried and screamed and grunted as every blow struck home, and though blood was fountaining everywhere, he did *not* die. Ronny Heard his Wind blowing weak but sure, and even as he Listened, he felt other, more distant Winds shift in his brother's direction and add their Strength, and he did not need to know that every one of those Winds blew from some distance Silence.

"The Luck," he whispered. "The Luck is protecting its own."

"What?" Winnie asked softly, looking up—apparently still too dazed by the carnage she had already witnessed to appreciate what was now going on.

Anson evidently had no idea what was happening either. He was still sitting astride his victim yelling over and over, as with each shout the knife found some new purchase in his cousin's body. "Why won't you goddamned *die*?"

But Lew *wouldn't* die, Ronny was sure of that now—though why not, given that Anson was certainly using the dagger Matthew had custom-commissioned to kill him, he could not even begin to imagine.

And then, to Ronny's amazement, Winnie rose abruptly, picked up the crutch, and turned to glare at Anson.

Unfortunately, Anson also saw her. Her gaze shifted to the crutch, which she stared at as if she expected it to turn and strike at her. But as she tightened her grip and started to draw it back, a fire of dread flashed into Anson's face, and before she could react, he snatched it from her startled fingers. "You'll die too!" he shrieked—but she managed to leap far enough to the side to avoid the swing he leveled at her; Ronny heard her fall. "Maybe I'll do your boyfriend first, though," he added, and switched his attention to Ronny.

—Who was almost fully conscious now, though every move still made his head swim, his stomach heave, and sent sparks flashing before his eyes. He had, however, at least got up on one elbow. But he would be too late, he knew: too late to stop Anson from shattering his skull with his own preposterous sculptures, and—theoretically immortal or no—he doubted he'd be able to survive such a blow. If nothing else, the pain would force him to will himself to die in order to escape it. Yet surely there was *something* he could do. *Surely* . . . He could not rise to face Anson in time, and doubted he could put up much of a fight even so. But . . . if there were someone to fight *for* him— shoot, if only the little guys on the crutch could come alive just long enough, *God* how he wished that would happen . . .

And at that exact moment Anson screamed. Ronny was so taken aback his arm gave way and he collapsed back to the rug, but as soon as his vision cleared again, he saw to his utter amazement that the figures on the crutch *were* moving: swarming across their metal battlefield in a quick-moving mass of brass and bronze and silver, their tiny weapons flashing, their miniature cloaks flapping in an unseen wind. Both Law *and* Chaos were on the march, and even as Ronny gasped out his surprise the first of them reached Anson's hand. Anson dropped the crutch reflexively and tried to shake the tiny warrior free—but could not; it had sunk its dagger into his sleeve and was hanging on for dear life. And by the time he *had* ripped it off and flung it to the floor, its fellows were upon him, climbing up his pants from where some had leapt or fallen. In no time at all, the warriors had engulfed him. They were obviously hurting him, too: stabbing at him with their tiny knives, slicing miniature half-moons from his flesh with their scythes and scimitars, even launching miniature arrows at his eyes. In no time at all, Anson Bowman was under siege by Lilliputians.

And he could not stand it. His eyes, already wide with frustration and anger, now took on the added wildness of unbridled terror. And though he tried to brush them aside, there were easily thirty of the little fellows, and some were beginning to find ways into his clothes.

"Get away from me!" he shrieked, dancing around as he tried desperately to avoid a hundred simultaneous stings and pricks and tickles. "Get off me! Go the hell away."

But the tiny army did not go away. If anything their movements became even more agitated, so that Anson could get no grip on even the slowest one.

"Get *away*!" he screamed. "I'm the Master of Cardalba, goddamn it!"

And with that he took the knife he had never dropped from his right hand and commenced stabbing at the tiny horde. His first blow ripped a major artery in his wrist. His second thrust deep into his thigh. And his third, fourth, and fifth all found his heart.

Whereupon he released one final ragged breath and collapsed.

And Ronny, to his utter surprise, heard him die.

Chapter 27

A Day Late

Cardalba Hall
The wee hours

Ronny was still lying on his side staring stupidly at the corpse of Anson Bowman sprawled across the floor two yards in front of him, when he heard a soft movement from the candlelit shadows beyond. He grunted and tried to rise, but slowly, stiffly, like the shell-shocked survivor of some vast battle that had swept over and around him but never quite engaged him, yet had been a cardinal threat to his very soul. Pain caught him as he lifted his head, shooting into his face and neck from where Anson had smashed his crutch into his temple. A wave of nausea came with it, so strong he had to swallow hard to keep from gagging. Darkness hovered near.

The movement again—and this time Ronny saw.

It was Winnie, blinking back horror and disbelief as she rose from where she'd scrambled to escape Anson's final blow. Her sweatshirt was splattered with blood, and she looked drained—and probably was, since Matt had been drawing on her Strength for days, never mind what Anson had used her for during the last few hours.

"W-Winnie?" Ronny croaked.

She stared at him uncomprehendingly. "Ronny?"

Ronny cleared his throat. "I . . . I'm still here, still alive," he managed. "Are you . . . ?" Words failed him abruptly, and before he knew it he was sobbing.

"I'm . . . fine," Winnie whispered, picking her way past Anson's body to kneel beside him. "Are you okay? Oh, God, your head . . . Here, let me get you up, and— Oh, Ronny, what's happened here? What's Anson done? What've *I* done . . . and what about poor Lew?"

"Lew?" Ronny sniffed dully, knowing there was something he was supposed to recall about his brother but not what it was. Another tide of darkness caught him as Winnie worked her arm under him and tried to help him rise. Then, when his vision cleared again: "*Lew!*"

Somehow he managed to sit up—and finally caught sight of his brother.

Lew was where Anson had left him: lying on his chest with his hands drawn protectively over his eyes. And though his clothing was completely saturated with blood, the pool beneath him in no wise reflected the number of wounds he had received. Or maybe the light was just bad, for he *was* lying in a shadowed area. Reflexively, Ronny tried to Hear him—and touched nothing. It was as if his brother did not exist—yet neither was there the resounding silence of *absence* he had felt when his mother had died. And there had been the strengthening Luck which must have come from other Listeners—which meant . . .

"*Lew!*"

Forcing back the nausea, the pain, the flashes of light that tried to draw him back down to darkness, he eventually made it to his feet. "I've *got* to get to him!" he cried, as he stood swaying in Winnie's arms. "I've got to! He may still be alive."

But Winnie continued to hold him. "You saw what I

saw," she whispered. "Could you have survived all that? Matt had a dagger made specifically to kill him, and Anson sure used it on him. You've got to accept that."

"But there should be a hole in my soul where he used to be and . . . and there isn't, and—"

Winnie held him firm. "No, Ronny, he really is—"

"Help me to him," Ronny interrupted. "I've gotta know."

Winnie bit her lip and nodded, and together they made their way past Anson's body—and Matt's—to crouch by Lewis's side. With Winnie's help, Ronny eased him over on his back and cradled the bloody body in his arms. Lew was completely limp, his flesh unnaturally cool. But when Ronny held his ear in front of his brother's lips he both felt and heard the softest hiss of breathing.

"Lew," he cried joyfully. "Lew!"

"But Anson *stabbed* him!" Winnie protested from beside him. "He stabbed him over and over. Look, you can still see the wounds."

Lew's sweater and T-shirt were so ripped and shredded and drenched with blood he might as well not have been wearing them. But when Ronny lifted a bit of the sopping fabric gently aside so he could see the flesh underneath, he got another shock. There were wounds, yes, lots of them. But the smallest had already drawn together, and the larger ones were in the act of closing.

Winnie suppressed a gasp.

"He's okay," Ronny whispered. "He'll live."

Relief flooded into him then, and he collapsed into Winnie's arms. For a long moment they simply knelt there, feeling each other's aliveness, holding each other close as if each feared the other might dissolve if let go. They were both crying, too overcome with emotion to speak further.

Eventually, though, Ronny eased gently away. He regarded Winnie seriously. "This doesn't make any sense at all, does it?"

She smiled wanly, blinking back tears. "Some. Anson

couldn't resist talking, and I couldn't help but pick up things. But . . . but the others—are they . . . ?''

Ronny shrugged. "Yeah . . . I think so. I . . . I kinda felt them die.''

"But . . . if they're dead, shouldn't we . . . ?''

"I will in a minute.'' Ronny sighed. "Just let me rest a little longer. There's more to me—and more to Lew—than either of us knew before tonight. And—''

But he could go no further, because a tide of nausea swept over him and for a moment the darkness reclaimed him. When he came to again, it was to feel something cool lying on his forehead, and to sense the warmth of Winnie's body sitting on the floor at his side. She had somehow managed to get him to a sofa. Ronny slitted his eyes open and gazed out at the room, and truly saw for the first time the carnage the last quarter hour had wrought. Anson was nearest, lying on his back with a knife still clenched firmly in his hand, its blade completely obscured by the same gore that stained his right pant leg and utterly obliterated the design on the paisley shirt. A larger pool was still spreading from beneath the corpse and across the rug toward him.

Matt lay beyond, with one foot somehow entangled with one of Anson's. Ronny was just as glad he could not see what he remembered: the red-white mass of blood and brains that had been the top of the old man's head.

It was too much, though, too goddamned much, and what would they do now? Call the police, he supposed, and then try to answer questions he knew he would not be able to.

"Winnie?'' he began, seeking her hand with his own and finding it polishing the blood off Elon: the chief of the miniature warriors, whom she had reclaimed from the floor. And only then did he recall how it was that Anson had been led to stab himself. Yet as best he could tell (for neither of them had had any urge to touch the brain-encrusted crutch), the rest of the warriors were exactly where they should have been—though many were now bent and twisted by the impacts they had received.

"Winnie?" Ronny tried again, forcing himself to sit up straight. "I guess we ought to . . ."

And at that moment the house resounded with a knock on the front door so thunderous the library windows rattled in their frames.

He glanced up at Winnie, who had already risen, and shook his head. "I'll go."

"Are you sure?"

"I'm a Welch," he said heavily. "Though I don't suppose you knew that—nor did I until a couple of hours ago. So I guess it's my responsibility."

"But . . ."

Ronny grimaced but got to his feet. "I'll be okay," he grunted, and limped—on his own two feet—for the door.

The knock had sounded twice more before they finally reached Cardalba Hall's main portal. Ronny hesitated there, wondering who might be on the other side and what could possibly bring anyone here in the middle of the night. Then something occurred to him. He had the Luck—of a sort. And so with that in mind, he Listened—and found a Silence so profound it was like falling off a cliff into empty space.

He gasped and drew back into himself reflexively, and without further ado, wrenched the door open.

The Road Man was standing there in his Night Man persona—except that for once he had added a pair of white painter's pants and a set of cheap rubber sandals to the long-tailed white shirt that usually comprised his sole post-sunset garment. He looked freshly bathed and combed—and was holding a narrow, foot-long box.

"Is Mr. Welch in?" the Road Man asked politely, peering over both their heads to probe the candlelit recesses of the hall with his guileless gaze.

Ronny was so taken aback both by the identity of the visitor and his request that he gaped foolishly for a moment before muttering a feeble, croaking "No . . . uh, not exactly." Only then did he recall that the Road Man was scarcely a friend anymore. In fact, by any reasonable assessment, he was a first-class traitor.

A shadow of disappointment crossed the tinker's face, which made Ronny curious in spite of himself. But before he could inquire further, the Road Man half-turned around, as if preparing to leave. "That's too bad," he murmured to no one in particular.

"What is?" Ronny asked, unable to restrain himself.

The Road Man flourished the box. "Mostly that I've just finished that knife he's been wanting in such an all-fired hurry, and now he's not here to pay me."

"Kn-knife . . . ?" Ronny stammered. "What knife?" Then, as realization dawned: "Goddamn it! You've got more nerve than anybody on this *planet* coming here talking about knives when I've already seen you sell him one tonight already."

"Ah, so that was you then?"

"It was," Ronny shot back acidly. "You fucking traitor."

But to his surprise the Road Man merely shrugged. "Mr. Welch asked me to make him a knife," he said calmly. "He said it should be made of gold and silver and iron, that it should be worked on under light of sun and light of moon and folded seven times under the influence of each. I agreed to make it that way, and we settled on the price I was to be paid. I then proceeded to prepare the knife. I finished the folding last night—the *seventh* night—but had not yet sharpened it, nor joined blade and hilt, which I did under the influence of tonight's moon."

"But," Ronny stammered, "I *saw* you! You sold—"

The Road Man shrugged again. "Mr. Welch came to my camp tonight and saw me working on a knife—the one *you* made, for I had decided to move on tomorrow and I knew you still wanted to file down that piece of silver inlay. He asked me if that were *it*, and I replied that it was—for it *was*: the knife you made, nothing more. Unfortunately, Mr. Welch was no more specific than that;

he did not *ask* if it was the knife he had commissioned me to make, for then I would have told him no. He then asked if it fulfilled all the conditions of the agreement, to which I replied, 'There was an agreement?' and upon being told there was—though *I* did not recall you and I making one about your knife—proceeded to inform him that in that case it had been fulfilled. At that point he wondered if it was constructed as required, which again it was—for your purposes. And finally he wanted to know if it would accomplish exactly what it needed to do— which I presume it will. Oh, and he said that it would be sufficient if it would kill what otherwise cannot be killed, and I told him neither yea nor nay.''

''You tricked him, in other words,'' Ronny said uncertainly. ''But why'd you take the money?''

Another shrug. ''Because he offered it and I needed it and seven thousand dollars twice is better than that much once—especially since I planned to share it with you to make up for the disappointment over losing your first complete work. And at any rate I still haven't collected my seed, but I'm in no hurry for that. But, as I said, I have now finished that strange knife he requested. And so I ask you again: is Mr. Welch within?''

Ronny felt as if he had been struck in the chest, and staggered back a step.

''So *that* explains . . .'' he managed, before Winnie hooked her arm around him and held him firm. And then the implications of the Road Man's words sank in. Without so much as a ''Hang on a second'' for their visitor, he turned and hopped/limped/ran back to the library.

''Jesus!'' Ronny murmured, as he stared once more at Lewis's body. His brother was still breathing, but still had not regained consciousness.

''I'd say more like Saint Sebastian,'' the Road Man opined disinterestedly from over Ronny's shoulder.

Ronny would have jumped about ten feet straight up— could he have jumped at all. Instead, he started violently, and twisted hard around to glare up at his mentor. "Jesus *Christ*, man, don't do that!"

"Don't do what?" the Road Man wondered innocently, carefully setting the box down on the blood-spattered cushion of the nearest recliner. "Oh, I see," he mused to himself.

Ronny, who was still glaring at him irritably, scowled uncertainly. "And what is it, *exactly*, that you see?"

The Road Man scratched his nose. "Well, one thing I see is a young man alive who should not be. And another thing I see is another young man dead who probably should be, and I think if you'll examine the knife in his hand, you'll find it was the one you've been working on." He picked up the box that contained the knife he had made for Matthew and dropped it atop the old man's corpse in disgust. "I guess I won't get that other seven thousand."

Ronny was trying hard to sort out the ramifications of what the Road Man had just told him. "You mean—"

The Road Man nodded toward Anson's corpse. "If I see things correctly, the knife *that* one was wielding could not have killed your kinsman because it was not meant to kill him. *This* one"—he pointed at the still-unopened box slowly becoming ensanguined by the gore in which it lay—"most certainly could have, though had I known it would be used so soon or so rashly, I would never have agreed to make it. Obviously the Masters around here aren't as reliable as they once were. I was foolish that night, I suppose. I imagine the Day Man will thrash me for it—probably preach me a sermon as well."

"But," Ronny said slowly, "but . . . if that was the wrong knife, how could it kill Anson?"

"Because it was the right knife to kill *him*, I suppose," the Road Man replied. "I imagine if you prowl deeply enough through the memories your mother this night stole from *her* mother and then passed on to you, you will find there how your uncle—or your father, whichever he was— tried to Fix—what's his name? Anson?—in secret, and obviously failed, at least as far as keeping him stable when the Luck manifested was concerned. But if memory serves, that's also the time they decide failsafes and that kind of foolishness, so he must have *succeeded* there, and probably then planted the form of the weapon that would kill him in your mind—which you then proceeded to execute. I *thought* you came up with that design too easily,'' he added absently.

But Ronny was still confused. ''Wait a minute. You're talking like you've known all along about me and the Welches and all. Are . . . are you a . . . a *Listener* too?''

The Road Man smiled cryptically. ''I Listen, though not in the way you do, nor do I always Hear what I ought, though I know about Voices and Silence. But then again, I know *many* things. I know the positions of the stars, but that doesn't make me an astronomer, nor does the fact that I have known two thousand and forty-five women in my life make me a father—or at least it hasn't so far.''

''But . . .''

''I have told you all I intend to,'' the Road Man said. ''Some things are not for the knowing, as you have ample evidence of here. And some things take a lifetime to discover.'' He sauntered over to Anson's corpse and started to pluck the knife from his death-loosened fingers, then thought better of it. ''You still want this?''

Ronny shook his head uncertainly, and cursed himself for not having noticed before that first Matt and then Anson had been using something he had made. Still, he hadn't exactly been *looking* for it, and the hilt, which was its most distinguishing feature, had been hidden in one hand or the other most of the time—or else had been completely covered with gore. ''I . . . don't think so,'' he whispered finally.

The Road Man shrugged again, and flopped down in the nearest chair. ''Odd it is,'' he mused thoughtfully, ''that the first thing you chose to make was a thing that kills; yet your true craft is to make things that heal.''

"Like what?" Ronny wondered, turning his gaze back toward Lew, who seemed to be breathing more strongly by the minute.

The tinker pointed toward Winnie's arm, where the bracelet still gleamed in the uncertain light of what were now guttering candles. "Like that."

"But . . ."

"Didn't I warn you, Ronny?" the Road Man said mischievously. "Didn't I tell you not to sing while you worked? 'Things have power because you give them power,' I told you. And yet I heard you singing, and—"

"I was humming," Ronny interrupted, but not with malice.

Winnie was staring at the Road Man now, and the tinker caught her at it and smiled back. "There is great power in that bracelet," he said, "for Ronny put great power in it: the power of his love. And when a *Listener* bestows his love, that can be *very* great power indeed."

Winnie did not reply, but Ronny saw her blush and look away.

"But what about Matt?" he asked suddenly. "And there was more about Anson too: like the fact that he had to die in his soul and his body both, or something."

"My, but you *have* been Listening to some strange Voices, haven't you?" the Road Man chuckled. "Maybe you should ask them."

"Give me a break!"

"I should," the Road Man replied promptly. "Maybe then you would stop *petitioning* me for one. Still," he continued, "I'm in an expansive mood this evening—or will be until I have to wake up the Sunrise Man and set him to packing. So I will only say three things: Both those men were full of wounds that *should* have killed them *by any criteria you choose*—so is there any wonder they therefore did? Secondly, if one is willing to kill *anyone* in cold blood, as Anson wanted to do, it pretty much means he's so full of hatred and bitterness he's *already* killed his soul. And the final thing is that dreams can be very real, and so can nightmares—especially when there is so very much in such folks as those two were for them to graze upon. Maybe they could not escape what they found they had made themselves into and simply wished themselves dead from guilt, and so died.''

"But you don't believe that, do you?" Ronny ventured.

"I believe many things, often several contradictory ones at the same time. But one thing I do not *believe* but yet *suspect* is that however the design for that knife came to be in your head, the little warrior—Elon is the name you have given him?—was created by much the same method, and for similar cause. And, if you'll notice, the wound in Matt's skull that killed him was made by a three-inch sword of solid silver—and that is *exactly* the sort of foolish thing a Listener would install as a failsafe. 'He can only be killed by a three-inch sword made of solid silver,' or some such. And who would make such a stupid thing as that?"

"Well, I'm glad I'm stupid then," Ronny replied grimly.

"I'm not," the Road Man said, standing again. "And now, if you'll excuse me, I have some more roads to wander—or Roads, if you catch the difference in meaning."

Ronny didn't, but tried not to show it, while Winnie merely looked puzzled. Poor girl, Ronny thought, he really was going to have to do some heavy explaining to her real soon. For the moment, though, his concern was for the Road Man.

"But you *can't* leave—not yet!" he cried. "I haven't learned anything at all to speak of."

"Have you not?" the Road Man snapped, his voice suddenly adrip with ill-concealed condescension. "I would at least have thought you had learned that things made with heart and soul can be stronger than those made by head and hands. As for the rest: all I can say is that you can learn as much from others as from me. And the things you *can't* learn from them—like how my machines work, for instance—will give you something to puzzle over for a very long time indeed. *Are* they perpetual motion machines? you will wonder. *Do* they put out more energy than they take in? You have the evidence of your senses. Are you going to believe them? If you do, then you know that some impossible things are not impossible, and if I have taught you nothing else, I hope you have learned that striving after impossible things is what keeps the best part of us alive. Reality never equals the ideal—yet by striving to make them one, both are exalted.''

''I'm confused,'' Ronny mumbled, starting to tug at Lew's sweater so he could begin the cleanup process.

''And so you were meant to be,'' the Road Man replied. ''And now I have to be going.''

''Will I see you again?'' Ronny asked suddenly.

The Road Man, who was now filling the doorway, only shrugged once more. ''You will doubtless see *many* things in what is left of your life. If I am one of them, then most certainly you will see me. Whether you will *recognize* me or not is another thing entirely. I have money now, you see: lots of it. And money has a tendency to warp things out of all recognition.''

''But—''

But before Ronny could blurt out his next perplexing question, the Road Man was gone. And by the time Ronny finally made it to the front hall, he was nowhere in sight.

For a long time Ronny stood there, staring through the tinted mullions beside the massive oak door. He was crying again, he realized, but for quite a different reason than before.

And when he returned to the library again five minutes later, he found his eyes a-brim yet again. For the first thing he saw was Winnie smiling, and the next thing he saw was his brother climbing shakily to his feet to stand beside her.

And between the three of them there was no trace of Silence at all.

Epilogue I

Clearing the Heir

Cardalba Hall
Sunday, April 22—morning

"So what do *you* want to do?" Ronny asked finally. He leaned back in the kitchen chair and yawned hugely, then looked at Lew through eyes still grainy-heavy from the unplanned nap they'd all just awakened from. His second cup of coffee steamed dreamily in his hand.

Sitting across what had been Matthew Welch's round breakfast table from him, Lew raised his freshly scrubbed head and tried at once to smile helplessly and shrug. Lew looked funny in Matthew Welch's clothes, Ronny thought—not that *he* looked any better in more of the same. But anything would have been an improvement on the wet, bloody rags they'd all been wearing. Besides, the oversized clothes covered Lew's wounds, and Ronny did *not* want to think about them—*or* watch them heal.

Winnie, who had been frying bacon and toasting Pop-Tarts (mostly to keep busy, Ronny knew; she was easily as tired, burned-out, *and* wired as he and Lew were), inserted a plate between them and pulled out a chair for herself. "You know we're going to have to do something soon," she said.

Lew nodded but did not reply. He looked pale, so very pale, but then again, he'd surely sustained more damage than any normal person reasonably could and survive, never mind that he had also lost his mother. Ronny tried not to think about that either, tried not to think about anything at all that had happened in the last twelve hours. And he *certainly* did not want to think about the future—except he knew that very soon they were all three going to have to. Two bodies here, a whole room practically soaked in blood, and a third body a few miles down the road assured that. And their period of grace was rapidly running out; soon they would have no choice but to report what had happened. Probably they should have already, since there was a good chance his and Lew's cars had been found by now, apparently abandoned up by the bridge. Never mind that Anson's mom—his *foster* mom—had surely missed him and started calling around by now as well. *Or* the extreme likelihood that some of Erin's cronies had also tried to get in touch with *her* and failed.

But how could they explain what had happened, and how could they cover for the fact that they had not notified the authorities sooner? The locals were tolerant of Welch-clan weirdness—including the police force. But Ronny doubted that even they would overlook one obvious murder and two very suspicious deaths. And he certainly doubted they'd accept as reasonable the fact that all three of them had been so drained by their ordeal that they'd fallen asleep in each other's arms on the floor of the parlor across the hall from the scene of carnage, only to awaken in the clear light of dawn to discover that all of the night's adventures had been real.

"So, Lew," Ronny whispered again. "What's it gonna be?"

Lew sighed resignedly. "Why're you asking me?" He took a sip of coffee and crunched a strip of bacon, then went on. "No, I know why, I guess. It's 'cause I really am Master of Cardalba now; I really am the Mr. Welch."

"That's right," Ronny acknowledged. "And you're the heir to great wealth and power—probably great knowledge as well."

"Which I neither desired nor need."

"But somebody has to keep the Luck up," Winnie pointed out. "Don't they?"

Lewis shrugged. "I dunno. Do they? It's a pretty strange situation, isn't it? One little corner of the world that's just a tiny bit skewed from all the rest."

"Maybe not," Ronny suggested. "We know there are other Listeners. We know there are at least some traditions and rules of conduct for them. Maybe Welch County isn't as unique as we thought it was. I mean, look at it this way: since there're some people with this kind of . . . of magic . . . in the world, doesn't it stand to reason that if they *weren't* carefully policed something would have slipped out by now? Think about Anson, guys; the temptation was there, but then again the same temptation would have to affect a lot of people if there were a lot more Listeners—if there *weren't* safeguards. One or two Lucky megalomaniacs per country would be enough to completely upset the world. On the other hand, there's a lot of good that's come from the Luck in some ways. I mean, the people up here really do live well. And the Luck doesn't ask of them more than they want to give—if it's used right. Maybe the notion is that little pockets of Luck build up and then slowly expand so that one day, poof, they'll meet and the whole world will be filled with Luck."

Lew rolled his eyes. "Dream on."

"You're just tired; we all are."

"I don't want to be Master, though; I know that much. I was never conditioned to be Master, my . . . my mother didn't *want* me to be Master. I don't know *how* to be Master.''

''But,'' Ronny told him, ''as you said a couple of hours ago: if not you, who? Look, *I* don't want it for you either. But maybe you *ought* to try it just for a little while. Think of the folks around here, for Chrissakes. What are they gonna do when they find out the Luck's gone? They're gonna look to you, and if they look to you for that, and you reject them, they're gonna hate you. Besides, you'd be a good Master, because you're a good *person*—and that may be what the county really needs. I think the reason things started warping up like they did was because Matt *wasn't*, in his heart, a good person. I've seen your heart, though, and it's true gold all the way through.''

Lew smiled wanly. ''You sound like a poet. You also sound like somebody who'd make a pretty good Master himself. I mean, you have *no* preconceived notions, and you're evidently the double-blooded heir. And I *know* your heart's at least as good as mine. Otherwise you'd never have done what you did for me.''

''And what was that?''

''Saved me about a dozen times, protected me at the risk of your life.''

''That was no more than anyone would do for a friend. But *you're* complete, I'm not—which is another reason I can't be Master.''

''Bullshit!'' Lewis said softly. ''The Luck had already started awakening in you before you lost your knee. It can ride those phantom circuits forever—if you're careful. Shoot, it might even repair you—I think it depends on exactly when it kicked in.''

Ronny regarded him strangely. ''You know this?''

Lew looked surprised. ''I . . . I guess I do!''

''You should!'' a new voice rasped authoritatively, as the door from the dining room swung open to admit a tall, stately, stern-looking woman Ronny had never seen before. He jumped reflexively—they all did. Winnie looked alarmed, but Lew, once he had regained his composure, mostly appeared relieved.

"Aunt Martha!" he cried. "What are you doing here?"

"I came to tidy up," Martha Welch replied matter-of-factly, though her eyes looked tired and Ronny suspected she had been crying. She snagged a coffee mug from the rack on the counter and helped herself to a cup, which she took black, before completing the square at the table. "My sources found several Winds unexpectedly gone awry when they checked in last night," she continued, "so they, quite naturally, let me know. And of course there's the rather remarkable vacuum that's created whenever a Master dies; *that* can be Heard a very long way indeed—especially when it's your son."

"Which is how—" Lewis began.

"Which is how I knew exactly when Matty died and had a good idea why," Martha continued, "since his last Wind blew by me in passing. I was far away, but not so far that I couldn't get here in six hours. —Not when you can make Lucky connections," she added with a twinkle in her eye that Ronny found both incongruous and vaguely inappropriate.

"Uh," Winnie began awkwardly, inclining her head toward the library. "I suppose you . . . saw?"

Martha nodded grimly. "Not pretty, though I've seen worse. I was afraid poor Matty would come to that, willful as he was, though I have to say I thought I was damned clever with that bit about the three-inch silver sword—until Dion tricked it out of me. Still, I'll do my mourning in private; we have more imminent problems to deal with now. *This* is going to take some explaining, even from me. I don't suppose *you've* come up with a plan yet, have you? —I thought not. Well," she went on, sighing, "I took the liberty of contacting a friend in the FBI when I arrived in Atlanta. He's—shall we say—also rather fond of Listening."

"Well, that's a relief," Lew said. "I mean it *is* your house, and all."

"Not *my* house," Martha corrected primly. "It belongs to the Master of Cardalba—the present identity of whom, I gather, is still subject to debate."

"Well, we've only *had* a couple of hours," Ronny grumbled.

"I know," Martha told him, taking another sip and snagging a Pop-Tart. "But enough of that. I'll handle things here. What you youngsters need to decide is the matter of the Mastership—oh, you don't have to do it now. But soon."

"Well," Ronny said slowly, "I think it ought to be Lew, if only because I'm not qualified."

"Why not?"

"You have to ask?"

"The leg won't matter in your case," Martha told him. "You couldn't have accomplished what you did without the Luck already working in you, therefore the channels were already mostly in place before the damage occurred; it only remains to be seen if you'll heal—that may still be a little iffy. Besides, while none of us has a clue what the Luck really is, we do know that it has a way of sensing when it's being manipulated. I imagine that since your damage was visited upon you from without, that'll pretty well clinch your claim—assuming you *want* the Mastership."

Ronny did not reply.

"Do you?" Martha asked pointedly.

Ronny shook his head. "No, I can honestly say I don't. I'm not sure what I do want, except that I seem to be happiest when I'm making things—*real* things, tangible things."

"And, at the same time, though you don't know it, you're making dreams," Martha told him. "Has it occurred to you that if you took on the Mastership you could, in effect, make the dreams of a great many people come true?"

Ronny shook his head. "I can't think about this now. I'm sorry. There's just too much going on."

Martha opened her mouth to reply, then closed it again with an almost audible pop. To cover, she took a sip of coffee. "I suppose you're right—from your point of view," she said finally. "And it was cruel of me to try to force you—any of you—to make any sort of decisions right now. What you all three need is sleep."

"You've got it there." Lewis sighed, exchanging glances with Ronny and Winnie, both of whom nodded emphatically.

"I'll see that you get some," Martha assured them. "You can use the room next to mine if you don't mind sharing. It's got a bathroom too," she added, "since I can't help but note a certain . . . sanguine air about the three of you that could use a bit more attention than it's had so far. And *surely* you can find some clothes that fit you better. Meanwhile, I suppose I should be about my business."

"Need any . . ." Ronny began.

"Help?" Martha finished. "Yes, but I won't accept any, at least not from the three of you."

Lewis, who had looked alarmed at Ronny's offer, relaxed immediately—but then his brow furrowed again. "Just one thing, Aunt Martha, before we go up," he said tentatively.

A steel-gray eyebrow shot up. "What's that?"

"What do *you* think about the Mastership? Who do you think should be heir to the Welch clan Luck?"

Martha scowled and pushed her glasses back up her nose. "Well," she said finally, "since you asked. There *are* other heirs, though most are either very distant or very dubious—and even that assumes they can be tracked down and convinced. I've got another son, for one thing; and then there're Donna's kids—Dion, for instance, who definitely has the brains for it, *and* the gift for clever behind-the-scenes deception. He *certainly* won't be in jail forever—but though his heart's good, I'm not so sure about his ethics, never mind that he's as willful in his own way as Matty was, and obviously a hell of a lot sneakier in the bargain.

"Of course there's also his brother Gil," she continued thoughtfully, "though *he's* probably a bit too randy; it'd be a real challenge to keep him in footholders and out of prison.

As for the two of you, that *has* to be your decision, though I'll be willing to talk to you again once the dust has settled and we've all had time to relax. For now, both you and Ronny have a year left in school, and neither of you should be Master until you've at least graduated from high school. Whoever takes it is going to need a huge amount of training and God knows where we'll get that. However, I also feel that neither of you should reject something—even something as tempting and as terrifying as the Luck—without trying it."

Ronny nodded thoughtfully, though he had the strangest feeling Martha was holding something back.

And then Lewis, to everyone's surprise, said, very quietly, "I think I'll give it a go."

Epilogue II

Epitaph

Erin Welch's house
Sunday, May 19—early afternoon

The sun was glinting so brightly off the eighteen-inch-square slab of cast bronze Ronny had propped between his lap and the picnic table before him that he feared he was going to have to go inside and retrieve his shades if he was going to finish the medallion he was making for Matthew Welch's tombstone before dark. Winnie was sitting beside him, ostensibly watching, but he knew by the way she was fidgeting that she was getting bored. Maybe he should ask her to fetch his Ray-Bans. At least that'd give her something to do. Oh, she still loved him, he knew, but there was a growing apprehension in her eyes, an ever-increasing distrust.

Not dislike: he knew her well enough now to know that. But he also knew that she'd been burned badly by her association with the Welches, and that as long as they were together the fact of his *difference* would forever be a barrier between them. Winnie's mind had been raped by Anson

445

and Matt, even if her body had not. And Ronny had finally admitted that a part of her feared, and forever would fear, the same from him. It was great now, of course, and would be good a long time after; he didn't need to Listen to know that (and would not, ever, Listen to Winnie, nor would Lew). But someday—in a year or so, when the time came for them to go to college—he and Winnie would part. He hoped it would be painless, a wistful acknowledgment of a wonderful time that had passed. Not for the first time, not even for the first time that hour or that day, did Ronny wish he could rip the Luck out of his body, tear away his entire cultural and genetic heritage and just be a regular guy. Maybe then Winnie could love him without fear or reservation. But that was impossible.

For the rest—for himself, here, today—he was complete, or at least content. It was a warm almost-summer day; the sky was clear and blue. And from where he sat on the back deck of what had been Erin's house and was now in all but title Lew's, he could take in one of those marvelous views that were so typical of Welch County. This one showed mostly riverbottoms and fields, with mountains beyond, and closer in the long low ridge that masked Cordova proper.

And to the left, he could just make out the jutting chimneys and high-pitched roofs of Cardalba Hall. He and Lew were both—officially—living there now, alone except for Martha, who had informed Lew in no uncertain terms that he was far too inexperienced to try anything with a foot-holder yet. Whether Lew was *happy* there, Ronny couldn't tell. *He* wasn't, and though most of Lew's other friends made a point of dropping by (Ronny preferred to sleep at Erin's place as often as Martha would let him, and kept most of his possessions there), he couldn't help wondering what must be going through poor Lew's mind on those long lonesome nights alone.

"What's the matter?" Winnie asked quietly, laying her hand on his free one.

Ronny put down the stylus he'd been using to clean up

the inscription on the new-cast bronze. "Nothing, really. What makes you think something's wrong?"

"You were frowning."

Ronny tried to shrug nonchalantly. "Sun got in my eyes and made me squint."

"Want me to get your shades?" Ronny was certain there was the merest twinge of relief in her voice. He resisted the urge to Listen, to Hear what hopes and fears underlay those words.

"Yeah, sure," he replied finally. "And could you maybe find me some lemonade? Get yourself some too, of course. Oh, and be sure you get the Ray-Bans. I think they're in my room. You may have to dig a little to locate 'em."

"No problem," Winnie replied easily. "I like prowling around in your stuff."

Ronny grinned back at her—completely sincere, in spite of his misgivings. "I *know* you do."

Winnie gave his arm a reassuring pat and rose. Ronny heard the sliding glass doors snick home and returned to his work.

He did not stay at it long, for his gaze kept drifting toward Cardalba Hall. Eventually he slid the slab of metal onto the table and pillowed his chin on his joined knuckles. And he was still thus engaged when he became aware of a presence at his back.

Once more he resisted the temptation to Listen, and instead eased his head around to gaze back toward the house and the short flight of railroad-tie steps that connected the herb garden to the ground-level western end of the deck. Whoever it was had been mightily stealthy. And then he caught a whiff of exotic, spicy perfume—and relaxed.

It was Aunt Martha. In the month of their association he had learned never to underestimate that old lady. It was too bad she could not have been Master of Cardalba; she would have been a wonder.

"Possibly." Martha chuckled. She had a disconcerting habit of answering questions aloud that had been officially, and often rhetorically, posed in private. "Unfortunately, women don't get the chance—or maybe that's fortunately."

Ronny nodded, but his gaze shifted back to the roofs of Cardalba. "I wonder if he'll be happy there," he mused. "After I leave, I mean."

Martha sat down beside him and absently traced the lettering on Matthew's epitaph with a sharp lacquered nail. "Does it really matter? He's a Welch, therefore he's Lucky. If he's doomed to be unhappy, it'll be because of what he does, not where he lives. What matters is doing what your heart tells you is the right thing. You're finding that out now, aren't you?"

Ronny nodded solemnly, but did not shift his eyes from the distant mansion. "Maybe. Trouble is, sometimes it's hard to tell what's really doing the talking."

"And therein lies both the joy and danger of living!" Martha cried. "Without that tension, there would be no excitement; and without that excitement, there would ultimately be no joy. Pain exists only when there is pleasure, remember. Without pain, pleasure is itself diminished; yet without pleasure there can *be* no pain."

"You sound like the Road Man."

"Sometimes. We've met, you know: he and I. Several times, in fact."

"Did you . . . did you *cleave* to him?" Ronny suddenly blurted out, then blushed. "No, I guess you're a little too—"

Martha fairly cackled her amusement. "*Old*? Am I? Money can change a lot of things, lad; including one's looks. So can knowledge. So can Luck. Besides, twenty goes into eighty a lot more times than eighty goes into twenty."

"I'm not going to get a straight answer out of you, am I?"

Another hearty laugh. "Not about that!"

"About anything?"

"Maybe."

"Prove it."

Martha remained silent for a long moment, then took a deep breath. "Ronny," she whispered conspiratorially, "aren't you even a *little* bit curious about where I was while Matty was playing his stupid games?"

Ronny shrugged. "Not really. You were just a name then; I didn't even know what you looked like. You were as remote to me as the Queen of England—more so, even, since I knew what *she* looks like."

"But surely you've wondered since then."

Another shrug. "I assumed you liked being mysterious."

"Want to know anyway?"

Ronny regarded his great-great-aunt askance. "Last time I heard somebody trying to bargain over a secret, they both wound up dead."

"Ah," Martha shot back. "But this is about *life*, not death."

"I'm listening." Ronny sighed warily.

"Very well," Martha confided, "as a matter of fact, I had gone . . . to check on your and Lewis's pregnant *sister*."

"*Well*," Ronny said carefully, after a very long pause. "So that means it's not over yet?"

"Nothing is *ever* over." Martha chuckled. "And you should thank your Lucky stars for that."

Ronny did not reply.

And when he looked up again, Martha was gone.

TOM DEITZ grew up in Young Harris, Georgia, and earned bachelor of arts and master of arts degrees from the University of Georgia. His major in medieval English (it was as close as he could get to Tolkien) and his fondness for castles, Celtic art, and costumes led Mr. Deitz to the Society for Creative Anachronism, of which he is still a member. A "fair-to-middlin'" artist, Mr. Deitz is also a car nut (he has lately acquired a black '62 Lincoln named Uriel which he hopes to restore someday), has recently taken up horseback riding and hunting (neither with remarkable success), and *still* thinks every now and then about building a castle.

In *Soulsmith*, Mr. Deitz has begun an ambitious new trilogy dealing with the powers—and the dangers—of one family's Luck. He is also the author of a very popular contemporary fantasy series comprising *Windmaster's Bane*, *Fireshaper's Doom*, *Darkthunder's Way*, *Sunshaker's War*, *Stoneskin's Revenge*, and the related novel, *The Gryphon King*, all available from Avon Books.

There are places on Earth
where magic worlds beckon...
where the other folk dwell

TOM DEITZ

takes you there...

SOULSMITH
76289-7/$4.99 US/$5.99 Can

STONESKIN'S REVENGE
76063-0/$3.95 US/$4.95 Can

WINDMASTER'S BANE
75029-5/$3.95 US/$4.95 Can

DARKTHUNDER'S WAY
75508-4/$3.95 US/$4.95 Can

FIRESHAPER'S DOOM
75329-4/$3.95 US/$4.95 Can

THE GRYPHON KING
75506-8/$3.95 US/$4.95 Can

SUNSHAKER'S WAR
76062-2/$3.95 US/$4.95 Can

The Epic Adventure
THE OMARAN SAGA
by
ADRIAN COLE

"A remarkably fine fantasy...
Adrian Cole has a magic touch."
Roger Zelazny

BOOK ONE:
A PLACE AMONG THE FALLEN
70556-7/$3.95 US/$4.95 Can

BOOK TWO: THRONE OF FOOLS
75840-7/$3.95 US/$4.95 Can

BOOK THREE:
THE KING OF LIGHT AND SHADOWS
75841-5/$4.50 US/$5.50 Can

BOOK FOUR: THE GODS IN ANGER
75842-3/$4.50 US/$5.50 Can